CORNERED

CORNERED

THREE ROMANTIC SUSPENSE NOVELLAS

LYNETTE EASON,
LYNN H. BLACKBURN,
AND NATALIE WALTERS

Revell

a division of Baker Publishing Group
Grand Rapids, Michigan

Published by Revell
a division of Baker Publishing Group
Grand Rapids, Michigan
RevellBooks.com

Printed in the United States of America

Library of Congress Cataloging-in-Publication Data
Names: Eason, Lynette. In the dark. | Blackburn, Lynn Huggins. Downfall. |
    Walters, Natalie, 1978– Perilous obsession.
Title: Cornered : three romantic suspense novellas / Lynette Eason, Lynn H.
    Blackburn, Natalie Walters.
Description: Grand Rapids, Michigan : Revell, a division of Baker Publishing
    Group, 2024.
Identifiers: LCCN 2024009874 | ISBN 9780800746087 (paperback) | ISBN
    9780800746339 (casebound) | ISBN 9781493447138 (ebook)
Subjects: LCSH: Suspense fiction, American. | Romance fiction, American. |
    LCGFT: Thrillers (Fiction). | Romance fiction. | Novellas.
Classification: LCC PS648.S88 C67 2024 | DDC 813.08720806—dc23/
    eng/20240508
LC record available at https://lccn.loc.gov/2024009874

Cover design and images by Kirk DouPonce

Baker Publishing Group publications use paper produced from sustainable forestry practices and postconsumer waste whenever possible.

24 25 26 27 28 29 30   7 6 5 4 3 2 1

Dedicated to our loyal readers.
We couldn't do this without you!
We appreciate you and love you.
Thank you for loving our stories.

IN THE DARK

LYNETTE EASON

ONE

THE SEPTEMBER SUN had barely risen over the mountain town of Lake City, North Carolina, casting a warm, golden glow that filtered through Stephanie Cross's kitchen window. She sipped her morning coffee, scanning the headlines of the *Lake City News* like she did most every day. Yes, she could read it online and sometimes did, but she liked the feel of an actual paper when she had the chance to do so. Her morning routine comforted her, anchored her for the day, and offered a moment of quiet before she headed to the office.

She flipped the page. "Local Woman Killed in Tragic Early Morning Car Accident."

CPA Brenda Hudson, her good friend and coworker at Blackston and Cosworth, had been confirmed dead at the scene. "What? No!" Steph jumped to her feet and scrambled for her phone. "No, it can't be." She dialed her friend's number and it went straight to voicemail. She hung up and called her boss, Stan Gilchrest.

Four rings, then voicemail.

"No, no, no."

She grabbed her purse and keys and darted out the door. Once in the car, she tried Stan again.

This time he answered just before the call slipped to voicemail. "Hello? Steph, that you?" His usually warm and confident voice sounded shaken. Wobbly.

"Yes. I just saw the newspaper. Brenda was killed in a car wreck? Tell me it's not so."

"I'm so sorry. Yes. I just got the news about an hour ago. Her husband called me at home to tell me."

"And it's already in the paper?"

"Yes, it is. As soon as the call came in to 911, that reporter, Cynthia Green, was right there. Probably heard it on the police scanner. Wrote her piece and sent it in on the side of the road."

"Unbelievable. But why?"

"It happened on Youngstown. You know how people are complaining about that road. Sharp curve, no guardrail. Claiming it's not safe and trying to get the city to do something about it. Cynthia is leading the way on that, and this is fodder to help push the agenda."

"Youngstown Road. Oh no."

"Yes."

"B-but I just talked to her yesterday. We were going to have lunch today."

"I know. I know." His voice caught and Steph swiped at the tears sliding down her cheeks.

She blinked, keeping the road in focus. "What happened?"

"Her husband said they suspect she was going too fast and lost control. Just like everyone else who's ever wrecked in that area."

"I just . . . I can't believe it." But what was Brenda doing on that road? She lived on the opposite side of town.

"I've got to go, Steph. I'll see you at the office."

Work. Right. "Yes. I'm on my way now." She hung up only to have her phone buzz with an incoming call from her brother James. She activated the Bluetooth once more. "Hey."

"I just heard about Brenda. Steph, I don't even know what to say. I'm so sorry."

She was going to have to pull over if she kept crying. "I'm in shock. I don't even know what to do."

"Are you driving?"

"Yes." She sniffed and swiped her eyes.

"Then pull over."

Right. She turned into a grocery store lot, parked, and rested her forehead on the steering wheel. Sobs ripped from her while James's soothing voice came through the speakers. Finally, she got herself together and pulled in a deep breath.

"You still there?" he asked.

"Yeah." She swallowed. "Okay. I'm going to work and trying to brace myself. It will be horrible. Everyone loved Brenda."

"Call me if you need me, Squirt. I'm here for you."

"I know. Thanks, James." She hung up and aimed her Subaru toward the office, dreading the coming hours, because while her heart pounded out a rhythm of grief, her mind whirled with questions. What had Brenda been doing on Youngstown Road? She, like everyone else in the city, hated it and avoided that route whenever possible. Parents forbade their teens to drive it—and the new drivers had often lost enough friends to obey. So *what* had compelled Brenda to be on it? And at that time of morning? Or rather night? She couldn't imagine.

She pulled into the parking lot of her office and parked.

And sat there.

Please, God, get me—us—through this day.

DETECTIVE TATE COOPER STOOD at the edge of the scene of the car accident, the flashing lights of police cars casting an eerie blue glow on the area around him. The air was thick with tension as his fellow officers worked to make sure they didn't miss anything that might help them understand exactly what happened. The tow truck had finally arrived and pulled the mangled vehicle up onto the bed. Tate was ready to head home and get some sleep. Except sleep was going to have to wait.

He glanced at his watch. In just a few short hours, he was supposed to meet Detective Cole Garrison at the station and begin his first day as a newly appointed detective. He should have scheduled some downtime between his last day as a patrol officer and his first day as a detective, but he'd been eager to get started. Who could have known he'd draw the night shift and have to work an accident with a fatality for his last day?

Tate walked up the slanted embankment and looked at the road. It hadn't rained in a few days, so the asphalt was dry. The curve was sharp, but Brenda had been a native to Lake City, knew the dangers of the curve, so it hadn't caught her by surprise. And yet she'd gone around it at a high rate of speed. One of her tires was blown and could have contributed to the accident, but—

"What are you thinking?"

He glanced at Jeff Goode, his partner of six years. "I'm thinking there aren't any skid marks."

"Suicide?"

"Maybe." No matter how many times he worked an accident scene, he always had the same sick feeling in his gut. "But I guess this case will stay with you while I move on. Keep me updated. I want to know why."

"Of course." Jeff planted his hands on his hips. "You ready for your big day?"

Tate gave a soft huff that was half sigh, half chuckle. "If I can make it through the shift without having to take a nap, then I'll call it a success."

"Yeah, you didn't plan that very well."

"No kidding."

"Hey, Cooper!"

Tate looked up to see one of the officers waving him over. Bobby Knight. He walked to the edge of the drop-off and looked down the path of destruction the runaway vehicle had left behind. "Yeah?"

"Come down here. Wanna show you something."

Tate turned and raised a brow at Jeff. "You want this one?"

"No thanks. I'm not into rock climbing."

Tate snorted. "This is a bit different. Just hold the rope and walk down."

"Pass. He asked for you."

Tate shook his head, grabbed the rope tied to the back of a fire truck, and belayed his way down. He landed on flat ground next to where the car had been stopped by a copse of trees. "What is it?"

Bobby pointed to one of the larger trees involved in bringing Brenda's car to a hard halt. Next to it were shards of glass and a hubcap. "That hubcap didn't come off her car."

Tate looked closer. "Could it have been here before she drove off the mountain?"

"Naw. Look at it."

He did and noted it was pretty clean. If it had been there before the wreck, it hadn't been long. "You think this is more than a one-car accident? That someone ran her off the road?"

"I'm speculating."

"Anything on the victim's car that might suggest that?"

"Yeah. Paint that wasn't there when it came from the factory. It's an olive-green color. Victim's car is white. But here's the deal. It's been bumped twice."

"Like someone hit it and then came back for another swipe?"

"Yep."

Tate snapped a picture of the hubcap with his phone. "Anything else?"

"Well, just one thing. There's a bullet hole in this tree right here."

Tate blinked. "Okay. Fresh?"

"As a newborn. Now, I'm not saying they were shooting at the victim, but I can't rule it out either."

"Right. So they were chasing her, bumped her—twice—then shot at her?"

"That's about how I'd put it together, but again, I can't say for sure. The victim didn't have any bullet wounds. Looks like she died from head trauma."

"Okay, thank you." Tate rubbed his hand over his bearded chin. "You bringing that hubcap up?"

"I am."

"Good." He sighed. "Best-case scenario in this tragedy is it really *was* an accident and someone got scared and ran. Maybe they'd been drinking or whatever. Knew they'd be in a world of trouble if they called it in. Worst case . . ."

"It was on purpose. The two hits kind of indicate this was intentional. And then there's the bullet hole in the tree."

"Right." Tate radioed Jeff. "Don't let the tow truck leave yet. I want a couple pictures of the car."

"Ten-four."

"Could have been a hunter or something," he said to Bobby.

"Could have been. It's archery season right now. Guns don't start till October. Of course, that doesn't mean someone forgot to read the calendar and didn't realize it."

True. Or just plain ignored the date. Some hunters thought risking getting caught and fined was worth it.

Tate finished examining the area and shook Bobby's hand. "Thanks. I'll pass this on to Jeff, and he can share with who-ever's going to be taking over the case." Tate made his way back up the incline, got the pictures of the paint on the white car and all four hubcaps still attached, then walked over to his partner to fill him in. He slapped him on the shoulder.

"All right, buddy, stay in touch. I'm out of here." He'd already gone through all the personnel stuff, getting his badge, gun, and everything else he needed for his first day on the job as a detective.

Jeff eyed him with an Eeyore expression. "I'm going to miss you. You always let me get away with not doing the hard stuff."

Like walk down the side of a mountain. Most stuff Jeff thought was hard . . . wasn't. "Because I knew you'd always have my back while I did it. Maybe your next partner will too."

"Take care."

"You too."

Tate went to his personal vehicle he'd driven up hours earlier and climbed behind the wheel. With a heaviness in his heart for the victim of the accident, he aimed his Nissan Armada toward the precinct and refused to feel nervous. He'd been working toward this moment his whole life. Since he was fifteen he'd been focused, one goal in mind. To be a detective and to put the bad guys away. To stop as many crimes as he possibly could before they were committed.

He drew in a deep breath. He'd done it. He was a detective. Now it was time to make his mark.

If he could just stay awake.

TWO

STEPH ARRIVED AT THE OFFICE, her heart still beating the rhythm only grief knew. Lela Simmons was at the reception desk, tears drying on her cheeks. When she looked up and caught Steph's gaze, the tears flowed once more.

Steph hugged her. "I know."

"I can't believe it."

"I can't either, but we'll get through this. Brenda would be the first one to tell us she's happy right where she is, but to take care of her family."

"That's very true, but it still hurts." Lela sniffed and snagged a clean tissue to mop up her face. The phone rang and she sucked in a breath. "I need to get that."

"Of course." Steph left her friend and pushed through the door that led to her office. Although "office" was a stretch. It was a cubicle. One of many in the center of the large open floor. The perimeter contained private offices.

But Steph didn't mind the noise, she relished it. She lived alone, and sometimes the quiet threatened to suffocate her.

Only today, for the first time in the five years she'd been an employee, it was quiet, the atmosphere thick, heavy with grief and disbelief. Coworkers exchanged hushed whispers and shared condolences, the tragedy casting a somber shadow over their usual bustling workplace. Stephanie settled in at her desk and tried to focus on her tasks, hoping to find solace in the familiarity of numbers and spreadsheets.

Unsure of how much time had passed, she finally blinked and realized what she'd done was going to have to be done again.

Stan walked over. "Steph?"

She looked up. "Yes?"

He cleared his throat. "I . . . uh . . . hate to bring this up in light of the fact that Brenda's only been dead for a few hours, but I need to clear out her desk and see where she is with different clients and notify them."

Steph blinked. Well, that was a little soon, but Stan was always worried about the clients more than propriety. Not that he didn't care, but . . . she had to admit, this rankled. "Stan—"

He held up a hand. "I know. I know. I'm a horrible person, but word is getting out and clients are going to hear and then the phone is going to start ringing, wondering who will be taking care of their money. They won't mean to be unfeeling, and neither do I, but I need to get ahead of this. We all do."

Steph blew out a low breath. "It's okay. I understand what you're saying." And she did, but it just seemed wrong somehow to be worried about clients and their money when Brenda was dead. But . . . "Okay. Someone has to do it and I know she'd want it to be me."

Alarm flashed in his eyes. "Oh, no, that's not . . . I mean, I've got this. I just didn't want to be harshly judged when I started working on her desk." He cleared his throat. "And reassigning clients."

"No one's going to judge you. I'll do it after everyone goes home so they don't have to watch me—or you—do it."

For a moment, she thought he might offer more protests, then he nodded. "All right. Thanks, Steph."

"Of course."

"And there's a basket of vegetables in the break room. Please take some home. I'm going to drop some off to Greg on my way home."

Greg. Brenda's husband.

"I know he'll appreciate the gesture," she said.

Stan's garden was legendary in the office. No doubt he'd already had his stash picked and loaded to bring in to the office before he'd gotten the call about Brenda.

He returned to his office but paced to the window instead of taking a seat behind his desk. He walked to his little watering pot and began to care for the multitude of plants in his office. His hand shook and he lowered the can. He was more upset than he was letting on.

For the next few hours, Steph worked, but her mind kept drifting back to Brenda. Why had she been on Youngstown Road, nowhere near her home? Had she been going to Bolin's? Bolin's Nature Nurture Expeditions, an ecotourism spot, was one of her favorites, and she worked there one weekend a month simply because she loved it. Youngstown Road would take her there, but so would one of the other safer roads. Granted, Youngstown was ten minutes faster, but still . . . No, there had to be another explanation. But what?

Steph finally pushed her chair back and stood, stretched out the ache in her lower back, and made her way to the break room for a cup of coffee. Brenda's mug had been rinsed out and placed on the rack next to the sink. The basket of fresh vegetables was right where Stan said it was.

More tears threatened, and Steph turned away to see Detective Cole Garrison and another man step off the elevator. The new partner James had told her about? He was handsome. About six feet tall with red hair, kind eyes, and a well-trimmed beard.

Stan walked over to greet them, then pointed in the direction of her cubicle with a frown. Steph took a deep breath and went to see what this was all about.

TATE LOOKED WITH ENVY at the steaming cup in the pretty woman's hands. She was about five feet six inches and had dark blue eyes and brown hair with subtle blond highlights. Definitely pretty. Gorgeous, actually. At the moment, however, he was more interested in her coffee. What he wouldn't give to be able to chug it. He cleared his throat and met her gaze while his partner took the lead on the case that had dropped into their laps as soon as they realized it was most likely a hit-and-run at the very least. Since Tate had been with it from the beginning, they'd agreed they'd be the best ones to see it through to the end.

"Hey, Steph," Cole said. "This is my new partner for the time being. Tate Cooper."

"Hello."

Tate nodded. "Good to meet you. Sorry it's under these circumstances. I've heard a bit about you from your brother."

"Don't listen to anything he says." She attempted a smile, but it faltered, her blue eyes sad and red rimmed.

Tate offered a smile in return, hoping his sympathy was reflected in it.

"Can we talk?" Cole asked.

"About Brenda?" Pain flashed on her face, but she kept the tears at bay.

"Yeah."

"Sure. Let's go back to the break room. It's more private." She shot a knowing look at Tate. "And there's coffee if you want it."

She'd accurately read his longing. He fell halfway in love with her just for that. "If it's not too much trouble."

He and Cole followed her into the small area equipped with a table and full-sized kitchen. She motioned toward the disposable cups and Keurig, and Tate helped himself. Cole did the same, then the three sat at the round table.

Cole leaned forward. "We're going to need to talk to her closest friends and coworkers."

"Well, then I'm a good place to start. She and I met at the gym twice a week, then worked together every day. We hung out some on the weekends. I even let her lead me down the river occasionally when she was working at Bolin's."

"The ecotourism place," Tate said. "I know it."

Cole nodded. "Yeah, me too."

"Then there's Stan Gilchrest, our boss. You'll need to talk to him if you haven't already."

Tate scratched his chin. "Not in detail."

"Virginia Carson and Patti Smith were also good friends with Brenda. What else do you need to know?"

"Did she have any enemies that you can think of?" Tate asked.

Stephanie blinked, then frowned. "Enemies? Brenda? No. She was the kindest, most gentle soul you'd ever hope to meet. She had an incredible mind for numbers and was very good at her job."

"Like you, I'm told," Tate said. At her questioning look he said, "James."

She sipped her coffee. "Hm. Well, I like to think so."

Cole set his cup aside. "Look, Steph, I hate to say it, but it's possible Brenda's accident wasn't exactly an accident. It's possible someone ran her off the road on purpose."

She gasped, then gaped. "What? You mean as in . . . *killed her*?"

"Maybe. We found paint from another vehicle on the side of her car in different places. Like someone bumped her twice and it was enough to send her over the side."

"B-but could it have been someone who was careless or drunk or—"

"It could be, but either way, they left the scene, so for now we're treating this like a homicide." At her stunned expression, Cole sighed. "I know it's terrible to ask this, but could you show us Brenda's workspace? We're going to need to go through it in case it was someone she knew. If it was just some weird accident by a stranger, that's one thing, but we've got to rule other stuff out."

"Stan was just talking about needing to clear out her desk this morning, and I told him I'd do it after everyone left for the day." She frowned. "It's right there in the middle of the room next to mine. If you guys start going through it, everyone will . . ." She shrugged. "I don't know."

"We get it," Tate said, "but it's possible she might have something in the desk that can lead us to why she's dead. The faster we find that, the faster we hope to find out what happened on the road."

"Right. Of course." Steph stood and waved for them to follow. Tate snagged his coffee and pulled up the rear.

She stopped at a cubicle that was neat and organized. Ready for its occupant to settle into the chair and start work. Unfortunately, Brenda wouldn't be coming back. Tate pulled in a deep breath while a sense of rightness settled over him in spite of the reason for his position being necessary. This was why he did this job. To get justice for those who couldn't get it for themselves.

THREE

POSSIBLY MURDERED? Steph couldn't process it. She moved the chair out of the way and motioned for Tate to help himself. Virginia Carson walked over to stand beside her. "What's going on?" her coworker asked in a low voice.

"They're investigating Brenda's death."

"They don't think it was an accident?"

Steph shrugged. "Apparently there's some evidence that warrants an investigation."

"They're going to want to talk to us, aren't they?"

"Yes. Do you know anyone who had it in for Brenda? Because I sure couldn't think of anyone."

Virginia shook her head. "No, not really. I know she was acting a little weird over the last couple of days, but when I asked her about it, she just shrugged it off and said, 'Family stuff.'"

Steph blinked. "What? I didn't notice— Wait, yes I did. She was on the phone yesterday, and I overheard her say, 'Not here. I'll call you when I finish up with work.' When I looked at her, she gave me a really strained smile and rolled her eyes like it was no big deal. So I didn't think anything about it . . . until now."

"What makes that stand out to you?"

"It wasn't so much the words as it was her tone. She sounded angry and resigned all at the same time."

"Hmm . . . guess we'd both better mention this. They're going to talk to her husband and anyone else she had contact with just before she died."

"And once we tell them about the phone call, they're also going to want to subpoena her phone records," Steph murmured.

Tate stepped back. "We'll take her laptop and files and see what we can find."

Cole laid a hand on her arm. "We have boxes in the car for this. I'll be right back. Tate's going to stay here with the desk." He nodded to Tate and headed for the door. Virginia squeezed Steph's hand and returned to her desk.

"So you're James Cross's sister," Tate said.

"I am. How well do you know him?" she asked.

"I met him a few times while I was working patrol. He's a stand-up guy and an excellent detective."

She smiled. "Yeah. He is." And Tate was going to be a good one too, if her instinct was correct. He had that look about him. Smart, observant, dedicated. Hunky. She cleared her throat.

Cole returned with the boxes, and he and Tate went through the desk. Surprisingly, Brenda didn't have a ton of stuff in the drawers. Just office supplies that they promised to return. And a couple of books.

"Brenda was a big reader," Steph said. "Loved all kinds of books. Fiction and nonfiction." She pointed to *Oliver Twist* and *The Old Man and the Sea.* "Her favorites were the classics, but she loved contemporary stuff too."

Tate smiled. "I actually liked *Pride and Prejudice.*"

"I'm impressed that you would admit that."

He grinned and her lungs stuttered a moment. *Focus, Steph.* She gestured to the computer. "All of her client files will be on the hard drive," she said. She handed him the paper with the laptop password. "We have backup copies on the server, of course, but I think you'll need a warrant to access them." He would know that. Duh. She ducked her head, hoping to hide the heat rising to her cheeks.

"Already gave that to your boss," Cole said.

"Of course."

Once they had everything they wanted, Tate nodded to her, his gaze lingering on hers. "Are you okay?"

She raised a brow. "No, not really, but thank you for asking."

He frowned. "I know you have your brother and Cole, but if you need anything, feel free to reach out. Or if you think of anything else that might be helpful." She told him about the phone call, and he nodded. "We'll talk to Virginia and get the phone records from her work line and cell. Thanks."

A memory floated back to her almost as quickly as it had faded only days earlier. "You know," she said, "you'll need to talk to her husband, but someone might have broken into their house a couple of weeks ago."

Tate's gaze sharpened. "What?"

"I just thought about it. Brenda told me about it the morning after it happened and brushed it off for the most part. She said it was her son sneaking back in after sneaking *out*. But she seemed shaken. Her German shepherd, Beau, pitched a fit barking and woke them all up, but if it was her son, he doesn't bark when Mark comes in. That was the one thing that bothered her even though she caught Mark red-handed." She bit her lip and shook her head. "She said she thought there might have been someone else outside but chalked it up to one of Mark's friends." Steph shrugged. "I don't know if that's important or not, but figured it wouldn't hurt to mention it."

"Absolutely. Thank you."

Steph nodded and watched them go, then turned back to

her desk, her mind unable to focus on work. Her attention kept straying to Brenda's desk. She walked over and sat in the chair, her gaze traveling over the empty spaces where pictures of Brenda's family had hung on the cubicle walls. "Oh, Brenda," she whispered. Surely they'd left *something* of her friend. She opened the top drawer and glanced inside, feeling as gutted as the empty nook was. They really *had* taken everything. She pushed the drawer shut.

Only to have it resist sliding back into place.

She tried again and got the same result. With a sigh, she wiggled the drawer out and looked inside. Something had fallen into the space at the back.

"What in the world?" she whispered. Steph slid her hand into the opening and grabbed the small notebook. She started to slide the drawer back into its home when she noticed tape on the side of it.

Tape that matched the residue left on the notebook she now held. A notebook Brenda obviously hadn't wanted found.

TATE LEANED BACK in his chair and fought the fatigue that threatened to pull him under. He could have happily put his head on his desk and fallen fast asleep, as it had been a long night and an even longer day. But he still had hours to put in before he could go home and find his bed.

"Go catch an hour nap," Cole said from the door.

Tate blinked at him. "I'll be all right."

"No you won't. I know you've been up way longer than you should, and if I have to trust you with my life, I want you to at least be able to see where to shoot."

Heat crept into Tate's cheeks. "Yeah, I guess I didn't plan the timing of this very well."

Cole waved his phone. "SWAT got a call to a scene. Take

the time to rest while I'm gone. Brenda's dead. Her case can wait an hour or two."

Tate nodded. "Be safe."

"You too."

Cole disappeared toward the SWAT HQ and Tate smiled. One day that would be him. At least he hoped.

But sleep sounded good. If he didn't rest, he wasn't going to be any good to anyone. He hurried out to his Armada. It was an older model, but he loved the spacious vehicle and refused his family's attempts to get him to upgrade. He aimed the SUV toward his apartment complex.

Fifteen minutes later, when he walked into his first-floor two-bedroom home, he made sure his phone was on ring, dropped into his recliner, and was asleep in almost an instant.

FOUR

STEPH PUSHED HER MOUSE to the side, rubbed her eyes, then glanced at her phone. Then at the little five-by-seven pink notebook sitting by her water bottle.

Still no return call from Cole. She'd give him another hour, then she was going to try James. But if James and Cole were together on a SWAT call, he wouldn't answer either.

She opened the notebook once more and tried to figure out the weird letters and numbers Brenda used. "*ENNB*," she whispered. "What's that?" Seems like she should know, but she didn't have a clue. They all had their own way of keeping up with their work, but this coded method was a new one, and Steph had no idea what made her friend use it—or how to decipher it. On a whim, she snapped pictures of each page. She was going to have to turn the book in to the police but wanted a copy for herself. Just in case she could figure it out.

Her phone stayed silent for the next ten minutes. "Oh bother." She pulled the other detective's card from her pocket and ran her thumb over the slightly raised black print. Detective Tate Cooper.

His gray eyes with a tinge of green still played in her mind. He'd been tired and hadn't tried to hide it, but he'd also been focused on the task before him. And he and Cole seemed to get along well despite the experience gap between them.

Then again, that was probably mostly due to Cole. He didn't have anything to prove, and Tate didn't act like he did either.

A throat cleared behind her and she turned to see Stan. "Hey."

"Hey, just walking around checking on everyone. How are you holding up?"

She shrugged. "I'm not getting much work done. I can't stop thinking about her."

"I know. I'm considering sending everyone home. It's Friday. We could all probably use the long weekend."

"Might not be a bad idea." She hesitated, then held up the notebook. "The cops missed this when they were cleaning out Brenda's desk. It was taped to the side of one of her drawers and came loose. I found it when the drawer wouldn't slide back in right."

"What is it?"

"I don't know." She handed it to him. "Have you seen it before?"

"No." He flipped through it. "Weird. None of that makes any sense."

"I think it's a code of some kind."

"*ENNB?* What's that?"

"Beats me, but I'll figure it out."

"Why don't I keep it? Maybe I can study it."

"The cops will want it. It's part of the contents of her desk." He frowned. "They're on the way to get it?"

"Not yet. I called and told them I had it, but no one's called me back yet. Someone will."

"Right." He passed the book back to her. "Well, let me know if they need me for anything. I'll be in my office for a little bit, then I'm taking off. I'm like you. Can't concentrate."

"Yeah." She studied him a moment. "Stan, are you sure

you don't know what Brenda was working on? I mean, did she mention a specific client she was having trouble with?"

He shook his head. "Nope, and that's what I told the police. I even went through her entire client load looking to see if a name jumped out at me, but"—he shrugged—"nothing."

"Okay. Well, thanks."

"And now, I'm going to make a phone call and take off. My kids said something about coming home for the weekend, so I want to help the wife get things straightened up for them. You should go home too."

"I will. Soon." She gave him a hug, then went back to work. After an hour of nothing, she finally gave up and dialed Tate's number.

He picked up on the third ring. "Tate Cooper here." His voice sounded different. A deeper bass than earlier. Like he had a sore throat.

"Did I wake you?" she asked.

"Yeah, but it's a good thing. I was taking a break and fell asleep."

"Sleeping on the job is allowed these days? I need to switch careers."

"Cute. I had permission due to bad scheduling on my part."

"Ah. You worked all night and then caught this case before you could go home."

He chuckled. "Exactly. Now you know my secrets. What can I do for you?"

"I found something that I think you need to see. It's a notebook that belonged to Brenda. I'm going to leave work in about five minutes if you want me to meet you somewhere."

"What if I just swing by your place?"

"That works." She gave him her address and hung up, gathered her things and Brenda's notebook, then waved goodbye to Stan, who was still on the phone and pacing his office.

He returned her wave, then went back to his phone conversation. And his pacing. He was usually so even-keeled it was odd to see him off-kilter, but Brenda's death had obviously thrown him. Like it had all of them. She almost stopped to ask if he was okay but didn't want to interrupt since he was obviously making a number of calls. Probably to clients who needed to know about Brenda's death. She'd catch up with him next week.

In the parking garage, she hurried toward her Subaru Outback, pumps clicking on the concrete floor. Leaving early meant getting a head start on the usual flood of traffic exiting the building, and it was eerily quiet except for the road noise two floors down.

And something else. Footsteps. Quiet ones, but nevertheless . . .

She stopped.

The footsteps behind her continued for a moment, then stopped too. Was she being paranoid or was it just someone else leaving early and the footsteps stopped because they'd arrived at their vehicle?

She scanned the area, her eyes sweeping right, then left. Nothing. Or was someone actually following her? She shivered. Brenda's death had spooked her, making her more jumpy than usual.

Steph picked up the pace, wishing she'd found a spot closer to the door, but she'd been running late this morning and the only spot available had been all the way at the end of the row.

Naturally.

Once again, she swore she heard footsteps and the rustle of pant legs rubbing together. Just a swish of a sound, but it was there. She clicked her remote to unlock her doors. Finally, she slid behind the wheel and slammed and locked the door.

She pressed the Start button and her engine purred to life. Steph aimed her vehicle toward the exit, faster than she should, but looking for anyone who might have been following her. And there. A man dressed in jeans, a blue short-sleeved shirt, and a baseball cap stood next to an older model SUV, head averted. She was tempted to stop and ask him if he was following her, but decided that might not be the smartest thing to do and kept going.

All the way home, she watched her rearview mirror, but finally pulled into her garage without incident. Only when the door was lowered behind her vehicle did she get out and scurry into her home. With the doors and windows checked and double checked, she stopped a moment to look at her phone.

Tate was on his way.

TATE PULLED INTO Stephanie's drive and cut the engine. She had a smaller home in one of the more affluent neighborhoods. It was a Victorian cottage–style house that somehow seemed to suit her. He propelled himself out of the vehicle and onto her front porch. It was nearing dinnertime, so he'd grabbed some Chinese from his favorite place after consulting with James about what his sister liked.

He rang the doorbell.

Seconds later, footsteps sounded and the door swung open. Steph stood there with a forced smile and pale face.

He frowned. "Are you all right?"

"I look that bad?"

"No, that's not what I meant. You just look . . . scared."

She waved a hand. "I just got home. I . . . uh . . . had a weird experience in the parking garage at work and it shook me."

He held up the food. "Want to tell me about it over sweet-and-sour chicken?"

Her eyes widened. "My favorite. How'd you know?"

"I called James and asked him."

She blinked. "Oh. Well, thank you. The kitchen is this way."

Tate followed her into the spacious area just off the den and put the food on the counter. "Now, tell me what happened."

She filled him in and he mulled it over. "And no one else was there?"

"No, no one other than the one man I saw as I was leaving. I mean, it was four o'clock in the afternoon. Most people don't leave until five or five thirty. Sometimes even later." She shuddered. "I've never been afraid in that garage. Not even at night. There are cameras and security patrolling—most of the time anyway. And before you ask, I have no idea where security was earlier. Probably on another floor." She sighed. "The point is, yes, it was weird, but the more I think about it, I'm pretty sure I overreacted. I'm actually a little embarrassed." She pushed a bag toward him. "Let's eat and forget about that while I show you what I found."

"Okay, sure." And while she could have overreacted, as she said, Tate wasn't sure he was comfortable just brushing off the incident. While she busied herself readying her food, he tapped a request for the security footage of the garage. Just out of curiosity.

He then grabbed one of the plates she offered, dumped his food on it, and carried it to the table. "You mind if I say grace?"

She smiled. "I'd love it."

He said a short prayer of thanks for the food and for guidance to find Brenda's killer, then looked up to find her watching him. Heat started to crawl into his neck and he cleared his throat. "What?"

"Sorry, I didn't mean to stare and make you feel uncomfortable. I was just thinking that you're a nice guy, aren't you?"

"I try to be."

She took a bite, chewed, and swallowed. "So, what got you into police work?"

His mind flew back to the incident that started it all. Did he want to get into that? He looked at her. She was waiting, expectant. Listening. "When I was fifteen, my best friend's father was killed in a grocery store holdup. The killer had just been released because of a technicality that very day." Tate rubbed his chin, wishing he could rub away the memories. "I saw what that did to my buddy and his family. It made me want to be the kind of cop who didn't make mistakes. The kind who got it right the first time so that no sharky lawyer could get someone off and put them back on the street to kill again."

"I'm so sorry, Tate. That's awful."

He blinked the past away and took another bite. "It was, but my buddy became a cop too and just testified at the killer's parole hearing, keeping him behind bars for another few years."

"Good for him," she said, her voice soft, eyes wide and focused solely on him, drawing him in, making him want—

No, that wasn't the plan. No romantic entanglements until he was settled.

You're pretty settled, Detective Cooper. You've reached your goal. You can—

He shut off the little voice in his head and cleared his throat. "Anyway, that's why I do what I do. Each time I catch a bad guy—and make sure I do it right—I think about the fact that maybe, just maybe, I kept someone else's family from going through what my friend's did."

"Very admirable."

"Thanks. Enough about me. Tell me what made you delve into the world of numbers."

She laughed and he was grateful she let him change the subject. "I was always good at math," she said. "I like things that make sense, and numbers make sense to me. When I found I could make a living helping businesses balance their books, it was a no-brainer. I love my job." She sighed. "And Brenda loved hers, but something was definitely going on.

I don't know what, but I think it's highly possible it's connected to someone running her off the road." She pulled a small pink notebook from her purse and handed it to him. "You missed this. It was taped to the side of the drawer at one point. All of the opening and closing must have loosened it. I went through her desk, looking to see if you left anything. You didn't. Anyway, when I opened and closed the top drawer, this was dislodged. I found it because the drawer wouldn't shut properly."

He frowned and opened it to the first page. "This looks like a bunch of random stuff." He looked up. "Code?"

"That's what I think."

"But why?"

"I don't know. If I had time, I might be able to figure out the key." She shook her head. "It's weird that she would feel the need to do this. She's not into conspiracy theories or anything."

"But she obviously came across something she didn't want anyone else seeing—or if they did see it—she didn't want them understanding it." He pressed his lips together. "All right, well, I already have a list of her clients, so we don't have to ask for them. Maybe if we go through this and the client names, we'll see something that matches?"

"Maybe. I have her clients too. We all have a list of each other's clients in case we have to handle something while someone is on vacation or . . . in case of an emergency."

She pressed her lips together for a moment and he placed a hand on her shoulder while she fought the emotion. "It's okay to cry and grieve," he said.

"I know. But not now. Crying won't find who killed her, and that's what I want to do more than anything at the moment." She glanced at him. "Have you talked to her husband, Greg?"

"We spoke with him briefly when we told him of her death,

but he was in no shape for questioning. We're supposed to go back in the morning for a more in-depth interview."

"Could I be there?"

"You're friends with Greg?"

"I am. I often babysit—sat—for him and Brenda when they wanted a date night." She offered him a sad smile. "Yes, I'm that single friend all married couples with children want." Tears appeared and she blinked them away. "But I didn't mind. Her children are precious, and I love them dearly. Greg is a wonderful man and husband. He'll miss Brenda terribly." She looked away and sniffed. "We all will." Then she straightened her shoulders and her eyes steeled. "Which means we must find the person responsible and get justice for her and her family."

"Yes," he said. "But not *we*. Me. And Cole."

She sighed. "I know you need to take this with you, but what do you say we spend a little while trying to decipher it?"

Her desire to help him get justice for her friend warmed him, and he nodded. "I think that's a great idea."

Maybe it was *we* after all. At least for the next little while.

FIVE

WHEN TATE LEFT, Steph shut the door behind him and pursed her lips. They'd worked on the code for the better part of two hours without a breakthrough, and now she was frustrated and tired. And grieving hard for her friend. She had other friends, of course. And family. All of whom had texted and called over the course of the day.

Lainie Jackson, soon to be Lainie Cross and Steph's sister-in-law when she walked down the aisle with James, had called twice while Tate was there, and Steph had let it roll to voice-mail. She dialed her friend's number.

"Steph, are you all right?"

Lainie's question in lieu of a greeting made her smile. "I am. I'm sad and mad and craving justice for Brenda, but I'll be okay."

"I'm so sorry."

"Thank you. And thank you for checking on me. It's a long weekend with Labor Day, so at least I have an extra day before I have to face her empty desk again." Not that the day would really help, but . . .

"I'm just sorry. I wish I had other words that were helpful, but I don't."

"I know. It's okay."

"I'm sure he told you," Lainie said, "but James said anyone who wanted to come to the lake house on Monday is welcome. Do you think you'll feel like coming?"

Her brother lived on Lake City Lake with his boat and other fun water accessories and enjoyed hosting his friends and family whenever possible. Lainie would move in after the wedding, but her two dogs, Rex and Tex, had already made the place their home. "I'm planning on it. What about everyone else?"

"Everyone who can will be there."

Which meant Kenzie King, Cole Garrison, Jesslyn McCormick, Kristine Duncan, and others. All close friends Steph usually enjoyed spending time with, but with the shadow of Brenda's death hanging over her, she'd almost feel guilty having fun. Not that her friend would want her to stop living just because she was gone. In fact, the opposite was true.

But still . . . "Okay, well, I'll just have to see how I feel, but I'll plan on doing my best to enjoy the day with you all."

"That's the spirit."

Her phone buzzed with an incoming call. "Hey, Lainie, I have another call. Let me grab this and we'll talk later."

"Bye."

Steph swiped the screen. Cherry Bolin, a longtime friend who worked just about every waking hour at her family's ecotourism company. They owned Bolin's Nature Nurture Expeditions, and she and her brother ran it while their parents did a lot of traveling. She'd also been Brenda's boss one weekend a month.

"Hi, Cherry."

"Hey. I'm calling to see if you're okay. I honestly don't even know what to think. I can't quite process that she's dead and won't be walking through the office door." The last word ended on a sob, and Steph closed her eyes to hold back her own tears yet again.

"I know," she said. "She loved working with you, though. Both at the business and having you for a client."

"And she was good at it too." Cherry cleared her throat. "Would you want to get together to just visit and have coffee sometime soon? Brenda and I were supposed to do that and . . . didn't. So, I'm just trying to . . . well . . . you know."

"Reach out to people you care about and let them know?"

"Yes. Something like that."

"I'd love to. Give me a couple of days and we'll figure out a good time."

"Sure."

They talked for a few more minutes before saying their goodbyes, and Steph hung up to sit in silence for a moment.

Yeah, that wasn't going to do.

She turned the television on low for background noise, then pulled her phone from the table to open it to the pictures she'd taken of the pages from the notebook. She squinted at the small print and huffed. "I'm too young to need readers," she muttered. But printed the pages anyway.

Once she had them from the printer, she curled up in the recliner with a pencil and stared at the letters and numbers. "What in the world were you doing, Brenda? All these letters. Two letters and four letters and random numbers and . . . ugh!"

She didn't even know where to start. With her earlier attempts, she'd tried the obvious—the alphabet for the first twenty-six numbers—and that had been a bust. She'd also tried it backward, and nothing.

So, what next? Every second letter? Every third? This was definitely going to take some time.

For the next two hours, she worked and came up empty. When she finally yawned for the third time in as many minutes, she put the pages aside and leaned her head back, eyes focused on the picture of her, Brenda, and Lainie on the mantel. They'd gone white water rafting and had laughed for hours. Steph loved the outdoors, but not like Brenda. The woman would have lived in a tent and off the land if Greg had been willing.

The Monday after the one weekend a month Brenda worked with the ecotourism company, Brenda would come to work refreshed and glowing.

"Why on earth would you choose to be a CPA when you love the outdoors so much?" Steph had once asked her.

"Because it takes money to raise a family." She shrugged. "And I love numbers. Truly, I have the best of both worlds. And the Bolins are wonderful." She nudged Steph, shoulder to shoulder. "Cherry babysits when you're not available."

"Ah, the truth comes out," Steph said with a laugh. "The real reason you spend as much time as possible there. Suck-up."

Brenda had laughed too, and they'd finished their lunch.

On that happy memory, Steph finally allowed her eyes to close and sleep to come.

Something woke her. A soft pop? Then a scraping sound that came from her bedroom on the other side of the wall next to her recliner. A window opening? She rubbed her eyes and sat up, papers fluttering to the floor and the soft drone of the television still playing in the background.

She stayed quiet, listening. Was someone in her house?

When nothing else reached her ears, she almost closed her eyes once more, then stopped. She couldn't just go back to sleep. Steph rose.

Another sound from the bedroom. Like wind blowing through an open window? She grabbed her phone and dialed James's number. When it rolled to voicemail, she started to dial 911, but at a footstep behind her, she spun to see a figure dressed in black wearing a ski mask, a gun pointed at her. She shrieked and raced for the back door even while knowing she wouldn't make it in time to flip the dead bolt, open the door, and get out.

He easily caught her sweatshirt and spun her to face him. "Where is it?" He was taller than she by several inches and his voice was a low, raspy whisper that grated over every nerve ending. And he was strong. Very strong.

"The police are on the way." The words came out in a rush, and he pressed the weapon against her chin. Terror flooded her and she froze.

"I'm only going to ask one more time," he said, his voice low. "Where is the notebook?"

"The—? I gave it to the police."

He cursed and she flinched. "Of course you did. What was in it?"

"I don't know."

"I know you read it." He slammed her against the island and the barrel of the gun jammed harder.

"I tried! But it was all written in code. I have no idea what it said or even what the key is!" She wanted to fight, to push him away, but was afraid she'd jar the finger on the trigger. A musky cologne registered, and all she could think was that he'd taken the time to smell nice before he killed her. *Get a grip, Steph!*

"The guy that was here earlier. He's the cop you gave it to, isn't he?"

Did she dare admit it? Did he know who Tate was? And why did something about her intruder seem familiar?

"Isn't he!"

"Yes! But he was taking it to put it into the evidence room! It's probably already there." She gasped the words, trying to force her fear-frozen lungs to work.

Another curse and he shoved her to a chair, the gun now in her face. When he pulled zip ties from his pocket, she trembled while her mind scrambled for an escape plan. "You don't have to do this."

"Shut up and put your hands behind the chair. I can leave

you alive or dead. Doesn't much matter to me. I'll do what's easiest."

Steph complied, and soon her hands were bound behind her. He secured them to the chair before he raced out her front door.

Tate! She had to warn Tate.

TATE COULDN'T SLEEP, so he'd been sitting at the kitchen island working on the code in the little notebook for the past two hours since he'd left Steph's place. He'd have to turn it over first thing in the morning and log it as evidence—probably should have done that tonight, but the truth was, he'd wanted a little more time with it.

Fat lot of good that had done him. Part of it could have been his splotchy concentration. He kept circling back to Stephanie Cross. Steph.

Despite her eyes and nose reddened from her grief, she was a beautiful woman who'd captured his interest the moment he'd set eyes on her. The professional in him wouldn't let that interest show. Not yet anyway. She was grieving and he needed to focus on finding who killed her friend.

But maybe in a couple of weeks there would be an appropriate time to ask her out.

His phone pinged and the security footage from the garage at Steph's office popped up in file format. He thanked the sender and pressed play. There was Steph, walking to her car. And then stopping. She looked behind her before walking once more, picking up her pace. The video stuttered, then shifted to a different angle. One that allowed him to see a man dressed in jeans, a blue short-sleeved shirt, and a baseball cap. He kept his head down, but he was definitely watching Steph. So something had happened since she left the office.

He picked up the notebook. "You're after this, aren't you?" Tate said aloud. Was that too much of a leap? From Brenda's death to Steph finding the notebook to the man in the garage being after it? The security footage showed him following her at a distance, the license plate covered with some kind of white cloth.

"Probably took that off after he got away from the cameras," he muttered. But he definitely believed the man not only was watching her but followed her home.

Which meant he knew Tate had been there if he kept watching for any length of time. He texted her.

> The guy from the garage could have followed you home. Make sure your doors are locked. I'm texting James and Cole to let them know and I'm sending a cruiser to your house. I'll be there soon.

Tate shut the book and patted his pockets. No keys. He walked into the den and grabbed them from the coffee table. Asking Steph out might not be okay right now, but he'd do everything in his power to make sure she was safe.

He hesitated. He should probably call her to make sure she saw the text.

A creaking sound came from the floor in his kitchen. He frowned, his hand automatically going to the weapon at his hip. Only to remember he'd taken it off and laid it on the kitchen counter.

The same kitchen with the floor that squeaked when someone walked across it. "Who's there?" He grabbed his phone and tapped 911, then turned the volume down so whoever was in his home wouldn't be able to hear the voice on the other end. But that voice would hear him. "Hello?" he said as soon as the dispatcher picked up. "I'm a detective with the Lake City Police Department. You're trespassing in my home. I'm also armed, so you might want to think about going back out the way you came in."

He grabbed the Louisville Slugger from the mount over his recliner and gripped it while he walked with slow, measured steps toward the now silent kitchen. Not exactly armed, but better than nothing, and the dispatcher now knew he was law enforcement. He just prayed the invader didn't pick up his weapon.

Before he could swing through the entrance, the intruder beat him to it, moving first and fast. Something slammed into the side of Tate's head, and he went to his knees while darkness swirled, threatening to suck him under.

This time the footsteps were loud as they rushed past him. Then his front door banged open, and the figure was gone before Tate could get to his feet.

When he finally managed to stand, the room spun, and he grabbed the nearest chair to hold himself upright. The wave of dizziness and nausea passed, and he pressed a hand to the goose egg rising. Sirens finally reached him, and after confirming his weapon and badge were still where he left them, he walked outside to sit in the wicker chair on his small front porch, empty-handed, bat at his feet.

Officers swung into the parking lot opposite him, climbed out, and walked his way, hands on their weapons. "You armed?" the nearest one asked.

"Just the bat." Not that it had done him any good. "My piece is on the kitchen counter." He kept his hands where they could see them.

"You're with the LCPD?"

"Yeah. First day as a detective. Badge is on the counter next to the gun."

The officer let out a low whistle. "You make someone mad already?"

Tate chuckled, then winced. "Looks like it."

"I'm Brad Covington. My partner is Elisa Sanders." He nodded to the officer at his side. "You mind if she checks your kitchen?"

"Not at all. Help yourself. I'm curious to know how he got in." Elisa walked through his open door and Tate touched his throbbing scalp. "And what he used to bean me with." The skin wasn't broken, but the lump kept getting bigger.

"You need an ambulance?" Brad asked.

"For this?" Tate almost shook his head, then thought better of it. "No. It was a pretty hard hit, but I know the signs to look for that indicate a concussion. If I have them, I'll get help."

"Good enough."

The officer returned and placed her hands on her hips. "Well, I know how he got in. He used a glass cutter on your window and simply flipped the lock, raised the window, and climbed in."

"Fabulous." Tate made a mental note to upgrade his alarm system to include the windows.

"You're the second one tonight."

"No kidding?"

"Yep, just as we pulled up to your place, a call came over the radio that a neighbor reported a break-in a couple of miles away in that fancy neighborhood."

Tate stilled. "Whose house was it?"

"Believe the neighbor said it was Stephanie Cross, James's sister. You met James Cross yet? He's a detective too."

His stomach dropped. Someone had hit Steph's house, then his? That was no coincidence. He stood and ground his teeth against the pain that spiked before it eased. "Yes, I know him."

He walked inside to the kitchen. The little pink notebook he'd set next to his gun was gone.

SIX

STEPH HAD MANAGED to walk the chair over to the counter where the knives were and, with a lot of maneuvering and failed attempts, finally got the paring knife under the zip tie and cut it.

She grabbed her phone mid-ring, noted the caller, and slapped the device to her ear. "Tate! There's a guy who's looking for Brenda's notebook. He broke into my home and now he's looking for you and—"

"Are you okay?"

"Yes, yes, but you've got to be watching—"

"He's already been here and gone. I'm okay, but he did get the book."

She snapped her lips shut. "Oh." She'd been too slow. Guilt slammed her hard. He could have been killed because she'd admitted she gave the book to him. "I'm so sorry. He knew I'd given you the book. I didn't want to tell him, but he knew. He just forced me to confirm it."

"I'm glad you told him. You're sure you're okay?"

"I am. And if it helps, it's not the end of the world—or the case—that the book is gone. I took pictures of all of the pages that had code on them."

He went quiet. "You did?" he finally said.

"I figured you'd have to take the thing and turn it in, and I wanted to work the code, so . . . yeah. Sorry if that was against the rules."

"No specific rule. And I'm grateful you did that. At least we have the copy if not the actual book."

"I have printed copies too."

"You're amazing. Can you send the digital pictures to me?"

"Of course. As soon as we hang up. I'm also saving them to the cloud just in case someone decides to steal my phone and burn the printed ones." She thought he might have chuckled at her disgruntled tone.

"I'm heading your way in about fifteen minutes," he said. "As soon as I can convince everyone I'm fine and that I'm not going to the hospital. Are officers there?"

Not going to the hos— Sirens sounded. "They're close. I hear them. Do you *need* to go to the hospital?"

"I don't. I'm fine. I have a headache, but I'm fine. You're sure *you're* okay?"

"Yes. I promise. He didn't hurt me." Not really. Not like he could have. Not like he would have if he'd felt the need. She shuddered.

"I'll be there shortly," he said.

She walked into her bedroom and glanced at the hole in her window. "Okay. I need to let James know. He'll probably be here when you get here." Maybe. Depending on where he was sleeping tonight. It was pushing one o'clock in the morning, and now that her adrenaline was crashing, climbing into her bed sounded better than calling James. But she had to report it, and if James took the statement, she could kill two birds with one stone. Get it on record and keep him from being livid that she didn't call him. Okay, three birds. She needed her window fixed. "I read your text, by the way. A little late, but thanks for trying."

"Sure thing. I was going to call, but that's when I heard the guy in my house."

"It's fine. Everything worked out okay. I'll see you in a bit."

When she hung up with Tate, she dialed James, who answered on the third ring. "This better be good," he croaked.

"Are you sleeping at your apartment or the lake house?" He kept a place in town close to the station so that when he was on duty he didn't have the long forty-five-minute drive to work.

"Apartment. Why?"

"Because someone broke into my house and tied me up before they went to Tate's house and stole evidence that was found after he and Cole cleaned out Brenda's desk."

"What?!"

It was a testament to how well he knew her that he understood that jumbled paragraph. "Since you're only ten minutes away," she said, "I need you to come take the statement so I can go to bed. If you were at the lake house, I was going to just get Cole to do it." Which, now that she thought about it, she maybe should have done. He'd probably show up anyway with Tate.

"I'm on the way."

"Bring a hammer. And maybe some nails. I have plywood somewhere in my garage. I have no idea where a hammer might be. Or nails."

"A ham—? Never mind. I'll be there soon."

True to his word, James was there in under fifteen minutes, took her statement, then declared he wasn't leaving.

And she was glad.

Tate arrived a short time later, and while the men talked, she busied herself in the kitchen, then stopped to lean against the counter and tried to grab a breath. The front door opened and James stepped outside to speak with the officers who were getting ready to leave.

The shakes set in and sobs gathered in her throat. She swallowed but couldn't seem to choke them down. Tears flowed and dripped into the sink. She pulled in a gasping breath, doing her best to stay quiet.

Warm hands landed on her shoulders, and she turned to see Tate's compassionate gaze welcoming her to use his chest to muffle her crying. She leaned in and let him encircle her shoulders.

"It's okay," he whispered. "Just let it out."

So she did for a few seconds, drawing strength and comfort from his presence.

"I prayed for you all the way over here," he said. "That you would feel protected and unafraid. That you would stay strong and be willing to continue the fight."

She sniffed. "I'm willing. And I'll be strong in just a minute."

"That works."

"Steph?"

James's voice ended her tears, and she stepped away from the shelter of Tate's arms and broad shoulders. "Thank you," she said.

"Of course."

James stepped through the door. "Hey, Steph?"

"Yes?"

He frowned when he got a look at her face. There was no way she could cover the evidence of her crying jag.

"Don't say anything," she said. "I'm okay. Really."

"Right." His gaze slid to Tate, then back to her. "I found the plywood in your garage and got your window fixed. You'll have to order a new pane for it, but you won't be trying to cool the outdoors with your AC."

"Thank you. I appreciate it."

"You want to come stay at the apartment with me? Or have me stay here?"

She sighed and raked a hand over her head. "I mean, I'm not in danger now, right? The guy wanted the notebook and he has it. So I should be fine?"

"Should be. But you're probably going to jump at every sound if you're alone. If I'm here, you'll rest better."

He wasn't wrong. And if she was honest, there was a fourth bird. She'd been waiting on him to offer so she could accept. The whole reason she'd wanted him to come take her statement rather than Cole or Tate.

"Okay. Thanks." She nodded. "Yeah, stay here if you don't mind."

"I don't. Your couch is more comfortable than my bed." He saluted Tate. "Cole is waiting for you in the car." He turned and headed to the den and settled on her couch.

Tate gave her a small smile that looked pained, and she gasped. "I'm a horrible person. I never checked to make sure *you're* okay!"

He touched his head. "Yeah. He got me with something that knocked me silly for a few seconds. Long enough to grab the book and get away, but I'm fine. It was probably the grip of a gun, which I prefer to a bullet." He reached out and squeezed her fingers. "Seriously. We'll talk tomorrow, okay?"

"We're still on to visit with Greg?"

"We are. I'll pick you up and you can ride with us."

"Then I'll see you in the morning."

He left and she turned to see James watching with an odd little smile on his lips. She huffed. "Stop it."

"I didn't say anything."

"Yes. You did."

He laughed and she walked into her bedroom, brushed her teeth, and fell across the bed. Knowing James was just in the other room allowed her to close her eyes and fall asleep.

TATE STUDIED HIS CEILING, then rolled out of the bed when no answers to his multitude of questions were forthcoming. He palmed his eyes and pulled in a breath.

He wanted to check on Steph. He couldn't get the woman out of his mind and that bothered him. For as long as he could remember, he'd avoided anything—including romantic entanglements—that would derail his push to become a police officer and now a detective.

Sure, he'd dated. He'd even had one fairly serious relationship with another career-minded officer. Thankfully, they'd both realized they were better off good friends than married to each other. It had been an amicable parting with no broken hearts involved. He'd been disappointed, of course, but had gotten over it fairly quickly.

He texted Cole, and the man said he'd pick him up, then they'd grab Steph before heading over to the Hudson home.

His phone rang and he swiped the screen. "Hi, Mom."

"How are you doing, Detective Tate Cooper?"

He smiled. "I'm doing okay, Mom. Thanks for checking on me."

"When are you coming for a visit?"

"Well, believe it or not, I started day one with a big case, so it might be a while."

"I understand. We miss seeing you, but your dad and I are proud of you."

Emotion grabbed him by the throat, taking him off guard. He'd always been close to his parents and he missed them. But the job was everything right now. "Thanks, Mom. I appreciate it." He glanced at the clock on the wall. "I've got to go. I'll try to find some time to come see you guys soon." They only lived forty-five minutes away.

"See you later, Son."

"Give Dad a hug for me."

"I will. Bye."

Tate hung up and, with a groan, headed for the shower. He dreaded talking to the new widower, but part of him was looking forward to seeing Steph again in spite of the circumstances.

Twenty minutes later, he hurried to meet Cole, who'd pulled in front of his apartment. Tate slid into the passenger seat and was greeted with the delicious aroma of fresh-brewed coffee with a hint of . . . something. Hazelnut?

Two cups from the local café sat in the cupholder. "I don't suppose one of those is mine, is it?"

Cole shot him an amused look. "You know it is."

"You're the best partner a guy could ask for."

Cole laughed. "Glad to be of service." He pulled out of the apartment parking lot and aimed toward Steph's home. "Question for you."

"Shoot."

"You like Steph."

Tate stilled and forced himself not to choke on the sip he'd just taken. After he swallowed, he looked at Cole. "That was a statement."

"Okay. You like Steph, right?"

"Hm. I do. I mean, I've just met her, but she seems like a nice person. A person I might like to get to know should I not be totally focused on my career right now."

"So, you're not interested?"

"I don't think I said that."

Cole laughed. "All right, then. I'll just say this. Steph is amazing, but you might want to keep in mind she has three older brothers who all know how to use a gun. And a knife if you count Keegan."

"A knife?"

"He's a surgeon."

Tate chuckled. "Warning noted." Then he sobered. "But honestly, right now isn't a good time for romance. She's grieving and I'm investigating her friend's death. I don't think it would be in good taste to ask her out in the near future."

"Maybe not, but there's no reason you can't be her friend in the present."

"That's the conclusion I've come to. So you can stop your copycat-big-brother-James protective routine."

Cole slanted him an amused look, then turned his attention back to the road.

"And frankly, I meant what I said. I'm focused on this job, you know? I just made detective. I can't let myself get distracted no matter how much I might like her."

"Well, there's that, but honestly, Steph has been around law enforcement forever, so it's not like she doesn't know what your job entails."

Tate nodded. "I'll take that into consideration."

"Then again, she may not be interested in going out with you, so it's a moot point."

"And there is that. So thank you." He paused. "Did she say that?"

"No. I haven't asked her and don't think anyone else has either. Would you like me to?"

"No!" Tate cleared his throat. "No. Thanks for the offer, but I'm a big boy. I can handle my own love life. Or lack of." He paused. "Just drive."

Cole chuckled and two minutes later he pulled into Steph's driveway. Tate's heart lurched when she stepped out of her front door and joined them by climbing into the back seat.

"Hey," she said.

They echoed their greetings, and she fell silent, her face a mask of sorrow.

Her grief reached deep into a place he thought he'd locked up nice and tight, but all he wanted to do was be there for her, comfort her while she processed the death of her friend. With each passing moment he spent in her company, she drew him to her, making him want more than just friendship. He kept his sigh silent. *Why now, God?* Because in spite of all Tate's protests, his heart was hoping it wouldn't be long before he and Steph could possibly explore options that went beyond friendship. And now Tate was restless, impatient with his wishy-washy feelings. He wanted to turn again and look at her, but refrained. He'd wait. Right now wasn't about him or what he wanted. It was about Steph and being part of the support system she needed. He'd wait. Be patient and see how things played out. She would heal and he'd give her all the time she needed for that.

Which was okay. His gut was saying she was worth the wait. But would she feel the same about him?

SEVEN

STEPH WAS GRATEFUL for her big brother, truly. But if James hadn't left when Tate and Cole drove up, she was going to have to kick him and his helicoptering out. And now she was in Brenda and Greg's home, struggling to hold it together.

Her heart broke at the grief etched on Greg's face as he led them into the den. Once seated, Steph held three-year-old Magda on her lap while six-year-old Vince played with his toy cars in the adjacent playroom, visible from where she, Tate, and Cole were. Fourteen-year-old Mark was nowhere to be seen.

An open book lay face down on the end table next to her. *A Christmas Carol* by Charles Dickens. Brenda's.

Greg swiped his eyes and cleared his throat. "Sorry. I'm still in shock." He waved to his mother in the kitchen, and she came to take Magda from Steph. The little girl protested until she was given a cup of juice and a handful of animal cookies. Beau, the well-trained German shepherd, raised his head from his bed, but when no one offered him anything, he settled back onto his paws with a disgruntled sigh.

Steph turned her attention to Greg. "I don't even have the words to express my sorrow or how much my heart hurts for you and everyone who loved her."

He shot her a sad little smile. "No one does. It's okay. You don't have to search for them. You won't find any that will help." He drew in a ragged breath. "What will help is catching who did this."

"That's why we're here," Cole said.

"Yes. Thank you. So, on the phone, you said someone ran her off the road. That there were traces of green paint on her white vehicle. I just washed her car the day before yesterday, and I assure you that wasn't there."

Tate nodded. "That's helpful to know. We thought the paint looked fresh, but your confirmation is good to have." He waved a hand to Steph. "She wanted to come along and offer support. She's also the one who found a pink notebook that Brenda had been making notes in. Last night, someone broke into Steph's house and then mine looking for it. They managed to steal it from my kitchen."

Greg's jaw dropped. "What?" he whispered.

"But I took pictures of it," Steph said. She scooted closer to Greg and held out her phone so he could see one of the pages. "Do you have any idea what kind of code this is?"

He took her phone and studied the pictures. "That's her handwriting, but I couldn't tell you what it means or why she would feel the need to use code."

"Do you know why she was on Youngstown Road at that time of night?" Cole asked.

Greg shook his head, then raked a hand over his short dark curls. "No. We had dinner and then she asked me to put the kids to bed because she had an errand to run. I tried to talk her out of going, but she said it was something that couldn't wait. I fell asleep in the recliner. Only woke up when an officer rang my doorbell to tell me she'd crashed her car on that curve."

Tate and Cole exchanged a look. Greg caught it. "What?"

"We've come to the conclusion that it wasn't an accident," Tate said, his voice soft. "We can't prove it, but evidence suggests someone deliberately made her crash."

Greg blinked. "Wait, what? How are you getting that from a side swipe? It could have been an accident."

"If there had just been one area where there was paint, then yeah," Tate said, "but there were two. Like Brenda managed to keep it on the road after the first one, so the person came back and tried again. This time succeeding in pushing her over the side."

Greg stared and Cole cleared his throat. "The ME will have more information on her exact cause of death, but I'm sorry, Greg, it looks like Brenda was murdered."

The man gasped and Steph's heart broke for him.

He looked at each of them and spread his hands. "But . . . but why?"

"We don't know," Cole said. "We think it may be related to something she was working on. Something she wrote down in that notebook, since someone went to so much trouble to steal it."

"I have no idea." Greg shuddered. "She never talked about her work much, but . . ."

"But?"

"But she was making and getting phone calls. Calls that she obviously didn't want me to hear. I never suspected an affair. Brenda wouldn't do that to me. Every time I asked her about the calls, she would just shrug and say, 'Difficult client.' Or 'Work,' and then go in another room to talk."

"We didn't find her cell phone in the vehicle. Do you have it?"

"No." He tapped his screen and turned it for them to see. "I tried to check her location. The phone is offline."

"Yeah," Cole said. "It's okay. Will you allow us access to her personal phone records?"

"Absolutely. I can print them off for you."

"That would be a huge time-saver if we didn't have to get them from the phone company. Can you go back three months?"

"Of course." Greg rose, went to the desk in the corner of the room, and with the click of a few keys, sent the printer whirring.

While they waited for the pages to print, Steph let her gaze roam over the pictures lining the mantel. So many of Brenda and her family and friends. Steph was in a few. Tears threatened and she sniffed. "Greg," she said, "are you certain the break-in a couple of weeks ago was Mark climbing back in his window and not something else?"

He frowned and rubbed his head. "I never saw any evidence that it was anything other than Mark. I'll admit, Beau barking like he did was disconcerting, but I walked around outside and didn't see anything or anyone else."

"Hmm. Weird, but okay."

"It was weird, but all was quiet up until . . . well . . . her accident." Greg went to get the papers from the printer and handed them to Cole. "If you need to go back farther, just let me know."

"Thanks." Cole stood. "Appreciate your time. And I'm real sorry about Brenda. I only met her a few times, but she was always so kind."

Greg nodded.

Tate stepped forward. "If you think of anything else, please give us a call." He handed the man his card and Greg slid it in his wallet.

Steph hugged Greg, then went to tell the children goodbye. Magda clung to her as expected, and she gave the little girl an extra hug and a tickle so she could leave her laughing. Magda ran to Tate. "Hug everyone goodbye?"

Tate smiled and dropped to his knees. "Goodbye, Magda. You sure are a cute little thing." The child wrapped her little arms around his neck and squeezed, then did the same for Cole.

Greg swung Magda into his arms and kissed her cheek. He looked at Steph. "Thank you all."

Steph, Cole, and Tate walked out to the car, and Tate looked at Cole. "Looks like we're going to be going through some numbers for the next few hours. Your place or mine?"

"Cornerstone Café?"

"Perfect."

"Is it okay if I come along?" Steph asked. "I can work on the code. And besides, I'm starving."

The men exchanged a glance and Cole nodded. "Let's go."

THE THREE OF THEM sat in a booth in the back of the café with another table pulled up to make room for all the papers. The waitress, Jenny, had finally just left a carafe of coffee on the table and said to wave at her if they needed anything.

Steph had pulled out the papers containing the code. She knew her friend best, and if she kept going over the code, she might figure something out. Tate watched her from beneath lowered lashes. It was more entertaining than going over the phone list for the fifth time. Steph was beautiful inside and out. She'd been so kind and gentle with Brenda's family. And little Magda. His throat tightened as he remembered the feel of the little girl in his arms and her sweet hug.

"Number, number, number, letter, letter, letter," she muttered. "Number number number letter, number number number, letter. And numbers with lines under them. What do the lines mean?" A groan slipped from her and she dropped her forehead to the pages in front of her. "It makes no sense. There's nothing consistent except the letters *ENNB* that are interspersed throughout the pages." She went still. "Wait a minute."

"What?"

She lifted her head. "*ENNB*. That's the initials for Bolin's Nature Nurture Expeditions, only it's backward. Maybe she did that as part of the code?"

Tate raised a brow. "Good observation. She worked there and they're one of her clients."

"Or it means something else entirely, but I'm going to play with that." Steph nodded and pointed to the page. "Then there are two letters together every so often and they all have a *B* in them. Like here"—she pointed—"*BG*. And two pages over, *BH*. And . . . a lot on the third page with *BB*—Benji Bolin? Gage and Helen's son, maybe? Continuing with the reversed letter idea, *BC* could refer to Cherry Bolin, their daughter. They all work at Bolin's and the reversed initials thing works for them all."

"You figured that out," Tate murmured. "You're brilliant."

She flushed and looked down. "Not really. Once I knew what to look for, it was easy. Also not sure if it's right, but it does work. I just don't know what the other letters are for. Or the numbers."

"Keep working. You'll figure it out."

Cole stood. "I'm not seeing anything on this list that's jumping out at me. Let's both take it with us and study it a little more at a later time. Maybe giving it some space will help. In the meantime, I think we might want to go talk to Gage and Helen. I know them in passing and have always thought they were good people. I have to admit I want to know why their initials are in a dead woman's coded note pages, though. I'll call them and see if they have a good time for us to come by."

"They may not be in town," Steph said. "They travel a lot. And I do mean a lot." She frowned. "Once Cherry and Benji were old enough, they dumped the business on them and started doing their own thing."

"How do Cherry and Benji feel about that?"

"Cherry's resented it from day one, but feels like she needs to be there to help Benji. She's always looked out for him and wouldn't think of abandoning him to run the place by himself."

Cole frowned. "I never knew all that."

Steph shrugged. "Cherry told me that a couple of years ago. I feel sorry for her. She's basically living her life for her parents and her brother. I tried to get her to take a trip to the beach with Brenda, Lainie, Kenzie, and me a few months ago, and she said she just couldn't leave Benji alone, that he'd run the place into the ground with his immaturity."

"Whoa," Tate said. "That's a pretty harsh statement."

"I know. When I asked her about her parents, she just rolled her eyes and said some people should never have children."

"What!" Cole raised a brow. "I always thought they were great parents."

"I did too until she said that. Then she laughed and said she was kidding, she was just tired and ready for a vacation that she could never take."

"Sad," Tate murmured.

"Very," Steph said.

Tate stood. "Now I want to talk to them more than ever. I'll take Steph home and we can go pay them a visit—assuming they're there. Even if they're not, I'd like to see the place through the eyes that Steph just gave us. I want to watch Benji and Cherry interact and all that."

Cole nodded. "I do too."

While Cole made the call, Tate and Steph walked out to the car. She looked at the pages she'd printed out and bit her lip. "Actually, you know what? While you guys do that, I'm going to investigate a little idea I've got."

"An idea?"

"Something that just occurred to me. I'll let you know if it pans out. I mean, don't hold your breath or anything since it will probably go the way of all of my other ideas, but I've got to try."

"Don't be so hard on yourself. You figured out the reversed initials thing."

She shot him a small smile. "Thanks." She hesitated, then said, "Like I said inside, Cherry and I are pretty good friends. Not as good as Brenda and I were, but she and I get together every so often for coffee and a chat. If you decide it would help to have me talk to her about anything, call me and I'll come on over. I'll be at the library. Bolin's is just a twenty-minute drive from there."

"I'll keep that in mind."

Cole joined them. Tate filled him in on the plan, and they dropped Steph at her home so she could get her car and go to the library.

With a frown, he watched her open her garage and climb into her car. "You think she'll be okay?" he asked Cole.

Cole rubbed his chin, a slightly concerned look in his eyes. But he said, "No reason to think otherwise. Whoever was after the notebook got it."

"I know, but I don't like leaving her alone."

"Because you don't think she'll be safe or because you just like being around her?"

Tate snorted. "Both."

"That's what I thought." Cole snagged his phone. "I'll ask a couple of buddies on patrol to follow her home from the library." He made the call, then looked at Tate. "Feel better?"

"Somewhat. Thanks."

Cole pulled away and headed up the mountain while Tate kept an eye on Steph for as long as she was in view. *Keep her safe, Lord. I'm not sure I like this idea.*

EIGHT

STEPH SPREAD THE PAPERS on the table in front of her and pulled one of the books off the stack she'd spent thirty minutes agonizing over and creating.

"All right, my friend, you love the classics, so if I'm right about this, you would use one of these. Now, the two books found at your office were *The Old Man and the Sea* and *Oliver Twist*, so we'll start with those. Of course, you could have used digital versions, but knowing your preference for a hard copy we'll just start here."

She opened *Oliver Twist* and went to the first set of numbers and letters.

"*472IH*," she muttered. "All right then. Page four, seventh row, second word." She sighed. "The *I* maybe stands for a word?" She tapped the page. "But that one does not start with I. Okay. Next book. *The Old Man and the Sea*." She kept trying until she'd gone through all the books.

With nothing.

"Ugh." She tossed her pencil down and looked around at the other patrons. The crowd had thinned the closer it got to dinnertime, but one young woman at the table in front of her looked deep in her research. She had several books open and flipped over, holding her spot until she was ready to come back to them.

The image of a book on an end table flickered in her memory. The one on Brenda's end table. And one she hadn't pulled from the shelf.

A Christmas Carol.

She rose, hesitated, then gathered the papers. No need to leave them where anyone could come by and grab them. She went to the aisle, found the book easily, and discovered it was the same edition that Brenda had.

Steph snagged it and glanced around, trying to stay aware of her surroundings. And the people in it. A figure wearing a hoodie stood next to the water fountain examining the announcement board. He caught her attention, but she hesitated, waiting to see what he might do.

He lifted his phone and snapped a picture of the library calendar, then turned and headed for the exit. Steph let out a low breath. She was paranoid. And maybe being a little paranoid wasn't a bad thing. But not everyone in a hoodie was a bad guy.

While the crowd in the library was sparse, there *were* other people around and he was gone, so she wasn't afraid to stay put and finish what she was doing. She chewed her lip and looked at the young man behind the desk. A woman in her twenties loaded books onto a cart. An older man mopped the floor of one of the glassed-in meeting rooms.

The library didn't have a security guard, but maybe one of the workers would help her out. She returned to the table and opened the book to apply the same key she'd been so convinced would work. And found the letter *I* on the fourth page, seventh row, second word. "Okay, maybe we're getting somewhere," she muttered. On the same line was a word starting with *H. Have.* Excitement swirled. And then the next part was *10 12 9F.* She flipped to page ten, counted down twelve lines, and over nine words. *Find!*

I have find.

Not exactly perfect grammar, but Brenda may have decided to pick words close enough to what she meant. She *could* have meant *I have found . . .*

Maybe.

But as long as she appeared to be on the right path, she'd keep going. She figured out the next few words.

I have find evidence of stolen money . . .

Steph sat back. That was it. She'd figured it out. It was so simple but would be a painstaking process to decipher every page. "What in the world, Brenda? Who were you so afraid would see this?"

She texted Cole and Tate.

> I have the key to the code. I think. I'm pretty
> sure. Anyway, I'm going to head home and if
> you want to come by, I'll give it to you.

She hit send. Then reconsidered. Maybe she should just take it to them. It was a twenty-minute drive . . .

Unless she took the shorter route. The dangerous one. She'd driven Youngstown Road before, of course. Very slowly and very carefully. And never in the dark. But she definitely didn't make a habit of it. Would it be worth the time saved to do so now?

Tate texted her back.

> We're leaving now. Not much light shed on
> Brenda's death. They don't know why she was
> on that road. Said she always avoided it.

Exactly.

Unless . . .

She'd been pressed for time and decided to risk it? Steph had just considered doing so.

Had Brenda?

But what would have caused her to be in such a hurry like that? What would have been worth the risk? And who had known she'd drive that route and had gone ahead to lie in wait for her to hit the curve before they pulled the trigger?

All questions without answers.

She texted her boss, the only other person who might have a clue about what Brenda had been working on. Cole and Tate had already talked to him, and he'd declared he had no idea about any of it, but Steph wasn't so sure. Maybe they just hadn't asked the right questions.

Stan, are you home? Do you mind if I stop by?

While she waited for Stan to respond, Steph worked a little more on the cryptic message, gaining confidence as the words appeared on the page.

I have find evidence of stolen money. I have talked to BH and asked her how business was. She said slow but all right. Money is being taken but I don't know who is doing it yet. Talk to GS . . .

Steph stopped. *GS?* If she reversed the initials that would be SG. Stan Gilchrest obviously. She checked her phone. Still no response from the man, and now she wanted to talk to him more than ever.

She called his number and it went to voicemail.

"Come on, Stan, this isn't like you. Call me back." But . . . it was a holiday weekend. One of his employees had been killed. Maybe he'd simply unplugged to hang out with his wife and any kids who were around. She couldn't blame him.

And if he didn't have any major holiday plans, Stan often liked to work in his garden on his days off. Maybe he was still outside in spite of the dark. He had floodlights. And his greenhouse was well lit. She'd just ride over there and see if he was available. But she wanted to decipher more and see what Stan had told Brenda. She worked on the next part.

SG said he would check probably mistake. I don't think mistake. I think SG knows something about missed money. Seemed scared. Frightened. Feel sorry for him. Will talk to him again.

In disbelief, she tossed her pencil onto the table and stared at the words.

And now Steph wanted to know what Stan knew. She took a picture of the paper and sent it to Tate and Cole.

She had to track him down. Now.

Relieved to have a plan, she packed up the pages of the journal and her notes and grabbed her empty Yeti cup. It was dark outside, but the parking lot lights were bright and the area fairly busy, so she clicked the fob to unlock her car and hurried to it. The officers in the cruiser parked near the door waved, and Steph relaxed then slid behind the wheel of her Subaru. She drew in a steadying breath, hating the feeling of lurking danger in spite of her temporary bodyguards. She longed for the days where she took her safety mostly for granted. Not that she didn't take precautions like any smart person, but she'd never felt that someone was out to do her bodily harm like she had over the last couple of days.

With the doors locked, she looked around and focused on the car in the corner of the parking lot. It was backed into a space, and she thought the driver was at the wheel. When he caught her looking, he cranked his vehicle, pulled out, and roared from the parking lot.

Steph frowned. While his features had been obscured by the glare on the windshield, she was sure it was the same guy in the library who'd snapped a picture of the bulletin board. Had he been waiting on her and, when he realized she saw him, gotten scared off?

But why? He had the book, so why keep tabs on her?

Unless he knew she had the printed pages and was working on deciphering them? She hadn't exactly hidden them while working on the code, and she'd been pretty absorbed in what she was doing, feeling safe at her little table in the library.

She swallowed hard, thinking she—and Cole and Tate—may have overestimated exactly how safe she was. Only the comforting presence of the police car behind her let her breathe normally.

TATE AND COLE had struck out with the Bolins, but Tate wasn't convinced they were being completely truthful in their protests that they had no idea what Brenda was doing on Youngstown Road or why she would have been headed to the facility at that time of night.

His phone chimed and he glanced at the screen while Cole drove.

"'Going to see my boss,'" he read aloud. "'Stan knows something. I deciphered more of the code, and Brenda said she went to him with evidence of theft and he said he'd take care of it, but she thought he might know something.'" Tate shook his head and glanced at Cole. "Is she serious?"

"Absolutely."

"I'm going to call her."

"Excellent idea. Then give me the phone so I can yell at her."

"I'll put her on speaker so you can judge whether that's necessary." Tate tapped her name in his contact list, thankful she answered on the first ring. "First, you're on speakerphone so Cole can hear, and second," he said in lieu of a greeting, "we have our forensic accountants working on this. You don't have to play amateur detective."

"I know. I'm not really. But Brenda was my friend, and I can't just sit on my hands doing nothing."

"Doing nothing is precisely what you need to do," Cole said, his voice slightly louder than necessary for her to hear it.

"And we need that key," Tate jumped in. "There's obviously a lot more she had to say by what's left to decipher."

"Well, then meet me there if you don't mind. I'm closer to his place than I am mine." She gave them the address, and Cole shrugged even though he shot a glare at the phone.

Tate frowned. "Fine, but if you think he knows something, it could be dangerous for you to confront him."

"Stan?" She laughed. "He wouldn't hurt a flea."

"Stephanie Cross," Cole said, "don't make me call James."

Another chuckle rippled through the line. "Is that supposed to be a threat? He doesn't scare me."

"Well, he scares me," Cole snapped, "and if something happens to you because—" He closed his eyes for a brief second while he ground his teeth against what he obviously wanted to say, and Tate almost felt sorry for the man. "Just stay put," Cole finally managed.

"I have my two watchdogs, Cole. They're right behind me. I'll be fine."

"Steph . . ."

Tate bit the inside of his cheek to keep a smile off his face. He really shouldn't be smiling. This was serious. But the interaction between these two was funny—and entertaining. James and Cole were best friends, so Steph had another older brother whether she wanted one or not.

She sighed. "Fine. I'll be waiting in my car."

"Thank you."

"Sure. I'll be there in about five minutes."

"We're closer to ten," Tate said.

"I can be patient for five minutes."

"Ten," Tate said.

"Ha!" Cole snorted. "In what universe?"

"I heard that."

"Wasn't trying to hide it."

This time Tate let his laugh break through. Cole shot him a scowl and Tate snickered.

"I heard that too, Tate Cooper. I'll be waiting." She hung up.

Tate laughed again and shook his head. "You think she'll wait?"

"No." Cole pressed the gas.

NINE

STEPH PULLED TO THE CURB of the very nice two-story farm-style home set on a two-acre parcel. Stan was married to Beth, and they had two sons in college and one married daughter.

Steph stepped out of the car, breathing in the scent of freshly mowed grass. Even though it was September in the mountains, it was still hot during the day. She gripped the driver's door and looked behind her. The driveway was long and winding, and the main road was empty. If anyone followed her—other than the two bodyguards right behind her—they were staying well back. She had to admit, knowing Tate and Cole were on the way eased her nerves. A lot.

Stan's garden was on the other side of the property at the back of the house. If he was here, that's where he'd be. The garage door was up, the lights on. Stan's weekday Mercedes was on the left side, and the right side that usually housed his wife's van was empty.

Where were the college kids' vehicles? Stan hadn't said for sure they were coming, so maybe they'd decided against it? And where was Stan's truck? He had an old beater that he used to haul stuff for his garden and yard. The sound of an engine caught her attention, and she turned to find Tate and

Cole turning in. As they drew closer, she was able to make out Cole's surprised expression.

He likely expected her to be inside or with Stan. She refrained from sticking her tongue out at him and simply raised a brow because . . . well . . . she couldn't really blame him.

He smirked and Tate looked amused as well. Cole had probably told Tate all about her impatient nature, explaining that she wouldn't have listened to him to wait. She almost wished she'd proven him right.

Cole parked and the two men climbed from the vehicle. Her gaze was immediately drawn to Tate, and she blinked, forcing herself to look away and turn to Cole. "I waited."

"I'm shocked," Cole said. He waved to the other officers and they drove off. When he turned back to her, his expression had softened. "But I'm glad, so thank you."

"Sure. The lights are on and it looks like someone's home, but he's not answering his phone." Steph turned her back on them and headed to the side of the house that would take her around into the backyard. "Stan? Are you here?"

"Steph?" Tate joined her, with Cole three steps behind him. "Do you always go dashing into possible danger?"

"Of course not."

"Of course she does," Cole said at the same time, all softness gone from his face.

Steph scowled at him, then focused on Tate. "Stan wasn't answering his phone and I just figured he was working in his garden or the greenhouse." The lights lit up the area, and she swept a hand toward the immaculate space that contained just about every vegetable and herb known to man. But no Stan.

Tate let out a low whistle. "Nice."

"I know. He brings stuff in all the time to share." She pointed to the vehicle at the edge of the garden. "Well, that answers the question about his truck." He'd pulled it around and looked like he'd been in the middle of unloading bags of mulch. "Wonder what interrupted him?" she asked.

"Maybe nothing," Cole said. "It's possible he simply stopped to go to the bathroom or take a phone call or get a drink or something." He clucked his tongue. "Always so suspicious. I'll check the house." He shot her a sideways glance. "Unless you've already done it and hightailed back to your car so I wouldn't know."

She rolled her eyes. "No, I haven't checked it, Mr. Smarty-pants." She'd had his friends watching her. Besides, there was no way she'd ever let on that she'd thought about it despite having eyes on her movements.

"But you thought about it," he said. Steph gave a short laugh and Cole shot her a knowing look, then nodded to Tate. "Ready?"

"I'm right behind you."

Her laughter faded quickly. The truth was, she was uneasy. Something just felt off.

Cole knocked on the door and they waited.

Steph shifted. Tate rang the bell.

Nothing.

"Stan?" Cole identified himself and Tate. "Steph's here too." He rapped his knuckles against the wood once more. "You home?"

No response.

Steph reached around Cole and twisted the knob. "It's unlocked."

"That's all well and good, but we can't go in there," Cole said. "We don't have a good enough reason."

"Exigent circumstances?" she asked.

"There aren't any."

"Well, I'm not bound by the same restrictions you are." Before either man could protest, she slipped past them and into the house. "Stan? Are you here?" She went right into the kitchen and noticed a pile of clothes on the kitchen table. Weird. But no Stan.

"Steph." Cole's exasperation rang clear.

She'd apologize later. She walked into the connecting den and gasped. "Stan!" He lay on the floor, next to a shattered glass coffee table. Blood had pooled beneath his head, the oriental rug stained dark.

Thinking he was dead, Steph nevertheless hurried forward and knelt by her boss to search for a pulse while Tate followed, and Cole called for an ambulance. Steph almost couldn't believe it when a faint thumping pulsed against her fingers. "He's alive. Y'all, he's alive." Barely. And not for much longer if he didn't get help.

"Ambulance is on the way," Cole said.

"What do we do now?" Because doing nothing wasn't an option.

"Keep him warm for one thing." Tate grabbed a blanket from the back of the couch and covered Stan. "Uh . . . ABC, right? Airway, Breathing, Circulation. Is he breathing?"

She checked. "Yes."

"And he still has a pulse," Tate said. "So we wait for the ambulance and pray it gets here soon."

Steph kept an eye on the clock. Three minutes later, paramedics arrived and got him stable enough to transport. Soon their taillights disappeared and the siren faded.

Tate returned to her side on the porch. "How did you know he was in trouble?"

"I didn't. Not really. Things just seemed odd. He was more stressed than usual. Yesterday I was leaving the office and he was on the phone and pacing, upset about something." She shrugged. "Individually, those don't mean much. Everyone has bad days and clients can really stress you out. When you deal with people's money, things can get hairy sometimes."

"Right."

"But just adding it all up and then Brenda's notes in the journal made me want to ask him myself. See his face when he said he didn't know what Brenda was working on, then show him her notes. The thing is, we *always* keep Stan up-to-date on stuff. He's a bit of a micromanager, so I know Brenda would have talked to him."

"Why didn't you tell us this?"

"I don't know. He said she didn't, and at the time, while it seemed odd, I believed him. Then I kept thinking about Brenda and Stan and how we all worked together, and I just . . ." She shrugged. "I thought maybe now that some time had passed, he might have remembered something—or would be more willing to share what he knew."

"Hmm." Cole looked at his phone. "Do you have any idea where his wife and kids are?"

"Maybe her mother's? I think she lives in Asheville. His sister-in-law lives in Black Mountain."

"Thanks. Those are good places to start. I can find names and addresses with that." He walked back into the house, dialing his phone on the way. The crime scene unit had taken over the den, and Steph was at a loss as to what to do next.

Tate started to say something, but Cole's appearance in the doorway stopped him.

Steph frowned. "What is it?"

With gloved hands, Cole held up a black ski mask and hoodie. "I don't suppose these look familiar?"

TATE SLID AN ARM around Steph's shoulder when she swayed and gaped. "Are you kidding me?" she whispered.

Cole grimaced. "I wish I was. They were right there on the kitchen table."

"Stan is the one who broke into my house? Tate's? B-but why?"

A shudder rippled through her, and Tate tightened his grip. "Unfortunately, only Stan can answer that."

She looked around, a slightly dazed expression on her face. "Then he's the one who stole Brenda's journal. It's got to be here somewhere."

"Assuming he didn't pass it off to someone," Tate said.

Cole nodded. "We'll turn this place upside down looking for it as soon as the crime scene unit is finished—which will be a while because now we're looking for anything that can give us a connection between him and Brenda that may not be work related." He paused. "At the very least, we need to finish deciphering the notes. It may tell us what made him so desperate to get his hands on it."

"I have a headache," she said.

Tate shot her a sympathetic smile. "Explain the key to us, and we have people who can finish decoding it. Fast."

She nodded. "All right."

Once they'd given their statement, Tate called to let Lainie know that Stan was being brought in and he and Cole needed to talk to him as soon as he was awake. And coherent. In the meantime, they'd be heading back to Bolin's for another visit first thing in the morning.

Steph pursed her lips and frowned. "I'm just confused. What was his connection to Bolin's? Other than the fact that they were one of Brenda's clients? Stan liked the outdoors, but he wasn't an outdoorsman. He'd never ride the rapids or do zip-lining or anything else Bolin's offers. Does that make sense?"

"Perfect sense," Cole said. "We'll figure it out when he wakes up."

"If he wakes up," she said. "What if he doesn't?"

Tate sighed. "I don't know. Maybe the crime scene unit will

turn up something here at the house. In the meantime, we need to get out of the way." Officers were doing as promised and tearing up the place, bagging evidence, and would let them know if the notebook appeared.

Steph continued to frown, then shook her head. "I just can't believe Stan would break into my house. And yours, Tate."

"What? You think someone is framing him by leaving the clothes?"

She shrugged. "I don't know. I just would have thought I'd have recognized his voice or the way he walked or even just the shape of his body. *Something.*"

Tate honestly didn't know what to think. He sighed. "You were scared. It's possible it just didn't register."

"I guess that's possible." Her furrowed brow said she was still thinking about it. "But suppose someone else is involved and is throwing the blame on Stan. Where does that leave me? Am I safe? Or does the person still want to come after me? And why?"

Tate rubbed his chin. "Good questions. Whoever was in our houses wanted Brenda's little pink notebook. And got it. If this was an attack on Stan and not a fall or an accident, then it's possible the person knew Stan had the notebook, attacked him, and got what he was after, assuming officers don't find it here." He looked around. "And so far, they haven't. I'm guessing Stan knew something and the person who attacked him—if it was an attack—wanted to shut him up. In that case, I'd think you're in the clear and safe."

"Right."

"We'll see what the lab says about the clothing. If they can pull some DNA off of it, then we'll have something to work with."

She nodded.

"I'm going to have a chat with Matt over there," Cole said.

"I need to tell him to be looking for the journal." He nodded to Tate. "I'll meet you at the car in just a few."

Cole walked off, and Tate led Steph back to her vehicle. She swiped a tear from her cheek, and he laid a gentle hand on her arm. "Are you sure you're going to be okay?" he asked.

A sigh slipped from her. "I'm in shock right now. And I may have been betrayed by a person who I thought was not just my boss but my friend as well. I've had lunch with his wife, they've given me Christmas and birthday gifts, and so on. I'm just . . . angry too." She ran a hand over her hair. "I'm sorry, I didn't mean to dump that on you. I normally vent to my girlfriends, but they're not here, so you're the lucky recipient."

"Hey, I'm here anytime you need to vent." He took her hand and gave it a light squeeze. "Steph, this may not be the best time to ask, but now that it looks like you're in the clear, would it be all right if I came over after I'm done at the hospital?" He ducked his head but looked up at her. "I'd like to get to hang out with you without the threat of someone trying to kill you."

She smiled at him. "I'd like that."

TEN

SUNDAY MORNING, Steph texted Cherry Bolin and asked to meet with her. While Tate and Cole had come up empty-handed after visiting the company again and were on the way to the hospital, Steph wanted to talk to Cherry personally. Now that the person who'd likely been after her was lying unconscious in the hospital, she felt safer driving to Bolin's Nature Nurture Expeditions without an escort or self-appointed bodyguard. Safer, but not completely relaxed. She'd keep her guard up.

Cherry texted right back and said she was at work and to come on by. They'd talk in the café.

Twenty minutes later, Steph checked the café and found it empty except for a young couple huddled over a laptop in the back corner. She went to the counter and ordered a mocha. Once she had the drink, she looked around. Still no Cherry.

Taking a seat, she considered whether to wait or let Cherry know she was there. She finally texted her.

Give me ten minutes, came her friend's reply.

"Fancy meeting you here."

She jumped and turned to see Benji Bolin, Cherry's brother. He was in his midthirties, tall, and in good shape, thanks to his physical lifestyle. He wasn't what she would consider good-looking, with the scruffy beard and shaggy hair, but he had a nice smile. "Hi," she said. "I'm just waiting on Cherry."

"She said you were coming by. Hold on a sec." He went to the counter and grabbed a water from the bucket, turned, and walked back to drop into the chair opposite her. "She got held up by a customer. I told her I'd keep you company."

"Well, it's good to see you. I hear you've taken over most of the operations of the place in addition to your guided hikes and rafting."

"I have. Mom and Dad wanted to slow down a bit, so I said I'd handle the business."

"Good for you." That all seemed kind of weird to her, though, because Cherry was the one who was more business oriented and stable while Benji . . . wasn't.

"Any news yet on what happened to Brenda?" he asked. "The detectives were here this morning again asking questions, but they didn't have much to share."

"No, they don't know yet, but they'll figure it out before too long. Brenda left a notebook that will probably lead them to her killer."

"Yeah, that's what the detectives said. You know what was in it?"

She raised a brow. Should she say? Probably not. She didn't want to lie, but . . . "Well, it was in code." Which was true.

"Oh right. They said something about that. They also said Bolin's was in it and that's why they wanted to talk to us. Wanted to know why Brenda thought she needed to write the information in code. It was all very weird. And kind of insulting."

She shrugged. "I don't think you should find it insulting. Brenda loved this place. She loved you and your family. I'm not surprised she would mention this place. Whatever she said in her notes might not be negative."

"Huh. Yeah, I guess." He sipped his drink and seemed about to say something more when Cherry rushed in.

"I'm so sorry, I got held up. Benji, your rafting party is ready to go. They're waiting on you."

Benji stood and saluted her with his drink. "Duty calls. Nice to see you again, Steph."

"You too."

He left and Cherry took his seat. "I'm so glad you called and came over. I hear you had quite the incident the other night. Someone broke into your house?"

"Someone did. Oddly enough, it turns out it might have been Stan, my boss."

"What! How do you know that?"

She sighed. "It's a long story—and I don't even know all the details—but I went looking for Stan and found him in a pool of blood on the floor. He'd hit his head on his glass coffee table."

"I'm so sorry to hear he's dead. That's terrible. Stan was a frequent customer here. He loved the zip line."

Steph stared at her. "He's not dead, but he's in the ICU. Cole and Tate are just waiting for him to wake up so they can question him. But hold on. Let's circle back to Stan and zip-lining. He hated that kind of stuff. What do you mean he *loved* it?"

Cherry frowned. "Well, he was here like clockwork every Sunday morning, signed up for the two-hour zip line package."

Steph groaned and dropped her head into her hand. "I'm so confused."

"Never mind that. Why on earth would he break into your place?"

Steph looked up, making a note to come back to Stan and zip-lining. Maybe his wife would know. "He was looking for a notebook I'd found hidden in Brenda's desk, but I'd already given it to Detective Cooper. And then Stan broke into *his* place and managed to steal it."

Cherry gaped and Steph sighed. "I know. It's all a bit much, isn't it?"

"A bit much for sure. And Brenda . . ." Tears welled in Cherry's eyes and she sniffed. "I don't even know what to think about that one." She brushed away a stray tear. "So they think she was killed because of the notebook?"

"It's just speculation, of course, but I can see it being the case if she was looking for something, found it, and recorded it." She paused and narrowed her eyes. "But it was a notebook no one probably knew about—not even her husband—until I found it and showed it to Stan." Stan, who'd been desperate to get his hands on it and had called someone immediately after their conversation. Well, Stan had gotten the book. But what about the phone call right after she'd shown him the journal? Coincidence? Maybe. Maybe not. Maybe his call had spurred the incidents that followed. Like her stalker in the garage and at the library. Because *that* person hadn't been Stan. And she still wasn't a hundred percent sure the person in her house had been Stan.

Steph grabbed her phone. "I'm sorry, Cherry, I need to make a call."

"Of course."

TATE'S PHONE RANG, flashing Steph's number. He tapped the screen. "Hello?"

"Hey, I just thought of something and it may be nothing, but I figured better to be wrong than right and say nothing. Right?"

He blinked. "What?"

"I'm at Bolin's—"

"What!"

"Uh . . . why are you shouting at me?"

Tate closed his eyes and counted to three. "Because," he said in a much calmer tone, "we're investigating the Bolins, remember?"

"I remember you came up here to chat with them, but I didn't realize you were doing a full-on investigation."

"That's because I can't tell you everything about what we're doing, but you need to leave there and don't go back until I or Cole give you the all clear. Can you do that?"

"Yes, of course. I'll just say goodbye to Cherry and text you when I'm on the way."

"Good."

"But first, I need to tell you about a phone call Stan made." She went on to explain about what she'd witnessed after Stan saw the journal. "It may be nothing," she said, "but I don't know. At the time, I didn't think much about it, but knowing what I know now . . ."

"Right." It wasn't a bad idea. "I'll see if we can find who he called around that time. Thank you for that. Now get out of there."

"I'm getting, I promise. I'll text when I'm in the car."

He hung up and said a quick prayer for the woman. He'd only known her a short time but was far more interested in spending time with her than he should be. Could he date her and still focus on his job? On climbing the ladder of success? Balance a relationship without sacrificing everything he'd worked for to get to this point?

He honestly wasn't sure, but for the first time since he could remember, he thought he might want to try.

He checked his phone. No text from Steph saying she was on her way home. He tapped on the screen.

> Steph, please. Leave. While I think Stan was the one causing all of your problems, we're not sure what role—if any—Bolin's played in Brenda's death. Or if someone from there was involved in Stan's "accident." Let me know you're away from there.

He hit send, then waited for the three little dots to appear.

How long did it take to walk to your car, climb in, and lock the doors?

ELEVEN

STEPH WALKED toward her car. She hated having to rush away from Cherry, but investigating Brenda's death wasn't her job. It was Tate's and Cole's and she was—*apparently*—interfering with that. "Not that I did it on purpose," she muttered. Her phone buzzed and she ignored it for the moment. She could check it once she was in the car with her seat belt on and the doors locked.

"Talking to yourself?"

Steph jerked to a stop three steps from her Subaru. "Benji, what in the world? You really have to stop sneaking up on people."

He laughed. "No sneaking involved. You were too busy having a conversation with yourself to notice me. Hope it was a good one."

She ignored his teasing. "I thought you were taking a team on the river."

"I was, but for the past two weeks, one of our new workers, Lila, has been insisting she's ready to go solo. After thinking about it, I agreed, so I sent her on her way." He shoved his hands in the pockets of his jeans and walked toward her. "And if you're finished talking to yourself, maybe we could continue our conversation."

She shrugged. "Okay." There was something to continue?

"Walk with me?" He gestured toward one of the hiking trails.

She glanced at her phone. Tate was getting impatient, and she needed to answer him before he had a coronary. She looked up at Benji. "I'm sorry, I really need to go."

"Just give me five minutes. Please?"

Steph hesitated. "Okay, but I need to text someone. He's waiting on me to let him know I'm leaving."

"Sure."

She tapped a quick text.

> I'm leaving in just a few. Talking to Benji for a minute and then I'll be on my way home.

When she finished, she tucked her phone into her back pocket and focused on the man in front of her. "Okay, what can I do for you?"

"I was just thinking. Brenda had a locker in the staff room. I don't think anyone has looked in it or cleaned it out yet. Maybe you can look and see if there's anything there that the cops might want?"

Steph raised her brows. "And you just now thought of that?"

He flushed. "I know." He shrugged. "But in my defense, I wasn't even on the property when the cops came the first time. The second time I was on the zip line."

"They talked to your parents. Why wouldn't they mention the locker?"

He gave a small shrug. "They, uh, don't know about it. It was just a couple of weeks ago that she asked for one. I got her a key and told her which locker to use."

"Okay. Why tell me? Why not call the cops?"

He spread his hands and sighed. "Because there was an envelope in there with your name on it." He ducked his head and shuffled his feet a bit. "I think she was having an affair, and if there's evidence in there to prove that, then I thought you could get rid of it when I gave you the envelope. I mean, the woman is dead. Why hurt her family by bringing all that to light?"

Steph gaped. "No way." He wasn't making a bit of sense. "Why not get rid of it yourself?"

"I thought about it but figured you could do it when I gave you the envelope."

"Benji, if you think she was having an affair and there's evidence in the locker, then the cops need to know. I'll call Tate right now and—"

She lifted her phone and stopped when he stepped forward, a scowl on his face. "No. Brenda was a friend. A good woman. She always treated me with kindness, and I don't want her name smeared. I only told you about this because of the envelope. Now, do you want it or not?"

She did, but Tate's warnings were echoing in her ears. "Does Cherry know about this?"

His frown deepened. "Cherry doesn't need to know everything."

"Why don't I wait here while you get the envelope for me?"

He hesitated, then scoffed. "Okay. Whatever." He walked away and she felt slightly guilty at her immediate assumption that he was trying to lure her into the locker room for . . . whatever purposes. But someone had killed Brenda and that someone may or may not have been Stan. If it wasn't Stan, then—

Cherry came out of the café, spotted Steph, and walked toward her. "Everything all right? You make your call?"

"I did and I'm not sure if everything's all right or not."

Her friend frowned. "Cryptic." Then her attention focused on a spot over Steph's shoulder and her eyes widened. "Benji? What are you doing? You're supposed to be on the river."

"Change of plans. Lila's got it covered."

Cherry groaned. "Are you kidding me?"

"Chill. She's got the sat phone and she's ready. It'll be fine."

A muscle jumped in Cherry's jaw, and she pulled in a deep breath. "Benji, I'm so tired of cleaning up your messes. If something happens—"

"Nothing's going to happen! Just let it go!"

"I've called Mom and Dad!"

Her brother stilled. "What?"

"They'll know how to fix this."

He called her an unflattering name, then stomped toward the office.

Steph turned raised brows to Cherry. "What messes are you having to clean up?"

Cherry ignored her and caught up with her brother, grabbing him by the arm and yanking him around to face her. "You can't run away from this."

"Watch me!"

TATE WALKED to his car and climbed in. He sent a text to Cole and let him know he was heading back up the mountain to bring a stubborn woman down it. She still hadn't texted him to let him know she was on her way home and she wasn't answering her phone.

He called her number once more and it went to voicemail on the fourth ring. At least the phone was still on.

His phone rang. Cole. "Hey, don't worry, I'm on the way to get her."

"Yeah, I'm on the way too. I just got the rest of the decoded contents of Brenda's book. She overheard part of a conversation between Benji and someone else. She said she had a hard time hearing the other person, but sounded like she was saying he needed to get his act together. In response, Benji said he had the money lined up, he just needed a couple more days to actually get it in his hands."

"What money?"

"Bolin's money. It's all here on the pages from the little pink book. Forensics found two sets of books for the company. One legit set and one that was tracking money being stolen and other money being laundered. It seems like Benji has a nice little drug operation going. Brenda found some wonky transactions—deposits and withdrawals that weren't actually made and other issues where the numbers didn't add up. Purchases of equipment, returns that were made but the refund was never deposited, et cetera. She went to talk to Helen and Gage, but they were out of town. She left messages on their voicemails that weren't returned. She finally said she was going to confront Benji and ask him to figure out a way to return the money so she didn't have to report anything to the police."

"Oh no," Tate said, his voice soft. "And Steph's up there with him."

"Try to get her on the phone. I'll meet you there."

Tate voice dialed her number and pressed the gas.

TWELVE

STEPH HAD LEFT the siblings alone for a few minutes, but now the argument had turned hushed. She was torn between leaving and trying to hear what they were saying. She drew closer to the locker room and hovered outside.

Silence.

Her phone buzzed, but she ignored it. It was probably Tate, Cole, or James, and they would be livid at her not answering, but right now she needed to figure out what was going on with her friend. She opened the door and found Cherry with her head bent, pulling in slow, deep breaths and letting them out through pursed lips.

"Cherry?" She placed a hand on the woman's bicep, and Cherry finally looked up, her jaw tight. "What's going on?" Steph asked. "What's Benji gotten himself into? What messes are you cleaning up?" She swallowed. "Did Benji have something to do with what happened to Brenda?"

Cherry slammed a hand against the nearest locker and Steph flinched. Cherry spun to face her. "You're the youngest of the kids in your family. You wouldn't understand."

"Try me."

"For as long as I can remember it's been, 'Cherry, you have to watch out for Benji.' 'Cherry, don't let anything happen to

Benji.' 'Cherry, Dad and I are going out with friends, keep an eye on Benji.' All day. Every day. Even when I was at school—Lake City Private Academy—I had to keep an eye on him and report back to my parents when I got home." She dragged in a ragged breath. "Do you know how much I came to hate my brother?"

"Oh, Cherry, I'm so sorry," she whispered.

"You hate me?" Benji's low voice brought gasps from both women as they spun together to see Benji in the doorway, eyes wide, face pale. "Wow."

Cherry groaned. "No! I mean I did. Yes." She waved a hand. "But not now. Now I just don't know what I'm supposed to do. What's my role? In trying to protect you, I . . ."

"You what?" Steph asked.

"Nothing."

"Something," Steph said. She slinked toward the back entrance, eyes bouncing between the siblings.

Benji's gaze swung to Steph and he scowled. "You just couldn't leave things alone, could you?"

Steph froze. "What are you saying?"

He took a step toward her and Cherry lunged in front of him. "Benji, don't." He pushed his sister aside and advanced. Cherry grabbed his arm and swung him around. "Benji, stop! What are you doing?"

He jerked out of her grip, and something fell from his jacket pocket.

A small pink notebook.

Steph let out a sharp cry, then snapped her lips shut.

But it was too late.

He grabbed for her, but Cherry was in his way, causing him to stumble, giving Steph just enough time to shove open the door and race out the back into the space between the locker room area and a large building that she had no idea what it held.

But the door at the end on the corner was open, so she bolted for it while reaching for her cell phone. She couldn't help a quick glance back over her shoulder. No one was coming after her at the moment, but she had to get away.

She slipped through the open door, looking for another exit that would enable her to route around to her vehicle. The place was an auto repair garage. Of course Bolin's would have their own mechanics. She glanced at her phone. She had service and—

A clatter up ahead sent her scurrying behind one of the Subarus. At least they had good taste in SUVs. She tapped a message into her phone to Tate.

> Still here. Benji and Cherry had something to
> do with Brenda's accident. Benji had the pink
> notebook.

So, how did Stan fit into all of this? The two had obviously been working together, but . . .

She hit send. Then dialed 911.

Then noticed neither her text nor her call had gone through.

The metal building. It was blocking the signal. Fabulous.

One worker went in the garage, but so far no one had spotted her. Heart pounding, she scurried across the floor, heading to the exit opposite the one she'd entered. At the very back, just before the door, she came to one of the SUVs that had been damaged.

White paint marred one side, along with a dent and broken headlight. "No," she whispered. "No, no, no." She checked the wheels and found one missing a hubcap. This was the vehicle that had sent Brenda plunging to her death. She needed to call Tate or James or someone and she had to get out of the metal warehouse to do that. Once she was outside, she lifted her phone to check the signal and found three bars.

Something hard pressed into the base of her skull and she froze. "Just keep walking," the voice behind her said. "Give me the phone."

She passed it to him.

"Walk."

"Where?"

"To your car."

The pressure on her head had moved to the vicinity of her left kidney. "Don't try to call out or alert anyone."

"You can't kill everyone here."

"I don't need to."

Meaning just her? Who was it? She didn't think it was Benji. It definitely wasn't Cherry.

"No!"

At her yell, he jerked her to a stop. She took advantage of his momentary surprise to yank out of his grasp and run for her car.

"Hey!" His shout echoed behind her.

"Someone help me!"

Only the place was a graveyard. Where was everyone? She continued her race toward her vehicle but took a circuitous route, dropping behind other cars and darting around anything that could offer her cover. When she finally made it, she threw herself into the driver's seat, locked the doors, and pressed the button to start the engine. The Subaru roared to life and she jammed the gas, spun the wheel, and aimed for the exit.

As soon as she was through the gate, she headed for Wilkins Gas station. She needed a phone. She'd have to take Youngstown Road, but it was the closest place to find help and—

She nearly jammed on the brakes.

Was this what happened to Brenda?

When she came to the curve, she glanced in the mirror and slowed almost to a crawl. It took mere seconds to get around it, but only when she was past it did she breathe again.

Another glance in the rearview mirror brought a scream to her throat.

The masked figure in her back seat pressed a gun against her shoulder. "Thank you for getting around that death trap. Now, here's the plan."

No, there wasn't going to be a plan. She stomped on the brakes and twisted the wheel away from the mountain drop-off. The sudden jerk sent him slamming back against the door and he let out a harsh scream. The car shuddered to a stop, and she shoved open the door, pushed out of the driver's seat, and headed for the tree line.

SHE WAS IN TROUBLE. Tate's gut screamed at him to hurry and he aimed his vehicle toward Youngstown Road. He hated that route as much as the next person, but shaving ten minutes off his time to get to Steph seemed like a good idea. *Please take care of her, God. She has people who love her and need her in their lives. I need her in my life too, God. Don't let me lose her when you've just introduced us. Let me get to know her. Please?*

Cole was about five minutes behind him, telling him more information, and James was bringing backup. "How is Stan involved in this?" Tate asked, taking another hairpin curve a little too fast. He pressed the brake and gripped the wheel tight enough for his knuckles to glow white.

"That's not clear. I'm hoping he can tell us when he wakes up. Also, I got a call from the lab. Stan's DNA is not on the clothing found in his kitchen. Then again, they were freshly washed so that's not surprising."

"You think someone set him up? Left the clothes there to redirect the investigation?"

"I'm leaning that way. I went back for a second look and couldn't find any other clean clothes. The dirty clothes basket in his bathroom was full."

"Could have just decided to wash those and not the others."

"True. How far away are you?"

Tate slammed on the brakes. "Found her car. This side of the curve on Youngstown Road. Doors are open. Front driver and back driver's side. I think she's on foot going through the woods somewhere."

"I'm almost there."

THIRTEEN

STEPH CRASHED through the underbrush with a quick glance behind her. The man who'd taken her was familiar, but she couldn't place him. The mask hadn't helped, but his voice . . .

It was the same man who'd spoken to her when he'd broken into her home. Definitely not Stan. And not Benji. She let her gaze bounce from tree to tree, desperately searching for something. Anything that would give her shelter from the man chasing her.

"Stephanie, stop! You're making this so much harder than it needs to be!"

She almost laughed through her terror. Should she apologize that she was making him work to snuff out her life? The ridiculous question flitted through her mind—a testament to her borderline panic.

Gulping a deep breath, she finally emerged from the trees and came to a wooden fence. She threw herself between the rails and beelined to the barn fifty yards away. She looked back and didn't see her pursuer, but that didn't mean he couldn't see her. Pulling on all her reserves, she put on a burst of speed and rounded the side of the structure. She paused, hands on knees while she thought. He'd expect her to go in. The structure was falling down, with rotting boards on the ground and the door hanging by one hinge.

And there were probably rats inside. And bugs and snakes and . . .

She shuddered.

Footsteps from around the corner hitched her breath in her throat, and she scurried around the opposite side, opting to stay out of sight and pray he thought she went in to hide.

"Come on, Stephanie," the voice said. "You don't want to be in here. You might get hurt. Just come on out and let's talk."

If she didn't get her pulse under control, all he was going to have to do was follow the *thud thud* of her pounding heart. And then she spotted the deer stand just beyond the barn and inside the tree line. If she climbed up and he spotted her, she'd be trapped, but she had nowhere else to go or hide. She was at a ranch that spanned at least thirty acres. But the deer stand was attached to the tree trunk and an idea took shape.

While he was busy looking for her in the barn, she raced across the open field and grabbed the ladder. It tilted back at her, and she gasped, then managed to steady it and scrambled up to sprawl across the wooden flooring. Gulping air, she peered through the rectangular gap that ran from one side to the other.

And saw him heading her way.

No, no, no.

She bit her lip. Okay then. She waited. Watched him get closer and closer. She climbed through the open space on the wall next to the tree, gripped like a true tree hugger, and inched down until she was between the open area and the bottom of the stand. Her long sleeves protected her forearms and her jeans her thighs, but she had no idea how long she could hold on because her biceps were already complaining.

Thank goodness for her twice-weekly workouts at the gym. She bit her lip and listened. When his feet hit the wood floor of the deer stand, he cursed. "Steph! Where are you, you brat? I don't have time for this."

His voice. She *knew* that voice. But who did it belong to?

She inched down the tree, whispering prayers, knowing he was looking out, searching for her. Thankfully she landed on the ground beneath the structure so he wouldn't be able to see her. She crept over to the ladder and knocked it over. His scream of rage followed her as she took off once more through the woods.

TATE AND COLE stomped through the underbrush, following the trail left by Steph and the person after her. At least Tate didn't need a degree in tracking to know which way they went.

"Left," Cole said.

Tate was already heading that direction. "You think it's Benji?"

"That's the way I'm leaning."

"He had help." Tate ducked under a low-hanging branch.

"Yeah. Stan."

"No, this has to be a whole ring. Brenda indicated she thought it was a whole group of people who worked at Bolin's that were involved."

"I'll admit that it occurred to me. Embezzlement, money laundering. What else?"

"Stan liked to grow things," Tate said. "What if he was growing more than veggies and herbs?"

"You mean like pot?"

"Yeah. It's still illegal here, but the demand is high." He paused. "No pun intended."

Cole snorted and Tate let his gaze roam the area. *Come on, Steph, where are you?* "There," he said, pointing, "through those trees."

Cole pulled up. "Wait. Look. That deer stand."

He hurried over to it and Tate followed. Cole nudged the ladder. "That's been recently moved. Look at the ground."

"Yeah, and footprints. Two sets leading away from here heading that way." He pointed to the tree line just beyond.

"Let's go."

FOURTEEN

STEPH WASN'T SURE how long she'd been hunkered down behind the large oak, but she no longer heard her pursuer and that relieved and worried her at the same time. She hadn't gone far from the deer stand, figuring Tate would come looking for her when she didn't check in. She just had to be smart and stay alive until he found her.

And that meant getting into the house that was about twenty yards in front of her. Twenty yards of immaculate and wide-open space all around the perimeter of the house. She'd had no idea this home was in the area, but someone lived there. And they had kids, judging by the play set and sandbox.

Which was why she was still sitting where she was.

She had no idea if the man had managed to climb down like she had or if he'd jumped or if he was still in the deer stand, but she was just about convinced no one was home, and if she broke inside, she wouldn't be putting a family in jeopardy.

She finally took a deep breath, pushed away from the tree, and bolted toward the house. Every second she was out in the open, she expected to feel a bullet slam into her. When she made it to the deck, she scrambled up the steps and tried the knob on the French door. To her amazement, it twisted, and she swung it inward, shut it, and locked it.

For a moment she stood in the den, taking in the emptiness of the home. No sounds of children playing or a parent in the vicinity. She went straight to the kitchen, looking for a landline phone.

Nothing on the wall.

"Home office?" she muttered. It didn't take long to find the room upstairs at the end of the long hallway. She pushed through the cracked door and scanned the mahogany desk. No landline phone. "Ugh!"

A floorboard creaked and Steph swung toward the open door to find herself staring down the barrel of a gun. She gasped and held her hands in the air and scurried backward behind the desk. "Don't shoot. Please."

"Who are you and what are you doing in here?" The man was in his early thirties with spiky, sleep-mussed hair, pajama bottoms, and bare feet. He held the weapon like he knew how to use it.

"I'm Stephanie Cross. A man tried to kidnap me and I got away. I ran through the woods and saw your house. The door off your deck was unlocked, so I came in. I didn't think anyone was here. I was looking for a phone. I . . . I . . ." She snapped her lips shut to stop the flow of words and took a deep breath.

"Steph Cross?" he asked. "Your brothers are Dixon, Keegan, and James?"

"Yes."

He lowered the gun and she sent up a prayer of thanks.

"I went to school with them. I've already called 911." He pulled a phone out of his pajama pocket. "They're on the way."

A shadow flickered behind him. Movement. She opened her mouth to warn him when there was an audible thud. He crumpled to the floor.

Steph grabbed a paperweight from the desk and threw it at the attacker's head. It slammed into his chest. A sharp gasp escaped him and he dropped his gun. Steph raced from behind the desk and jammed her fist into his throat. He went to the floor gagging. She zipped past him, but he swung a leg out and caught her foot, sending her sprawling to the polished hardwood with a pained grunt. When she rolled, she kicked the weapon and it slid under the armoire.

He growled a curse, snagged her leg, and yanked her back to his side. Then with a quick move landed on top of her, his hands around her throat. She reached up to grab his wrists while the pressure increased.

TATE SCANNED the property line, seconds ticking past while he made sure the figure who had entered the home a few seconds ago was alone. "That's the guy who broke into Steph's house and mine." He started forward, racing across the open backyard.

Tate and Cole came up on the guy just after he'd slid a hand into the hole he'd cut in the glass. Within seconds he was inside. Sirens echoed in the distance. Backup was close.

"He's the one who tried to frame Stan," Cole said.

"Yep."

Tate stepped through the door the guy hadn't bothered to close, the hole in the glass mocking him. Too bad the homeowners hadn't had an alarm on that door.

"Police! Show yourselves!" Cole and Tate called out twice.

"Tate! Cole! Up here!"

Tate's heart lurched. "Steph!"

FIFTEEN

STEPH GASPED FOR AIR. Somehow she'd managed a well-placed knee that had him howling and loosening his grip. Then Cole's and Tate's shouts had frozen him long enough for her to snag the paperweight she'd thrown from the desk and slam it into the side of his head. Now he lay on the floor, stunned but not unconscious.

She scrambled away from him and swept her hand under the armoire, just as Tate entered the room, his weapon on her attacker. She found the gun and shoved it to the side, not wanting to pick it up in front of two cops—regardless of who they were—whose adrenaline was probably flowing as fast as hers.

Cole went straight to the masked man, cuffed him, and ripped the mask off.

Steph gaped. "Gage Bolin!"

He glared at her while Tate checked on the unconscious homeowner. "Pulse is strong," Tate said. "But he's going to have a nasty headache when he wakes up."

"At least he'll wake up," Steph said, still gazing at her attacker while her pulse thrummed in her ears and her throat ached. "It was you all along?"

"I want a lawyer."

Paramedics hurried through the door while Cole grabbed Bolin's arm and passed him off to a uniformed officer. "Make sure he gets his lawyer." He looked at the man. "And go round up his kids. Maybe they'll talk if he won't."

The flash of fear in Bolin's eyes made Steph believe Cole might be onto something. She cleared her sore throat and walked over to Gage. "I saw the vehicle in the warehouse," she said. "That wasn't you who ran Brenda off the road, because Cherry said she didn't call you until the day before yesterday. So who was it? Benji? Or . . ." She hesitated. "Cherry?"

His shoulders twitched.

Cherry.

Her heart plummeted. "No."

"It was an accident," Bolin muttered, his voice low.

"Sure it was," Cole said.

"Cherry killed her? She wouldn't. No." Her sore throat tightened even more and tears gathered. "I don't believe you. You're a liar!" She backed away.

"Steph . . ." Tate held out a hand, but she ignored it and shoved out of the room. She needed space, room to breathe, to process that one of her friends had killed another. She made it outside to the front yard and bent double, hands on her knees. *No, God . . . not Cherry.*

A gentle hand on her shoulder pulled her up and around. She looked up through her tears to see Tate's compassionate gaze, and she leaned her forehead on his shoulder while silent tears dripped down her cheeks. "I want to hear her side of this."

"Of course."

"I don't believe him."

"I know you don't."

She wanted to punch him for sounding so pacifying, but deep down she realized he was just trying to offer some comfort. And while she appreciated it, she pulled back and swiped her palms across her cheeks. Paramedics loaded the home-owner into the ambulance.

Steph stopped the nearest one. "How is he?"

"He'll be all right as far as I can tell, but a CT scan is probably a good idea."

"Any idea who he is?"

"His ID was in his wallet. One of the officers called his wife. She's meeting us at the hospital."

"Oh good." When the ambulance pulled away, she turned to Tate. "Okay, now what?"

"Now we—as in Cole and I—go find the other three Bolins and figure the rest of this thing out."

TATE COULDN'T LEAVE Steph without a way home. At least that's what he told himself when he led her to his unmarked vehicle. She climbed into the back seat, buckled up, and rested her head against the headrest. He still wasn't sure she shouldn't go to the hospital, but she refused and he wanted to keep an eye on her. The fact that Cole didn't argue said he felt the same.

While she rested, he and Cole mapped out a plan, alerted SWAT and other backup, then made their way across the mountain to Bolin's Nature Nurture Expeditions.

Cole parked just outside the entrance. "All right, Steph. You stay put, and I mean that."

"I'm not going anywhere," she muttered. "I'm done playing investigator."

"Good." Cole popped the trunk and went to don his SWAT gear.

Concerned at the ring of defeat in her tone, Tate turned to look at her.

She met his gaze and narrowed her eyes. "But if you need

me, I'm here. You know. Just if you need me to talk to Cherry. I think she'd listen to me. Benji won't. You have to take him first. If you do that, Cherry will want to protect him."

Tate nodded, relieved her momentary surrender to the stress seemed to be gone. "Noted." Reluctantly, he left her and followed Cole through the open gates. They headed for the office, keeping in contact via comms. Tate joined Nathan Carlisle, one of the other detectives, and waited until everyone was in place. Steph's brother James was there with his team and gave the signal that they were ready.

"Benji's in the back office," he said. "We have eyes on him through the window."

"Copy that. Where's the sister?"

"Reported to be on the grounds near the zip line tower. Can I get an affirmative?"

That came and Cole said, "Take the brother in the office first. Once he's contained, on my signal, take the sister."

"Copy."

Tate and Nathan walked up to the office door and Tate tried the knob. Once it twisted, he pushed the door open, then swept inside with Nathan right behind him. "Hands in the air." He kept his voice low, not wanting to alert the man in the back room.

The woman at the desk gasped and shot her hands up while her wide eyes darted to the closed door that had been confirmed to be Benji Bolin's location. Tate held a finger to his lips and motioned for her to come out from behind the desk and join him.

She gulped, nodded, and did as told. Nathan moved to the door and glanced at Tate. Tate nodded. Nathan pushed the door open and Tate swept inside, weapon on the man at the desk.

Benji yelped and jumped to his feet, backpedaling toward the exit behind him.

"Police, Benji! Freeze!"

But he kept going, throwing open the door only to come to an abrupt halt when he stared down the barrels of the officers there. "What is this?" He spun back to Tate and Nathan. "What's going on?"

"On your knees. Cross your legs at the ankles and put your hands behind your back. Now!"

Benji looked like he might run, but after a few seconds of hesitation, lowered himself to the ground and did as instructed.

"You're under arrest for the murder of Brenda Hudson, conspiracy to commit murder, and a host of other charges," Cole said.

"No, wait, you don't understand." He looked up over his shoulder at Cole. "No one meant for Brenda to die. It was an accident."

"Of course it was. That's what your father said too."

The man paled. "My father?"

"Yep."

"Where's your mother?"

He shrugged. "I haven't heard from her since they got back from Aspen. She hates this place. Only tolerates it because it pays for her lifestyle."

"Fine. We'll find her with or without your help. Let's go. Your sister will be joining us shortly."

"Cherry?" He laughed. "Are you kidding me? She won't tell you anything."

"Not a bit kidding. And guess we'll find out if she has anything to say or not."

"I'm not saying anything more. I want a lawyer."

"Smartest thing you've said so far."

SIXTEEN

STEPH BOLTED OUT of the car when she spotted officers escorting a handcuffed Cherry to the nearest cruiser. Other workers had been rounded up, but she'd ignored them. There were only a few customers and they'd been cleared and escorted to their vehicles to leave the area.

"Cherry!"

Her friend looked up, caught Steph's eye, and burst into tears.

Steph started to run to her, but Tate appeared and snagged her arm. "Not right now, Steph."

She jerked away from him and shot him a hard glare. He frowned but didn't flinch. Steph backed down. He was just doing his job.

His stance softened. "Come on, I'll take you home."

"No, please. I want to go to the station with you. I know I can't talk to her, but maybe it will help if she knows she's not alone. That I'm there. That I believe in her."

He sighed, then offered her a faint smile. "You're a good friend."

"Thanks."

It didn't take long to arrive at the station, where Tate escorted her inside and allowed her to sit outside the interrogation room Cherry had been led to.

Benji was next door, their father in yet another room. Their mother had yet to be found.

Tate and Cole had disappeared into the room with Cherry fifteen minutes ago. Steph reached for her phone, only to remember Gage Bolin had taken it and probably tossed it somewhere. She sat back with a huff, then leaned her head against the wall and prayed.

She wasn't sure how much time passed, but she might have dozed mid-prayer because the next thing she knew Tate was calling her name. She blinked and stood. "What is it?"

"Cherry insists she will only talk to you."

"What? Why?"

"Because you're her friend and she needs to tell you what happened. According to her."

"Oh. Okay. Is that allowed?"

"It is. Follow me."

When Steph stepped into the room, Cherry brought her handcuffed wrists up to swipe her cheeks. Steph walked around to hug her, and Cherry let loose with a sob followed by tears that seemed to have no end.

But finally, she stopped, drew in a deep breath, and took the handful of tissues that Steph gave her, compliments of the box on the table.

"Okay," Steph said, "I'm here. Talk to me."

"They want me to tell them where my mother is, but Steph, I promise I don't know. She and my dad have been cagey my whole life, but I never knew about their illegal activities until about three weeks ago."

"But Benji knew."

"Yes. Apparently."

"How did they hide it all from you?"

"I guess it all started after I went to college. Then when I came home, they were knee-deep in it. To be honest, I knew something hinky was going on, but just ignored it. I was so busy trying to keep the business going that I convinced myself I didn't have time to worry about people on the property after hours. Or strange calls in the middle of the night. Or my parents constantly traveling." She shrugged. "Maybe I just didn't want to see it." She scoffed. "You can't imagine how stupid I feel." Tears welled once more. "But they're my family," she whispered. "I love them."

"I know," Steph said. "I never would have thought they'd be involved in anything illegal." She hesitated. "Well, Benji maybe, but not you or your parents. They were always involved in charities and—"

"Charities that they used for money laundering."

Steph sighed and raked a hand over her hair. "I'm sorry, Cherry."

"I am too."

They fell silent a moment, then Steph bit her lip, pondering how to approach the next subject. She reached out and squeezed her friend's fingers, always aware that Tate and Cole and who knew who else were watching from behind the two-way mirror. "Cherry, tell me what happened with Brenda."

Cherry drew in a sharp breath and gulped air. "That was all just a horrible accident. Horrible and no one will believe me. They won't." She hiccuped and dropped her face into her palms.

"Tell me."

"I can't," she whispered.

"You have to." Steph sat for a moment, thinking. Then took a wild stab. "Cherry, you've protected him your entire life. You've always put his needs ahead of your own. Always. Truthfully, you've basically sacrificed your life for his. It's time to reclaim your life."

"At the expense of his?" She mumbled the question.

"He hurt, probably killed, someone. If you continue to protect him and don't tell the truth, he's going to hurt someone else. Can you let that happen?" Steph didn't bother to add that Benji probably wouldn't be hurting anyone for the rest of his life if convicted of all the charges against him.

After a few seconds, Cherry lifted her head, her tears gone, but grief still in her eyes. "She'd discovered everything. The crazy numbers in the accounting, the fake sales to various customers, the return of equipment but the refund was never deposited. Everything. She was suspicious for a while, but she took her time and put together hard evidence against my parents and Benji—and brought it to me. I didn't know what to think. I told her she was out of her mind. That she was making it up or lying or . . . I don't know. While I yelled at her, she just sat there, this sad expression on her face. One of indecision and pity. Benji overheard the argument and stormed in. He grabbed Brenda and locked her in the office closet." Cherry shook her head, her eyes wide with the memory. "I didn't know what to do. I reached for my phone to call the police and Benji grabbed it from me. He was furious, in a panic, unsure what to do." She swallowed hard. "But he wasn't letting Brenda go, that was clear."

Steph gritted her teeth hard enough that her jaw ached. "Go on."

"He left, never thinking I'd go against what he planned." A low scoff escaped her. "I admit I've protected him and covered up a lot for him since he was a child, but murder? There was no way I was going to let him do that to Brenda. To our friend. The person who came to me, begging me to get Benji to do the right thing so she didn't have to turn him in."

"Oh, Cherry . . ."

"A couple of hours passed. Benji paced the office, tossed threats in my direction, but he wouldn't leave. He even cut the cord to the phone line. And I didn't dare try to go anywhere to find another phone or involve one of the innocent guests. I worked the front desk—minus answering calls—until closing, knowing that time was running out for Brenda. Benji canceled all of the activities that would involve him leaving the area—and me. But finally, he stepped outside to talk to someone, and I hurried to let Brenda out of the closet. I shoved her out the office's back door and got her to her car. She was practically hysterical. I told her to go to the police and tell them everything and I'd back up her story. Just as she was leaving, Benji came back and realized what had happened. He raced to the nearest vehicle, one of our SUVs, and climbed in. I knew he was going after her. Unfortunately, I had no way to call for help, so I jumped in the passenger seat, begging him to stop, but . . ." She shook her head and tears tracked her cheeks once more. "He was determined and took off after her. I was horrified to see her go in the Youngstown Road direction. I guess she was hoping that Benji would be too scared to follow."

"Benji took her phone?"

Cherry nodded.

Of course. "Then help was closer. The store at the bottom of the hill."

"Yes. I thought about that too. Anyway, Benji bumped her car toward the drop-off, but she managed to stay on the road. I grabbed the wheel and he pushed me off, screaming at me he was going to kill me next. My head hit the window, and it dazed me for a few minutes. He took advantage and bumped her one more time. That time she went over." Cherry lowered her head to her hands and wept. When she regained control, she sat for a brief second, pulling in gasping breaths. "Then he stopped," she said into the table, "got out of the car, and fired a gun at her." She sniffed, lifted her head, and grabbed another handful of tissues. "I didn't even know he had a gun on him. The rest of that evening is a blur. I was screaming at him that he'd crossed a line and I wasn't going to be a part of it. He put the gun to my head and told me to shut up. So I did. Then we drove back to the office and he told me to think good and hard about reporting him to the police. Because our parents would go down too. It was then that I realized my whole family were crooks. And now . . . killers."

TATE LOOKED AT COLE, who couldn't seem to take his eyes from the drama unfolding in the interrogation room.

James had come from Benji's room just in time to hear the full story. "Wow," he said. "Benji wouldn't say a word and Cherry can't seem to stop talking." He glanced at his phone.

"Shows which one of them has a conscience," Tate said.

Cole nodded. "Must have been killing her keeping all that bottled up inside."

James glanced at his phone again. Tate raised a brow. "You expecting a call?"

"Lainie's coming by. She said she'd text when she got here."

Tate shoved his hands in his back pockets and nodded to the two in the other room. "Cherry would have come to us eventually."

"You believe her?" James asked.

"I do." He pursed his lips. "She won't walk away from this without some consequences, though. I'm guessing she'll have to face some charges for covering up a crime."

James crossed his arms after another look at his phone. "Maybe she can get those reduced for testifying."

"You think she'll do it?" Tate asked.

Cole shrugged. "Only one way to find out. Let's see if we can get a deal worked up fast while she's still getting all of this off her conscience."

"Cherry." Steph's soft voice reached them once more. "What was Stan's role in all of this?"

"I asked Benji that after the detectives left. He found out about the money laundering before Brenda did and came to

Benji, wanting in on everything . . . especially the profits. He demanded a percentage for his silence."

"Ohhh, I see. So, all of his zip line adventures . . ."

"Yeah, just a cover-up. He never paid for that stuff, but it was a way to account for some of the money coming in. Just a small part, of course, but . . ." She shrugged. "It kept him quiet, according to Benji. And culpable should he ever decide to turn." She swiped a hand over her hair. "I can't believe this," she whispered. "I just can't."

James nodded. "I'll call the ADA."

He left to contact the assistant district attorney, and Tate turned to focus on Steph. She was sitting quietly while Cherry continued to weep. He couldn't imagine it. Finding out your whole family was involved in something so awful. And then trying to cover up the murder. He sighed. "I'll get Steph. We'll let Cherry sit there and get herself together while James gets in touch with the ADA."

"Works for me."

Tate went to the interrogation room, opened the door, and motioned for Steph to join him. When she did, the grief in her eyes hit him. She'd suffered too much of that over the past three days. But at least Brenda and her family would have closure. He touched Steph's cheek. "I'll call you and keep you updated, okay?"

"Sure."

"I was invited to the lake house. Do you think you're going to go after all of this?"

She shrugged. "Yes. As much as I might want to hide under the bed at the moment, I won't do that."

He offered her a faint smile. "Good for you."

"See you there." She headed for the lobby.

Tate watched her go for a brief moment, then walked back to let Cherry know they'd have some information for her soon. He stepped inside. "Hey."

She kept her gaze on the table.

"I just—" An alarm sounded, cutting him off.

A gunshot followed somewhere beyond the room.

Cherry jerked her head up. "What's going on?"

Tate ran from the room and locked it behind him while James and Cole rushed past him, headed to the front lobby.

"Stay with her," Cole said over his shoulder.

"Where's my family!"

Tate was opening the door to the interrogation room just as the scream ripped through the building.

Cherry jerked. "Mom? Mom!"

"Put the weapon down!"

"Put the gun down!"

"Drop it!"

The shouts echoed over the blaring alarm.

"I want to see my daughter! Just let me see Cherry and I'll drop the gun!"

Cherry turned pleading eyes on Tate. "Don't let them kill her." She yanked at the handcuffs attached to the table. "Let me talk to her! Please!"

After a split second's worth of hesitation, Tate unlocked her from the table but kept her cuffed. He led Cherry down the hallway, stopping just beyond the lobby where James and Cole were covering the situation, out of the way of any stray bullets.

"Shut that thing off so we can hear," James said into his radio. The blaring alarm stopped seconds later.

Just beyond them, officers were hidden behind anything that might offer cover. James looked like he wanted to puke. Cole didn't look much better. And finally Tate saw why.

Helen Bolin stood just inside the front door, her eyes wild, gun clutched in her right hand. The gun rested against Steph's temple. Officers had closed in behind the woman, blocking her, but she had the upper hand at the moment.

Cole looked at Tate. "You heard all the commotion?"

"Yep. So did she."

Cherry stepped forward, stopping only when Tate wouldn't let her go any farther. "Please," she whispered.

"You think you can talk her down?" James asked, a muscle jumping in his jaw.

"I don't know. All I know is I have to try. You have to let me try."

They didn't let family negotiate with family except in extremely special situations. This might qualify.

"Cherry!"

Cole nodded to her.

"I'm here, Mom!"

At the sound of her daughter's voice, the woman froze. Steph stayed perfectly still, her eyes searching. Finally, her gaze landed on Tate and almost instantly, the fear in her eyes lessened. He suppressed a shudder. She trusted him to get her out of this. Her family, James, was right there. Tate couldn't let him watch his sister die. Live with the grief, the regrets, the what-ifs. *Oh, God, help me . . .*

He could hear Benji banging on his door. The father was quiet.

"Mom, please, don't do this," Cherry said. "You know Steph. Please."

"Where are Gage and Benji?"

"They're here. They're just answering a few questions."

"Don't lie to me! Where are they? Get them out here."

"They're in the rooms here. Just answering some questions."

Tate had to admit he was impressed with Cherry's composure. He wouldn't have thought she had it in her after the breakdown with Steph. Her gaze clung to his and her pulse thrummed visibly in her throat.

"I saw them get arrested," Helen said. "I want them released! Now! Or I'm going to start shooting people. Starting with this one!"

Steph closed her eyes and Tate's breath hitched.

"No, Mom! She's my friend!"

Cherry broke away from Tate and rushed toward the lobby.

"Stop!" Tate yelled.

She stopped several feet from her mother and Steph. Tate and the nearby officers held their fire. The officers at the glass doors behind Helen and Steph wouldn't shoot for fear of the bullet going through Helen and into Steph. A head shot from a sniper could cause her to jerk her finger in reflex and send a bullet into Steph's brain.

Panic swirled. How could he help resolve this?

Steph's eyes were open and locked on Cherry.

Cherry walked forward. "Mom, I need you to put the weapon down."

"Cherry . . ."

She ignored James's tone full of warning. This was about the worst situation Tate could imagine playing out. Nothing was going according to the rules. Well, it didn't matter at the moment. Right now, they had to get Steph away from the woman—and Cherry might be their best chance of making that happen.

Cherry's mother hesitated. "What are you doing? Stop right there! I'm your mother. You do as I say!"

"I want to help you, Mom. I want to help Steph. Do you understand? I want to help. Steph, she's not going to hurt you. Are you, Mom?"

Cherry took another step, and Steph gave a faint nod at whatever she saw on Cherry's face. Cherry finally stopped about three feet away, and Tate grabbed a breath into air-starved lungs.

"You told me to take care of Benji," Cherry said. "All my life, you've told me to take care of him. But I can't do that if I'm in prison, can I?"

Confusion flickered on Helen's face. "What? I . . ."

"Drop, Steph!"

Cherry's cry sent Steph down like her legs had turned to wet noodles. The weapon slid away from Steph's temple and time slowed. Cherry launched herself at her mother and the two women joined Steph on the tile floor.

Tate bolted toward them.

A gun went off.

Everyone went still.

"Steph!" His shout echoed in the split second of silence, then chaos erupted.

Steph rolled one way. Cherry the other. A red stain on her green business shirt.

Then time sped back up. Cherry's mother had a matching red stain on her abdomen, only hers was growing. But her hand still searched for the weapon, closed her fist around the grip, and yanked it up to aim it right at Tate.

Cherry threw herself in front of him as two shots sounded. One hit Cherry and she dropped.

The other hit her mother right between the eyes.

Cherry slapped a hand to her side and met his gaze while tears slid down her cheeks. "I had to make it right," she whispered. Then her eyes closed and she went limp.

SEVENTEEN

One Month Later

STEPH WAITED while Tate pulled to the curb of her home, then went to join him. He hugged her. "You look amazing."

"Thanks. So do you." A wave of shyness swept over her. Which was incredibly weird because she'd never been shy a day in her life. She pulled her coat tight and slid into the passenger seat. He waited until she was buckled to shut the door.

Gentlemen did still exist.

Tate settled into the driver's seat, his leather-gloved hands gripping the wheel. "Sure is nice of James to have us all over again."

"The weather's been so good I'm sure he wants to take advantage of it."

"He and Lainie set the date for their wedding, did you hear?"

"Of course." She shot him an amused look and realized he was slightly nervous as well for some reason. "New Year's Eve. I can't think of a better way to spend the evening."

"Yeah, me too." His fingers flexed on the wheel, and he aimed the vehicle toward the road that would take them up the mountain to the lake house. "Cherry coming?"

"She is." Could this conversation get any more awkward? What was going on with him? She didn't think he *did* nerves. "This is her first outing since . . . everything. Thank goodness Lainie was there. She and her medical expertise are the only reasons Cherry lived."

"I heard."

More stilted dialogue. Steph decided to just go with it if it made him feel better. "Anyway, she's finished with her rehab and ready to start living again. I think she's excited and terrified all at the same time."

"I know the feeling," he muttered.

"Sorry? What was that?"

He cleared his throat and shot her a sideways glance. "Nothing." He paused. "I know she visits Benji and her father—or tries to. They still won't see her?"

"Not since they heard she was going to testify at their trials. She still has a hard time reconciling that her father was the one in the parking garage looking for a way to attack me. And was also the guy at the library. And the one who attacked Stan, trying to frame him. Talking about all of that on the stand . . . well, it's safe to say she's dreading it."

"I'm sure that's hard for her."

"Terribly, but she's determined."

"Tell me about Stan. How's he doing?"

Steph often visited Stan in the rehabilitation center and was touched that Tate asked about him when he knew she'd been to see her former boss. "Recovering. He's still got some memory loss. I honestly don't know what's going to happen to him." The man had basically been a stooge, but he'd also made his choices.

"Time will tell."

They fell silent, but finally, it wasn't awkward or uncomfortable. Quite the opposite. She found she enjoyed being in Tate's company whatever they were doing.

Except dodging bullets and people trying to kill her. "When you texted last night, you said you wanted me to meet your parents. Tell me a little more about them. What are they like?"

"They're awesome. Mom's a high school science teacher and Dad's a financial advisor." He glanced at her. "I can't believe we haven't already had this conversation."

"We've been a little busy."

"True. Anyway, I believe you'll really like them. They're good people and they're very excited for me to introduce you."

Her stomach fluttered at the thought and what it all could mean. But she was excited too.

He cleared his throat. "I have a question."

"Sure."

"I know we haven't seen much of each other since the . . . event, but I keep wondering how you knew to drop like you did when Cherry was talking to her mother."

That was his question? Maybe the silence was more awkward for him than it was for her. "I don't know," she said. "I just felt like she was trying to tell me something even while she was keeping her mother mostly calm. Then when she said 'drop,' I dropped. I had no idea she was planning on tackling her and wrestling with the gun, but I think she saved me."

"She definitely did."

"So now I have a question. How'd she get away from you?"

He cleared his throat. "Ah, well . . ."

She studied the flush creeping up his neck and into his cheeks. "You knew she was up to something, didn't you? You *let* her go."

"I can neither confirm nor deny that." He paused. "But yes, we needed to calm Helen Bolin down and give her something to make her believe we were listening."

"Well, it worked. So thanks."

He finally pulled into the lake home driveway, parked, and came around to open her door. Then he took her hand, his warm and endearingly a little damp, and led her down to the dock.

"Wait," she said. "Where's everyone else?"

"They're coming. I wanted to get here a little early so we could talk."

"Okay, sure."

On the deck, the wind was chilly coming off the water, and she pulled her gloves from her pocket.

"Too cold?"

"No, not at all." She walked over to the firepit and cranked it up. "We have it all to ourselves." She chose the cushioned love seat–sized swing hanging from the wooden structure James and Cole had built last month. He sat next to her as she'd hoped he would.

He turned to face her and took her gloved hand in his. "I'm not very good at small talk, Steph. You probably noticed that in the car." She chuckled and he quirked a small smile at her. "So I'm just going to throw something out there."

"Throw it."

"I like you. A lot." He drew in a deep breath.

"I like you too, Tate." Then she stayed quiet, letting him figure out how he wanted to say what he wanted to say.

"For what seems like my entire life, because of what happened to my friend, I've been focused on making detective. I've been determined nothing would derail my plan and I've sacrificed a lot. Including personal relationships. And since I've met you, I've realized something."

"What?" She kept her voice low, almost a whisper.

"That I don't want whatever might be there for us to be part of that sacrifice." He cleared his throat and squeezed her fingers. "The last few weeks have been so busy I haven't had time to really see straight, but when the day is done and in those moments before I drift off to sleep, you're on my mind. I think about you, I want to see you, to talk to you.

More than can be said in a few short texts. And I wonder about you."

"You wonder about me? What do you wonder about?" This she had to hear.

He laughed. "What you're doing, who you're with, if you've had a good day. How you're doing processing Brenda's death and everything else that went on."

"I see."

"Full disclosure?"

"Absolutely."

He pushed stray hairs behind her ear, leaving a trail of heat that had nothing to do with the flames from the firepit.

"Mostly, I wonder what it would be like to kiss you."

She let a smile curve her lips and leaned toward him. "Then why don't you find out, because I've been wondering that too."

Apparently, that was all the encouragement he needed, because his lips were on hers almost before she finished the sentence. His kiss was sweet, respectful . . . and hot. Definitely hot. Holy wow. She kissed him back, feeling his simmering passion and restraint while they both reveled in discovering the wonder of that first kiss and all the questions it answered.

Like she could do this for the rest of her life and die a happy woman.

He finally lifted his head and let his eyes lock on hers. "That was better than what my limited imagination came up with."

She laughed, a sound that came from her soul. "Same."

"Think we need to do that again and make sure it was real?"

"For sure."

He started to pull her in for another round when the sound of footsteps on the dock stilled them both. "Later," he whispered.

"Later."

James and Lainie stopped next to the swing. "Glad you feel

comfortable enough to make yourself at home," he told her. But the look in his eyes said he was happy for her.

Lainie elbowed him and he caught her to him and kissed her forehead. "I'm going to get stuff for the s'mores." He eyed Steph and Tate. "You two don't look like you want to move, so . . ."

"Yeah," Steph said, "why don't you and Lainie go get the goodies while Tate and I finish our conversation."

"That's what it's called these days?" He narrowed his eyes at Tate. "Remember that's my baby sister."

"A baby sister who's about to start telling all of her brother's secrets if he doesn't go away."

James frowned. "Now, see here—"

Lainie giggled. "Stop it. Both of you." She dragged her fiancé back toward the house. "Oh, look, Jesslyn, Cole, and Kenzie are here. Let's go keep them away from the dock for a few more minutes." She looked back at Steph and mouthed, "You're welcome."

Steph laughed and Tate chuckled, then gazed down at her. "Now, where were we?"

"Winding up a conversation if I recall correctly."

"Ah yes." He kissed her again. Long seconds later, he tipped his forehead to hers. "I like conversing with you."

"I see. So how should this conversation end?"

"With, 'Where would you like to go on an official first date?'"

"I don't care as long as it's with you."

He grinned, and Steph couldn't wait to see how the rest of their story unfolded. If it should end with "and they lived happily ever after," filling in the details sounded like a lifetime she could look forward to.

Lynette Eason is the *USA Today* bestselling author of *Double Take* and *Target Acquired*, as well as the Extreme Measures, Danger Never Sleeps, Blue Justice, Women of Justice, Deadly Reunions, Hidden Identity, and Elite Guardians series. She is the winner of three ACFW Carol Awards, the Selah Award, and the Inspirational Reader's Choice Award, among others. She is a graduate of the University of South Carolina and has a master's degree in education from Converse College. Eason lives in South Carolina with her husband. They have two adult children. Learn more at LynetteEason.com.

DOWNFALL

LYNN H. BLACKBURN

ONE

CASSIE QUINN DROPPED her speed as she approached the employee entrance to The Haven. Everyone in the small town of Gossamer Falls knew Cassie had a lead foot. But violating the fifteen-mile-per-hour speed limit within the gates of The Haven was a one-way ticket to unemployment.

And Cassie wasn't about to risk that. Especially today, when she was on her way in for a meeting with The Haven's CEO, Bronwyn Pierce.

She waved her badge in front of the sensor and gave a tiny salute to the security guard she knew watched from the cameras placed along the top of the walls. The massive iron gates opened, and she drove her Jeep inside.

No one could get inside the grounds of The Haven without permission. Bronwyn had a zero-tolerance policy for trespassing. That didn't mean people didn't try, but the few who managed to get a toe across the property line found themselves spending the night in a Gossamer Falls jail cell.

The last time it happened, she'd still been dating Officer Donovan Bledsoe.

Don't go there. Memories of the three months they'd dated last winter had been shoved into the same vault where she'd stuffed the four months of stress followed by twelve hours of intense trauma that she'd experienced in Atlanta a year ago.

Heartbreak came in many forms. Some, like the Atlanta fiasco, she'd never put herself through again. That was in the vault because she didn't need to relive that. Ever. But Donovan? He'd never been anything but a dream come true.

Right up until the night he ended everything.

So he'd gone into the vault that held the dust of her dreams.

Would her time as chef at Hideaway join him there? Maybe. But when Bronwyn had called her a month ago, desperate after the head chef had a heart attack while The Haven was at capacity with late summer guests, Cassie hadn't had to think twice before she took the risk.

Just like deep down she knew if Donovan ever came to her and said he'd made a mistake, she'd give him another chance.

Because some dreams were worth it. Weren't they?

How incredibly stupid was that? He hurt her. He made her fall head over heels, and then he walked away like it was no big deal. How could he do that?

And why hadn't she insisted that he explain? Instead she'd just let him go.

Five minutes later, she pulled into her reserved parking spot and checked her watch. She was early, but not by much. She checked her makeup in the mirror and climbed out. She was reaching into the back seat to grab her bag when a horn beeped. A few seconds later, Bronwyn parked beside her.

Cassie waited for Bronwyn to exit her car and smiled at the woman who'd given her an opportunity she'd never dared dream of. Would that end today? If it did, she had no idea what would come next. She'd spent the year since she'd come home running a small weekends-only restaurant in town and supplementing her income by working as a personal chef for a few clients in Asheville. She could make the personal chef gig permanent, but she didn't want to.

"Cassie! Great timing!" Bronwyn's grin held no tension.

Lord, please let it be good news.

"Want to walk with me over to the breakfast kitchen? I need coffee."

"Sure." Cassie fell into step with Bronwyn.

The Haven catered to an exclusive clientele. Celebrities, politicians, and business moguls came to the mountains of North Carolina to get away from it all. But just because they wanted a mountain escape didn't mean they wanted to rough it. They wanted luxury linens, high-end everything, and room service. Three years earlier, Bronwyn had a separate kitchen built to accommodate the myriad requests for everything from chocolate milk to The Haven's most popular dish—a fried green tomato BLT.

The breakfast kitchen handled room service requests twenty-four hours a day. Breakfast, lunch, and snacks were provided through the breakfast kitchen and delivered to the individual cabins by resort staff.

Dinner was another matter entirely. The Haven's fine dining restaurant, Hideaway, had made a quiet name for itself for its intimate atmosphere, professional service, and unique seasonal menu, which featured sophisticated Southern cuisine. Reservations were required and were only available to The Haven's guests. Dinner was served from six to nine. No exceptions.

Cassie loved everything about it. Well, almost everything.

"Thanks for meeting me so early," Bronwyn said. "When did you get out of here last night?"

"I left around one."

Bronwyn tugged on her arm and stopped them in the middle of the path. "One—a.m.? Why? You should be out of here long before then."

Cassie couldn't meet Bronwyn's eyes. She'd been hoping to avoid this conversation.

"Cass? What's going on?"

Cassie stared at the ground and tried to come up with an

answer that wouldn't get anyone in trouble. "I didn't want to say anything. It's a temporary situation, and I can handle it."

"Explain." Bronwyn's voice had shifted from concerned friend to concerned CEO.

But Cassie wasn't prepared to give in. "I'm not a rat. And it isn't my kitchen. If it were, I'd handle this differently. But Chef Louis has been nothing but gracious, and I won't ruin what he has worked so hard to put together."

Bronwyn shook her head, her frustration obvious. "We can table this discussion temporarily. But after we talk, we will be revisiting this topic."

That didn't sound ominous at all.

Before Cassie could ask what she meant, Bronwyn pasted on a smile. "Let's grab our food and go back to Hideaway to talk. I don't want to be overheard, and my office will have too many people there now."

They chatted about safer topics as they picked up coffees, a muffin for Cassie, and a chocolate croissant for Bronwyn.

"I heard you had a date last week." Bronwyn's oh-so-casual tone didn't fool Cassie.

"Who told you that?" It had to have been Cal or Meredith. Cassie's cousins—technically they were her cousins once removed, but seriously, who could keep up with all of that—Cal, Meredith, and Mo had grown up with Bronwyn, then in their teens they'd drifted apart. Everyone was back in Gossamer Falls now, and Cal and Meredith got along with Bronwyn fine. Mo was another matter entirely.

Bronwyn's laughter held so much mischievous glee that Cassie groaned. "Spill it." She took a bite of her muffin and stared Bronwyn down until she answered.

"I heard it from our very own police chief."

The muffin went down all kinds of wrong. Cassie coughed and spluttered, and tiny crumbs flew out of her mouth. She wanted to die of embarrassment. She couldn't stop coughing, but Bronwyn was laughing so hard, she was doubled over. Hopefully she'd missed the crumb debacle.

Police Chief Grayson Ward was Donovan's boss. If Gray knew, then . . .

Cassie finally got the coughing under control and ran a finger under each eye in hopes of preventing her makeup from running down her cheeks. When she refocused on Bronwyn, it was to see that the laughter had been replaced by concern.

"I'm sorry." There was no way to miss her sincerity. "I didn't expect you to nearly choke to death. And I've just realized why this isn't funny to you. Gray heard it from Cal at breakfast. Donovan was on a night shift, so I doubt he heard anything about it. If you care about that?"

Cassie took a sip of her coffee. Then another. She didn't respond until they were almost to the back door of Hideaway's kitchen. "I don't know why I reacted that way. I'm free to date whomever I want. And it shouldn't matter if anyone"—she refused to say his name—"overheard or knows."

Bronwyn put an arm around her and squeezed. "I understand so much more than you know." With a final squeeze, Bronwyn slid her ID card in front of the security sensor to unlock the door. "So, how was the date? Good?"

Cassie followed her inside. "It was—"

Bronwyn had flipped on the lights and they both stared at the kitchen. A kitchen that had been pristine when Cassie had left it a few hours ago but now looked like someone had taken a chain saw to the appliances.

The kitchen had been destroyed. Knives lay in pieces on the warped counters. Shelving had been overturned. The refrigerator door had a hole large enough for a gallon of milk to fit through it.

Cassie didn't even know how that was possible.

On the floor, written in a red sauce, was one word.

Oops.

TWO

OFFICER DONOVAN BLEDSOE took a sip of his tea—sweet iced tea, the way the good Lord intended it to be—and then set the tumbler on his desk. At the moment, he was the only officer in the building. Their police force was small. Too small for their population. But his boss, Grayson Ward, believed in quality over quantity. Gray had been hired to fix the mess the previous chief had made of law enforcement in this small community, and the day he was hired, over half the force turned in their resignations. Those who could took early retirement while others sought employment elsewhere.

Chief Ward was rebuilding, but it was hard to find people who wanted to protect and serve in a small community. And while he'd interviewed a number of candidates over the past few years, only a handful had made the cut.

Donovan was delighted that he was one who'd been brought on board. He felt nothing but pride in his work, the team of officers he served with, and the people he was getting to know better as he settled into life in Gossamer Falls. He'd been here eighteen months, and if it was up to him, he'd retire here.

These people were, for the most part, what his grandpa would have called "good folk." Crime was present, but it wasn't unusual for him to go through an entire shift with nothing more problematic than a disabled motorist or a cow on the loose.

Hopefully today would be as slow. By the time he went off shift tonight, he would have put in sixty hours for the week. Not that he minded. Extra shifts meant overtime pay. And long hours at work meant fewer hours at home staring at the walls.

All he had on his agenda was to clear out some paperwork and then walk up and down Main Street. There were two other officers on duty today, but both were tied up until midafternoon. They were providing security for a chili cook-off sponsored by the Chamber of Commerce.

Donovan had still been in Chicago when it happened, but two years earlier, a questionable judging decision led to a full-on brawl with pots of chili, bowls of cheese, sour cream, jalapeños, and at least one cast iron skillet of cornbread being thrown about. The melee appeared to be transitioning from a food fight to a fist fight when one of the town's elders hopped on his Harley and drove it into the crowd. Somehow there were no injuries.

Since then, the mayor had insisted on a police presence. Which left Donovan as the only officer available if they had a call for most of the day. Normally, Gray would fill in if needed, but today, the chief was off somewhere playing bodyguard to Dr. Meredith Quinn, DDS, town princess, and do-gooder extraordinaire.

Donovan liked Meredith, but he didn't love her penchant for going off by herself into areas that held hidden dangers she wasn't prepared to handle. Gray had finagled a promise from her that the next time she decided to run a charity dental clinic in the more remote nearby counties, he'd get to tag along. And while it was clear to everyone in a twenty-mile radius that she wasn't happy about it, she'd stayed true to her word.

Donovan hoped Gray could keep Meredith out of trouble.

Cassie would be devastated if anything happened to Meredith, who was more big sister to her than cousin. Truth be told, the Quinns were pretty loose about how they defined family relationships. Cousins, first cousins, aunts, uncles, brothers, sisters . . . it didn't matter. They were Quinns.

His own family of origin had given him no framework to understand the kind of loyalty the Quinns gave each other. Now, a year and half after moving to this tiny village in the mountains of North Carolina, he'd experienced the full force of the Quinn family.

When he'd been dating Cassie, he'd been welcomed. After he broke up with her? No one had shunned him, but there'd been a shift in the Quinns' reactions to him. They smiled. They shook hands. They nodded when they saw him or raised a hand in greeting when they passed by.

But he was very much on the outside looking in.

He'd hurt a Quinn, and they'd closed ranks around her. He didn't blame them. In fact, he admired them for it.

"Donovan?" The stricken features of Glenda Justus, their secretary, came into view moments after her voice had reached him. "You need to get out to The Haven."

A chill skittered across his body. Was Cassie in trouble? No. She wouldn't be there this early. He stood and grabbed his keys from his desk drawer. "What's happened?"

"Bronwyn called. She and Cassie found the kitchen at Hideaway vandalized."

The chill returned as a wave of ice.

Glenda wrung her hands and kept talking in a pitch higher than he'd ever heard from her. "Bronwyn said everything's destroyed. You'll need the camera to document it."

Donovan didn't fuss at her for telling him how to do his job. "Are they okay?"

"Bronwyn said they're fine. But, Donovan . . . what if whoever did this is still there? What if it's a trap?"

She'd been watching too many crime shows for her own good.

"I'll check it out." He could call the two officers who'd worked the night shift if he needed them, but he'd wait to do that until he evaluated the scene. "Please let Gray know what's going on."

"Will do."

He didn't run lights or sirens, but he did exceed the speed limit on his way to The Haven. The security guard at the gate waved him through without a word, and he made his way down the winding entry road, slowing only when he approached the populated areas.

When he came to a stop at the back of Hideaway, he paused to let Glenda know he'd arrived and was leaving his vehicle.

He grabbed his small forensic kit, camera, and notebook, then stepped out of his car, nodded at the two security guards flanking the ladies, and focused on Bronwyn and Cassie. "Are you okay?"

Both nodded. Both wore matching expressions of barely contained fury mixed with a splash of fear and a healthy helping of confusion.

"Give me a few minutes to see what we're dealing with, and then we'll talk." Donovan walked into Hideaway's back entrance. He paused at the door and put on booties.

He looked around as he entered the space. Lockers filled the walls on his left. To his right was a long hanging rod filled with the white jackets the serving staff wore.

Two more steps and he hit the swinging doors that opened into the kitchen and came to an abrupt stop. He studied the scene. He didn't want to jump to conclusions, but this kind of destruction looked like the work of an angry individual. It felt personal.

And the word "oops"? That was a taunt.

Would property destruction be as far as they went?

He took several minutes to investigate the space. He squatted down and shone a light on the floor, but there were no footprints. In fact, with the exception of the word "oops" and the random cooking implements that had been tossed around, the floor was pristine.

He formed a plan for how he wanted to proceed, then walked back outside. Bronwyn and Cassie leaned against Bronwyn's BMW. When he joined them, Bronwyn made eye contact. Cassie did not.

He pointed back to the kitchen. "I need to document the scene first. Then I'll need to talk to both of you."

"Of course." Bronwyn looked around. "Do you mind if we come inside with you? The two of us hanging out on the sidewalk might generate questions I don't want to deal with."

"That's fine."

"What would you like us to do, ma'am?" The question came from one of the security guards and was directed at Bronwyn.

She turned to Donovan. "Do they need to stay?"

Before he could respond, Bronwyn's phone beeped. She apologized and answered. She hadn't put it on speaker, but it didn't matter. He could hear every word.

"Are you okay? Is Cassie okay? We're headed your way." He recognized the voice of Cal Shaw.

"Cal, we're fine. You don't need to come. Donovan's here."

Cal said something that Donovan couldn't make out, but the tone hadn't been complimentary. Bronwyn handed her phone to Donovan. "Cal wants to talk to you."

He took it. "Bledsoe here."

"Officer." Cal's voice was as chilly as Gossamer Falls in January. "Bronwyn called Landry." Of course. Landry Hutton Shaw, Cal's new wife, was the artist in residence at The Haven and good friends with Bronwyn. "Landry called me. I called Gray. Now Mo and I are headed to The Haven."

"I—"

"I don't care if you want us there or not. We told Gray we'd help."

"I—"

"Unless you've found a way to clone yourself, you need help. We're not interested in taking over the investigation." A muttered sound that might have been Mo disagreeing with Cal's statement filtered through the air, but Cal didn't acknowledge it. "And as soon as word spreads to the family, you're going to need help keeping everyone from storming the castle."

Donovan pinched the bridge of his nose. The Quinns invading the Pierce stronghold? Wouldn't that just be pouring fuel on the fire.

He didn't like bringing civilians in, but Cal Shaw and Mo Quinn, Cassie's cousins, were both former military and were paid consultants with the Gossamer Falls Police Department. He could use them to secure the scene *and* they could keep the Quinn family in line without hurting feelings. "Fine. Come to Hideaway."

"We're ten minutes out." Cal disconnected the call.

Donovan handed the phone to Bronwyn. "The cavalry's coming."

Cassie and Bronwyn groaned in unison.

"You're loved." Donovan's words came out more sharply than he'd intended. He tried to soften his tone. "It's a gift, ladies."

Cassie made true eye contact with him for the first time since he'd arrived. She knew about his family, and the smile she gave him was far more tender than he deserved. "You're right."

Donovan turned to the security guards who continued to wait. "I'll need to talk to you later. For now, put everyone on high alert, and keep guests and staff away from this area."

"We'll do that." The men shook hands and left.

Bronwyn's phone rang again. She looked at the screen and sighed. "Excuse me." She answered the call and then took several steps away.

Donovan turned in the other direction to give her additional privacy. Cassie did the same.

Filling the silence would be a mistake. But he hadn't spoken to Cassie in months. And he had questions. So many questions. But he couldn't ask any of them, so he went with something safe. "How's Chef Louis?"

"Good. I went to see him yesterday. He's showing off his scar to anyone who walks in the door. Tells everyone he's a walking miracle. Says God left him on this earth for a reason and he's going to figure out what it is and do it."

"He wasn't already doing it? I've heard that his food is an almost spiritual experience."

Cassie glanced in his general direction at his words. "Oh, it is. There's something sacred about a delicious meal that provides nourishment in a way that speaks to all the senses. And Chef Louis is one of the best."

"So why does he think he isn't doing what he's supposed to do?"

"It has more to do with having time for family. He never married or had children. He told me once that he fell in love in his early twenties, but the lady didn't return his affections. He said he left his heart with her and transferred his passion to his food." Cassie slid her thumbs into the belt loops of her jeans. "He regrets that now. Not that he could do anything about her. You can't make someone love you back. But he poured so much of himself into his art that he never gave anyone else the chance to touch his heart."

"You can't make someone love you back." Cassie's tone had hardened when she said that, and Donovan knew that little speech had been for him. But she kept going, her voice light and airy as she said, "He told me he knows he's too old and

grumpy for romance, but that doesn't mean he can't be a good uncle and brother. He's trying to talk his family into going on a cruise next summer."

Cassie met his eyes and there was a spark of mischief in them. "We were in his kitchen at home, and he was teaching me how to make his secret chocolate sauce for the cream puffs when he shared that. I risked ruining my already tarnished résumé by joking that he should go on a singles' cruise and see what happens."

The thought of Chef Louis on a singles' cruise made Donovan laugh despite the seriousness of the current situation. He'd missed Cassie more than he'd even admitted to himself.

THREE

WHY HAD SHE COMMENTED on her tarnished career? She never spoke about that day or what had happened after. But today, amidst this new chaos, she felt like she was back there again. It wasn't an exact replica of what had happened, but the overtones were eerily similar.

The arrival of Cal and Mo pulled Cassie solidly back to the present.

Many people who didn't fully grasp the complexity of the Quinn family tree assumed her cousins were brothers. Both Cal and Mo were tall, currently clean shaven, with dark hair cut military short, matching sets of the Quinn blue eyes that came from Granny Quinn, and strong chins that mirrored Papa Quinn's.

At the moment, those eyes were hard, the chins were set, and their mouths bore similar expressions of disdain. And she knew why.

She and Donovan had dated. They weren't dating now. End of story. No need for drama. Especially not the big-brother-ready-to-beat-you-up vibes these two were sending toward Donovan.

"Thanks for coming." Cassie gave Mo a hug. Mo's eyes flicked over her shoulder and then back to her. "Y'all okay?"

"Yeah."

Cal pulled her away from Mo, threw an arm around her shoulder, and pressed a kiss to her temple. "Do you have any idea who did it?"

Donovan cleared his throat. "A little too soon for speculation, Cal."

Cassie stepped away from Cal and was relieved to see that he didn't glare at Donovan, which was good because Mo was giving him a death stare.

All three men stood ramrod straight, but that was where the similarity ended. Mo and Cal could pass for brothers, especially with the blue eyes that Cassie had also inherited from the Quinn side of the family.

And then there was Donovan. He was close to the same height as her cousins, but with his uniform, vest, and the muscle she knew was underneath, he was just . . . more. Bigger body, darker skin, deep brown eyes that could be warm and inviting but at the moment were focused and intent.

He looked from Cal to Mo and clearly wasn't cowed by either man. "I appreciate you coming by to help out."

That earned him two barely there nods. "Of course." Mo pointed to the restaurant. "How do you want us to do this? How many entrances are there?"

Cassie answered his last question. "This is the employee entrance. There are several customer entrances, and there's a loading entrance."

"I trust you both to handle it however you see fit. We need to prevent anyone from entering until we give the all clear." Donovan's voice was so stiff and professional that Cassie almost didn't recognize it. Then he turned to her. "Cassie, ba—" His eyes held hers, and she thought there was an apology in them as he swallowed what he'd been about to say. She didn't know if Mo or Cal caught it, but she knew. She knew because she'd heard the words "Cassie, baby" come from him so often while they'd dated that she'd thought he would always call her that.

He pinched his lips together for a second before he continued. "How much trouble will this cause you? Even if you brought in your entire staff, I'm not sure you'd be able to get the kitchen back up in time for the dinner service."

Cassie hadn't expected Donovan to be concerned about that. She'd just reached the point where she could think of him without tearing up. This reminder of how thoughtful and gentle he'd been with her was not what she needed now. "I need to talk to Bronwyn. But I think there's a way to make it work. We're fully booked this weekend, but fortunately we only have a handful of guests."

All three men gave her quizzical looks, but it was Mo who spoke up. "How can you be full but not have a lot of guests?"

"It happens. As exclusive as things are here, sometimes we have guests who require, or think they require, total privacy. They'll book the whole place and then bring a handful of friends or family."

"How many do you have to feed tonight?"

"Twelve. They're coming in this afternoon and they requested to dine in their rooms tonight. Everything is being served around eight. Tomorrow they have reservations for dinner at eight, and while I'm sure they were planning to be inside, if the weather cooperates we might be able to convince them to dine outside so we can use the breakfast kitchen." If the guests were nice, it might be okay. But if they weren't? Ugh. She didn't want to think about it. "We could set up a tent. We've done it before. If we pitch it to them as a special thing we're doing exclusively for them, it might fly."

She tried not to let the chaos and ugliness in the kitchen mess with her mind. "If the food I need for tonight and tomorrow night's meals hasn't been ruined, I can prepare the meals from the breakfast kitchen. But after that, things get dicey."

"More guests?" Donovan didn't look up from the notepad he'd pulled from his pocket while she spoke.

"We're booked solid Monday night through next week. I haven't looked beyond that. But I need *this* kitchen operational by Monday." The low-key panic she'd been fighting since she walked into the kitchen threatened to overwhelm her. "And I need to see my pantry and cooler as soon as possible. If the food has been tampered with . . ."

Should she even try to cook with the fresh food she had on hand? The sealed items would be fine, but what about the produce? The meat? Did she have time to buy more for tonight?

"Cassie?"

She looked up at Donovan's question and realized he must have been talking to her and she'd zoned out. "Sorry. What was that?"

"I said we'll do our best to get your kitchen back to you by to-morrow. I'm not sure about tonight though. And I'm not sure about the food either. That's going to be your department."

Bronwyn rejoined them as he finished speaking. "My apologies, everyone."

Cal pulled her into a hug. "You okay?"

"Honestly? No. I'm not okay. Thanks for stepping in." Her thank-you somehow managed to include Mo even though she didn't look at him.

Donovan took photos of the word "oops" and then set the camera down. He pulled some kind of collection tube from the bag he'd brought in and scraped up several samples of the red sauce. Once they were labeled and secured, he took one more sample and raised it to his nose.

"I don't know if huffing the evidence is the best plan." Mo's voice was low and lazy, and the laughter in it was heavily veiled. But it was there.

Donovan shot Mo a glare. "I'm not going to huff it. Or taste it." He held out the small sample. "I'm not an expert. But it smells like sriracha." He looked at Cassie. "Do you use it?"

"Yes. I make it from scratch, and we have multiple squeeze bottles in the cooler and the prep areas."

Donovan finished up with the sriracha and then grabbed the camera again. He took a photo of the hole in the refrigerator and asked, "Bronwyn, what kind of video surveillance do you have for this space?"

Bronwyn groaned. "Not as much as you'd think."

Donovan shifted and took a photo of a mixing bowl that last night held a salad and today looked like someone had taken batting practice on it. "I know Gray's talked to you about this. I assume nothing has changed?"

Bronwyn leaned against a counter and dropped her head back. "The situation with Landry highlighted the need for more surveillance but to be honest, I haven't made it the priority I should have."

Cal frowned at her. "You have to stop taking on all the responsibility—"

"Stop trying to give me an out, Cal! I'm the CEO. Who else is responsible?" Her frustration was evident.

"You have a board," Cal responded with the same tone. "You have people who work for you. I assume this means that most of them continue not to do their jobs."

Cassie looked between the two of them, then to Mo and Donovan, who looked on with identical expressions of concern.

Bronwyn gave Cal a tight smile. "None of that is important right now. What matters is that we don't have cameras inside. And the cameras we have outside don't record constantly. If the security guards didn't see anything from their live feeds in the control room, there's not going to be anything else to show who was here last night."

She pulled the card on the lanyard around her neck and

showed them her security badge. "We do track who enters and exits all of the controlled entries. But I can't imagine that anyone would be foolish enough to scan themselves in and then destroy the kitchen."

"I'll need those logs, regardless." Donovan snapped more photos. "We might catch a break."

"I'll get them for you this morning."

"And any video you do have."

"Of course."

There was a long pause where the only sound was that of Donovan's camera shutter. Then Mo stepped forward. "Cal, how about you and I go make a pass through the dining area. Check all the doors. That okay with you, Donovan?"

"Go for it."

Mo stalked out of the kitchen. Cal followed him.

Donovan set the camera down and pitched his voice low. "Bronwyn, is there something I need to know? I can ask them to leave."

So, Donovan had picked up on the tension too. Cassie shouldn't be surprised. It was so thick she'd been tempted to smack Mo on general principle. He radiated frustration and what Cassie was almost certain was a barely contained fury.

Bronwyn looked toward the dining area. "They can stay. It's a private war. And it won't bleed into this. We need the help."

Cassie considered her options as Donovan finished documenting the scene. He dusted for prints in a few places, but as far as she could tell, he didn't find anything useful. When he finally put everything away, she was prepared to be told her kitchen would be off-limits indefinitely.

"Bronwyn, do you want the good news or the bad news?"

"The bad news."

"Fair enough." Donovan stood and surveyed the room. "Because they entered the premises and destroyed property, this is a burglary. Unfortunately, I couldn't find a single usable footprint or fingerprint. I've taken a sample of the sauce, and we'll have it analyzed, but it will take weeks before we have results back from the lab." He pulled first one glove off, then the other. "If you want to bring in a private lab, or a private investigator, I wouldn't fault you for that. But no one can find what isn't here."

Bronwyn shook her head. "No. I don't want to do that."

"I need to interview both of you on the record, as well as the security guards and the restaurant staff. I'll write up a report. But unless we unveil a smoking gun in the interviews, there's nothing more I can do."

"Please move on to the good news." Cassie tried to keep her voice light.

"Of course." Was it her imagination, or did his voice drop into an even lower register when he spoke to her? Imagination or not, she liked it.

"The good news is that unless you plan to bring in someone else to investigate, I'm prepared to release the scene. That means you can get some staff in here to sort through the mess and get this place cleaned up."

Bronwyn let out a weak "Yeah."

Donovan frowned. "I thought that would be good news."

"It is. But everyone who could work any extra time was already tasked with other things today."

"Have no fear." Cal spoke from where he leaned into the swinging door. "Landry's been on the phone. The Quinns are ready to roll. Just say the word. And, you know, tell the guys at the gate to let them in. We'll have a crew here in an hour."

Cassie squealed and ran to Cal. "You're the best!"

"Hey now," Mo's rumble came from the other side of the door. "I'll have you know it was my idea."

She stepped through the door and hugged Mo. "You're the best too."

"Don't you forget it, sweet girl."

"Thank you."

Mo winked at her. "Don't worry, Cassie Lassie. We've got you."

She stepped back into the kitchen, Mo on her heels. "Bronwyn? Is that okay?"

"Let them come."

Donovan looked around the space once more, then nodded. "Excellent. If you'll hold down the fort here, I'll get these two lovely ladies interviewed so Cassie can get back and figure out how to feed tonight's guests."

FOUR

BRONWYN LED THE WAY, and they walked the short distance to her office. No one spoke as they walked or when she led them into the conference room. She paused and spoke to her secretary. "Could you bring water and coffee? And then hold all my calls. Thank you."

They entered the conference room, but Donovan hung back by the door. "Ladies, please understand that I'm just doing my job. But I need to speak to you individually." He pointed to Cassie. "Would you be willing to wait outside while I speak to Bronwyn?"

A host of emotions flitted across Cassie's face. He hoped she understood.

"I'll wait—"

"In my office," Bronwyn cut in. "With the door closed. I don't want anyone harassing you."

Donovan didn't like the sound of that at all. "Is there a chance she'll be harassed?"

"It depends on which members of my family show up this morning," Bronwyn answered. "I'd rather not have a decades-old family feud flare up."

"Agreed." Cassie reached for Bronwyn's hand and squeezed it. "Thank you."

Donovan watched her until she disappeared behind Bronwyn's office door. Then he joined Bronwyn in the small conference room, waited for her to sit, and took the chair across from her. He pulled a small notebook and a voice recorder from his pocket. He hit record, stated names and basic information, then turned to Bronwyn. "Why were you and Cassie in the kitchen this morning?"

Bronwyn pointed to the voice recorder. "I understand the need for that, but I would appreciate it if you would let me tell her what I'm about to share with you."

"I can't commit to that until I know what it is."

"Fair enough. Chef Louis called me yesterday. He wants to retire. Well, mostly retire. Sort of retire." She waved a hand in the air. "It depends on what Cassie says. But if Cassie is willing to work with him, he would like to take a significant step back and turn the kitchen over to her."

Donovan had to focus on the words he was scribbling in his notebook. Bronwyn was going to offer Cassie a chance to stay in Gossamer Falls? Permanently?

He tried to keep his voice steady. "Interesting."

"Yes." She dragged the word out. "I thought you might think so."

There was something in her voice that set Donovan on edge. "I'm not sure I know what you mean."

"You know exactly what I mean. Take some advice from someone who knows. You blew it, but I don't think you've done irreparable damage. Beg, plead, grovel, do whatever you have to do. Just fix it."

Had Cassie told her? That seemed unlikely. Bronwyn was Cassie's boss, not a confidante. Or she hadn't been while he and Cassie were dating. "I'll take that under advisement, but we need to focus on the situation in the kitchen."

Bronwyn straightened, and when she spoke, she was the CEO again. "My plans for Cassie may or may not be relevant to this. I haven't spoken to anyone about Chef Louis—not my staff, no members of my family, and not the executive board. When he had his heart attack, I brought her in fast and without consulting anyone. Given the need for immediacy, no one could complain about it at the time. But if I make it permanent? They'll throw a fit."

"Really?" He'd thought the feud was dying down.

"Oh yes. There will be a fight with my family, and I *will* win the fight. In fact, I'm happy to fight them over this. It's worth it to me. But"—she tapped the table—"I won't put those cards on the table, or burn the relationship capital it will require, if Cassie isn't interested."

Donovan couldn't blame her for that.

"This morning I planned to make a proposal to her, and then give her a few weeks to consider it. And before you ask, I don't think Chef Louis spoke to anyone, although you'll have to confirm that with him. He and I met for coffee in town yesterday. It *is* possible we were overheard, although he was very discreet. And we were tucked in the back corner."

There was only one coffee shop in Gossamer Falls, and Donovan knew the back corner she was talking about. It would be difficult to overhear any conversation taking place in that space.

"I didn't even tell Cassie what I wanted to talk about. And unless Chef Louis called her, she remains unaware."

"If anyone in your family knew about your plans, would it make sense for them to vandalize the kitchen?" Donovan didn't think so, but he had to ask.

Bronwyn stared at a point somewhere behind him, and there was so much old pain in her expression, it made him want to pat her hand and tell her everything would be all right. Not that he did either of those things because he didn't make a habit out of touching people, and the sad truth was that he had no idea if things would be all right or not.

"My family can be devious and underhanded. And a few of my cousins despise the Quinns in a way that simply isn't healthy and could lead them to make foolish decisions. But the guests that are arriving this afternoon are very high profile, even for us. When the current guests check out at noon, The Haven will be crawling with staff doing everything they can to make this place sparkle even more than usual. There've been multiple strategy sessions focused on this weekend's guests, which makes me think that even the most cantankerous Pierces wouldn't choose today to cause a scene."

She huffed out a small chuckle that held no humor. "My family has always done a good job of setting aside petty things like family feuds and personal ethics if it means protecting the bottom line."

Donovan tapped his lip with his pen. "Given that you're planning to make Cassie's position permanent, is it safe to assume that she's working out well? No one has any beef with her as a chef, or with her personally? Besides those with an aversion to her last name."

When Donovan moved to Gossamer Falls, one of the first things covered in his orientation briefing was the feud between the Quinns and the Pierces. Both families had been around since the founding of the town. Both families were devoted to Gossamer Falls. Between the two families, they owned almost half of the property in the area.

But somewhere in the early 1900s, there'd been a falling-out. If anyone knew the exact nature of the dispute, they kept it to themselves. From then on, there'd been a low-level tension simmering any time Quinns and Pierces interacted.

They kept it civil. A few of them even went into business together.

All that changed when the Pierces decided to take a large portion of their land and turn it into an exclusive enclave for the wealthy, connected, influential, and famous people who craved a healthy dose of privacy along with their luxury accommodations.

The Quinns had been horrified by the decision. They were convinced that bringing outsiders to their mountain would ruin their way of life and corrupt Gossamer Falls until it became an unrecognizable tourist trap. The resulting arguments took the feud to a whole new level.

It had never been violent. But all ties had been severed. Business partners dissolved their contracts, children were encouraged to find others to play with, and the two families continued to live side by side with as little interaction as possible.

Life carried on in Gossamer Falls, and Donovan's briefing had concluded with the interesting tidbit that the feud was losing ground with a few of the family branches. In particular, Bronwyn Pierce had been close to three Quinns since childhood—Cal Shaw (his mother was a Quinn), Meredith Quinn, and her brother, Mo Quinn. But there were rumblings that while the Quinns seemed willing to let bygones be bygones, there was a contingent of Pierces who clung to their hatred.

Despite what Bronwyn said about the business side of things, could one of those Pierces be behind the vandalism? The timing was interesting, coming as it did right before Bronwyn offered the job to Cassie.

Bronwyn glanced over her shoulder and leaned across the table toward Donovan. Her voice was loud enough for the voice recorder, but just. "If you'd asked me that question yesterday, I would have told you that Cassie has been an unqualified success. That she's universally adored by the staff, and our guests have been delighted with her approach to the menu."

Donovan kept his voice low. "But you can't say that now?"

"There's a problem, but I don't know what it is. I tried to get her to tell me this morning, and she said she had it under control. I was hoping that after I offered her the position, she'd be willing to tell me what's going on."

Bronwyn leaned back. "You probably already know how much Cassie abhors conflict. But when you talk to her, don't let her off the hook. Something's hinky in her kitchen. I want to know what it is and who's behind it."

FIVE

HOW LONG DID IT TAKE to discuss what happened this morning?

Cassie paused her pacing in front of the window in Bronwyn's office and soaked in the extraordinary view. Hideaway's dining room sported a breathtaking vista as well. It was too bad the kitchen didn't have a window.

When Bronwyn finally entered the room, she held the door open and waved Cassie toward the conference room. "I'm not supposed to talk to you again until Donovan completes his interviews. But I have to say this." Bronwyn reached for Cassie's arm and squeezed it. "It's none of my business, but I'm pretty sure being alone in a room with Donovan isn't exactly what you were prepared for today, and I'm sorry."

Cassie felt her face go up in flames. "I can handle it."

Bronwyn squeezed once more and released her. "Oh sweetie, I know that. Quinn women are fierce and strong." She leaned toward her. "But even the strong can fall when someone cuts their legs out from under them."

So, so true.

Bronwyn stepped back. "You've got this. And when you're done, we still need to talk."

Cassie walked toward the conference room. Donovan stood

by the open door, and after she was inside, he closed it. She took a seat and waited. He stood, his back to the room, his shoulders rising and falling as he took a few deep breaths.

What was that about? "Donovan? Are you okay?"

He turned and gave her a smile. If that smile had been a paint color, it would have been called busted-by-my-ex-girlfriend sheepish. He took his seat and finally met her gaze. "Just needed a second."

"Why?"

He scooted his seat back from the table, far enough that he could rest his elbows on his knees. He laced his fingers together and spoke to the floor. "I'm not sure I can do this."

"Do what?"

"Interview you."

"Why not?"

"I'm not as unbiased as I should be."

Cassie leaned back in her seat and crossed her arms. "Unless you think I'm responsible, there's no reason any biases you have against me should make any difference. Welcome to small-town life, Officer Bledsoe. You don't get to pick and choose who you defend and protect."

He stood and ran his fingers through his hair. It had grown out some since—

She pulled back from that thought so fast her mind provided her with sound effects for a needle scraping across a record.

He put his hands on the table, and with his height and general disposition, she probably should have been a little concerned about the way he was towering over her. What did it say about her that she'd always liked it when he got riled up? Worse, what did it say that she *still* liked it?

"Cassie."

Her name was practically a growl. And why did she have to like *that*?

"I'm concerned for your safety." His hands flexed on the table. "You could have walked in on that burglary. The vandalism could be directed at you. And I'm not sure I can investigate this without letting my personal feelings interfere."

Cassie kept her arms crossed so he wouldn't see her hands trembling. "I fail to see how this is an issue. I assume you want all of your constituents to be healthy and happy."

"You are *not* the same, and you know it."

"No, Officer Bledsoe. I'm *exactly* the same as anyone else. At least as far as you're concerned. So I suggest you sit that cute little butt of yours down, conduct the interview, and allow me to get on with my day. I'm sure my cousins will be anxious to get to work, and I'm sure you have plenty of other things to do today."

She took a breath and gave herself a mental high-five. Of course she knew he was referring to their dating history, but playing dumb, or at least refusing to acknowledge that he might have a valid point, made her feel like she had the upper hand.

She tried to focus on that and not on the way she'd be spending the next six months trying to erase that growly "Cassie" from her memory. Or the way his struggle to hold it together made her wish for things that she couldn't have.

Like Donovan Bledsoe.

A Donovan Bledsoe who currently looked ready to rain down death and destruction on anyone who got in his way.

He sat, turned on his voice recorder, stated their names and the date, and then held his pen against his notepad. "Ms. Quinn, do you have any quarrels with anyone in the kitchen?"

Bronwyn. That rat.

When she regained motor function of her mouth, she gave Donovan a sugary sweet smile. "How would you define quarrel, Officer Bledsoe? Chefs are as temperamental as any other artist. No one expects everyone to get along."

"No one expects a coworker to destroy the kitchen, either. But given that it's a very real possibility that one of your co-workers did exactly that, it's one we have to explore." Donovan's tone was even. But there was a muscle jumping in his neck.

What was wrong with her? Shame flooded through her as she thought about her reactions to Donovan in the last ten minutes. He'd been nothing but kind. While she'd been . . . awful. She leaned forward and rested her forehead on the table. "Could you turn off the recorder? Just for a minute?"

He didn't answer, but she heard the recorder move. Presumably he'd turned it off.

She didn't look up. "Could we start over please? I don't know what's wrong with me. You're concerned, and I appreciate your worry. I apologize for being such a shrew about it." She sat up but kept her head down. "This is harder than I anticipated it would be. If you could restart the voice recorder, I'll answer your questions without the attitude."

"Cass." This time, there was no growl. There was tenderness. And drat her stupid, idiotic, traitorous, glutton-for-punishment heart, but she liked that too. "You don't owe me an apology. Your day ran off the rails, and then I took it and threw it over a cliff."

She didn't want to laugh. He wasn't being funny. But her heart still ached. Because Donovan was funny. Kind. Protective. Caring. Compassionate. And for all his macho manliness, he wasn't afraid of apologizing or of expressing his emotions. He'd been practically perfect in every way.

Right up until the day he wasn't.

And she still didn't know why.

But she wasn't going to find out. Not today. Today, she was

going to put on her big-girl panties and deal with the situation. "I'll accept your apology if you'll accept mine."

"Deal."

She pointed to the recorder. "Let's do this."

He gave her a look that said the conversation they were about to have wasn't the one he wanted to have. But he hit record. "Cassie, could you tell me if there are any issues in the kitchen that I need to be aware of?"

"Bronwyn ratted me out, didn't she?"

He smirked. "She indicated that she had concerns, and you'd been unwilling to discuss them. She also indicated that while she respected your decision at the time, circumstances being what they are, it would be wise for me to find out what's going on."

"You aren't going to like it."

"I don't have to like it. Doesn't mean I don't need to know."

"Fine." How to put this . . . delicately? "The sous-chef, Amos Cartwright."

"Yes?"

"He, um, well . . . he either wants to date me or kill me. Honestly, it could go either way. I'm not quite sure."

Donovan's jaw worked. She waved a hand at him and mouthed, "Relax before you break your teeth." Somehow she didn't think it would be appropriate for that to be on the recording, but seriously, he was going to need to see Meredith and get a night guard if he did that kind of thing in his sleep.

He unclenched his jaw and indicated that she should continue. "To be clear, I'm not interested. I don't date my sous-chefs. It's a firm rule. But even if he wasn't my sous-chef, I wouldn't date him. He isn't my type."

One eyebrow lifted. He went with a different approach. "Can you describe this chef? What was his name again?"

"His name is Amos Cartwright. He's from West Virginia.

Chef Louis hired him two years ago. He's an excellent sous-chef. He claims that he doesn't want Chef Louis's job. But I think he was caught off guard when Bronwyn brought me in rather than promoting him to the role of head chef while Chef Louis is recuperating."

"Okay. What does he look like?"

"He's maybe five ten? Two hundred pounds? Brown hair. Brown eyes. May or may not be emotionally stable."

AN UNSTABLE CHEF? In a kitchen, night after night, with Cassie? No. Donovan did not like the sound of that.

Cassie had the bubbly, girl-next-door good looks that made people underestimate her. They saw her blond hair and blue eyes and easy laughter and didn't realize that she was a woman driven to be the best. Mentally, she was a force. But physically? She wasn't much over five feet tall. A two-hundred-pound man with anger issues could be a big problem.

Cassie ran her hands over the smooth tabletop. "But I don't see him doing something like this."

"You said earlier that he either wanted to date you or kill you and you weren't sure which."

"Oh, I stand by that."

Donovan's blood ran cold at her matter-of-fact statement. "Why, exactly, do you say that?"

"Because one day last week, he told me he wanted to marry me. This was after I made breakfast for supper for the staff after a long night. But then a few days later, he half jokingly, half seriously threatened me with a chef's knife. So I'm not sure how he feels about me. But I do know that he loves that kitchen more than he loves anything else. He'd never damage it. He might damage me, but not the kitchen."

How could she say that so flippantly? "He might damage you?"

Cassie shrugged. She shrugged!

Donovan squeezed the arms of the chair where he sat and forced himself not to move. "Cass, could you go back to the way he threatened you with a chef's knife?"

Cassie glanced at the recorder. Then back at Donovan. "This is one of those things that could get blown way out of proportion. I don't want him to lose his job over what was probably a joke to him."

"But it wasn't to you?"

She shook her head, and when she met his eyes for a fleeting moment, there was something he'd never seen in them. It might have been shame. Or fear. Whatever it was, it was bad.

"Cassie?"

She took a gulp of air, and the words tumbled out so fast he was thankful the recorder would capture everything. "It was late. We were all tired. Everyone gets punchy sometimes, and the diners that night had been . . . challenging."

"Define challenging."

Cassie stood and paced around the table like a caged animal. "Okay." She pitched her voice low and leaned toward the recorder. Clearly she wanted her words recorded, but didn't want to risk anyone overhearing. "It shouldn't come as a surprise that in order to keep them happy, some of our guests require special handling."

"You mean because The Haven caters to people who almost never hear the word 'no' regardless of what they ask for?"

Cassie smirked. "Something like that." Her shoulders relaxed a fraction. "We had a guest who complained about everything we served him. The salad dressing had too much salt. The shrimp was too spicy. The dessert"—she paused and held her hands out in a circle the size of a small dinner plate—"was too small."

"Too small? How do you put up with that?" He would have told the guy to go make his own dessert.

"Your world is black and white. There are laws. People follow them or they break them. If they break them, there are consequences. But my world isn't like that. Taste is subjective. One person's spicy is another person's bland. It doesn't mean one person is right and the other is wrong. It's a matter of opinion."

"People can have a difference of opinion without being jerks."

"True. And if it had just been about the seasoning of the food, I could have attributed the behavior to someone with a vastly different palate than mine. But when he pitched a hissy fit about the size of his dessert? That's when I knew there was no pleasing him. We aren't running a buffet here. This isn't a cruise ship where people can request three entrées and four desserts. We typically don't plate the desserts until it's time to take them to the diners, and we only make what we need. But in this case, someone had miscounted and we had another dessert plated, so I told the server to give him another one, no charge. I didn't realize that Amos took it upon himself to hand deliver it. When he returned to the kitchen, he was so angry he took a knife, whacked a few onions, a couple of potatoes, and then came toward me with the knife in his hand, point up."

Donovan had never believed it was possible to feel his blood pressure rise. Until today. He was pretty sure he was approaching stroke levels. Only the obvious proof that Cassie had walked away unscathed from the encounter kept him in his seat.

She carried on, seemingly oblivious to the mental, emotional, and physical distress her story was causing him. "When

I asked him what had put a twist in his toque, he told me the guest took two bites of the second dessert before declaring himself too full to eat any more. Then Amos waved the knife around, a bit too close to my jacket for my liking and went off. He ranted about the guests and the kitchen and my handling of the entire situation."

She paused, her brow furrowed. "I'm not sure how to explain it. Even while he was spewing about everything wrong in our kitchen, it still wasn't clear if he was angry *at* me or *for* me."

Donovan took a swig of water from the bottle on the table and was pleased to see that his hands weren't shaking in rage. "Cassie. The knife pointed at your chest probably should have clued you in on that."

"He didn't attack me with it."

"No? Were you afraid?"

She dropped her gaze.

That was all the answer he needed. "Terrorizing someone with a weapon is aggravated assault. No physical harm is required. You could have him arrested for that."

Her eyes widened. "I don't want him arrested. He was angry. He'd had a long night. He was tired and frustrated, and that particular guest was loud and drunk and completely out of line."

"None of that gives him the right to come at you with a knife!" Donovan wasn't sure when he'd stood up, or when he'd leaned toward her. But Cassie didn't flinch from his nearly shouted response.

"I know that! But it isn't my kitchen." She pressed a hand to her chest. "I'm filling in. I'm in charge of the food, not the staff."

"I doubt Bronwyn would see it that way."

Cassie flopped into her chair. "I've handled far worse and lived to tell about it."

This was a thread Donovan desperately wanted to pull. But he knew from past experience that it wouldn't get him anywhere but annoyed and frustrated. Cassie had a story. But she hadn't confided in him while they'd been dating. She certainly wouldn't confide in him now.

"Bottom line—Amos has been a problem from the first day I came in. But like I said, I don't see him destroying the kitchen."

SIX

"CASSIE." DONOVAN'S VOICE was calm. Too calm. She braced herself for whatever was coming next. "Why didn't you confront him? Why didn't you tell anyone? If this guy's unstable, you're putting yourself and the entire kitchen staff at risk. Maybe even your guests."

"I have reasons. Good ones."

"Care to share?"

She couldn't tell him. It was too embarrassing. And they didn't have time to discuss it now anyway. "It isn't relevant."

"I'm going to have to disagree with you."

"It's a free country." Great. Now she was spouting junior-high-quality insults. No. She'd been more articulate in junior high. She fought the panic creeping through her at the memories the events of this morning had pulled front and center.

She stopped those thoughts and focused on what Donovan wanted to know. "There have been . . . other incidents. Things messed up in the kitchen. Small nuisances. I didn't think they were anything more than petty annoyances. But now?"

"Could Amos have been responsible for all of it?"

"No. Sometimes it happened before Amos arrived. Once it

was when he was gone. And once he was the one who found the mess. Amos doesn't like messes. At all."

Donovan tapped his pen. "Would you please tell me exactly what's happened?"

"It's small stuff. So very small."

"I don't care."

"Fine." She counted on her fingers. "First, one of my paring knives disappeared."

Cassie could see by the look on Donovan's face that he understood. They'd talked about it before. A chef's knives were sacrosanct. No one touched the chef's knives without permission.

"When was this?"

"My second week on the job."

"You didn't tell anyone?"

"No. I was trying to keep my head above water. New kitchen, new staff, new menu. I didn't have the energy for causing drama over a paring knife, especially when I couldn't be sure it hadn't been taken by accident."

Donovan's face told her that he found her reasoning weak, but he didn't push it. "What happened next?"

"A few days later I planned to use the ice cream maker to make a special dessert. It's mine. I brought it from home."

"I'm guessing this is a very expensive ice cream maker."

"Yes. I got it for my birthday."

Donovan didn't ask who'd given it to her.

"Right before we got ready to start making the ice cream, we realized the power cord was missing. And of course it has a specific adapter that isn't common. We didn't have anything like it in the kitchen. Had to completely change our plans."

Cassie hadn't realized before now that it was possible to convey emotion by breathing, but Donovan was managing it. His expression was calm and his hands were steady, but the way he inhaled through his nose was . . . aggressive. There was no other way to put it.

He blew out that breath, also aggressively, and asked, "What else?"

Cassie tried to keep her tone even. "Well, a few nights after that there was a mean message in the bathroom on the mirror, and then—"

"What did it say?"

Cassie swallowed. "It suggested that I should leave. Using multiple expletives."

Donovan's lips flattened. "Go on."

"And, uh, one of my jackets was cut up."

Donovan dropped his head and took several slow breaths. "Anything else?"

"Well, really just one other thing. I had a flat tire on Monday. I mean, it could happen anywhere. I didn't think anything of it. I took it to Mr. Monroe's shop the next day to get a new one. I left the old one with him. But then he called yesterday and said he wanted me to know that when he looked at it more closely, he realized it had several small punctures. He didn't think it was from road debris."

Donovan pressed his palms to his temples and didn't speak for a full ninety seconds. She knew because she was watching the second hand spin around on the clock over his head.

"Cassie." He stopped. Shook his head. Started again. "Please tell me that you've told someone about this before now."

She stared at the table. "When I said it all out loud just now, it seems so obvious that I should have. But when each incident occurred, I . . ." She groaned. "No one else knows. Except Amos. He knows about the missing knife. And he knows about the sliced-up jacket."

She reached for her water and took a sip. "You probably won't believe me, but when I found out about my tire, I knew it was serious. I was going to tell Gray today, but then I found out he was going to be with Meredith all day. I didn't think one more day would matter."

Cassie couldn't sit still any longer. She shoved the chair back and stalked to the window. When had she turned into the stupid chick in a horror movie who didn't have enough sense to stay alive?

But she knew. She knew the date, the time of day, what the weather had been like outside, the way the kitchen had smelled of garlic and onion and celery, and the way the screams echoed around the stainless steel the second before the gunshot that ended a life. She pressed her head to the glass.

"Cassie, this paints everything in a new light."

"I know."

"I'm trying to understand. I really am. You are loved by so many. What would make you think that you have to handle this on your own?"

"Because—" The words refused to come. "I'm sorry. I . . . I can't get through the day if I have to dredge all that up. I'm riding a very thin edge at the moment. I can't . . . not right now."

A wall of heat behind her was her only warning that he'd approached her. She must really be messed up if she hadn't heard him move. "I'm going to give you a hug, Cassie."

He waited, and she realized that he was giving her time to tell him no. She *should* tell him no. Having him hold her would be a mistake. So why wasn't she saying anything?

His hands closed over her upper arms and he pulled her back against his chest. His chin rested on her head and his arms wrapped around her. The hold was familiar. He was a big guy, and she relaxed into the safety of his embrace.

She wished she knew why he'd ended things between them. When he'd told her they would be better off as friends, he'd been so calm, so gentle, but so firm in his decision that she hadn't been able to argue with him. At first she was completely stunned. Then the hurt and humiliation seeped through her so fast that she could barely breathe through the pain of it.

He didn't know, of course, but when he said he wanted to talk to her that night, she'd been expecting a very different conversation. She wasn't expecting a marriage proposal, but she thought the conversation would be about exclusivity and commitment.

Instead, he told her he was so happy to have gotten to know her and that he knew this was ultimately best for both of them. And she . . . sat there. On the inside, she was confronting him and demanding an explanation. Had he been lying when he'd held her and told her she was the most beautiful thing in his universe? It hadn't felt like a lie. She almost found the strength to call him on his behavior.

But then her mind flashed to the last time she'd confronted someone and everything that followed, and she froze. She said something stupid to Donovan like, "I understand. Thank you for telling me."

She was so terrified of confrontation that she thanked him for breaking up with her! How messed up was that?

By the time she got her head on straight, he was gone. The opportunity had passed. Their relationship was over and it had been too late for her to get the answers she needed.

Although right now, it strangely didn't feel like anything was over or too late.

"Donovan?"

"Yeah."

She blinked the sudden moisture from her eyes. No. She wouldn't cry. She was tired of being afraid. Tired of tiptoeing around everyone and everything. Tired of being pushed around by her own feelings.

His arms tightened as he waited for her to speak.

But the words weren't there. How could she tell him that she *had* pulled on her big-girl panties and called someone out for their behavior? And her bravery led to her being so traumatized that she'd turned into a sniveling coward who would rather put up with being mistreated and disrespected than risk being hurt that way again?

How was she supposed to say that to a man who had never been a coward a single day in his life?

"You wouldn't understand."

There was a weighty pause before he said, "I wish you'd give me the opportunity to try."

She didn't owe him an explanation. Or a conversation. Or . . . anything.

But maybe if she told him what happened, she could somehow bring the conversation around to them and why he'd decided they should be friends. Because despite her attempts to get over him, their current position made it clear that she was nowhere close to being over Donovan Bledsoe.

And if she didn't get some answers, she might never be.

"Tonight then. Right now, I have to figure out how to prepare a meal that will blow our guests away without the use of the kitchen."

"I'm going to hold you to it." He squeezed her tight and then released her. "Let's get back over to Hideaway."

She stayed facing the window until she heard him gathering his things at the table. Then she turned and joined him. They didn't speak until they were outside and headed back to the restaurant.

"Is there any chance of us finding out who did this?" she asked.

"There's always a chance."

She cut her eyes at him. "Like if this guy confesses?"

"That would help." He finally cracked a smile, albeit a teeny, tiny one. "Confession *is* good for the soul."

"Subtle."

He winked.

They didn't talk anymore, and when they returned to Hideaway, it was to find several more cars than had been there before.

"I see the Quinn cavalry is here." Donovan shook his head.

She opened the door to the back entrance, and what she saw brought tears to the surface. She retreated, closed the door, and leaned against the exterior wall.

Donovan immediately stepped in front of her, shielding her from view. "What is it?"

"My family is awesome." She sniffled and blinked and ran a finger under her eyes. "They always come to the rescue. Whether I'm in Atlanta or a traitor on Pierce land."

A door opened, and she felt Donovan's body shift and his low "Give us a second."

The door closed.

"You aren't a traitor."

She laughed and sniffed. "It was a joke. But did you ever expect to see so many Quinns at The Haven?"

"I don't know." Donovan's voice was low and soothing. "Things are changing. Cal lived here for a few months before his and Landry's house was ready. And Meredith and Bronwyn are together a lot."

"The Pierces don't like it."

"I don't know that they have much choice."

"Maybe."

"What do you mean?"

"Not everyone is happy about me being here. They'll be super thrilled"—she layered every word with sarcasm—"when they find out my parents, grandparents, cousins, a few aunts and uncles, and who knows who else decided to save the day."

SEVEN

CASSIE'S WORDS SPUN in Donovan's head. Her parents were in there? Great. They weren't his biggest fans. And he didn't blame them.

He looked down at the top of Cassie's head. He'd pulled some idiotic stunts in his day, but telling her they could only be friends? That he thought she was awesome, but he couldn't imagine their life together? That had, without any doubt, been his dumbest move. Ever.

It had been a lie. He *could* imagine their life together. He could see getting down on one knee, proposing, and living in Gossamer Falls with her forever.

He would be ecstatic to wake up with her every single day for the rest of his life.

But Cassie? She would wither. And eventually, she would resent him. Cassie was a shooting star, destined for amazing things. Her genius was with the food she prepared, and she needed people who could eat her creations. More people than could be found on the streets of Gossamer Falls. And until today, Donovan hadn't been able to imagine a scenario where she could possibly be fulfilled if she stayed here.

He'd experienced the bitterness that came when people who claimed to love you stifled your dreams. And he'd seen a life cut short because the pain of trying to please others had been too much. He couldn't do that to her. He had to let her go so she could achieve everything she wanted. She was young, beautiful, fun, and talented, and she would find someone who could live in a place like Charlotte or Atlanta, or even New York or LA.

He wasn't that person. He'd nearly died trying to be that person, and he knew he couldn't go back. He certainly couldn't ask Cassie to do what he wasn't able to.

So he'd made a decision.

He'd let her go.

He hadn't prayed about it. Hadn't sought any kind of counsel. Hadn't explained himself to Cassie. And when she didn't fight for him? When she didn't make any effort to hang on to what they had? He'd held on to the idea that no matter how much it gutted him, it was the right decision.

But now she was here. Her body inches from his own. She'd let him hold her earlier, but she undoubtedly assumed it was a friend offering comfort and nothing more.

She couldn't know how much he wanted to pull her into his arms, claim her lips, tell her he was sorry, and beg her to be his.

He was sorry about her kitchen. Sorry about this Amos Cartwright character who was giving her a hard time. Sorry that she'd been traumatized.

He couldn't do it now, but they were going to talk. And when they did, he would come clean. Worst-case scenario, she'd hate him. He'd deserve it if she did. He'd nearly lost his mind when he heard about her date last week, but he knew from his sources around town that it had been a bust. So maybe it wasn't too late.

Cassie took in a few more shuddering breaths and wiped her hands on her pants. Donovan held his position, with his hands braced on the wall above Cassie's head while she pulled herself together. He had to focus. Her comments about the Quinns and Pierces had sent warning bells chiming in his mind. Could some of the grumpier Pierces be behind this?

She looked up at him. "Does it look like I've been crying?"

"No."

"Okay." She sniffed once and shook her shoulders. "Let's try this again."

He moved aside and held the door for her as she walked into the restaurant. She'd barely made it three steps before she was engulfed by family. The cacophony of voices reached a peak before a shrill whistle brought them all to silence.

Donovan almost dropped his notepad when he realized the sound had come from Rhonda Quinn, Cassie's grandmother.

"She doesn't need you to hover over her. She needs you to get to work. So get back to it." The crowd dematerialized and Rhonda strode toward him. This could be . . . uncomfortable. "Young man, I understand that you are in charge of the investigation."

"Yes, ma'am."

"I expect you to protect my granddaughter. She's been through enough."

"Nana." The word held a touch of outrage and a healthy dose of exasperation as Cassie put a hand on her grandmother's arm.

"Hush, child." The words were brusque, but the hand that patted Cassie's was gentle. "Let me talk."

Cassie threw him an apologetic look but said no more.

"I'm sure you're an excellent officer. But if you need anything at all, you let us know. We protect our own. And Cassie is precious."

"Nana." This time the word was full of tenderness.

Donovan placed a hand over his heart. "I won't let anything slip through the cracks, ma'am."

"Good. Now, Cassandra?"

"Yes, ma'am?"

"You need to go somewhere where you can figure out tonight's menu. You can't do that in here."

"Mom." Cassie's dad had joined the fray, and the look he gave Donovan was so flat it sent an unpleasant sensation crawling over Donovan's skin. Very few people scared him. But this man did. Not because he expected John Quinn III to behave in anything other than a calm manner. But because that look told Donovan that Cassie's father had classified Donovan as a man who could not be trusted with his daughter. "Cassie's an adult. She can figure this out."

"Of course she can, John. I never said she couldn't. I said she needed some space and that we will handle the cleanup."

Cassie's dad turned his full focus on Donovan. "Is there any reason Cassie needs to be here?"

"No, sir." Donovan kept his tone professional and respectful. "She needs to be nearby in case we have questions, and under no circumstances should she be alone."

Cassie's eyes flashed, and she hissed out a low "Traitor."

"Oh, she won't be." John Quinn pulled Cassie against his side.

Cassie had told him she was a daddy's girl. But while he'd spent some time with her grandparents, and even her great-grandparents, he hadn't had much opportunity to see her interacting with her immediate family while they'd been dating. Her parents had been away for ten weeks visiting with missionaries who were supported by their church. When they returned home, he'd already known he had to end his relationship with Cassie, so he'd managed to avoid the handful of invitations to attend family gatherings.

John Quinn gave him a nod and pulled Cassie away, toward the opposite side of the restaurant, in a not-at-all subtle move to remove her from Donovan's space. If he did manage to get Cassie back, restoring himself to the good graces of the extended Quinn family would require a deft hand. And patience.

He spent another hour in the kitchen and dining areas of Hideaway. He talked to cleaning staff. He talked to servers, and he talked to cooks.

And then Amos Cartwright walked in the door.

"What on earth is going on?" Amos wasn't tall, but he was a solid guy, and the thought of him waving a knife anywhere near Cassie's skin made Donovan wish he could arrest him on the basis of being an overbearing jerk and nothing more. But the man, for all his size and volume, stood frozen in the space—and unless he had an acting background no one was aware of, simply could not make his mind process what had happened.

"Mr. Cartwright?" Donovan approached him. "Could we speak over here?" He pointed toward the dining area. He'd appropriated a few tables where he could interview the staff.

Amos gave Donovan a once-over. His gaze lingered briefly on the gun, and the badge. Then he met Donovan's gaze. "Where's Cassie? She should be here."

Donovan couldn't tell if he meant that in a hostile way, or if he was concerned for her.

"She's been here. She's currently in the breakfast kitchen trying to figure out how she's going to make dinner work tonight."

"I need to talk to her."

"You can talk to her *after* you talk to me." Donovan sunk all his authority into those words.

"What happened?" Amos asked.

"We're still not sure."

Amos took a few steps toward the dining area, then caught sight of the refrigerator. "Why would anyone do this?"

"We don't know." Donovan pointed to the doors again. "Come on. Let's talk."

The big man deflated with each step, and by the time he reached the table, he sank into a chair and dropped his head into his hands. "We don't need this. Not this weekend. There's so much to do. I need to talk to Cassie."

Donovan didn't want to take this guy off his suspect list. But Amos was sure making a compelling case for Cassie's assertion that he would never do anything to harm the kitchen.

"Let's talk about Cassie for a minute."

Amos's face was infused with what looked a lot like shame. "I bet she named me as her prime suspect."

"Actually, she said she didn't think it was you."

Amos lowered his hands and his voice. "But you do, don't you?"

"I'm undecided. Why would Cassie assume it was you?"

"Because I'm a jerk. And I've made every day difficult for her. And I've done it on purpose."

Donovan had a lot of questions, but if this guy was willing to talk, he decided to go with the simplest one. "Why?"

"Why?" Amos waved a hand around the room. "This is practically my home. I've worked here for years. Sous-chef to Chef Louis. We've collaborated on menus and he's let me experiment with dishes. He's my mentor. And this place . . . I don't have children. Or a spouse. I have Hideaway."

That didn't sound depressing at all.

"When Louis had his heart attack, I assumed I would step in. I know everyone thinks I do, but I don't want the job full-time. I have . . . issues. I don't need the pressure of being the head chef. But I could have managed it while he recovers."

He ran a shaky hand over his chin. "But instead there's this little girl. She's barely out of culinary school."

Donovan didn't point out that she'd been out of school for over five years and had an impressive list of restaurants on her résumé.

"She's cute and perky and the polar opposite of Chef Louis. Have you met him?"

"Briefly. Once."

"Well, he's a grump. He has a heart of gold, but he's a little salty. And he runs the kitchen a certain way."

"And Cassie runs it a different way?"

"So different! Some days I can barely stand it!"

Donovan made a note to ask Cassie and Bronwyn how often Hideaway staff were drug tested. He didn't think Amos was high. But there was something going on with him.

EIGHT

CASSIE WALKED into Hideaway in time to hear Amos's outburst. She froze, undecided. She shouldn't eavesdrop. But she really wanted to know what his deal was.

"Is different so bad?" Donovan wasn't being nearly as harsh with Amos as Cassie had expected him to be.

"Yes! No. I don't know." Amos ran his hands through his hair. "Listen. I didn't do it. Can I please go talk to her? She's a phenomenal chef. But I've been here longer. I might be able to help. And she'll need to start prepping as soon as possible."

"I can't let you go work with her until I'm confident that you aren't a threat to her safety."

"I'm not." Amos sat straighter. "I know what happened to her. And I know she's scared. But she needs to be more confident. More assertive."

"And you think waving a knife at her will help her with that?" Donovan's face was so serene that Cassie knew it for a mask.

"Of course not. But she should have called me on it. She should have told me to put the knife away. She also should have told that guest that he could take his dessert and be grateful for it. The one she gave him? That was hers. I'd made it *for her*. She loves chocolate and raspberry, and she works hard. But instead of standing up for herself, she gave it away."

Cassie turned and ran out of the restaurant. And she kept running until she came to the rock wall by the small creek that ran through The Haven's property. The wall was just two feet high, and she climbed over it and slid down on the other side.

This wasn't her first time in this spot. There were trees and mountain laurel and large rocks everywhere and it felt like her own little secret garden.

She brought her knees up to her chin, wrapped her arms around her legs, and stared at the water. Her tears were silent and she made no move to halt them.

When had she become this person? Someone who couldn't see the good in others? Who didn't believe in herself enough to fight for what she wanted?

She knew the answer.

And she hated it.

Father, please forgive me.

She owed Amos an apology. He was a fragile spirit, and instead of trying to find out what was going on, she'd let him disrespect her and her role. From what she'd overheard, he wasn't even all that angry about her taking Chef Louis's position.

Father, I don't want to be afraid all the time.

Her phone vibrated in her pocket. She pulled it out to look. Donovan.

Time to face the music. "Hello." Her voice was scratchy and sounded awful. She cleared her throat and tried again. "Hello."

"I don't think Amos is going to give you any trouble. Would you like me to send him to the breakfast kitchen?"

"Yes."

"Would you like some company?"

She stared at the river. She shouldn't. But . . . she did. "Yes. I'm—"

"I know where you are. Mo followed you out."

"And he told you?"

"Shocked me too. Be there in a minute."

When he climbed over the wall to join her, he muttered, "When in Rome," and took a seat on the ground beside her. "I may be seeing things, but isn't that a swing over there?" He pointed to the porch swing that had been hung from a tree near the river.

"It is. But sometimes I need to feel the ground." She patted the grass where she sat. "Some people call it forest bathing."

Donovan snorted. "You made that up."

She bumped his shoulder with hers. "It's a goofy name for getting out in nature. I try to spend some time outdoors every day. It's good for my mental health. And"—she pointed to the garden around them—"I feel closer to God in a garden like this."

"Fair enough."

They sat in silence for several minutes. "My apartment in Atlanta had no green space. I couldn't afford one with a garden roof, and the grass nearby was used by every dog in the building."

He turned toward her, his face wrinkled in disgust.

"Exactly. No sitting in that grass. Ever."

"Wise decision." He turned his attention back to the river, but he scooted his body a fraction closer to her.

His voice had always been one of her favorite things about him. He could make her feel safe just by saying her name. But now, it was his willingness to sit in silence that kept her talking. "It was probably the only wise decision I made while I was there."

He stiffened but didn't speak.

"Chef Albert had been one of my dream chefs. The person I would do anything to work with, to learn from, to have the opportunity to absorb his culinary genius. So when the offer came, I didn't think about it. I said yes, found a cheap place to live, and hauled my stuff to Atlanta so fast that I was already on the job before most of my family knew anything about it."

"Risky."

"Stupid." She pulled a few blades of grass and began to twist them together. "Three days in, and I knew I'd messed up."

"Three days?"

"Okay. Fine. I knew on the first day. But it took me to the third to accept it." When he didn't prompt her, she realized he wasn't going to push for more than she was willing to give. And she gave more. "Kitchens are notorious for being hotbeds of addiction. Alcohol and cocaine are so commonly abused that no one bats an eye. Some chefs don't think they can maintain the pace if they don't snort some cocaine before they start. Line cooks and the front of house staff will close up a kitchen, then go party until dawn. Sleep it off during the day, but then need something to help them make it through a shift that night. It's a vicious cycle."

She tossed her little grass circle to the side, grabbed another handful, and started over.

"Chef Albert was an addict. He could be kind. He could be cruel. I never knew which version of him would be there when I walked in. But I didn't want to say anything. He was Chef Albert. I kept hoping that maybe I'd caught him at a bad time, and he'd string together a few weeks of sobriety."

"He didn't?"

"Nope. I started looking for other opportunities in the city. I didn't want to move again so soon. But I knew I couldn't hold out for much longer. My goal was to suck it up for six months. Then leave."

DONOVAN TRIED to remember what he knew of Cassie's work history. She'd been in Atlanta for four months. Not six. And when she left, she returned to Gossamer Falls.

He hoped she would tell him the rest of it, but if she didn't, he'd keep his mouth shut and wait.

Her grass weavings grew increasingly frenetic. "But then one of the servers started dealing. Or maybe he'd been dealing all along. Regardless, he started bringing the drugs to Chef Albert at the restaurant. I never knew if the problem was that he had a different supplier and he reacted differently to the drugs, or if the dealer intentionally laced the cocaine with something else. Or maybe the longer you do a drug, the more erratic your behavior gets. Who knows? What I did know was that Chef Albert's behavior became unpredictable. He was frequently manic after a hit, but he'd always funneled that energy into his cooking. But he became more and more angry. And when he offered me some cocaine and I refused, he screamed at me for a solid ten minutes."

Donovan clenched his hands together. It had taken him no time at all to discover that while Cassie could appreciate constructive criticism, she took it hard every time. She'd told him more than once that she didn't have thick skin, but she made up for it by being too stubborn to quit.

"I went home that night and considered all my options. The owner of the restaurant was a good man. And didn't have a clue what was happening in the kitchen. The quality of our food was going down. I'd caught multiple mistakes in the previous few weeks, and while I'd been able to fix a few of them, more than one dish had gone to a customer in a way that Chef Albert would have normally fired someone over."

She gave a weak laugh. "I was terrified, but I decided I had no choice but to confront him. It was a tough decision. Like I said, drug use is an open secret in the industry. Has been for decades. I couldn't tell him that I had an issue with his cocaine use. He would tell me to find another job. End of discussion. But I thought if I called him out on the quality of his work, maybe he would listen. I took photos of some of his dishes, made notes about customer complaints, and spent another week compiling my arguments."

She stretched her legs out in front of her and folded her body almost in half, reaching for her feet. She turned her head to face him. "It was so stupid. I should have kept my mouth shut, taken the hit to my résumé, and moved on."

Donovan couldn't sit still anymore. He reached toward her and twirled her hair around his finger. "Standing up for what's right, trying to make a difference for good—those are not stupid things."

"No?" She looked so very young and so very lost when she spoke. "Tell that to the man who died that night. I'm pretty sure he would disagree."

Donovan tried to keep the shock from showing on his face. He'd known it had been bad, but he hadn't expected it to be that bad. All he wanted to do was to pull Cassie into his lap and hold her and make every bad thing that had happened go away. But since he couldn't do any of that, he traced her jaw with his hand. "Oh, baby. No. I'm sorry."

She sat up and crossed her legs. "I walked into the chef's office and asked if we could talk. He said yes. I sat down and shared my concerns. I hoped he would listen. I was prepared for him to fire me. But when I told him I'd documented the food mistakes and customer complaints, something in him snapped."

She closed her eyes and spoke quickly. "He pulled a gun from his desk. Told me to get out of his office. Long story short, he took me and every chef, line cook, and two of the cleaning staff hostage."

Donovan bit back the words he wanted to say.

"One of the line cooks, Jaime, argued with him and he shot him." Cassie's tears fell and she made no attempt to stop them. "We all saw it. And there was nothing we could do."

Donovan couldn't sit there while she cried. He put an arm

around her and pulled her closer. She sobbed into his chest. "It was my fault."

"It wasn't."

"Jaime died. Chef Albert came down from his high, realized what he'd done, and let us all go. Before the police could get to him, he died by suicide. He left a short note. Said he couldn't live with himself for killing Jaime."

He held her and murmured, "It wasn't your fault" and "You aren't responsible for other people's bad choices" and "You can't carry this on your shoulders," and he prayed for wisdom when none of his words felt like the right ones.

NINE

CASSIE HAD NO IDEA how long she sat on the ground, snuggled into Donovan's arms, crying like she hadn't cried since she'd moved home. When she sat up, he pulled a handkerchief from his pocket and handed it to her.

When she thought she could speak without falling apart, she said, "You asked me why I didn't speak up about what happened here. Now you know. I'd rather deal with bullying and intimidation and stress and drama a million times than be responsible for anyone's death. I know what I can handle. And I can't handle that. Not again."

She stared into the blue Carolina sky and took a deep breath. "There has to be a balance, but I haven't found it yet. I have to be able to stand up for myself. And I can see how, in this case, I should have spoken up sooner. But it's going to take me a while to figure out where my personal boundary lines are."

Donovan tilted his head and gave her a nod that said he understood. "I have faith in you. You'll figure out what you need. And you'll be okay. And I want you to know how much I appreciate you sharing this piece of yourself with me. It hurts to know it, but I don't think I ever could have truly known you without it."

"I'm afraid knowing me isn't all that big of a prize."

"We'll have to agree to disagree there."

"There's still more we need to discuss. I have questions."

"I'd be happy to answer them."

Donovan got to his feet, then extended a hand to her and she gladly took it. Her rear end was cold and stiff from sitting on the ground, but her heart felt lighter. She still needed to talk to Donovan about their relationship and why he'd ended it. But for now, she had to get back to her kitchen.

CASSIE RETURNED to her car at ten o'clock. The security guard patrolling the parking area gave her a small salute.

She wanted to believe that increased security would make a difference. But she couldn't shake the suspicion that the destruction of the kitchen had been an inside job. Either someone had figured out how to avoid the security at The Haven or someone who understood the security at The Haven had helped. She had no idea which was more problematic.

She slid into the driver's seat and rested her head on the steering wheel. She'd had days where she'd put in more hours, but she wasn't sure if she'd ever put in a longer day. Every part of her hurt. Her head, her heart, her body.

She started the engine and put her high beams on, then began making her way through the winding roads that sang to a place in her soul that had been parched and miserable in big cities.

She came around a curve and slammed on the brakes, barely avoiding the deer lying in the middle of the road.

The Jeep shuddered to a stop and adrenaline coursed through her system as her heart slowly returned to a normal rhythm. She slid her foot from the brake and gently pressed the accelerator, taking her time as she was forced to move into the opposite lane to skirt around the carcass. She used voice commands to call Donovan.

"Cassie? Everything okay?"

"Yeah. Sorry to bother you with this, but there's a deer in the middle of the road. Two miles toward town past The Haven gates."

"Did you hit it?"

"No, but I almost ran over it. It probably would have bashed up my Jeep."

"Where are you now?"

"On my way home."

"But in relation to the deer?"

"Oh, half a mile?"

"Are you going straight home?"

"That was the plan."

"Okay. I know we have more we need to discuss, but I've been thinking, Cass. I think we should talk tomorrow. Or maybe Monday."

Cassie squeezed the steering wheel so hard that her finger-nails pressed into her palms. "Seriously? You want to wait?"

"You have to be exhausted. Right now I think the priority should be for you to get the sleep you need."

"Fine. We'll talk next week."

She disconnected the call. "Next week?" She spoke into the empty air around her. "He wants to talk next week?" She'd been so sure that he was sorry about what had happened between them. So sure he wanted to talk about them.

But a few minutes earlier she'd been desperate for sleep. So why was she upset now?

She slammed her hand on the steering wheel. When would she learn? When would she speak up? When would she stop letting people push her around?

DONOVAN STARED at his phone.

What had just happened? Aside from the situation with the deer, Cassie sounded mad. Why would she be mad? He was trying to look out for her.

Or, a small voice whispered, *maybe you're trying to do what you think is best for her without giving her an opportunity to decide for herself. And maybe she doesn't like that.*

He called the fire station nearest The Haven and gave them a heads-up about the deer. Most of the time when a driver hit a deer in the mountains, they would call the police if for no other reason than to document it for insurance purposes. It was weird for the deer to still be in the middle of the road like that.

He turned back to his kitchen counter. He had his report from today's incident pulled up on his laptop. Gray was picky about reports. He expected them to be clear, concise, and complete within twenty-four hours whenever possible.

But by the time Donovan finally left The Haven, he'd returned to the office and didn't stop until he'd handled three more calls. Which was why he was sitting at home trying to finish his report, instead of sleeping like a reasonable person.

A sharp rap on his front door had him reaching for his gun.

"I know you're in there, Donovan Bledsoe. Open up."

"Cassie?"

Donovan reached the door in record time and pulled it open. Cassie stormed in.

"We are going to talk tonight." She pulled off her sweater and threw it on his sofa. She kept talking as she entered his kitchen. "I don't know why you think I can't talk tonight, but I can." She opened his fridge and removed a small can of Coke. "And I want to." She cracked it open. "I'm not going to have this hanging over my head all weekend." She took a sip. "That's not fair to me." She walked back toward him. "I have enough to deal with, and you owe me some answers."

By the time she stopped talking, she was standing right in front of him. He reached out, took the Coke from her hand, placed it on the nearby coffee table, pulled her against him, and pressed his lips to hers.

For a moment, she blinked at him, clearly confused. Then she pushed him away. "Oh no you don't, mister. No. Huh-uh. No way. You can't shut me up like that." She reached for her Coke, and Donovan was pleased to see that her hand was trembling as she took another sip. "You don't get to kiss me whenever you want to. You didn't want that privilege. Remember?"

"I was an idiot."

"No doubt." Cassie waved the can in his direction. "But your idiocy is *your* problem. Not mine. Do you walk around kissing women you aren't in a relationship with?" Her brow furrowed in real concern.

"No! Of course not! I haven't kissed anyone since the last time I kissed you. I haven't wanted to kiss anyone but you."

She frowned. "Well, that's good, I guess."

"You guess?" Hmm. Had he misjudged this whole situation? "Do you not agree?"

"Of course I agree. That isn't the point."

"That is exactly the point!" Donovan reached for her hand, but she pulled it away.

"No touching."

He raised his hands in surrender. "Yes, ma'am."

He wasn't quite sure where this attitude had come from, but he was quite sure that as much as he'd liked gentle, quiet, calm Cassie, he was absolutely smitten with feisty Cassie.

"I want to know why you broke up with me."

"I'm not sure if you noticed, but I'm trying to undo that action."

"Not a chance."

Donovan's mouth went dry. She couldn't mean that. "Cassie, please. Let me explain."

"I asked you for an explanation, and rather than explain, you said you wanted to undo it. That's not an explanation."

"You're right." He pointed to his sofa. "Can we sit? And talk?"

Cassie narrowed her eyes, then took a seat in a chair. Fine. She was sitting. He could work with that. "Would you like another Coke?"

"Yes. Please." Her voice was low and quiet. Whatever rage had fueled her decision to come bursting in to confront him, it was fading. He took the empty can from her, tossed it in his recycling bin, and grabbed another from the fridge.

When he handed it to her, he knelt by her chair. "Cassie. I *am* sorry."

Her hand shook as she opened the drink, but her voice was steady when she asked, again, "Why?"

Donovan sat on the spot on the sofa that was closest to her. "I need to tell you a story."

"Okay."

"It's not a fun story."

"Okay."

"There's a longer version, and I'll be happy to share it with you in the future, but for tonight, I'll keep it as short as I can."

"That's probably wise."

Donovan opened the Coke he'd brought for himself and took a sip. "I'm not sure how to say this without it coming across as super arrogant, but I'm pretty smart."

Cassie didn't say anything.

"Like, straight A's in school. Valedictorian. Total nerd."

That earned him a raised eyebrow.

"It's true. There are photos to prove it. I was the president of the chess club."

Cassie didn't manage to hold in her little snort of laughter.

"Oh, it gets better. I was freakishly skinny. And we don't want to talk about my hair."

At that, Cassie closed her eyes and shook her head. "I can't see it."

He pulled his phone from his pocket, scrolled through to social media, and found the photo he'd been looking for. He handed her his device, and she took it. Then her mouth fell open.

TEN

CASSIE STARED at two boys. One was a pretty average-looking teenager. The other was a skinny kid with thick glasses and acne and a truly awful haircut that made him look like he was sixty instead of sixteen.

"This is you?"

He nodded.

"Are you blind without your glasses?"

"I was. Had surgery a few years ago. Now? Perfect vision."

She looked from the photo to the man sitting two feet away. Then she looked back at the photo. "Um . . ." She was truly at a loss. He'd shocked her into a land of confusion and curiosity. "I'm guessing you discovered the gym at some point after this photo was taken."

Donovan smiled, and the smile finally convinced her that the boy in the photo and the man beside her were the same person. "You guessed correctly."

Cassie was intrigued, but Donovan's glow-up wasn't an excuse, or an explanation, for the end of their relationship. The boy in the photo stood before a large home. And while the clothes weren't to her taste, they screamed expensive. "You told me that you come from a well-off family who didn't approve of your career choices and that you don't have much to do with them."

"All true. When I told my parents I wanted to be a police officer instead of a doctor, my mother told me that it was noble to want to help people, but that I would regret it if I, and I quote, 'failed to live up to my potential' and 'turned my back on the hard work of the generations that came before me' by choosing a profession that was both dangerous and, in my family's view, menial. And then my mother cried. A lot."

Donovan took a drink. "I still don't know if I was weak-minded, or if they were just that good at manipulating me. Either way, I went to college and got my degree in biochemistry. Was accepted to med school."

His hand clenched the can, and Cassie reached out and pried it from his fingers. Then she leaned toward him and took his hands in hers. "What happened?"

He nodded toward the photo that still glowed from his phone on the coffee table. "That kid in the photo. His name was Chris. We were best friends. Did everything together. Neither of us wanted to be doctors, but we knew we'd be letting everyone down if we didn't pursue medicine. Our senior year of college, Chris started acting strange. I couldn't figure out what was going on, and I was busy with school. I missed it."

Cassie braced herself for what was coming.

"I found him the night before graduation. He'd overdosed. I found his journals. He'd been miserable since he was in junior high. He wanted to pursue music. He was a talented cellist, but his family told him he couldn't make a living that way. At least, not the kind of living he was supposed to make. In his case, they'd played the family card in a different way. Told him that as an only child, it was his responsibility to have a career that would make it possible for him to take care of his parents."

Cassie squeezed his hands. "I'm so sorry."

He gave her a humorless smile. "I joined the Marines the next day. I didn't tell anyone. I packed up my apartment and made my plans. I knew my parents would be angry, but I thought they would come around. I was going to be an officer. I expected them to roll with it. Instead, my father contacted our congressman and spent two years trying to get me out."

Cassie couldn't wrap her mind around parents like that.

"I tried to keep the door to them open. Tried to find a way to bridge the gap between what they wanted me to do and what I needed to do. When I got out of the Marines, I joined the police force in Chicago. I thought if I moved up the ranks and worked in a big city, maybe it would give my profession some validity in their eyes." He stared at the floor. "Turns out that even though all I've ever wanted to do was to be a police officer, some of what I experienced in Afghanistan messed me up enough that the level of violence and corruption in Chicago brought me to a breaking point. My therapist told me I had two choices: find a different profession or find a way to practice my profession in a safer place."

"That's why you came here."

"Yeah. I knew Gray from the Marines. Reached out. He had a place for me, and I've never regretted it. I feel so fulfilled here. Like this is what God put me on this earth to do. I can help protect this town and the people here. I won't ever be rich or famous. But I'm completely okay with that."

"And your family?"

"I talk to my mom a couple of times a year. Never talk to my dad. He says he'll talk to me when I come to my senses. But the relationship is shattered. It took me a long time to see it, but it's all about control. I wouldn't do what they wanted so they won't have anything to do with me. They claim if I loved them, if I was a good, respectful son, if I was a good Christian, I would bow to their wishes."

DONOVAN WAS emotionally drained from the retelling, but the fury on Cassie's face was worth it.

She jumped to her feet and paced away. "What is wrong with them? How could they not see that trying to force you to conform to *their* idea of what you should do would destroy you? How could they try to make you feel like you had to do that to show them you loved them?"

"I grew up with them, and it surprised me too." He stood and walked until he was standing in front of her. He reached for her hands, and she didn't pull away. "What I do know is that I swore I would never ask someone to change their dreams for me. Love isn't making someone do what you want them to do. Love is setting them free to do what makes their soul sing."

A knowing settled over Cassie's features. "No." She pulled her hands away.

Donovan waited.

"Please tell me you didn't decide something like this without talking to me first."

"I didn't want to pressure you. I tried for so long to do what other people wanted me to do. People who loved me. People I loved. And in the end, it made me bitter and ruined our relationship. I couldn't do that to you."

Cassie practically vibrated with rage. "I'm sorry to say this about your family, but that wasn't love. Love is always looking out for someone else. Love doesn't seek its own."

"Exactly. Love doesn't seek its own. I couldn't ask you to stay here for me. I thought you needed a bigger city. The possibility to grow. Maybe even leave the country. I'm eight years older than you are, and I spent a good part of my twenties figuring out what I need and where I belong. If I thought there was any way that I could follow you all over the country, I would do it. But if I tried, it would destroy me. And it would destroy our relationship. I'm going to be a small-town cop for the rest of my life. And I'm great with that. I love what I do, and I'm happy here. Honestly, the only thing that could make me happier would be if you were with me. But I didn't see any way for us to stay together and live out the lives God has for us. Walking away nearly killed me, but it seemed like the best solution."

Cassie walked around the coffee table and picked up her sweater from the sofa. "Let me get this straight. You broke up with me because you were afraid that at some point in the future, either *I* would resent *you* or *you* would resent *me*. Do I have that right?"

Donovan had no good answer. "Well, obviously, when you put it that way, it doesn't sound great."

She was edging closer to the door. "You chose the nuclear option over the possibility of future pain. You left me wounded and wondering what I'd done wrong, when I hadn't done anything wrong at all." Cassie put her sweater on.

"Cassie, please."

"I need to think. And I think I need to think somewhere other than here."

Donovan's phone rang, but he ignored it. "Think here. Don't leave. Don't do what I did. Don't make decisions without talking them through. Please. I'm sorry."

Cassie's face crumpled. "So am I, Donovan. So am I."

She opened the door and ran down his porch steps. His phone rang again. He glanced at it and saw the number of the fire station. He accepted the call. "Bledsoe."

"Hey. This is Stu. Hope I didn't wake you up, but I thought you'd want to know."

"What?"

"That deer in the road? It wasn't hit by a car. It was shot."

Donovan didn't hesitate. He sprinted after Cassie and stepped in front of her Jeep. "Cassie. Stop!"

She froze and the car shook as she slammed on the brakes.

She rolled down her window and yelled at him. "What is wrong with you? I could have hit you."

"I need you to come back inside."

"I'm not coming back in tonight."

"Fine. Then I'm following you home."

"You'd better not."

"Cassie, someone shot that deer."

All the fight went out of her as the implications sank in. She put the Jeep in Park and dropped her head to the steering wheel. "Why me?"

"I don't know, baby. Come back inside. Please. Just until I can figure out what's going on. I'll call whoever you want and you can go home with them."

Cassie unbuckled her seat belt, and Donovan opened her door. She took the hand he offered, and when she was on her feet, she didn't let go. "This doesn't make any sense." She dropped her head against his arm as she walked beside him.

He paused to let Cassie walk through his open door. He followed and took a look at the phone he still clutched in his hand. The screen told him the call was active. He hit the speaker button and spoke. "You there, Stu?"

"What was that, man?"

"I'll explain later. For now, tell me what you found."

"That's what I was trying to do when you disappeared."

"Well, I'm back now."

"Fine." It was clear Stu was wondering what had happened and was annoyed that Donovan wasn't sharing. "We went out there like you asked, expecting to find a deer versus car situation. Needless to say, we were a bit surprised to find a deer that had been shot. And she wasn't shot on the road. She'd been moved."

"How sure are you?"

"You do much deer hunting?" Stu's question held more than a hint of condescension.

"Not much." While Donovan had gone on a few hunts that had been held with the specific purpose of thinning the local deer population, he found no enjoyment in the activity. He preferred fly-fishing.

"I've been hunting in these parts since I was old enough to climb a tree stand. That deer was shot somewhere and dumped on the road. I shouldn't say dumped. She was placed. Carefully. And given that Cassie was the first one to report it, I'd be willing to bet she was put there just a few minutes before Cassie drove up on her. There's no way she could have been there for any length of time without someone slamming into her."

Cassie sat in the same chair she'd been in earlier as Stu continued.

"I took pictures of the scene. We did a little video so you can see how close it was coming out of the curve. Even knowing she was there, we almost hit her." Stu chuckled. "You given Cassie a speeding ticket lately?"

"What does that have to do with anything?" Donovan hadn't, but he knew she'd gotten one in Asheville a few weeks earlier.

"Please." Stu scoffed. "Everyone knows Cassie Quinn has a lead foot. If she'd been flying through there the way she usually does, she'd never have had time to stop. If she'd slammed into it at her normal speed, she could have flipped that Jeep. She's lucky she's in one piece."

ELEVEN

CASSIE COULDN'T STOP the tremor that shook her body at Stu's words. She'd been embarrassed and more than a little annoyed about his comments on her driving.

Not that he was wrong. But still . . . She'd been about to chime in and remind him that she knew what he'd done during the Homecoming game their senior year. A spectacular stunt that still reigned as the best Homecoming prank ever pulled off at Gossamer Falls High.

Now? She sat frozen in her seat as he continued talking.

"No kidding, Donovan. If we have some fool doing this as a prank, they're going to get somebody killed."

"I agree."

A screeching sound came through the phone. "I'm back at the station. What do you want me to do with the deer?"

Donovan looked like he wanted to throw something through a wall. "You can't eat it, Stu."

"I may not have a fancy college degree, but I'm not an idiot. I'm asking if you're gonna do some kind of forensics on it."

"Can you hang on to it for a few hours? I'll have to let you know what we're going to do with it."

"Sure thing. No problem. I'm on a twenty-four so I'm here all night."

"Thanks, Stu."

Donovan disconnected the call.

Cassie couldn't stand the look on Donovan's face. "Is it too soon for me to make a joke that if you'd done what your family wanted and gone to medical school, you never would have had to figure out what forensics to do on a deer in the middle of the night?"

Donovan met her gaze. "Too soon."

"But is it? Really?"

The tiniest twitch at the corner of his lips was the only hint she had that he didn't think she was an idiot.

She stood and walked to where he was standing by his kitchen counter. "No kidding. What do you have to do now?"

He ran a hand through his hair. "Instead of going to bed, I have to go get a dead deer and take it I have no idea where and do I have no idea what with it." He punched the screen on his phone with enough force that she wondered how often he broke them.

She shamelessly looked at the screen to see the text he was sending to Gray asking for guidance. When he hit send, he set the phone on the counter and looked at her. "I think it should go without saying that I'm very uncomfortable with the idea of you being alone tonight."

"I won't be alone. You haven't seen the setup I have now. I'm surrounded by family."

Donovan didn't look convinced.

"If it will make you feel better, we can call Mo and make sure he's home. But he's always home. Unless he's at his mom and dad's. But he doesn't spend the night there."

"It would make me feel better."

"Fine." She pulled her phone from her pocket and scrolled to Mo's number. She put it on speaker while she waited for him to answer. He picked up after three rings.

"Cassie? Why aren't you home, sweetheart?"

She leaned against the counter. "I've got you on speaker. I'm at Donovan's."

There was a pause. "Lots to unpack there. How about we start with why you've put me on speaker?"

"I almost hit a deer on the way home from work."

"Did you get a ticket?"

"Why does everyone assume I'm going to get a ticket tonight?" She threw her hands up in exasperation. "No. I didn't get a ticket. I didn't wreck. I wasn't speeding. Look, I'll explain it all when I get home. Right now, I'm confirming that you're home for the night. Donovan doesn't want me to be by myself."

"Yeah. I'm home. So is Meredith. We're out here by the firepit. Cal and Landry just left. But I can get them back if you need me to."

"No. I'll be home in a few minutes."

"I'll be following her. Don't shoot." Donovan's words had a hint of military command in them.

"Then I guess we'll see you both. Be careful." Mo's tone matched Donovan's.

Lovely.

She disconnected. "Please don't pick a fight with my cousins."

"I'm not trying to pick a fight. But I'm not going to step aside and let your cousins bully me into staying away from you." He checked his weapon, keys, phone, and hat. "Let's go."

"Donovan?" She paused at the door.

"Yes?"

She'd wanted nothing more than to get away from him just a few minutes ago. So why was she suddenly compelled to hash everything out now? She had no idea, but she couldn't fight it. "Should we, you know, maybe, talk? Before I go home?"

"No."

His abrupt response cut her more deeply than she'd thought

possible. She didn't know what her face looked like, but whatever he saw made him close his eyes for a brief moment and shake his head. Then he reached for her.

And like the total pushover that she was, she let him pull her against him. "We can talk all night if you want *after* we get you safely home. Part of my job is to think of the worst-case scenarios and not to make assumptions. It's possible that the deer was bad timing and some teenagers are out there thinking they are funny when they aren't. But I don't like the timing. So I'm following you home. When we get you on Quinn land, we automatically make you safer." He ran a thumb across her cheek. "When you're safe, I'll be able to think straight. And then we can talk. Yeah?"

Her body was reacting to his proximity. Her mind was screaming reminders of how he'd hurt her. And her heart was telling her mind to shut up because no one else made her feel this way.

DONOVAN STEPPED AWAY from Cassie. "Let's get you home."

He didn't think it was his imagination that she didn't want to move out of his embrace. Good.

He stayed close, one hand on her lower back, as they locked up his house and walked back to her car. He opened her door. She climbed in. "Please stay close."

She rolled her eyes. "What do you think I'm going to do? Floor it and force you to give me a ticket?"

He couldn't stop himself from grinning. "Might be fun."

"For you maybe. My insurance is already sky high." Cassie was still grumbling as he closed her door and left to climb into his own vehicle.

He flashed his lights at her when he was ready, and to her

credit, she kept it in the vicinity of the speed limit as they maneuvered through town and toward Quinn land.

His phone rang. Stu again.

He didn't bother with a greeting. "I'm still not sure what I'm going to do with the deer. I'm working on it."

"Yeah. I don't care about the deer. It's fine for now. Listen, I need to ask you something." Stu's voice was low, as if he was trying to keep anyone from overhearing.

"What do you want to know?"

"Do you think the deer being in the road right when Cassie drove by was random? Because I don't."

"What makes you say that?"

"That mess at The Haven is all over the county. Everyone knows the kitchen was trashed and Cassie and Bronwyn found it."

"I'm not surprised. What does that have to do with the deer?"

"Because when I got back to the station with the deer, I was telling the other guys what happened. One of our volunteers got a funny look on his face. He said he'd heard some talk at The Dry Gulch tonight that Cassie was the target."

"I'd like to know why a volunteer was at The Dry Gulch before his shift, but even more than that, I'd like to know who was talking."

Stu snorted. "I tried to get something for you. He said he heard it from the bartender who heard it from a mysterious somebody who'd heard it from some other somebody. And he wasn't drinking. He was playing pool with his brother."

"Sure he was. If you hear anything else, holler."

"Will do."

Donovan followed Cassie down the long driveway to the tiny house where she now lived. She pulled into the space that was obviously hers. Two other vehicles were already parked under the carport. A red Jeep that belonged to Mo, and a deep blue Toyota 4Runner that was Meredith's.

The tiny house compound had been built by Cal, Mo, and Meredith so the cousins could have their own space but still be neighbors until they decided to build their forever homes. So far, Cal was the only one who'd made the leap. And rather than have his tiny house sit empty, the cousins had offered it to Cassie.

When Donovan heard about it, he'd assumed it had been because she planned to stay in Gossamer Falls for only a short period of time and didn't need a long-term lease.

Now? He wasn't so sure.

He climbed from his SUV and joined Cassie. He walked beside her but didn't touch her, and when they reached the firepit, he found that Mo and Meredith had called Cal and Landry back after all. The four sat around the firepit. Cal's dog, Maisy, sat at his feet.

"Where's Eliza?" Cassie asked as she walked around the circle giving hugs.

Cal had taken to fatherhood like everyone had always known he would, and he was extremely protective of his daughter. The adoption wasn't final, but she'd started calling him Daddy even before the wedding and as far as everyone was concerned, she was his and always would be.

Landry, Eliza's mother and Cal's new bride, spoke up from her perch on Cal's lap. "She's with Abby."

Abby Shaw, Cal's niece, and Eliza were the best of friends. And Donovan knew that Cal's brother and sister-in-law were happy to have Eliza over frequently to give the newlyweds some precious time alone.

Cal pointed to a chair. "Let's hear it."

Cassie laughed. "Ready to go home, Cal?"

"Yes I am." There was a distinct tinge of exasperation in his voice. "I was almost home when Mo called. What's going on?"

Donovan filled them in on the deer in the road, the phone

call from Stu that Cassie had heard, and then the one he'd received on the way to their house.

"I'm feeling like I might need to spend a few hours in The Dry Gulch." Mo stretched his arms above his head.

"Oh no you don't." Meredith gave her brother a flat look. "Leave it to Donovan."

Donovan didn't miss the look that passed between Mo and Cal. And based on Cassie's squared shoulders, neither did she.

Meredith patted Cassie's hand. "Don't worry. Gray and Donovan will handle it. And Cal and Mo will have to be content with making themselves a nuisance as they provide a protection detail for you. Please note that your desire to have this protection detail will not be taken into consideration."

Maisy stood and walked to where Cassie sat, and then put her head in Cassie's lap. Cassie ran her hands over Maisy's head.

Donovan had never known a dog as sensitive as Maisy was. She was most attuned to Cal. But she'd picked up on Cassie's stress and decided she needed to do something about it.

While Cassie argued with her cousins, Donovan kept his mouth shut. He was in no position to get involved. And when his phone rang, he didn't hesitate to answer. "Bledsoe."

"I leave you in charge for the day and the whole place implodes." Gray's amusement was clear, as was his fatigue.

"That'll teach you," Donovan fired back.

"Where are you now?"

"At Cassie's."

"Oh really?"

Donovan ignored Gray's innuendo. "What do you want me to do with the deer?"

"I've already sent someone to get it."

"We have a procedure for this?"

"Yep. Don't worry about it. Tell me why you're at Cassie's."

This time, the comment held nothing but a request for

information and Donovan didn't hesitate to respond. He stepped away from the firepit and shared the story for the second time in the last few minutes.

Gray's response was similar to that of Cal and Mo. "I would give up a month's pay to get an informant in at The Dry Gulch. But that will have to wait. Talk to Cal and Mo about sticking to Cassie. I'll call Bronwyn and tell her what's going on. She already has security ramped up at The Haven, but I'll make sure she doesn't drop her guard."

"Sounds good."

"Then go home and sleep. Tomorrow I want you to talk to Chef Louis. And talk to Bronwyn about the possibility of putting you in the kitchen while Cassie's working. You might need to dress like a server to keep from standing out, but I'd like you close."

"Okay." He was going to do that regardless. But having permission made it easier.

"Unless"—Gray drew out the word—"you want me to hand her over to Brick."

"Gray—"

"Think about it. He's on this weekend. Cassie knows him, and I doubt she'd mind."

"Absolutely not. No one else is handling Cassie. She's mine."

TWELVE

"OH REALLY?" Cassie stood three feet away from Donovan, and the look in his eyes when he turned around and saw her wasn't one she'd ever seen before. She didn't hate it. But she didn't quite understand it either. She was pretty sure he was angry. But not at her. Or at Gray. But at someone.

He kept his eyes on her as he spoke into the phone. "Well, if she wasn't aware before, she is now." A pause. "Because apparently she's part ninja and she's standing three feet away from me."

Cassie heard Gray's laughter through the phone but couldn't make out what he said. Donovan's response was a grunt. Then a "Yeah." And finally, "Later."

He slid his phone into his pocket and faced her, hands on his hips. "Didn't your mother teach you not to eavesdrop?"

"I'm sure she tried."

What was she doing out here? Why had she followed him?

She needed to think. Needed to process. Needed to figure out why the sound of his deep voice telling Gray that she was his had turned a university-sized marching-band drumline loose inside her.

"Cards on the table, Cassie. I hurt you. And now you don't

trust me the way I want you to. That's my fault. I did that. And now I want to fix it. With that said, I'm well aware of the fact that your need to put up boundaries is completely legitimate. I won't push you into anything you don't want. But I also won't lie about what I want."

He took one step toward her, and even though he didn't touch her, she could feel the heat from his body and the energy that twined around them.

"What is it that you want?" she asked.

"I want you. I want you to stay in Gossamer Falls, with me. I want you to be mine. And I want to be yours."

The drumline went completely bonkers and she found it difficult to catch her breath. She wanted to throw herself into his arms.

But she stood there. And tried to keep her voice steady even as her breathing turned jagged from her own fear. "There's something I need to know. Something I still don't understand."

"Ask me. I'll tell you." Donovan sounded like a drowning man who'd been thrown a lifeline.

"Why didn't you try to fix it before now? If I mean so much to you, why did it take this mess today for you to decide that I was worth the risk?"

"Seriously?"

"Yes, seriously."

"When I broke up with you, you acted like it didn't matter! You were icy and calm and I thought I'd misread everything. I thought if you really cared about me, you'd put up a fight or at least be a little upset. But you weren't. You didn't even *try* to get me to change my mind. I know it was my decision, and I broke us. But when you just let me go? It hurt. And it confused me. And I thought that maybe it was for the best because clearly my feelings ran a lot deeper than yours did."

She shoved at his arm. "I was faking it, you idiot. You crushed me. If you didn't want me, I certainly wasn't going to let on how much it hurt! A girl has to have some pride!"

Donovan's phone rang.

Cassie closed her eyes and turned her back to him, attempting to hide her threatening tears. She wasn't sure if she'd ever been as angry as she'd been at Donovan Bledsoe.

But she wasn't angry anymore.

He'd walked away from her when he answered the phone, but his voice grew closer as he returned. "Yeah." A pause. "Okay." A longer pause during which he came to stand a foot away from her. "Got it. I'll be there in fifteen. Yeah."

He tapped the screen and his shoulders slumped. "I have to go. There was a fight at The Dry Gulch. Brick and Tony arrested half the people there. Gray had to call in everyone available."

Fights at The Dry Gulch weren't uncommon. But it didn't usually require this much manpower to handle them.

"Someone got stabbed."

That would explain it. Fights were usually more about people needing to sleep it off and property damage and everyone agreeing not to press charges for assault.

"Brick says the knife was a fancy knife—smaller than a chef's knife, but definitely something from a kitchen."

Cassie couldn't stop herself from reaching for Donovan's arm. She grabbed him and held on. "Was it . . ."

Donovan placed his free hand over hers. "The description matches, but I won't know for sure until I see it."

"The person who was stabbed?"

"On the way to the hospital. Dr. Shaw is riding with the ambulance." He hesitated. "They aren't sure if he'll make it."

Cassie couldn't get her mind to settle on anything. Thoughts. Emotions. Questions. Fears. Everything was a maelstrom in her mind.

"Hey."

She looked up into Donovan's face.

"I have to go, but this, you and me, us, we aren't done. I'm going to fight for us. Fight for the right to love you the way you deserve to be loved. Fight to be a man worthy of you. So be careful. Stay here. Keep someone with you if you leave. We'll figure out what's going on, but until I know for sure, please promise me you'll do everything you can to stay safe."

Cassie couldn't do anything more than nod.

"I need to hear it, baby. Because for all I know, you're just nodding to get me to leave."

Donovan's voice held a touch of humor, but mostly it was concern.

"I'll be careful. You be careful too. I'm . . ." Cassie swallowed. "I'm not through fighting with you."

He ran a thumb across her cheek. "Don't you mean fighting for you?"

She shook her head. "Not yet."

Her intransigence should have been frustrating, but his smile was glorious. "I like this feisty version of you, Cassie. I really do."

Then he was gone. And Cassie stood in the woods alone until Mo found her.

"You okay, kiddo?" He put an arm around her and led her back to the firepit.

"I'm not sure."

"We all heard. You weren't being very quiet."

She tried to bury her face in his chest. "Shoot me now."

"Can't do it, sweetheart."

They walked on, and when they stepped out of the woods, all the chairs around the firepit were empty. "Where'd everyone go?"

"Meredith said to tell you good night. Cal and Landry went home because they're newlyweds and that's what newlyweds do." He winked at her. "But you're too young for such things."

"I am not too young."

He put his hands on her biceps, and he looked so sad that she wanted to ask him what was wrong. Before she got the chance, he leaned close and whispered, "I'll always be in your corner. Always. No matter what. But don't let your stubbornness keep you from giving Donovan a chance to make things right."

"I'm not stubborn."

"You're one of the most stubborn people I know. And that isn't always bad. But when it comes to this? Maybe you should let go of the anger and give him a chance. Meredith was rooting for him. I thought she was going to blow a gasket when his phone rang."

Cassie could picture them sitting around the firepit, straining to hear every word.

"He messed up. But so did you." Mo's smile was gentle, and she dropped her head against his chest and let him give her a hug. Mo gave the best hugs, but he was stingy with them. She'd learned to savor each one. When he released her, he pointed to the door of her home. "Go to bed. Sleep. And don't leave the property unless someone, and by someone I mean me, knows where you are and where you're going. Whatever this mess is, it's escalating, and I don't want you out on the mountain alone until we've resolved everything."

Cassie wanted to tell him she was an adult and didn't need him bossing her around. But he wasn't wrong. And she'd already promised Donovan the same thing.

She'd almost reached her door when Mo called out, "Cassie?" He was standing on his porch, hand on the doorknob.

"Yeah."

"I love you, sweetheart."

"Love you too, Mo."

DONOVAN ARRIVED at the police station to discover that every parking space was full, and most of the vehicles were trucks with varying degrees of cleanliness. He had to park two blocks away and walk back to the station, and when he arrived, he had to flash his badge and put on what Cassie called his "mean cop face" to get the crowd to clear enough for him to get inside.

He went straight to Gray's office, stuck his head in the door, and said, "For the record, none of this was my fault."

To which Gray replied, "Try again." He wasn't kidding.

"How is this my fault?"

"Your girl. Your fault."

Donovan stepped inside the office. "What are you talking about?"

"Cassie Quinn has been a hot topic tonight. Apparently, the fight broke out over her. And of the five men currently behind bars, three of them told me they have info on the threat to her."

"Do they?"

"Sure they do. One guy said she's in danger from a guy she dated in high school, but then he said maybe it was from a girl who's married to a different guy she dated in high school. He was fuzzy on the details. Of course, he was fuzzy on pretty much everything."

Donovan groaned.

"Then we had the guy who blamed the sous-chef at Hideaway—"

"It wasn't him."

Gray held up a hand acknowledging Donovan's interruption but continued. "He claims it's a conspiracy between the sous-chef, Chef Louis, Bronwyn, and other members of the Pierce family."

"That makes absolutely no sense."

Gray talked over him. "And last but not least"—he tapped the desk—"you."

"Me?"

"Yeah. Apparently you're all kinds of jealous and you've gone psycho. Those are direct quotes, by the way."

Donovan couldn't figure any of this out. "We're missing something."

Gray cleared his throat and sat straighter in his chair. "So far, everyone here is either drunk, high, or a truly disturbing combination of both, which has led to everything from belligerence to begging. Nothing that has been said can be used against them or anyone else. I doubt most of them will remember what they told us."

"How many arrests?"

"Twelve. So far."

Donovan sat in the chair across from Gray. "Twelve?"

Gray blew out a slow breath. "I've never seen anything like this here. But I've heard of something similar."

"What happened?"

"Last year, a new dealer came to the city where a friend of mine is a deputy. This dealer decided to offer free samples. It took a while to figure it out. And they didn't catch a break until the third event. Six people died over the space of a month at four different bars around the city."

Donovan considered it. "So a guy comes in, offers a few hits. Then a few more. Maybe people try it who wouldn't normally or who never had before? Things get out of hand. Or maybe it wasn't someone who wanted to establish himself. Maybe it was someone who wanted to stir things up."

"Either one is a valid possibility." Gray pulled something from the printer behind his desk and handed it to Donovan. "I want you to look over the list of everyone who was there tonight."

"What am I looking for?"

Gray shrugged. "I have no idea. But I think you'll know it when you see it."

Donovan studied the list. At first glance nothing jumped out at him. "Is this everyone?"

"Probably not. That's just the first list I've compiled. When the dust settles, I'll have Tony start looking through the footage." Gray pointed to the door. "Close that, please."

Here we go. Donovan closed the door, then returned to the chair.

"The knife." Gray shoved another page toward him. On it, a picture of a knife. Thankfully it was not covered in blood. "We need to ask Cassie if it's hers."

"It is." Donovan handed the photo back.

"How do you know?"

"Chefs are serious about their knives. Cassie would bring her knives to my house when she cooked for me. That knife has a small mark near the end." He pointed to the spot on the photo. "It's on both sides. She told me the story that when she was in culinary school, she somehow managed to pinch it in a press of some kind. Honestly, I don't know how she did it. And this is the knife that went missing her second week at Hideaway."

"So this knife has been missing for two weeks? Why didn't she report it?"

Donovan rubbed the back of his neck. "She said that she couldn't be sure she hadn't lost it."

"So, she used it, and then she couldn't find it. So she assumed it was misplaced in the kitchen?"

"Yeah."

"This sounds like the beginning of a bad joke. A guy walks into a bar with a paring knife . . ." Gray stabbed the photo. "How does a guy walk around with that? It's not like he could slip it in his pocket without stabbing himself in a delicate area."

"I don't care so much about how he got it in the building as I do about why he had it with him. It's not like he could use it to frame Cassie for something. She has an airtight alibi. She was with me."

"She was with you when the fight went down. But what about later tonight? What if the plan was to commit a crime with the knife and try to frame her for it?"

"What kind of a fool plan is that?"

Gray frowned at him. "If you're expecting rational behavior from drug addicts, then you've been spending too much time helping little old ladies and not enough time with the darker elements around here."

"Shows what you know. I'm 99 percent sure that the grand-mother of the guy who owns The Dry Gulch is the one who manages their backroom poker games. Granny Lucas is al-ways carrying. And she's mean."

"She's also too smart for this." Gray spoke with certainty. "But it could be some of the young guys who think they know what they're doing but don't."

"Stupid mistakes can get smart people killed."

"Which is why you're going to stick to Cassie Quinn until we figure out what's going on."

THIRTEEN

WHEN GRAY TOLD CASSIE that Donovan was going to be her shadow, she hadn't been completely surprised. Everyone was convinced that someone was out to get her, and it was definitely freaking her out.

Having Donovan around on Sunday had been nice, but she'd been so busy that she'd barely had time to do more than nod in his direction.

Now it was Monday. Her kitchen was far from being back to normal, but they'd bluffed their way through the weekend by offering the guests an "exclusive" alfresco dining experience. It had been an unparalleled success.

Her kitchen. In all the chaos of the weekend, Bronwyn had made time to offer Cassie a permanent position as the chef at Hideaway, and it had taken an extraordinary amount of self-control for her not to immediately say yes.

She wanted the job. But could she stay if someone was so determined to get her off the premises that they would steal things, vandalize the kitchen, possibly stab her tire, and then try to cause a car wreck?

She forced the questions and doubts from her mind and went to work. Her staff was on fire tonight, and even with the inconveniences of working in less-than-optimal conditions, they were killing it. Even the servers had gotten in on the action by delivering beverages to the chefs. They made to-go cups filled with sweet tea and the house special that Cassie had introduced on her first night—honey lemonade. They'd decorated each cup with the names of each chef and line cook, and included little slogans like "You're the best" and "Foodies forever" and her personal favorite, "The chef is always right."

She plated her last dish and accepted a refill on lemonade. "Thank you." She took a long drink and watched the server as he returned to the kitchen. He looked so familiar, but she couldn't place him. If she decided to take the job permanently, she'd have to find a better way to interact with the servers. She didn't like not knowing everyone's names, but in the month she'd been here, she'd only interacted with a handful of the front of house staff.

She stifled a yawn. Maybe she should have gone with tea instead of lemonade. The caffeine jolt might have helped her power through. Although based on how heavy her head and neck were feeling at the moment, there wasn't enough caffeine in the universe to keep her going for much longer.

"Cassie! One of the guests would like a photo."

She blinked several times. Was the room spinning? She focused on the server who'd made the request. "Give me a second to change my jacket."

Cassie was a neat chef. It was a point of pride to keep her chef whites white. But that didn't mean she didn't look a little rough around the edges by the end of the night, which was why she always kept a sparkling clean chef's jacket at the ready for the always photo-hungry guests. The guests weren't allowed to post the photos on social media during their stay. But that didn't mean they didn't post when they left. And she wanted to represent The Haven well.

She fumbled with her buttons as she walked to the back of the kitchen.

Donovan, her perpetual shadow, followed her. He'd done a good job of being unobtrusive. But she was starting to chafe at his constant presence since the tension between them continued to increase. Had they made up? Were they back together? She honestly didn't know. They'd been interrupted before they'd had a chance to define the relationship. And she needed that conversation to happen sooner than later.

"You're tired." Donovan's observation carried nothing but concern.

"Yeah." She wanted to say more, but her mouth wasn't working quite right.

"Is it always this busy on Mondays?"

"No." Mondays at The Haven were typically the slowest night of the week. But tonight she'd been booked solid from six to nine. She got the final button off and Donovan helped her take off the jacket. When she reached for the photo jacket, all crisp and professional looking, he took it from her and held it out.

"Thank you. I don't know what's wrong with me."

"You're allowed to be tired, Cassie. You aren't normally here eighteen hours a day the way you've been since Saturday. You haven't had a chance to catch your breath."

She rubbed her forehead. "You've been putting in even longer hours. Why aren't you about to fall asleep on the floor?" Because she seriously was. She swayed and bumped into the wall. "Whoa."

Donovan was in front of her. When had he moved in front of her?

He took over the buttons, and she let him. "Cassie? Are you okay?"

She blinked a few more times and the room stopped tilting sideways. "I don't think I realized how tired I am." She had to concentrate hard to form the words, and she wasn't sure if they were coming out quite right.

Donovan finished the buttons. "Promise me you won't drive yourself home."

That was a promise she had no difficulty making. "Promise."

Donovan didn't look convinced, but he stepped back and followed her into the kitchen. "I have a question."

"What's that?"

"Is it normal for Steven Pierce to stop by?"

Cassie couldn't tell if Donovan was asking as a cop or as a jealous, well, whatever he was. "He pops in a couple of times a week. Technically, all dining at The Haven falls under his purview."

"What did he want tonight?"

"Um?" What did he ask? Her head was so fuzzy. Oh. Steven. "He said he wanted to tell me in person how much he appreciated my efforts over the weekend."

"Huh."

They hit the swinging doors that led out of the kitchen and into the main dining room. She tried to hurry to the photo op, but her legs and arms didn't want to move the way she wanted them to. What was going on with her? The guests were going to think she'd been sipping on more than lemonade tonight.

DONOVAN STAYED OUT of the range of cameras and phones while Cassie accepted kudos from a movie star who'd recently won an Oscar. One of the servers leaned around the group taking photos and pointed toward the door. "I don't want to intrude, but the porch with the fireplace makes for some gorgeous evening photos."

Donovan watched as the whole crowd immediately abandoned their meals and trooped outside, Cassie companionably squashed between the Oscar winner and his producer girl-friend. At least they were almost done for the night. Amos had finished plating the desserts, and he could handle closing up the kitchen. He and Cassie were on much better terms now. They'd had a little chat on Saturday, and as far as Donovan could tell, Amos was Team Cassie all the way. He hoped he wasn't wrong about that.

Donovan slipped outside and paused by the door to the restaurant. In between the crush of guests, he could just make out Cassie posing for a photo with yet another celebrity.

He doubted anyone else would be able to tell, but he could see the strain on her face and the way her smile was forced.

That decided it for him. He was taking Cassie home after she came back inside. She was so tired she was starting to slur her speech. He made a mental note for the future: Cassie Quinn would quite literally work herself to death if not protected from her own off-the-charts work ethic.

A few minutes later, a wave of laughing guests returned to the dining room. He held the door open for the first guest, then the next. One man who looked vaguely familiar extended his hand.

"Thank you, Officer. I don't suppose you'd be willing to let me come do a ride-along with you sometime?"

The other guests swirled around them and continued to filter inside.

"I'm playing a cop in my next movie. My agent's lined up a few things for me in LA, but I'd really like to get the small-town experience."

The last thing Donovan wanted to do was chauffeur an actor for a day, but he forced a polite smile. The line of returning guests had almost dissipated. Where was Cassie?

Of course she would agree to take pictures until the last guest was satisfied, even though she could barely stay upright.

Donovan focused on the man. "I'm afraid that's not my call to make. Have your agent call our chief of police, Grayson Ward."

"I'll do that, man. Thank you." He shook his hand again, and when Donovan looked back to the fireplace, the porch was empty.

He walked all three sides of the porch.

No Cassie.

He called her phone. A male voice answered. "Cassie Quinn's phone. Donovan?"

"Amos? Why do you have Cassie's phone?"

"It was in her coat pocket. I heard it ringing, looked at it, and saw it was you. So I answered it. Where are you?"

Donovan walked off the steps and into the green space around the restaurant. "Did Cassie come back in a side door?"

"No. I assumed she was with you."

"She isn't with me. I'm outside, and I don't see her anywhere."

"Well, she has to be out there somewhere. It's not like she could disappear into thin air."

TEN AGONIZING MINUTES LATER, Donovan no longer agreed with Amos. Cassie Quinn had most definitely disappeared into thin air. She was gone. He stood in the security office and fought back panic as one of the guards whose name he'd already forgotten pulled up the footage for the camera near Hideaway.

"There." The guard pointed to the screen. On the far edge of the back parking lot, a small person in a white coat climbed into the back of a white van. She didn't appear to be under duress, but the image was too far away to be certain.

"What is that vehicle?"

"Give me a second." The guard's hands were a blur as he typed something and then used the mouse to click through several screens. "That's the laundry service we use. They provide overnight dry cleaning for the guests."

"Are they usually here at this time?"

"Yeah. Standard stuff." The guard turned, and Donovan saw his name tag. Larry pointed to the screen. "The housekeeping staff brings out the bags, loads them onto the van, and they take them away. I'm not sure where. They make two stops here each day. The first stop is around 3:00 p.m. Then they keep going to some other places dropping off and picking up. They stop here again in the evening because our guests are special, and we offer a last-minute option. I'm pretty sure we're the last stop on their route."

"Find out where they go from here."

The guard didn't balk at the order. Thanks to a unique set of decisions made decades earlier, The Haven, while quite a few miles from the main part of town, was under the jurisdiction of the Gossamer Falls Police Department. And that meant Donovan could take charge of the investigation.

"Larry, get the make, model, and license plate for that van while you're at it." Donovan pointed to another guard. "What's your name, ma'am?"

"Belinda."

"Okay, Belinda. You're going to get on the phone. You're going to call Bronwyn Pierce and get her over here. Then you're going to call the front gate and tell them to let in any official who shows up." He paused a second. "Or any of the Quinns." Because they were going to blow a gasket.

Both Larry and Belinda got to work.

He called Gray. "Gray. Cassie's missing."

FOURTEEN

DONOVAN HAD SURVIVED some tough stuff, but the twelve hours following Cassie's disappearance would forever rank at the top of his "worst ever" list.

He stared at the laptop he'd set up in the dining room of Hideaway and accepted a cup of coffee from Amos. The poor man had stayed all night. At some point in the wee hours of the morning, he'd decided to bake. Cassie had been right when she'd said the man was a genius with pastries. He'd been plying the team with food since dawn, and it was the only thing giving them any energy right now.

Because they certainly weren't running high on the adrenaline of leads.

They had nothing.

As far as they could tell, Cassie had willingly climbed into the van around 9:30 p.m. The dry cleaners were based out of Canton, about forty-five minutes away. Brick had pulled the van driver over thirty minutes outside of town.

And what he'd told them had made absolutely no sense.

The driver claimed that he'd been checking his phone before beginning the last leg of his route. Cassie had knocked on the door of his van and told him she needed to get off the property. She handed him a hundred-dollar bill and said all he had to do was drive through the gate and then let her out at the trailhead to Gossamer Falls.

"I figured it wouldn't hurt to give her a ride."

Donovan had never felt compelled to strangle someone before. But this guy? "I bet the hundred bucks wouldn't hurt either."

The driver had the decency to look ashamed. "Well. No. But I didn't hurt her or anything, man. She was kind of manic. Like she couldn't figure out if she was tired or wired. I drove her to the trailhead, and when we got there, she looked at me kind of funny. She said, 'Why did you stop?' and I told her that she'd asked me to."

"You didn't think maybe she needed a doctor or something?"

"Man, I didn't know! But I wasn't gonna leave her there alone. I told her she could wait in the van for a few minutes. So we sat there. About ten minutes later, this car pulled up. A guy got out and came to the door. He was all smiles and happy. He opened the door, said, 'Man, thanks for getting her out. 'Preciate it.' Then he took her hand, and she went with him."

By this point in the interview, Donovan had lost all faith in humanity. "And you just let her go."

"Well, yeah." As if that was the obvious answer. "She seemed to know the guy. He took her hand and he was real gentle with her. He helped her get in his car and drove off."

"What did he look like?"

The driver wrinkled his face in concentration. "It was dark, man. I don't know. I think he was a White guy. No facial hair. He had very white teeth, I remember that. He was probably six feet?"

He made his last comment a question, and Donovan didn't try to get more of a description. "You didn't happen to notice anything about the car, did you? Make, model, tag number?"

"Nah. He parked close but not that close. And out of the

lights. It was an SUV. Smallish. Not like a Suburban. More like a RAV4. Maybe? Dark?"

His description gave them nothing to go on. Eyewitnesses were notoriously inaccurate, and the only thing this guy seemed confident about was that it wasn't a car, van, or truck.

"Did you notice which direction he went?" Donovan didn't expect an answer, but this time he was in for a surprise.

"Yeah. He went back toward Gossamer Falls. I kept going toward Canton. Until I was pulled over." At this the driver frowned. "Which was completely bogus. I didn't do anything wrong."

Donovan let all his fury and frustration bleed into his voice. "A woman is missing and you are the last person known to have seen her."

The driver paled. "I didn't hurt her."

"You didn't help her, either."

At that point, Gray had stepped in. The driver had been allowed to go home, but it was with the understanding that he might be facing charges.

Donovan had gone outside to try to pull himself together . . . just in time to come face-to-face with Cassie's mom and dad. Her mom had been crying. Her dad looked like someone was burning him alive from the inside out.

"I'm so sorry." What else could he say? "So sorry." His own voice broke.

And then John Quinn III pulled him into a bear hug. "Gray told us what happened. Wasn't your fault, son."

Smaller hands around his back, a softer voice murmuring against him, "There's no blame here. Nothing you could have done."

He wiped at his eyes. "I'm going to find her." To consider any other outcome was a fast track to a nightmare.

The hours that followed had been fruitless. He still believed that he would get her back, but now he couldn't stop the gnawing terror that threatened to overwhelm him.

He would find her. And no matter what, he would stay by her side.

CASSIE'S MOUTH FELT like someone had forced her to eat cocoa powder. Her head pounded. And her stomach churned.

She blinked and tried to shift into a more comfortable position. There was a weird lump under her back. Had she gone to sleep on a pile of clothes or something?

She went to roll over onto her left side but came face-to-face with the back of a leather sofa. She didn't own a leather sofa.

She attempted another swallow, and her tongue glued itself to the roof of her mouth. The split second of panic at the unexpected issue cleared a few cobwebs from her mind.

And a whole new level of panic washed over her.

Where was she? Why was she on a couch? What had happened to her? Her mind frantically searched for the last memory she could claim and came up alarmingly blank. She tried to slow her breathing and focus.

The concentration sent a shock of pain through her head, and she remembered she'd been at work and she had a headache. And . . . nothing.

Voices filtered through to her consciousness, and she strained to hear what they were saying.

"You imbecile." Male. The voice wasn't deep and resonant. It had a thin tone that was familiar. The unmistakable sound of a hand meeting flesh. "What exactly was your plan?"

"You said you wanted her out of the picture." Male. Not Southern. And slurred. Maybe the slap she'd heard hadn't been the first one he'd been subjected to. A coughing sound. Then spitting. "I'm bleeding."

"A busted lip is the least of your worries." The first voice. "Again, what are you planning to do with her? I told you I wanted her off the property. I didn't say anything about kidnapping her."

"She wouldn't quit." The second male was angry. And defensive.

"Yeah. I noticed. And I told you to let it go. I wanted her gone, but she's a good chef. She's so good that despite your efforts to make a royal mess out of everything, the entire weekend was an unmitigated success." The first man was icily calm. "Which is why I told you to wait. We needed to leave her alone for a while and let things cool off. But instead of waiting, you kidnapped her."

"There's no proof of that. None. She was a willing participant."

At those words, Cassie almost lost the battle with her roiling stomach.

"So help me, if you touched her—"

"I didn't." The second man sounded a little desperate now and his words came faster. "I picked her up from the spot, drove her here, and put her on the couch. I haven't laid a hand on her."

Cassie wanted to cry from relief, but the possible horror had jolted her into full consciousness. She sat slowly, careful not to make any sound that would attract her captors.

The second man was still talking. "But I *didn't* kidnap her. Don't you see? That's the beauty of the plan. She got in that van of her own free will and asked the driver to give her a ride."

"Because you suggested it."

"Well, yeah, but she did it."

"Sure she did. But there's only one reason she would agree to such a ridiculous request. What did you give her?"

A pause. "GHB. In her lemonade."

"Idiot." This time the word was low. "You could have killed her."

"But I didn't. And GHB is perfect for this. She won't remember anything. She won't be able to testify about anything. She's in there asleep. All we have to do is dump her somewhere. The whole town is looking for her. She'll be found."

Cassie took her time but got on her feet and looked at her surroundings. The room she was in looked like a bedroom that someone had converted into a small den. There was a recliner, a TV, bookshelves, and enough drug paraphernalia to get half of Gossamer Falls high.

"Yeah. And what happens when she's found?" The first guy again. Cassie struggled with the voice. She knew that voice. Why couldn't she remember? *"You're* the one she's going to remember. And when she does, you'll be arrested. Or have you forgotten about what happened the last time you were in the same space as Cassie Quinn? Huh? Oh, that's right. An innocent man was killed and then the man who killed him later killed himself because he couldn't live with himself when he found out what he did while he was high on drugs. Drugs that *you* sold him."

The words fell like tiny little grenades all around her heart.

The second man started talking, and Cassie had to concentrate to hear him. When he finally stopped cursing, he said, "I have a good thing going here. And so do you. So I suggest you help me figure out how to handle this, because if they take me down, you can be sure I'll take you with me."

In the silence that stretched between the two men, Cassie fought to process what she'd heard. The second man had been in Atlanta. He was the one who'd been selling the drugs? How had he wound up in Gossamer Falls?

And now he was back in the drug business. And he believed that Cassie would recognize him. Cassie sat back on the sofa and tried to breathe.

"Fine. How much longer do you think she'll sleep?"

"Who knows? I didn't think I'd dosed her that much, but she's a lightweight."

"She's probably never done anything stronger than a Tylenol. The Quinns don't do drugs."

There was venom in his voice when he said "the Quinns," and it was in that moment that she recognized the voice.

This was bad.

This was very, very bad. *Oh Father, help me. Please.* Cassie knew that prayers weren't always answered in the way she wanted. She'd prayed her heart out for twelve solid hours that night in Atlanta. No one could have prayed with more desperation or faith than she had.

And while she'd survived, she'd lost friends, and for a while, she'd lost part of herself. But she knew that prayer mattered. She knew that it was a declaration, albeit a silent one, of trust in her heavenly Father.

Her mind flashed to Donovan. *Help him, please.* He would be a disaster by now. Her parents and family. Cal, Mo, Meredith. Bronwyn. They would all be devastated. She had no doubt that they were turning Gossamer Falls upside down and inside out to find her. And she knew they would succeed.

But if she didn't stay alive for the next few minutes, they might find her body after it was too late.

She had way too much living to do. She wanted to kiss Donovan Bledsoe and tell him that she loved him. She wanted to build on what Chef Louis had done, but also make Hideaway her own.

And she wanted to be sure Steven Pierce and his mysterious accomplice went to jail.

"Do you think we can leave her here?" Steven's voice was closer to the room than it had been before.

Cassie made the only choice she could. She lay back down on the sofa and tried to get herself into the exact position she'd been in when she woke. She closed her eyes and waited. *Father, protect me* was on a permanent loop.

The door opened moments after she settled in. A pause, then it closed. "She's still breathing, she hasn't moved, hasn't puked. So yeah, I'd say we can leave her. What do you have in mind?"

"We're going to have to figure out a way to kill her but make it look like an accident. Which means both of us have to be far, far away from here."

"You know someone who can do that?"

"I do." There was no hesitation in Steven's voice.

FIFTEEN

DONOVAN GLANCED at his phone. The number wasn't familiar, but it was local. He couldn't risk missing something important. "Bledsoe."

"Donovan?"

He sat down hard in the chair that, thankfully, was right beside him. "Cassie? Baby? Is that you?" Every person in the room went silent.

"I need you to come get me."

"Where are you?"

"I'm at Mrs. Cagle's. I think I scared her half to death. Might want to send some paramedics."

"Are you hurt?" He grabbed his keys and waved for everyone to mobilize.

"No. But she seems a little short of breath."

"You aren't hurt?"

"I . . ."

The hesitation sent a spike of dread through him.

"They drugged me. I have a raging headache, and I threw up while I was running away."

She sounded so calm. Was she in shock?

"Cassie, don't hang up." He turned to the room and gave them a brief rundown.

Gray pointed to him. "Go. I'll send backup. Find out what happened and loop me in."

Donovan was already out the door by the time Gray finished talking. "Okay, baby. Talk to me. What do you remember?"

Cassie filled him in on what she'd heard. "They left, and I knew I had to get out of there. Once I was outside, I knew where I was. I had a friend in elementary school who lived near there. So I cut through the woods. Figured it would be safer than being on the road. And I didn't want to risk staying inside to call you. I saw Mrs. Cagle's front door was open, so I knocked on her screen door. She let me in." Cassie's voice dropped. "I really do think I frightened her. But she's been so sweet. She gave me a toothbrush and a washcloth and a glass of tea, but her hands are still shaky. I'm worried that I've put her in danger."

"We won't let anything happen to her or you. We've got people headed your way." A transmission came through his police radio, and he relayed the information to Cassie. "Not sure if you could hear that, but you'll have company very soon. Your cousins were nearby."

Cassie stayed on the phone, even after Cal and Mo all but burst through poor Mrs. Cagle's front room to get to her. Donovan heard the whole thing go down, and he didn't blame them for their hurry. When he heard Mo say, "You're really okay?" and Cassie's "Yes," he could have cried in relief.

By the time Donovan pulled into Mrs. Cagle's driveway, there were already four vehicles parked in the yard. Everyone who'd been searching for Cassie had heard the news.

Mrs. Cagle had apparently recovered her good spirits and was now ensconced in a rocking chair on her front porch with a quilt over her lap. The four men standing around her made her look like an ancient queen surrounded by her courtiers. The air vibrated with palpable relief, but with a sense of contained urgency.

Because Cassie Quinn knew who'd taken her.

And when the news got out, Gossamer Falls would never be the same.

SIXTEEN

CASSIE LAUNCHED HERSELF out of the chair she'd been sitting in, and she didn't stop moving until she was in Donovan's arms. He wrapped her in his embrace and pulled her tight against him. His lips brushed her temple, he took a shuddering breath, and then his big body shook around her.

She sensed more than saw the room empty around them as her cousins gave them privacy, and for several moments, the room was completely silent. She held him and he held her and it was impossible to know who was holding on tighter.

Eventually he released her, only to cradle her face in his hands and use his thumbs to brush away her tears. Cassie placed her hands over his wrists and leaned into him. "We need to get something out of the way right now."

He tensed.

"I'm never letting you go."

A faint smile flirted with his mouth and his thumb brushed across her lips. "Good." The word came out deep and certain. "Then you won't mind when I tag along wherever you go." He swallowed hard. "Because you're never getting rid of me."

"Good."

He brushed her nose with his, then placed the softest of kisses on the corner of her mouth. When she chased his lips with hers, the laughter that rumbled in his chest sent a shiver through her. "Later, baby." He tucked her hair behind her ear. "Your family needs to see you alive and well, and while I have a lot of questions, we need to get you checked out by a doctor."

If they tried to make her go to the hospital in Asheville, she was going to refuse. "I want Aunt Carol."

"She's on her way here." Cal's voice came from the doorway. When she turned to face him, she kept her body aligned with Donovan's, and he didn't release her. Cal quirked an eyebrow and huffed out a breath that spoke volumes.

"Don't go big brother on me, Cal." She didn't want to fight with him. He and Mo were her favorite cousins. But she would do what she had to. She wasn't going to tolerate them hassling Donovan.

"Sweet girl, I'll go big brother on you every day and twice on Sunday." Before Cassie could protest, Cal pointed at Donovan. "'Bout time you got this sorted. Hurt her again and we won't be forgiving."

"Hey! I'm standing right here!" Cassie would have said more, but Donovan squeezed her close, and when she looked up, he gave her a wink before focusing on Cal.

"There's no need to worry. I learn from my mistakes. I don't repeat them."

"Glad to hear it."

Cassie buried her face in Donovan's chest. "Make him go away."

Not only did Cal not go away, but the next few hours were a blur. Her parents arrived and there was more crying. Then Aunt Carol, who was technically her great-aunt, Cal's mom, and the town doctor, came to examine her and take so much blood that Cassie asked her if she had a secret life as a vampire.

When they got to the police station later, she settled in on the cozy couch in Gray's office while Gray and Donovan asked her questions for what felt like forever. Nothing they asked helped narrow down the search for Steven's accomplice. Nothing made any sense. And then Donovan handed her an iPad. "Bronwyn sent me a file with the photos of everyone on staff at The Haven."

"I'm not sure if this will help." Cassie studied each photo. She'd only been on staff for a month, and her interaction with employees had been extremely limited. "I haven't met most of the people who work at The Haven. I haven't even met all of the front of house staff at Hideaway."

"How is that possible?" Gray asked. "Are there seasonal workers or . . ."

"No. Well, I mean, maybe there are some students who are only there during the summers. But The Haven doesn't have an offseason so it's not like anyone is getting laid off in the winter." She pointed to the screen. "This girl. I've seen her. But I can't tell you where. Maybe she's a server. Maybe she's a housekeeper."

She scrolled through more photos and tried to concentrate. Even with nearly twelve hours of drug-induced sleep, her head still pounded and she needed more rest.

Her hand hovered over the screen, and she stared at the photo that filled the space. "This is Wyatt Patterson. I know him." She shuddered at the thought of how and why his voice had been so familiar. How could he be here? "This is the man who was with Steven. He's the one who's been trying to get rid of me. What does he do at The Haven?"

Gray placed a call to Bronwyn. The answer was unexpected and unwelcome. "Bronwyn says he's been a server at Hideaway for six months. His file says he has a good rapport with the guests and with his coworkers."

"I bet he does." Cassie had to force herself not to throw the iPad across the room.

"Why do you say that?" Donovan took the iPad from her.

"Because he's a drug dealer. He's the one who was supplying Chef Albert in Atlanta."

Gray was typing away on his computer before she finished speaking. "Then why isn't he in jail?"

"They couldn't get proof that would stand up in court. But in the restaurant, it was an open secret. Lots of the staff got their cocaine from him. Can I see the photo again?"

Donovan returned the iPad, but not before he studied the photo for a while. "Something about this is off."

Gray gave Donovan a shrewd look. "Even if Cassie hadn't seen him before, you should have. You interviewed everyone, didn't you?"

Donovan grabbed his laptop. "I did. But I don't recall seeing this man." His voice trailed off, and Cassie and Gray shared a look but didn't interrupt. Then Donovan turned his computer around and a new photo appeared. "This is who I saw."

Cassie stared in shock. "Oh! I *have* seen him. I didn't recognize him. But that's him with longer hair. He didn't have the mustache in Atlanta. Or the glasses."

She tried to find a memory of Wyatt in the events of the previous evening, but they were gone. But his voice wasn't gone. And what she'd heard later wasn't gone.

"I don't know how he did it, but he's the one who drugged me."

Donovan sat on the sofa beside her. "I know he is. This is the guy who refilled your lemonade last night."

IT HAD NEARLY KILLED Donovan to let Cassie out of his sight, but he had a job to do. And she was safe with family.

His phone dinged.

Please be careful.

He texted back.

I will.

A photo came through, and Donovan couldn't help but chuckle at the sight of Cassie's grandfather and great-grandfather, sitting on the porch of her parents' home, shotguns across their knees.

He showed the photo to Gray, who gave him a pointed look. "You sure you want to marry into that family?"

Donovan grinned. "If she'll have me? You'd better believe it."

Five minutes later, there was no smiling and no thought of proposals or gun-toting octogenarians. The house where he stood was small, the wood siding was rotten in places, and what landscaping there might have been at one time was overgrown. He stepped onto the porch with caution. It wouldn't have surprised him if his feet had slid right through the boards.

When he knocked on the door to Wyatt Patterson's home, he was prepared for anything.

But there was no answer.

He knocked again.

Still no answer.

Gray communicated with the officers behind the house. There was no movement. But there was a window with no curtain or blind over the kitchen sink. Donovan waited in tense silence as Brick approached the back of the home.

"We've got a body."

They breached the house from every entrance and found Wyatt Patterson slumped over his kitchen table. Cocaine and other drug paraphernalia lay everywhere. Donovan reached toward the man.

"He's still warm." He searched for a pulse. Nothing. No. Wait. He shifted his hand. "Get the paramedics in here. I've got a pulse."

THERE WAS NO HONOR among thieves, and when Wyatt Patterson regained consciousness, he rolled over on Steven Pierce faster than the district attorney could say plea bargain.

After he'd been implicated in the hostage situation that Cassie had been involved in, Wyatt decided Atlanta was too hot for him. A music producer had shared all about the drug action he'd been surprised to discover while at a secret resort in the mountains of North Carolina.

Wyatt claimed that he'd planned to go straight and work at The Haven, but no one believed that part of the story. Especially since he'd managed to not only find the local drug dealers but also use his position at Hideaway to provide drugs to the guests at The Haven who were interested in purchasing everything from meth to crack.

He also sold cocaine to none other than Steven Pierce. And he had proof by way of some video he'd recorded. He explained that when he saw Cassie for the first time, he expected her to recognize him immediately and he knew he would lose his job. He ran into Steven and told him that he had to quit.

He claimed that it was Steven who suggested that Wyatt should get Cassie to quit, and that Steven volunteered to help. Wyatt didn't think Steven needed him to be there just so he could get his drugs a little easier, so he questioned him about why he was doing this. Steven explained about the enmity between the Quinns and the Pierces and said that Wyatt would be doing the whole family a favor.

Wyatt started small. He began a process that he hoped would convince Cassie to leave. He admitted to taking her knife, but he claimed he'd wiped it clean and left it on a table at The Dry Gulch the day before the stabbing there. He insisted that his ideas were more about intimidation and fear, and that it had been Steven who had given him access to Cassie's kitchen and suggested both the deer in the road and the kidnapping.

Given that Cassie had overheard Wyatt confess to drugging her and had heard Steven Pierce say that he thought kidnapping Cassie had been a terrible idea, it threw his entire testimony into question.

It might have ended there, but Wyatt was a paranoid guy—not surprising, given his occupation—and had hidden security cameras in his home. While the evidence against Steven Pierce in the kidnapping of Cassie Quinn was virtually nonexistent, there was unmistakable video evidence that Steven had attempted to kill Wyatt. The cocaine he'd used before he passed out at his table had been provided by Pierce and had been heavily laced with fentanyl. The doctors speculated that if they'd been even an hour or two later in finding Wyatt, it would have been too late to save him.

To firm up the case further, Mo was asked to take a look at The Haven's security log-in system. Donovan had no idea how it all worked, but Mo found a back door in the code that had given Steven a way to hide an hour's worth of keycard access information. The missing hour coincided with Wyatt's destruction of Cassie's kitchen.

Two days later, Donovan took extreme pleasure in placing Steven Pierce under arrest.

EPILOGUE

"**WE HAVE MUCH** to be thankful for." Papa Quinn's voice had a quaver to it, but it was still strong. Cassie leaned into Donovan's side as they stood around the table at Papa and Granny Quinn's on Thanksgiving Day.

He reached out and took Granny Quinn's hand. "This year has brought new family into our circle. Some by marriage." He winked at Cal's wife, Landry, and their daughter, Eliza. "Some by the bonds of friendship and faithful service that we will never forget."

Cassie knew he was talking about the men and women from the Gossamer Falls police force who had been invited to dinner with their families, all sprinkled in among the Quinns.

"We know that God is good. We know that he works for our good and his glory." Papa Quinn choked up a little and took a deep breath. "Through all of the pain our family has been touched by this year, still he is faithful. And we choose to offer up a sacrifice of praise."

More than one person, male and female, dabbed at their eyes. Papa Quinn raised Granny's hand to his lips and pressed a gentle kiss there, then turned to the rest of the family. "We love you all. We're so thankful for you. Now let's eat!"

In the chaos of over sixty people helping themselves to

turkey, dressing, mashed potatoes, and gravy, Cassie slipped her hand into Donovan's and pulled him toward the edge of the property and into the woods. As soon as they were out of sight of the main house, his arm slid around her waist, and he dropped a kiss to her hair. "Cassie, baby. I hope you know that this is a testament to my love for you. Because your granny made her homemade dressing and those people"—he nodded toward the house—"are vultures. There won't be anything left when we get back."

Cassie grinned. "I'm not going to keep you long."

"Oh?" He pretended to pout. "Well, to be honest, I'm a little disappointed."

She led him to the bench that Papa Quinn had made for Granny, and they sat. Cassie twisted her body around so she was facing him. "I've decided to take Bronwyn up on her offer."

With all the chaos and upheaval after the attacks on Cassie, she'd told Bronwyn that she needed time to think and consider before she accepted the position as head chef.

Those first few weeks after the arrests had been brutal. The press had descended on Gossamer Falls. Their quiet town became the focus of the national news and brought the worst kind of attention to The Haven. The relative anonymity that had long protected Gossamer Falls was destroyed.

Bronwyn told Cassie she could take all the time she needed, as long as she treated the kitchen and the staff like they were hers and made whatever changes were necessary.

Cassie needed the time to be sure that she wasn't using Hideaway to, quite literally, hide away from her own life. And she'd wanted time to think about what she would need to be truly happy as the chef.

"As of yesterday, I'm officially the head chef at Hideaway. Bronwyn said they'll be changing all the letterhead and menus and everything next week. So apparently my first order of business is to approve the font. How crazy is that?"

PEACE AND CONTENTMENT like he'd never known flooded through Donovan. But he kept his voice as noncommittal as possible and asked, "Are you sure?"

She was radiant as she nodded and said, "So sure. It's perfect for me. Bronwyn agreed to everything I asked for. I can stay here, close to my family, and you."

He cupped her face with his hands. "If you ever change your mind—"

"I won't."

He rubbed his thumb across her lips. "If you do, I'll go with you. These past months have shown me that the thing I need most is you. The rest I'll figure out. As long as we're together, I'll be fine." He pressed a kiss to her lips.

"I need you too. More than I need fancy kitchens and accolades. I'm not giving anything up by staying here. I'm getting everything I could have ever dreamed of."

Donovan had been wondering when the time would be right. He'd been ready since September but hadn't wanted anything about their relationship to sway Cassie in her decision. But now? He couldn't wait another second.

He reached into his pocket and pulled out a ring.

Cassie looked down and then back up. "Donovan!"

"I know everyone will say it's too soon. And maybe you think it is too. You don't have to say yes right now, but—"

"Yes. Yes. Yes." She punctuated each word with a quick kiss. "Forever. Always. Together. Yes."

Lynn H. Blackburn is the bestselling author of *Never Fall Again*, the Defend and Protect series, and the Dive Team Investigations series. She loves writing swoon-worthy Southern suspense because her childhood fantasy was to become a spy, but her grown-up reality is that she's a huge chicken and would have been caught on her first mission. She prefers to live vicariously through her characters by putting them into terrifying situations while she sits at home in her pajamas. She lives in Simpsonville, South Carolina, with her true love, Brian, and their three children. Learn more at LynnHBlack burn.com.

PERILOUS OBSESSION

NATALIE WALTERS

ONE

"BUT WHY WOULD they put a flamingo in jail?"

"Did he lie?"

"You don't go to jail for lying."

"I lied to my mom about hitting my brother—am I going to jail?"

Lahela Young clapped twice, cutting into the rising excitement leading dangerously close to uncontrol. From the learning carpet, twenty-three sets of hands clapped twice back. The eyes of her second-grade class all on her. Well, except for Blaise, who had just plucked his finger from his nose and was inspecting his treasure.

"No one's going to jail." Lahela tried again to explain what she learned about the story behind the infamous Pink Floyd— the flamingo, not the 1960s rock band. A fact she discovered through the cackling laughter of Mrs. Margo Bell, Cottonwood Elementary School's eighty-year-old librarian. "Pink Floyd wasn't put in jail. He escaped the zoo."

A second before another round of chatter erupted, the familiar tune of "Aloha Friday" started playing from the timer Lahela had set on her phone to indicate five minutes before the end of school. "Okay, my little coconuts, all pau. We're done, back to your desks."

Twenty minutes later, Lahela's students were on their way home and she was back in her classroom straightening everything in sight—all to avoid looking at the text message from her friend Daphne on her cell phone. Again.

As if it wasn't already ingrained in her brain.

I think Briggs is going to ask you out tonight.

Briggs Turner was going to ask her out? The possibility made her head fuzzy and the rest of her warmer than a sunny day on Waikiki Beach.

"Looks like you're glad it's Friday too."

Standing in the doorway of her classroom was Nancy Bart, wearing bright pink flamingo sunglasses on top of her head. The bubblegum color complemented the teal-green dress she wore with a pair of shiny patent-leather boots.

"My students would've loved to see you wearing those sunglasses today." Lahela tossed the trash she collected and made sure her computer was shut off before grabbing her bag and meeting Nancy at the door. "All they could talk about today was Pink Floyd."

"That's better than what I caught two of my students writing on their desks."

"Uh-oh." Nancy was a great fourth-grade teacher who Lahela always thought would make an excellent kindergarten teacher with her quirky personality and matching style.

"You know . . ." She sighed, stepping back into the hallway so Lahela could turn off the lights and close her door. "I thought once I was an adult I'd hear less 'Nancy Bart likes to fart.'"

They started walking down the hall toward the exit next to the faculty parking lot. "At least they're generationally consistent?"

Lahela glanced at the woman walking next to her. Her brows

were pinched together, and she had a distant look in her eyes. Had her students' juvenile remarks truly bothered her? She gently elbowed Nancy in the arm. "You're a great teacher."

Nancy flipped her sunglasses back down to her nose. "And I'm fun."

"That you are."

"What are your plans tonight?" Nancy held out her key fob and her yellow VW bug beeped. "Want to grab a pizza and watch a scary movie?"

Lahela wrinkled her nose. "I can't tonight. I have plans."

"Oh, okay," Nancy said, but something in her tone said it wasn't. "With Daphne?"

Ugh. Had Nancy meant to say Daphne's name like that? If fourth-grade boys never matured past fart jokes—and Lahela's older brother, Kekoa, was proof they didn't—then fourth-grade girls never matured past the fear of rejection and being the girl left out.

It wasn't intentional. When Lahela moved to Miracle Springs, Texas, in January, Kekoa made sure she met his friend Colton Crawford's cousin, Daphne, and they clicked immediately. Nancy was nice and fun, but Lahela's friendship with Daphne just felt more . . . natural. Like they'd been friends forever.

But it still bothered her that this felt like she was picking one friend over the other. "It's a birthday dinner for Nash. I'm sure no one will mind if you join us."

"Oh, no. It's totally fine." She slid into her car. "Maybe I'll see you at the festival tomorrow or something."

"Yeah." Lahela felt like she was letting Nancy down somehow. "But we're still on for Mocha Monday, right?"

Nancy's face brightened. "Yep! I have a feeling I'm going to need extra caffeine if I'm going to survive this year as Ms. Fart."

It helped that Nancy was quick to laugh at herself. It eased some of Lahela's guilt as she watched Nancy zoom off in her little car with a wave. On Lahela's first day, the woman had quickly made it her mission to make Lahela feel welcomed at Cottonwood Elementary. She'd personally introduced the entire faculty, invited her to coffee dates and lunch, and even talked Lahela into signing up for spin class. Lahela regretted that last decision immediately after a sculpted man named Basil tortured her via stationary bike for thirty-three minutes and nineteen seconds. She counted down the seconds and then waddled up to the front desk afterward, politely canceling her membership.

Nancy had even been there for her after Trevor.

Maybe she should've insisted Nancy come to dinner with her and her friends. She didn't think any of them would've minded . . . except . . .

Lahela opened the text message from Daphne.

Reading the message again turned her insides tingly. But she was also conflicted.

Lahela placed her phone in the cupholder, started her car, and then twisted her long, dark brown hair off her shoulders and up into a bun on the top of her head. It was October and summer had *finally* ended in Texas, bringing cooler temps—but thinking about Briggs had suddenly driven up the temperature for her.

Or maybe that wasn't it at all.

It'd been six months since she'd had her world flipped and the man she thought wanted a future with her—the man she'd left her home on the islands for—had decided he wasn't ready to commit.

A different kind of heat flooded her face. Embarrassment.

This was when homesickness hit rock bottom. When she missed her family the most. Buckling her seat belt, she stared at the two-story brick building where she taught. Even if she wanted to go back to O'ahu, she couldn't afford it. She'd spent most of her savings to move across the Pacific Ocean, find a house, and fill it with furniture in the hope that she'd one day be sharing it with the man she'd loved.

So what made her think dating Briggs was a good idea? Clearly, she'd made a huge mistake with Trevor. What if she did the same with Briggs? They were friends—good friends. And she literally had only a handful of them here in Miracle Springs. Was she willing to risk it for the hope of something more?

The warmth blooming in her chest said yes. But the reality of her past with Trevor echoed in her head like a tsunami warning. Briggs, Daphne, and Nash were a group of friends before she came into their lives. If things didn't work out, she could lose them all.

Reaching for her phone, she decided inviting Nancy might not be a bad idea after all. Her text message was interrupted by a call. Lahela's breath stalled in her chest at a number she didn't recognize. She swallowed, debating whether to answer it or not. *It's been weeks.* And she'd changed her number . . .

"Hello."

Silence. A chill skirted down the back of Lahela's neck and stretched down her spine.

"Hello?"

Nothing. A stinging sensation burned at the back of her eyes, but she didn't know if it was fear or frustration. Was it the same person? How would they have gotten her new number? Why were they doing this?

Pulling the phone away from her ear, she stared at it a second before ending the call and immediately blocking it. Her eyes moved across the now-empty school parking lot, and she suddenly felt not only alone but exposed.

TWO

BRIGGS TURNER'S PULSE thumped louder in his ears when he saw the torn piece of clothing on the branch. A quick look at the photo on his phone confirmed it was a match for his missing hikers.

"This way," he called over his shoulder before clicking his tongue, sending Durango, his quarter horse, down the rocky slope. Durango's hooves slipped as the dry earth gave way beneath them. Briggs grabbed his radio and called back to let the rest of the Search and Rescue team know they might be close to finding the two missing teenage girls.

This part of Esperanza National Park had seen record flooding in the spring, which had changed the topography of the area, destroying some of the man-made trails and closing off others due to mudslides. Smart hikers avoided the area, but a few wanting to see or swim in the spring-fed pools would ignore posted warnings. That meant they'd forge their way into terrain unsafe for the other members of the SAR team to get to on foot.

Behind him, he heard the soft snort of Jett's horse, Duke, and Jett steadying the four-year-old gelding who was still new to off-trail riding. "Do they have any idea how dangerous this is?"

"Probably not." Branches scraped against Briggs's pants. He kept guiding Durango forward, but honestly, he could let go of the reins and his horse would know where to go. "Chief said the last photo the girls posted on their Instagram was about a half mile from the north parking lot."

"We're about two miles in." The trail was wide enough for Jett to walk Duke forward. "Seems like a lot of effort for two sixteen-year-old girls, if you ask me."

"You must not realize the importance of the perfect social media photo." Briggs scanned the landscape ahead of him, searching for where two image-obsessed teenage girls might brave for the most likes.

Jett tipped his Stetson low over his forehead. "I don't."

Briggs slid a glance to the man who not only was his partner for the mounted Search and Rescue team but was also his parents' ranch hand. The former Texas Rangers' first baseman had left the MLB five years ago, and it took Briggs less than a second to find salacious details on him. When he questioned his parents' decision to hire him, his father said, "It's settled," and Briggs knew better than to push Lee Turner. Instead, on his days off from the Dallas Police Department, he'd come down to the family ranch under the pretense of missing home, but both parents saw right through that and decided to work him.

It was on those weekends sweating side by side working the land and cattle with Jett that Briggs learned the man was not the aggressive maverick the media portrayed him to be. He was quiet, dependable, and had a streak of humor Briggs had come to appreciate.

He'd also realized how much he appreciated being back home, which made his decision to leave the Dallas PD that much easier.

"There." Jett gave a short whistle that encouraged Duke forward.

Durango followed, and when the elevation dropped, Briggs spotted what had caught Jett's attention. Ahead of them was a rock outcropping where boulders turned Esperanza Springs into a waterfall during high rain seasons, but after the dry summer it was just a steady flow. At the base, he saw the two girls—sunbathing.

IT WAS A TWENTY-MINUTE RIDE back to the east parking lot, where Kailey and Bethany were embraced by their worried family members. Briggs and Jett loaded the horses up in the trailer.

"Tanning," Jett grumbled. He pulled a small apple from his pocket and crushed it in half with his hands before handing a piece to Briggs.

"They're young." Durango's velvet lips quickly snatched the treat out of Briggs's hand. "I'm glad you only gave them half a lecture."

Jett sent him a hard stare. "They're old enough to understand the risks and they're lucky to hear my lecture." He scratched Duke's forehead. "Those girls need to recognize that's not always the case."

"They told me about your safety lecture." Barrett Brown, their incident commander, walked up to them. "Pretty sure they're not going to be venturing out on their own for a long time just to avoid it."

Jett tipped his head. "Then I did my job."

"Such a good job, in fact, I think those girls might've had a little crush on you," Barrett said. "Asked if they could get a picture with their 'knight in Wrangler armor.'"

Briggs coughed to cover up the laugh that wanted to escape. It wasn't the first time a female hiker *appreciated* being rescued by Jett. Earlier this spring seventy-three-year-old

Edna Lewis faked a fainting spell just to keep Jett holding on to her.

Jett flexed his jaw, looking unamused. "I don't do photos."

"Don't worry, that's what I told them. But we've been looking for a way to raise funds for new tack. Maybe we could create a calendar and you could be our model. Twelve months of you in Wranglers."

"I'd rather have my teeth pulled, Chief."

Barrett released a hearty chuckle that echoed around them, and Briggs couldn't help laughing too.

"I appreciate you boys coming out so quickly," Barrett said. "Let's pray this is the most exciting thing we see this weekend."

The high season for hikers was only picking up as Texas temperatures finally dipped below melting, which meant their season as volunteer SAR was also picking up.

Barrett backed up toward his Chevy. "Will I see you boys at the festival?"

Jett shook his head. "Not if I can help it."

Briggs opened the door to his truck's cab and dropped his backpack on the floor. "I'll be there."

"Sounds good." Barrett climbed into his truck and pulled out of the parking lot.

Briggs checked the time. If he hurried back to the ranch, he could help Jett unload the horses, get the gear put away, and have time for a quick shower before heading out to meet his friends for dinner.

He climbed into the driver's side of the truck, as thoughts of Lahela filled his mind, along with a nervousness he hadn't felt since he crushed on Jessica Coleman freshman year of high school.

Even though it was Nash's birthday, he was hoping tonight might be the right opportunity to see if Lahela would go to the festival with him.

There was something about his feelings for Lahela that had him seeing his life—his future—differently.

The soft caw of crows pulled his attention to the nearly cloudless blue sky. It was the same beautiful sky over Dallas, but somehow the weight of the job there had dimmed the grandeur. Here, even with sweat dripping down his back, blisters on his hands, dirt covering his skin, and mud on his boots, everything around him was a technicolor of God's artistry.

As beautiful as it was, he couldn't wait to get back to the woman who unexpectedly had him wanting to explore more than their easy friendship. And his plan tonight was to take that first step.

THREE

"YOU LOOK GORGEOUS." Daphne Crawford crossed the parking lot, her brown hair swishing behind her in a ponytail. "And that dress is the perfect color."

Lahela looked down at the yellow sundress she'd finally selected after an hour of going through everything in her closet. October in Texas was still warm enough for a sundress but also cool enough she needed a jacket, so she'd paired her favorite dress with a denim jacket.

The decision only took fifteen minutes, but the other forty-five minutes she'd sat in said pile of clothing talking herself into coming out tonight, trying not to panic that the person behind the random phone calls haunting her life was back.

"Hello?" Daphne met her halfway in the parking lot of Juana's. The touch of her hand on her shoulder was enough to bring Lahela's attention to the present. "You okay?"

"Yeah." Her cell phone felt like a brick in her purse. After blocking the number, she hadn't received any more calls. Maybe it was a mistake.

"Lahela, girl, you're worrying me." Daphne tipped her head so that she was looking right into Lahela's eyes. Her expression shifted from concern to amusement. "Wait, you aren't nervous, are you?"

Briggs.

"When he sees you"—Daphne stepped back, giving her a once-over—"I bet he doesn't waste a second asking you out."

"Well, look at these beauties just standing in the parking lot." The voice and a wolf whistle turned them to find Nash Martin walking toward them. "I appreciate Juana's new marketing choice to lure customers in."

Daphne rolled her eyes. "Is flirting in your DNA?"

Nash wrapped an arm around Daphne's shoulder. "My grandmother doesn't seem to think so since I'm"—he placed a hand on his chest and looked up into the sky—"woefully single." He dropped his voice and his gaze to meet theirs. "Her words, not mine."

"You're terrible." Daphne slapped her hand playfully against Nash's chest. "Happy birthday."

Lahela studied her two friends and wondered again that if Nash wasn't Daphne's brothers' best friend, *their* friendship might cross into romantic territory someday.

"Happy birthday, Nash." Lahela handed him her gift bag. "You don't look a day over twenty."

"I'm cursed by good genes." Nash accepted the gift and gave Lahela a hug. "Though it would be nice to have your naturally tan skin tone so I wouldn't burn in the summer."

"Aww." Daphne pinched Nash's cheek. "I think lobster red really brings out the gold flecks in your brown eyes."

"Gold flecks?" Nash sent Lahela a look before turning an impish smile on Daphne. "So, you're checking out my eyes?"

Daphne recoiled, her face twisting into playful disgust as she shoved Nash. It didn't even move him an inch, a testament to the time he put in at the gym to stay physically fit for his job in the FBI.

"Ew. No. I mean . . . I just . . ." Daphne stumbled over her words before relief flashed across her face. "Hey, Briggs!"

And just like that, the world seemed to shift on its axis.

Lahela turned and her pulse picked up at the sight of Briggs in his signature jeans, boots, and T-shirt with the Mounted SAR emblem on it. If sexy-casual was a thing, he nailed it.

Add the baseball cap he tugged over brown hair just long enough to brush the tops of his ears and collar, and she'd be lying if she said that the first time they met there wasn't a tiny moment of appreciation. But it was his easy friendship coupled with the countless ways he'd shown up for her over the last ten months that had her taking Daphne's words to heart.

Briggs strode toward them in a casual swagger, the setting sun highlighting his form. His gaze snagged on her and held. Her shyness kicked in, pressuring her to break eye contact, but she ignored it. If she hadn't, she would've missed the appreciative glint in his expression as he took her in, the slight uptick of his lips in a smile that seemed only for her.

Heat blossomed everywhere across her body, and she dipped her chin, not wanting anyone to catch the blush warming her cheeks.

"Y'all weren't waiting on me, were you?"

"No. Daph just admitted she's been checking out my eyes," Nash said. "Tell me again how pretty the golden flecks are."

"You're so annoying. I have no idea why my brothers like you."

"For my gold—"

"Stop." Daphne waved her hands in the air. "I regret so many things," she mumbled, reaching for Lahela. "Let's go inside and eat." Looking at Briggs, she said, "You're welcome to join us." And to Nash, "You're one second away from me taking back my birthday gift."

"Aw, Daph, your compliment about my glittering eyes is gift enough."

"So. Many. Regrets." Daphne groaned.

Lahela laughed as the four of them started for the restaurant entrance and finally felt herself relax. A hostess showed them to a round table, and Briggs pulled out her chair the same as Nash did for Daphne.

"You look great tonight." His low rumble whispered over her shoulder. "I like the flower too."

She absently touched the plumeria flower hairpin she'd added above her right ear. Grateful to focus on anything else. "Thank you."

His fingers brushed against the side of her arm, sending a delicious chill skirting through her. He sat down on her right, bringing with him the woodsy scent of his cologne that swirled around her, tempting her to inhale. No, she would not sniff the man. This wasn't the first time she'd been around Briggs and his cologne.

So why was she suddenly too shy to meet his gaze? On her left, Daphne wiggled her brows suggestively, like she had read Lahela's thoughts.

Thankfully, the waitress arrived with a basket of tortilla chips and bowl of salsa she set in the middle of the table before asking if they wanted their usual. Dinner at Juana's had become a tradition from the first time Daphne invited her to meet Briggs and Nash, whenever he could make it down from Dallas, and there wasn't a bad thing on the menu.

"Finn sends his apologies for not being here tonight to celebrate your big day," Daphne said and pulled an envelope from her purse. "And Fish is running late, so this is from all three of us."

"Aww, Daphne." Nash reached for the envelope she slid across the table. "You—"

Daphne's hand slapped down on the envelope. "If you bring up golden flecks one more time, Nash Martin, I'm not kidding, I'll keep the gift."

"You're so sweet to think of me." Nash picked up the envelope. "Thank you."

"My gift goes—" Lahela was cut off by her cell phone. Anxiety slammed back into her like a tidal wave. "S-sorry. Let me just . . ."

Reaching into her purse, she pulled out her phone just enough to see the screen. Cold dread instantly raced through her. Unknown caller. *No.* This couldn't be happening again. Her fingers shook as she hit the ignore button.

"Who was it?"

Lahela met Daphne's gaze and forced herself to smile, but it must not have been very convincing because her friend's expression shifted into concern.

"What is it?"

"Nothing." Lahela licked her lips and dropped her gaze to the table. Daphne was the only person she had confided in when the anonymous calls started coming, and only after nearly a dozen of them interrupted the middle of dinner with Daphne's family. And that was after a weekend of random calls in the middle of the night. But there was no way to figure out who it was or why it was happening, and it wasn't worth burdening her friend with something Lahela could easily block and ignore.

"What's going on?" Briggs said. There was a protective edge in his deep tone that made Lahela want to melt into it. If there was one difference between Briggs and her ex, it was the way Briggs always made her feel safe. Even as just a friend, he watched out for her in ways Trevor never did.

Another shrill ring of her cell phone cut into her thoughts, causing her to jump in her chair. She looked down at the phone ringing and vibrating in her palm. It was another number she didn't recognize. *Don't answer it.* Lahela's thumb hovered over the screen as her pulse pounded in her ears. *Don't answer it.*

"Lahela."

She jerked when Daphne's fingers reached for her arm, and both Briggs and Nash were now watching her. The phone gave a half ring and then stopped. Lahela exhaled, but it did nothing to loosen the tight band across her shoulders. She stared at the phone, half expecting it to ring again and praying it wouldn't.

Her phone chirped with a new text message. Impulse caused her to swipe open the message. Lahela's breath came out ragged when she saw the photo. It was of her watering her plants on her porch that morning before school.

Another image appeared on the screen, this time a close-up of her arriving at school later that morning. And then another of her at home as she was leaving to come here.

Lahela dropped the phone on the table, and she didn't even try to stop Daphne from grabbing it. Instead, heart racing, she searched the restaurant around her. Someone was watching her. Maybe watching her now.

"What's going on?" Briggs said, scooting his chair closer to her side. He looked across the table. "Daphne?"

Knees trembling, Lahela couldn't shake the feeling that someone was out there, watching her, calling her, and she had no idea who or why they were doing it.

"Lahela." Daphne's voice pulled her attention to her friend.

When they'd first met, Lahela was captivated by the color of Daphne's eyes. They were the same emerald green as the Koʻolau mountainside. And right now, those eyes were brimming with a dark current that was as dangerous as a riptide.

"It's time to go to the police."

FOUR

THE SECOND BRIGGS TURNER saw the unmistakable look of fear flashing in Lahela's brown eyes, his instinct went on alert. "What do you mean, go to the police? What's going on?"

"Lahela, are you in trouble?" Nash's attention was no longer on his birthday gifts. "How can we help you?"

Briggs appreciated the level of concern radiating from his friend, but it wasn't a surprise. In the short time they'd known her, Lahela's friendship felt so natural, like she'd always been a part of their lives. It was one of the reasons Briggs hesitated to ask her out. Their friendship was relatively new, and he didn't want to risk losing it if she wasn't in the same place he was. He may not have known Lahela long, but it only took a few hours with her to see the way her bubbly personality lit up the room. Nearly as bright as her smile. Both were missing in this moment, and it didn't sit well with him.

His eyes searched Lahela's face for an indication of what was going on before sending a pointed message back to Daphne.

"It's okay, Briggs," Lahela said, catching him in the act. She offered him a half smile that was no match for the wattage of a real one. She looked to Daphne, who gave a small nod, before continuing. "I started receiving some weird phone calls from someone who doesn't say anything."

"From who?" His nerves were already firing in the offensive. All he needed was a name and he'd put a stop to it.

"I don't know." Lahela twisted her hands together. "I thought it was someone dialing a wrong number."

"Okay." Briggs leaned his elbows on the table. "Start from the beginning and tell me everything."

"No. We're here to celebrate Nash's birthday dinner." Lahela shook her head and took her cell phone back from Daphne. "This is probably someone's idea of a weird joke." Her voice lacked the confidence of her words as she dropped her cell phone into her purse.

"No, we should talk about these calls."

"And photos," Daphne added.

"Photos?" Briggs practically growled, and it drew startled looks from both ladies. "They sent you photos?"

His imagination was taking him places he did not want to go, places he'd witnessed when he worked with the Dallas Police Department, things he wished he could scrub from his eyes and brain.

Lahela's eyes rounded. "No." Her hand reached over to wrap around his forearm, and his skin instantly reacted to her touch. "Not *those* kinds of photos."

Relief spread through him even as he watched Lahela shudder, likely her mind going to the same place his did.

"They're photos of Lahela"—Daphne held up a hand when his gaze swung to hers—"at school and outside of her house."

Lahela dropped her hands to her lap. "Daph."

"What?" Daphne folded her arms. "This guy is stalking you."

Stalker. A dull throbbing began in the back of his head. He was glad the photos weren't the worst he'd imagined, but this wasn't much better. He didn't know what was driving Lahela's hesitancy, but in his experience, it was better to tread lightly. "Anywhere else?"

Lahela reached for a chip. "Those were the only ones from tonight."

"Tonight?" Nash asked. "How long has this been happening?"

Lahela exchanged a look with Daphne before meeting his eyes. "A while . . . and before you read me the riot act, I did go to the police when it started happening, but without any proof or ideas of who it was, there wasn't much they could do."

Briggs blew out a breath. She wasn't wrong. Stalking cases were some of the most difficult to prosecute, which made them not just frightening for the victim but, if they escalated, often deadly.

"You have no idea who it might be?" Nash asked.

"No," Lahela said quietly.

Briggs wanted to press her on that, but he was interrupted when Fisher Crawford showed up at the table.

"Happy birthday, big man." Fish wrapped an arm around Nash's neck in a playful back hug, his eyes landing on the envelope still sitting in the middle of the table. "Did you like it? If you need someone to—" His eyes moved around the table. "What's with the serious tone? Wait, are they out of tacos? Because I just spent the last two hours helping Mom flip her office upside down looking for Celery only to find the little rodent hiding in the art closet covered in blue paint. Washable paint is only washable when the subject *wants* to be washed. So, if they're out of barbacoa tacos I might throw an adult-sized tantrum."

The magnitude of the interrupted conversation hung between Briggs, Daphne, Lahela, and Nash as they all stared up at the man who looked a little unhinged.

Nash frowned. "Are you saying that you have a *blue* prairie dog?"

"Actually"—Fish flashed his painted palms and fingers at them—"he looks a little green now, but yeah."

Lahela and Daphne burst into laughter. Even Briggs couldn't help but crack a smile as Fish dropped into his chair.

Their laughter slowed when the waitress arrived with a tray of Juana's tacos along with bowls of rice and refried beans, and Fish looked like he wanted to kiss her. He filled his plate, only pausing when he realized he was the only one. A taco hovered in his hands, inches from his first bite, when he glanced around the table again.

"What's wrong with you guys?"

"We should eat before it gets cold." Lahela set a fish taco on her plate. "We can talk about everything else later. It's Nash's birthday. Let's celebrate."

"*Taco* 'bout what?" Fish crunched into his taco and smiled. "See what I did there?"

Briggs loved Fish, but reading a room wasn't where he excelled. He looked over at Lahela, who was pushing her rice around on the plate. It wasn't his place to bring up the calls and texts right now, but he wasn't done discussing it.

AN HOUR AND A HALF LATER and with restrained patience, Briggs had forced himself to eat if only to encourage Lahela to do the same. Nash opened his gifts. They laughed, they talked, they ate tacos, and to anyone seated around them they seemed like a group of friends enjoying a normal night out.

What they wouldn't see was the angst turning Juana's delicious tacos into something tasteless and heavy in his gut. Or the places his mind was taking him as a former police officer. It was enough that when they had finally paid the bill and were walking through the parking lot to their vehicles, he'd

NATALIE WALTERS

kept to Lahela's side and vigilantly surveyed the area. Was the person behind the calls and photos out there watching her now?

"So, you're picking me up tomorrow for the festival?" Lahela asked Daphne when they got to her car.

"Yep." She looked at Briggs and then back to Lahela. "Are you sure you don't want us to go with you to the police station?"

"You already know they can't do anything."

"But you need to report this." Nash slid a look at Briggs, understanding passing between them before he said, "Especially because whoever is calling you has changed their tactics with the photos of you at your work and home."

Lahela's chin tipped down and her features shifted into worry. Nash wasn't trying to scare her, but his job with the FBI gave him the same insight Briggs had into these types of cases. Briggs hated that someone was doing this to her and hated it even more that she wasn't wrong. He'd worked stalking cases, and without any names of possible suspects, there wasn't a lot the police could do, which put her at a disadvantage.

Briggs put a hand on her shoulder. "I agree with Nash."

"Listen, guys, I appreciate your concern, I do. And I'm taking it as seriously as I can, but I know"—she looked at Nash and then Briggs, her eyes lingering on his for a few seconds—"there are a lot bigger crimes that need the attention of the police, and I'm not going to distract them with a potential prank caller."

"We just want you to be safe." Fish hugged Lahela. "You call us anytime you need us. We'll be there for you."

Nash voiced his agreement and then pulled Briggs aside while Daphne and Fish said their goodbyes. "If you can get her to give you a list of potential suspects, I'll do whatever I can from my position."

265

"Thanks, Nash." Briggs fist-bumped his friend. "Happy birthday, man."

When Daphne, Fish, and Nash left for the night, Briggs turned to Lahela. "Listen, I know you don't want to go to the police right now, but I care about you." There was a shift in the way she was watching him. A softness in her gaze that had him remembering what he'd been hoping to do tonight. The timing wasn't right in her vulnerable state, but he did need her to listen to him. "If you get another call or text, you'll go to the police immediately. It's their job. These kinds of cases can become dangerous, and I need you to understand that."

"I do." Her tone wasn't defensive like he expected. It was assenting, and it made him see that she wasn't trying to defer the seriousness of the situation so much as maybe she was trying to assure him she was okay. "Is that all?"

He swallowed and fought back the urge to ask her out right now just so he could spend every second with her and keep her safe. Instead, he reached to her cheek and brushed her hair back behind her ear. "I'd also like to make sure you get home safely."

"I'd appreciate that." Her eyes dipped to his lips and then back up again. "Thank you, Briggs."

Relief swelled through him, fighting for space with the mix of attraction and protection already battling in him. For the first time all night, he thought he saw a glimpse of the emotion that made him believe they shared the same feelings for one another. Any other night, he wouldn't waste another second, but tonight . . . tonight hadn't gone as planned.

FIVE

"YOU HAVE NO IDEA who it might be?"

It wasn't like she hadn't asked herself the same question dozens of times since the calls started, but it was the very last thing she had wanted to focus on tonight while they were celebrating Nash.

Lahela's gaze moved to Briggs's headlights in her rearview mirror. It was hard not to let the guilt ripple through her, but at least her house wasn't far away so Briggs could do his good deed and then be on his way back home.

Any hope she had that Briggs would ask her out disappeared the second she saw his frustrated concern at her decision not to report this latest incident to the police. But he wasn't there the last time she went in and made a report, only to be told they couldn't do anything without a list of people to investigate. When the calls started four months ago, she'd only been living here six months and honestly had no idea who would do this. The police officer was kind and patient, but Lahela couldn't help feeling like she was wasting their time.

Lahela pulled into her driveway and grabbed her purse. Briggs was already parking his truck when she got out of the car and started across her yard to let him know he was fine to go on home. Then her attention snagged on something on her front porch.

Redirecting her steps, she hurried toward her home, not believing what she saw.

"Do you like 'em?"

Lahela turned on her heel to see her neighbor Mr. Dunn coming up her walkway. "Did you do this?"

"I heard you mention to Rosemary you thought this porch was perfect for a swing." He stuffed his hands into his jeans, looking bashful. "'Fraid I'm a bit too old to manage a porch swing, but I saw these at the feed store. All they needed was a good stain and some polish. Figured an old man could do that for his neighbor."

Rocking chairs. Lahela climbed the steps, remembering her conversation with her next-door neighbor. She ran her fingers along the curve of one of the chairs and set it to a gentle rock. "They're beautiful, Mr. Dunn."

"Well, now I'd thought this would at least get you to start calling me Jesse." He joined her on the porch and pulled a rag from his pocket. He ran it over a spot. "I put the last coat of polyurethane on this morning, but that smell should go away soon and be ready to enjoy tomorrow or the next day."

"I don't know what to say."

Lahela had fallen in love with this cottage home the second she drove up the tree-lined street and saw the wide porch. It had been listed as rent-to-own, and she thought it would be the perfect starter home—all it needed was a porch swing and a family.

A pinch of melancholy threatened to steal this moment, but Lahela wouldn't allow it. It didn't matter whether it was a porch swing or beautiful rockers, the thoughtful gift from her elderly neighbor reminded her that she did have family here.

Briggs stepped next to him and shook his hand. "This was thoughtful of you, Mr. Dunn."

"Thank you." Mr. Dunn pushed the rag back into his pocket and swiped a hand through the halo of wispy, white hair. "Well, I guess I better let you young'uns get back to your night." He eyed Briggs, and a paternal look took over that Lahela thought was cute. "If you need anything, I'm just across the street."

"Thank you so much, Mr. Dunn. These are beautiful and I can't wait to invite you over to sit in them with me and tell me more stories about your wife, Janine."

"I'd enjoy that."

Lahela watched Mr. Dunn cross the street and enter his house before she gaped at Briggs. "Can you believe this?"

"They're nice."

There was something off in Briggs's tone, and when she looked back at him, her happy moment faded. If she had hoped Briggs would let her come home and forget about the earlier incident with the calls and texts, the steely look he was giving her now said she was in for another lecture.

"Briggs . . ."

"Lahela."

Why did he have to say her name like that? Low and broody. It made her want to change her mind and invite him in, but it was highly unlikely their conversation would go where her heart wanted it to.

"Thanks for escorting me home." Her attention slid to his hand and the memory of his fingers brushing her cheek. *Be strong, Lahela.* She used her house key to unlock the door and flipped on the inside lights. "I'll see you tomorrow at the festival."

A few seconds passed where only the sound of crickets filled the air. Enough time for her to search his face and see the genuine concern drawing his brows low over his hazel eyes that leaned greener when he was upset. Like they were now.

"I'll be fine, Briggs." She smiled at him. "I've got great neighbors who are always looking out for me."

Briggs's frown deepened, and he looked up and down the quiet neighborhood. "Aren't most of them in their sixties and seventies?"

Her laugh cut through the night, and she covered her mouth. The corner of Briggs's lip lifted, and it made her happy to return to the easy banter they shared.

"Yes," she whispered. "Which makes them bored and the first to call the police if anything is amiss. Just ask Mr. Dunn. Rosemary called the police because she thought he was watering on the wrong day of the week."

Briggs's face split into a grin, and it was the best thing Lahela had seen all night. "Fine. I'll trust the senior citizen brigade for now, but promise me you'll call the police yourself . . . for any reason."

Lahela nodded, surprised at the emotion swelling in her throat. With a wave, she closed the door, bolted it, and then watched Briggs drive away before closing her blinds. She'd always felt safe in her home, but tonight . . . tonight she turned on all the lights and left the television on all night.

SATURDAY MORNING, Lahela woke up with a new focus—and it wasn't going to be on harassing phone calls or texts. Thankfully, her phone remained silent.

Crossing the street, she carried the tray of homemade pumpkin muffins she made for Mr. Dunn to thank him for the beautiful rocking chairs. Waiting for them to bake, she'd dressed up her porch with a wicker table from her back patio and a fake fern because she still hadn't figured out how to keep outdoor plants alive in the Texas heat. She was already imagining nights spent here with the soft glow from the lights strung on the railing. Maybe with Briggs.

"Good morning."

She found Mr. Dunn wiping a soapy sponge over the hood of his wife's car just like he did every Saturday. He looked up, his eyes brightening with his smile. "Good morning, Lahela. You're up early this morning."

"I made you these." She lifted the tray. "To thank you for the beautiful rockers."

"You didn't need to do that." He dropped his sponge into a bucket and wiped his hands on a towel. "Those look delicious."

"I hope you enjoy them."

He grabbed one and bit into it. "Just like my Janine used to make."

Lahela's heart ached for her neighbor. Janine had died almost thirty years ago and yet he'd kept remnants of her around, like her dark-green Volvo, caring for it and protecting it like she was still around to drive it. It was both sweet and sad. And sometimes brought up the painful memories of losing her brother Ikaia.

A cool breeze drifted through the trees and she shivered. This was not where she wanted her thoughts to go on such a beautiful day. After praying last night and again this morning, she was leaning into the truth that God made all things new—including her hope that there was nothing behind the calls.

"Was that your fella?"

Lahela shielded her eyes against the sun. "My fella?"

"Last night."

Oh. Briggs. "We're friends."

"I remember when I was sweet on my Janine. Never could get enough of her, and when we were apart, she's all I thought about." His gaze turned teary, but he offered a smile.

Lahela thought about Briggs. Her cheeks bloomed with a heat that had nothing to do with the above-average temps.

Her cell phone rang and a chill sliced through her. *I'm not going to be afraid of answering my phone.* But her words held no sway over the twisting in her stomach. She turned from Mr. Dunn, pulled her phone from her pocket, and nearly cried out in relief when she saw that it was Daphne.

She took a step to the side and answered. "Hello."

"Hey—what's wrong? You sound funny."

"That's the sound of relief." The back of her eyes burned. Would she ever be able to hear her phone ring without fear pulsing through her?

"You haven't had more calls, have you?"

Lahela inhaled deeply to settle her nerves. "No, thank goodness."

"Good. So, the reason I'm calling . . ." Daphne's voice did that thing where it went high because she was about to say something unlikable, but it was usually reserved for Nash. "I can't come pick you up."

"Oh . . . Okay."

"But . . ." Daphne's tone changed. "Briggs is coming to get you."

"What?" Her raised response pulled Mr. Dunn's gaze to her, and she offered him a smile. "Daph, what did you do?"

"Nothing," she said on a laugh. "Something came up and I'm not going to be able to join you today. That's all."

That didn't feel like *that's all,* and a flight of nervous energy moved through her. Briggs was taking her to the flamingo festival and Daphne wasn't going to be there. *Wait.* "Is Nash meeting us there?"

"Uh, no . . . I think he had something come up too."

"Daph—"

"So, are you dressed and ready?"

Lahela looked down at the jeans and pink sweater she'd chosen for today. With the sun bearing down, she was already wondering if she'd need to change her top. Fall weather in Texas was as unpredictable as second-grade show-and-tell.

"I hope it's something cute because Briggs is already on his way."

"Wha—"

But her question was left unfinished when she spotted the familiar truck coming up the street. A breeze swept through the cottonwoods, sending a fresh batch of leaves swirling through the sky just like the emotion in her chest.

"Have fun and know that I'll be calling you bright and early tomorrow for all of the details."

Lahela might've said something else to Daphne, or maybe it was just incomprehensible noise coming from her lips. It didn't matter because suddenly all she could focus on was Briggs walking over to greet her, in a Stetson.

SIX

BOOTS. Some guys liked a woman in heels, but for Briggs, it was always boots. He tipped his Stetson back a bit to appreciate the way Lahela looked in them. Jeans tucked in, a light pink sweater that highlighted her skin tone, dark hair twisted in a braid with a flower over her left ear. *I owe Daphne big time.*

"Daphne said something came up and asked if I'd pick you up for the festival." Why was his throat so dry? He swallowed, eyes moving for a second to her neighbor before finding her again. "I hope that's all right?"

"Yes, sure. Daphne just called." She turned to her neighbor. "I hope you enjoy those."

"I'm sure I'll have these polished off by noon." He looked over at Briggs, and his features shifted from friendly to something guarded . . . or maybe protective? Fatherly? He remembered what Lahela had said about her neighbors always looking out for her. It was the only reason he'd felt comfortable heading home last night after circling her neighborhood a few times just to make sure there was no one lurking about. "Good to see you again."

"You too, sir." Briggs looked at Lahela. "You ready? I don't want you to miss the great flamingo release."

"I can't wait." Lahela smiled, and unlike last night, it lit up her face, and he was glad to see it return. "Let me grab my purse."

Briggs was struck again by her beauty when she reappeared on her porch. She locked her door and then turned, catching him watching her. "You look really pretty today."

She smiled and surprised him when she grabbed his hand and tugged him toward his truck. "Let's go, Briggs. The flamingos are waiting."

In his years as a police officer, he had busted several drug rings, been involved in multiple car chases, and had a whole host of dangerous assignments, but winning Lahela's heart seemed by far the most challenging.

Today he intended to bust the barriers of the friend zone.

It took ten minutes to drive to downtown Miracle Springs and another ten to follow the line of traffic to the open fields near the Brazos River. He jumped out of his truck and rounded it to get the door for Lahela, which earned him a shy smile.

Last night hadn't gone how he hoped, but he woke up this morning with a new hope. Give Lahela the best day and gather the courage to put his heart on the line. And possibly their friendship.

"This is the craziest thing I've ever seen." Lahela accepted his hand as he helped her out of his truck. "There's so much . . . pink."

The touch of her hand in his didn't last more than a few seconds, but man, he liked the feel of her skin against his. Her fingers were soft and smooth, such a contrast to his calloused ones.

Around them citizens of Miracle Springs and plenty of tourists from the Central Texas area were wearing pink shirts, pink boas, and hats that looked like flamingos sitting on their heads. A few dedicated fans were lounging along the banks of the river in those giant, inflatable pool flamingos.

"There's even a carnival?" Lahela clapped her hands. "I had no idea it was going to be this big."

"You know what they say about Texas." Briggs walked her through the park where local craft vendors, game booths, food trailers selling fried everything, and carnival rides had been set up. "So you know the story then?"

"Only what I've looked up on the internet," Lahela said as they weaved through the crowd. The cloudless sky, moderate temps, and yearly anticipation felt like it had lured the entire city here. "A flamingo named Pink Floyd escaped a zoo in Denver and flew to Texas where he's regularly spotted in Galveston or here in Miracle Springs."

"One time." Briggs joined a line near the suspension bridge crossing the Brazos. "Pink Floyd was spotted here, confirmed by his tag, but no other sighting has ever been validated by wildlife experts. I'm pretty sure he sticks to the Texas beaches, but it doesn't stop people here claiming they see him from time to time. Our last mayor was looking for a way to ramp up tourism and decided to lean into all the false sightings and create this."

Lahela watched as a group of college-aged kids wearing flamingo sunglasses, two of the males shirtless and painted pink, left the line and headed to the river. She smiled widely at Briggs. "I love it!"

He stepped up to the table and paid for two rubber pink flamingos. "Now let's go dress up our flamingos."

"What?"

"Pink Floyd's festival has grown." He gestured to the crowd. "But more than the traffic headaches it brings in is the money donated to support various local charities." He walked her to another table filled with tiny hats, sunglasses, and clothes. "This year it's for children's literacy."

"Our school librarian, Mrs. Bell, mentioned that, in between laughing at me for thinking this was a concert for the band."

Briggs covered his own laugh after she narrowed her eyes at him, but the playfulness dancing in them thrilled him. "Okay, now what do you want your flamingo to wear so you can spot him in the river?"

"Her." Lahela picked up a tiny crown of daisies. "My flamingo's a girl and I think I'll name her Daisy."

Briggs selected a cowboy hat and paid the girl behind the table. Another girl took their flamingos to another table to attach the accessories with super glue. Lahela watched, her expression bright and full of the life he'd watched drain from it last night. He'd be lying if he said a part of him wasn't dying to bring up the calls and texts, but Daphne made him promise not to discuss it unless Lahela did first. He wanted to respect Lahela's boundaries and would, of course, but he couldn't just turn off the instinct or experience he carried with him from his time as a police officer. And it didn't prevent him from subtly scanning the area for anything suspicious.

"Oh, they're so cute!" Lahela accepted her flamingo, Daisy, and his cowboy flamingo, holding them up for him to see. "Do we have time to take a photo of them before the release?"

"If we hurry." The speakers overhead were already encouraging everyone to deliver their flamingos to the race line, which was a quarter mile up the river.

They found a grassy spot near some trees, and Lahela set their flamingos on the ground and started to pull out her cell phone before hesitating. Not long, maybe a fraction of a second, but enough that it pushed his gaze to the subtle worry in her eyes. That instinct to talk to her about the calls returned, but it was interrupted when Lahela took hold of his hand.

She handed him his cowboy flamingo and then squeezed in next to him, positioning them so the river was behind them. "Say 'Pink Floyd.'"

He obeyed and smiled at the camera, his eyes captivated

by the image of them together. *This.* This was what he was wanting—hoping for. *So what am I waiting for?*

It wasn't that he'd had a bad experience with women he dated before. All of them were sweet, kind, and fun. But none made him see a future with them. Lahela . . . she was different. It was the potential hurt that worried him. Not his, though he'd be crushed if it didn't work out, but it was the pain he'd witnessed in Lahela when her ex broke her heart. He wouldn't do that to her.

"There's no way we're going to be able to track our flamingos." Lahela's laugh pulled his attention to a giant net where thousands of small, rubber flamingos were hanging over the river. "How will we know if we win?"

"Just like Pink Floyd, our flamingos are tagged." He showed her the number on the bottom of their flamingos.

"Cool. Well, Daisy, it's been nice knowing you." She lifted his cowboy flamingo and looked it in the wide, rubber eyes. "You take good care of her, Cowboy."

Lahela's words to a toy flamingo somehow claimed a space in his chest. *"You take good care of her, Cowboy."* It was a charge he was going to take personally, whether he won Lahela's heart or not.

SEVEN

IT WAS THE STUFF of Hallmark movies. From the top of the Ferris wheel, Lahela had a bird's-eye view of downtown Miracle Springs and the festival below. That is, if she wasn't sneaking peeks at Briggs sitting next to her. Or thinking that with his right arm stretched behind her, she'd only need to scoot a little to her left and she could tuck herself into his side.

It surprised her how much that's where she wanted to be . . . almost as much as the anxiousness that had her doubting Daphne's assertion that Briggs might like her as more than friends. If he did, why hadn't he asked her out yet?

The ride slowed to a stop at the platform and the ride attendant let them out. Briggs reached for her hand to help her out. Good manners, that's all. Yet, his fingers lingered around hers as they walked back into the crowd still enjoying the day.

"Would you like to go for a walk along the river?" Briggs's voice, impossibly deep but somehow tender, sent an undercurrent of excitement charging through her. "Or we can go, if you're ready?"

"No." She squeezed his hand. "I'm not ready to leave yet."

Briggs's lips tipped up at the edges, and with a nod, he walked her to the river's edge.

Lahela's heart thumped a little heavier behind her rib cage.

Why was something so simple as hand-holding enough to drive up the level of attraction? It didn't just make her feel wanted but also protected.

"Are you having a good time?"

Lahela watched a family on bikes ride past them. The park on the other side of the trail was filled with people enjoying the day. Carefree smiles, laughter, and squeals of delight from the kids on the rides filled the air. Briggs's thumb brushed across the top of her knuckles and a burst of sweet contentment rushed through her. "The best time."

"How about I go get us something to drink? Lemonade? Sweet tea? Soda?"

"I'd love some lemonade."

Briggs tipped his Stetson and it made her smile. "Two lemonades coming up."

"And I'll find us somewhere to sit." Lahela eyed the mostly full picnic tables around them. She pointed to a spot beneath a large cottonwood tree. "What about over there?"

"Perfect."

Their eyes lingered for a few seconds before he backed up, and Lahela couldn't help the wide smile filling her face as she started for their spot. *Their spot.* She could get lost in those hazel eyes.

"Ms. Young!"

She turned and recognized the towheaded boy running across the grass toward her and two more of her students running behind him.

"Samson!" He stopped short of crashing into her. Lahela's smile moved to the sibling pair. "You guys having fun?"

"Yes!" Ginny Allen gave her a gap-toothed smile. "My flamingo escaped."

"Mine too," her twin brother, Hudson, said. He waved Lahela closer and cupped his hands near his mouth. "Mom said that so Ginny would stop crying."

"I didn't cry," Ginny protested and gave her brother a shove.

"Okay, well . . ." Lahela knelt to get to their eye level. "Just think of all the new friends Pink Floyd has now."

Lahela's cell phone rang in her purse, and her smile tightened for a second until she remembered Briggs was getting their drinks and maybe had a question. She pulled her phone out and the hope that it was Briggs vanished.

"Are you going to answer that?" Hudson asked.

"Yeah, um, no." She declined the call and was about to drop her phone back in her purse when she got the notification of an incoming text. She swiped it open, then regretted her action immediately.

It was more photos like last night. A photo of her outside her house carrying the muffins to Mr. Dunn. Unable to stop herself, she swiped to the next photo. Her and Briggs with their flamingos by the river. Them on the Ferris wheel. Her breathing turned shallow at the last one of her with Samson, Hudson, and Ginny from seconds ago.

Her gaze shot up, protectiveness surging through her as she stepped closer to her students. They were chattering about something, but she couldn't make sense of it over the buzzing in her ears.

"Where are your parents?"

"Sitting over there." Hudson pointed to a picnic table near the food vendors. "Samson came with us."

"Okay. How about we head over there."

Lahela walked them that direction, her eyes stopping on every person holding a cell phone up. She fought for any sign of recognition or at least some kind of awareness that they might be watching her. It wasn't so much fear as it was anger pulsing hot beneath her skin.

Whoever was doing this to her had crossed the line. Harassing her was one thing, but taking photos of her students?

She wasn't going to let them get away with that. As soon as she found Briggs, she'd talk to him about going to the police station and filing a report.

"Why are we walking so fast?" Ginny asked, her freckled cheeks flushed.

"Sorry, sweetie." Lahela took hold of her hand but didn't slow down. Should she tell their parents about the photo? Guilt ripped through her. *I should've listened to Briggs. I should've reported this last night.* But would that have stopped whoever it was?

Mrs. Allen rose from her seat and waved. Lahela forced a smile to her lips and hoped she didn't look as freaked-out as she was feeling on the inside. Where was Briggs? He'd know what to do.

"Hey, Lahela."

She paused, looking over her shoulder at the familiar but unexpected voice of her ex, Trevor West. Once upon a time the sight of him thrilled her, but it was dread coiling inside of her now. What was he doing here?

Lahela shifted her attention back to the kids. "Go back to your mom, kiddos. I'll see you on Monday."

All three kids skipped off, unaware of the tremor in her voice. She searched the area again for Briggs.

"You look nice." His hand wrapped around Lahela's arm, and she twisted herself away from his light grip. "Real nice."

He was holding one of those tall plastic cups some of the vendors sold, filled with colorful blends of alcohol. In the time they spent dating, she'd never witnessed him drunk, but from the slight glaze to his eyes, he was well on his way.

"I've missed you." Trevor took an unbalanced step toward her. "I'm glad I found you here."

An unsettling feeling shot through her. *Found her?* What did that mean? Her mind went to the photos on her phone and a sudden realization turned her blood cold. Was Trevor behind the calls, texts, and photos? She started to step back, but Trevor caught her arm again and pressed in close to her.

"We were good together." His foul breath was hot against her skin. "Why did you have to end it?"

Lahela reared her head back and tugged her arm free again. "What are you talking about? You broke up with me!"

Trevor looked confused. "Me?"

"I need to go." She twisted on the heel of her boot and made her way through the crowd. The adrenaline was making her sweat and she felt nauseous. She needed to get away from Trevor and find Briggs. Her first thought was to go over to where Mrs. Allen was sitting with her kids, but if Trevor was behind the calls and photos, she wasn't going to put him anywhere near her students.

"Hey, wait up." Trevor followed. "Let's just talk."

She hooked a right around a corn dog stand and came to an abrupt stop. An ice machine blocked her from escaping and forced her to face Trevor again.

"Look, Lahela" —he began backing her into the tight space—"I know you want to talk about—"

Whatever Trevor was about to say was cut off with a yelp when a hand yanked him backward. The sudden movement sent Trevor's bright pink drink flying out of his hand and across the grass. Briggs had Trevor's shirt twisted in his hand and the darkest look she'd ever seen locked on Trevor.

"What're you doing, man?"

"I could ask the same of you," Briggs growled. His gaze shifted to Lahela, searching hers. "Are you okay?"

"Y-yes."

The commotion had garnered some attention, and Lahela recognized one of Trevor's friends—she couldn't remember his name—walking over. Was he drunk too? Would he try to start a fight with Briggs?

Lahela stepped forward. "I'm okay, Briggs." She put a hand

on his arm, and the touch was enough to make her believe her own words. "Let him go."

"Yeah," Trevor seethed. "Let me go."

"Wait." Lahela eyed him. "Where's your cell phone?"

Trevor smiled at Briggs like he'd won. "In my back pocket."

"Let me see it."

Trevor reached around, retrieved his phone, and handed it to Lahela. She held the phone up to his face so it would unlock and then opened his messages.

"Hey, what are you doing?" Trevor grabbed for his phone, but Briggs blocked him. "You can't go through my messages."

A quick glimpse and Lahela didn't see what she was looking for. She wasn't sure if she should feel relieved or bothered by the fact that Trevor hadn't sent her the message with the photos.

"What's going on over here?" Trevor's friend arrived.

Lahela reached for Briggs's arm. "Let him go."

"I think I might escort him to the PD for a little chat."

"For what?" Trevor nearly screeched. "I didn't do anything, just ask her."

Briggs's gaze slid to hers again, and she gave a subtle shake of her head.

"He's just drunk, man. Had a bad week." The friend took Trevor by the arm. "I'll take him home."

Trevor did look a little different, but she couldn't quite identify what it was. Whatever had turned him into this must've been bad. Regardless, it wasn't her place to figure it out, because she had basically eliminated the only person who she'd thought might be behind the calls and texts. And that meant there was someone else—watching.

EIGHT

AS BRIGGS DROVE away from the police department, his knuckles tightened over the steering wheel. Lahela had filed another report and that should've made him feel better, but he was still reeling over what happened.

He'd seen Lahela with her students and decided to grab a stupid bag of kettle corn, thinking maybe they could linger a little longer in the park. He wasn't ready for their day to end just yet, but when he'd turned around, she was gone. The panic set in, and he had discarded their snacks in search of where she went. Motion from the corner of his eye had him turning to find her being backed into a corner. Even from a distance, he identified the alarm in her expression, and his fists were ready for a fight. "You're sure it's not him?"

"I looked at his phone, Briggs." She ran her hands down her jeans. "I didn't see any messages to my number."

"He might've used a different phone."

"Officer Sandberg said they'll talk to Trevor." She exhaled. "But unless there's some kind of evidence . . ."

"There's not a lot we can do."

Briggs wanted to be upset with the officer's response, but how could he? Hadn't he said similar things to other victims of stalking who made reports? He'd encouraged them to file an Order of Protection, but even if a judge were to grant them that piece of paper, it wasn't enough to stop someone who was obsessed.

He throttled the steering wheel again. The images of the photos on Lahela's phone flashed through his mind as he drove up her street. His gaze sharpened on the houses, the cars driving by, and anyone out in their yard like he expected to see someone watching them.

The photo of her with her students was especially disturbing, but at least she'd been in public. His experience told him most stalkers wouldn't try anything around other people, but he still had his doubts about Trevor. And his concern was leaving Lahela at home alone. Maybe he could just park outside her house and keep an eye on things.

"Would you like to stay for a while?"

Briggs pulled into the driveway behind Lahela's car and cut the engine. "I wouldn't mind that at all."

Her smile returned, but it wasn't the same as earlier that day. "I don't have kettle corn, but I can make us some popcorn and POG juice. Maybe we could watch a college football game?"

"POG juice?"

"Papaya, orange, and guava juice. My parents sent me some packets from Hawai'i." But she eyed him with a flash of amusement. "Only in Texas would a guy not blink twice at a girl's offer to watch football."

"Football is a way of life here."

THE INSIDE OF LAHELA'S HOUSE was cheerful and bright. The cottage home had original oak floors and white shiplap walls. Lahela used throw pillows and artwork to add pops of color. *And plants.* Briggs had never seen so many plants tucked into corners, near windows, hanging on the walls. It felt lush and like the space was full of life.

"Sorry for the mess." Lahela picked up a sweater from the back of a dining room chair and collected math pages it looked like she'd been grading. Nothing Briggs would consider a mess at all. "The remote's on the coffee table."

Briggs turned on the TV and left it on the first game he could find before he joined Lahela back in her kitchen. He admired the natural way she moved about her home, taking command of the space, so different from the hesitant version only moments ago. It pulled at something deep within him.

"So, football isn't big in Hawai'i?"

Lahela set two glasses of a pinkish-orange juice on the peninsula between them. "It is but mostly between rival high schools, and most of the really good players leave the islands to play for colleges on the mainland."

Briggs was about to ask if her brother played football, but an acrid smell filled the air like something was . . . burning.

"The popcorn!" Lahela rushed to the microwave and pulled out the half-popped bag.

The gray smoke clouding the room wasn't coming from the popcorn. Briggs pivoted toward the living room. Through the large picture window behind Lahela's couch, he saw orange flames dancing with black smoke on her front porch.

"Lahela, get out of the house!"

"What?"

He reached for her hand and pulled her to the back sliding glass door. That's when she saw the flames on her porch.

"No!" Instinct or shock stopped her movement, her eyes widening in horror.

"Come on." Briggs tightened his hand around hers. He already had his cell phone out and was dialing 911. "We need to get out of the house."

Outside, Lahela pulled away and ran around to the front of

her home. She gasped, covering her mouth, her eyes glued to the fire engulfing her new rocking chairs.

A flash of movement sped around him, and Lahela cried out as her neighbor charged up the steps with a fire extinguisher.

"Mr. Dunn, stop!"

The old man either didn't hear her or ignored her as he kept spraying the flames, but the extinguisher wasn't enough.

"Stay here." Briggs handed her his phone and ran up the porch steps just as Mr. Dunn tossed aside the extinguisher and reached for a burning rocker with his bare hands.

"Mr. Dunn!"

Briggs tried to stop him, but Mr. Dunn's hand was already deep into the flames as he tried to grab for the chair. He yelped and pulled back, sending the chair tipping to its side with a crash.

The black smoke was thick and the fumes were choking him, but Briggs took hold of the man's shoulder and yanked him back down to the lawn. Anger flashed bright in Mr. Dunn's eyes before resignation filled them as he stared at the flames consuming the rocking chairs.

Lahela rushed to their side with tears streaming down her face and fear blazing in her eyes. This didn't feel like an accident.

NINE

"IT HAS TO BE an accident, Briggs." Lahela's voice raked over the emotion that had been building in her throat since she watched her poor neighbor get taken away in an ambulance. He assured her he was just fine, but the EMTs wanted to take him in to be sure. "Mr. Dunn said—"

"I know what he said." Briggs looked over at her. His expression was a mix of concern and frustration that softened once more, making her think he wanted to pull her in and wrap his arms around her. She wished he would. But instead, he ran one hand through his hair and the other moved to his hip. His attention shifted to the firefighters on her porch. "I'm sure they'll let us know."

"Excuse me, Ms. Young." Officer Blair, the police officer Lahela had spoken to minutes ago, reappeared at her side. "I talked with Captain Riser from the fire department, and the earliest he can get an arson investigator here is tomorrow. Will that work?"

"Sure, yeah." *Arson.* She rubbed her arms, but it did nothing to remove the goose bumps. While firefighters worked to extinguish the flames, Captain Riser approached and began asking her questions she couldn't answer about the fire, despite Mr. Dunn's claim of responsibility.

"So you think it's arson?"

Briggs's question snapped her focus back to Officer Blair, but he only gave an apologetic shrug. He wasn't the same officer she'd spoken to at the police station, which meant she'd had to explain the calls, photos, and what happened earlier with Trevor all over again.

"Until we get the report from the investigator, we won't know," Officer Blair said. "If it turns out to be arson, it'll bump your case up as a priority."

Briggs's posture stiffened next to her. He was growing increasingly agitated, and it made her feel even worse than she already did. "And what about finding out where Trevor West is? Is someone from the department making that a priority?"

Officer Blair gave Briggs a look that could be interpreted as annoyed tolerance. "We have the information and will look into anyone who might be involved."

Lahela stared at the charred remains of the beautiful rocking chairs. She hadn't even gotten a chance to enjoy them once. And not only were they destroyed, but her porch was charred and the rest of her plants and decor were marred ash.

Neighbors had gathered around the perimeter of her property to watch the commotion. Most were retired, and some elderly, like Rosemary. She stood on the porch in her robe with the red and blue lights of the fire truck flashing against her skin. What if they hadn't stopped the fire in time? What if a gust of wind sent the flames in the direction of Rosemary's house? She was close to eighty and didn't move fast . . . Lahela's throat burned.

"Why?" She looked between Briggs and the officer. "If this is arson and if it's related to the calls and photos, why would they suddenly do something so . . ." Devastating? Dangerous? Criminal? The right word failed her. "I don't understand why."

Officer Blair didn't look very old, maybe in his forties, but he had the weary expression of experience. "Sometimes the stalker will escalate their intentions if they don't get the attention they're after. We'll be posting a police officer here until the investigator arrives and finishes their job, but I think it might be a good idea for you to stay with someone else until we have some more answers."

Lahela's stomach twisted with guilt. As scared as she was, she couldn't burden her friends. She'd dip into her meager savings and get a hotel if she had to.

"Daphne's already on her way." Briggs fixed his attention on her. "You're going to stay at her place until this gets resolved."

Even if she'd wanted to argue, the energy to do so slipped away the second his hand moved to the small of her back. Emotion—or maybe the acrid smoke she inhaled—scratched at her throat, and immediately she wanted to fold herself into his arms and pretend like all of this was a terrible dream.

Officer Blair took her silence as an answer and handed her his business card with the report number on it. He said something else, and Lahela heard Briggs answer, but the words were nothing more than a muffled sound in her ears.

How had the day gone from so wonderful to this?

If this wasn't an accident . . . Was Officer Blair right? Was the person behind the calls escalating their efforts? Her eyes moved from the damage on her porch to her innocent neighbors. *Mr. Dunn.* She could still hear his frantic apologies assuming the fire was his fault. He'd come racing over to protect her, but what if he'd seen the person who started it and tried to stop them?

A chill spread across her skin and she rubbed against her arms again, but her hands were shaking and the fear swirling inside her threatened to steal her breath.

"Lahela." Briggs's strong arms wrapped around her. He pulled her against his chest, and she melted into the warmth like it was a security blanket. His steady voice spoke into her ear. "Slow, deep breaths."

She tried, but the vise around her chest just seemed to tighten. Tears burned the back of her eyes, and embarrassment flashed hot in her cheeks. *Breathe. You can't fall apart.*

With great effort, she peeled herself away from Briggs and felt the void of his protectiveness immediately. His hand still lingered on her back, his thumb rubbing a soothing track back and forth that helped her keep time with the breaths she had to think to take.

"Are you okay?"

"I don't know." The words slipped out honestly, and when Briggs's hazel eyes darkened with concern, she wanted to take them back. "I'm fine. I mean"—she scrambled for her thoughts to make sense—"I'm just sorry all of this is happening."

Briggs had her back in his arms again, his breath warm against her forehead. "Why are you apologizing? None of this is your fault."

"Mr. Dunn's in the hospital, Briggs." Her voice warbled against his shirt. "My porch looks like a bonfire was set on it, and tomorrow an arson investigator is going to tell me if someone did it on purpose."

"Mr. Dunn's going to be all right." Briggs held her tighter as his voice rumbled through his chest. "The paramedic said the burns look superficial." That should've made her feel better, but all she could think about was what if it had been worse? "And I've heard fire investigators are pretty cool. Maybe they have a sticker?"

Lahela couldn't help but smile. She knew what he was doing and it eased her anxiety. Lifting her head from his chest, she met his eyes. Even though the timing was the worst, the tension began shifting from fear to something else entirely.

The sound of a car door closing jerked her attention to the figure jogging around Briggs's truck. Lahela stepped back and out of Briggs's embrace, feeling the disappointment she saw in his face.

"Lahela!" Daphne jogged across the yard. "Are you okay?"

"I'm fine." This time she half believed it as she returned her friend's hug.

"Briggs?"

"All good."

Daphne hugged him and then looked at the house. "Do they know what happened?"

"Not yet," Briggs said.

"Mr. Dunn thinks he may have used too much polyurethane on the rocking chairs he gave me." Lahela ignored the look she felt coming from Briggs. Until it was proven otherwise, she could only hope this was a freak accident. "Captain Riser said it was possible with the heat it could be spontaneous ignition."

"Spontaneous ignition?" Daphne asked.

"Under the right conditions there are some chemicals that can ignite on their own," Briggs answered. "But they haven't ruled out arson. They're bringing in an investigator."

Daphne's brows scrunched together, and familiar worry creased the edges of her green eyes. She turned them on Lahela. "Maybe it's time you call Ke—"

"Absolutely not." Lahela cut her off. "I've already spoken to the police *twice* tonight and we don't know this wasn't an accident." She put as much conviction in her words as she could, even as she saw Daphne and Briggs exchange a look that said they didn't believe her. It didn't matter though. Kekoa was already busy with his job, and she wouldn't involve him in her problems. *I've already burdened too many people.*

"I'm just saying it wouldn't hurt to have Kekoa's expertise on the matter."

"Daphne, please." Lahela's voice cracked and Briggs started to reach for her, but she took a step back. Her focus remained on Daphne. She was the only one who really knew her brother and what he did for a living. And she wasn't wrong. One call to

Kekoa and it wouldn't take him long to find answers. *So, why am I not asking him for help?* That same question lingered in Daphne's confused expression. "He's working on a big case." Probably not a lie. "And if the investigator determines the fire was—" She didn't want to say the word. "*If* it's not an accident, then I will call Kekoa if necessary."

A tense second passed between them before Daphne smiled gently, wrapping an arm around Lahela's waist. "Okay."

Relief tried to fight its way through the stress coiled tightly around every muscle in her body, but it was a lost cause. She wasn't going to call her brother, because if she did, it meant she'd have to admit she needed help and it wasn't the kind Daphne or Briggs might think—it was the kind that would take her back home to Hawai'i.

TEN

EVERYTHING WAS different now. Lahela sat in her parked car looking at the home that once made her feel welcomed and safe. A home that she'd believed was full of promises and potential.

Now . . . all she saw was the fire and fear. Oh, and the police officer standing watch over the possible crime scene.

When the nightmares wouldn't let her sleep, she had sat up in bed and began grading papers and working on this week's teaching schedule. By six, she couldn't take it anymore and decided to get up, shower, and get ready for church even though she attended the late service at eleven.

The conversation with Captain Riser last night had her feeling restless. He seemed skeptical about Mr. Dunn's theory of spontaneous ignition and mentioned the possibility of an electrical fire caused by the string lights on the railing, but there was something in his explanation that told her he wasn't buying that theory either.

Emotion burned the back of her eyes. How had her life become so . . . chaotic? Ever since her little brother died, everything in life just felt harder. Like she was always holding her breath, waiting for the next wave to roll and toss her in the ocean of life.

Movement caught her attention, and she spotted Mr. Dunn walking across the street toward her. Lahela picked up her guilt offerings and got out of her car.

"Oh, Mr. Dunn, how are your hands?" It was a silly question when she saw the bandage wrapped around his left hand and the angry red marks on his right forearm. Nope. The Shipleys' donuts and coffee weren't going to be enough to ease the guilt that had been haunting her all night. "Mr. Dunn, I'm so, so sorry."

"What are you apologizing for? This wasn't your fault." The words were a familiar echo of Briggs's from the night before, but they didn't squelch the ache in her chest that *yes, this might very well be my fault.* "I saw the flames and came to warn you, but then . . ." Mr. Dunn's teary gaze moved to what was left of his gift to her. "I thought maybe if I could put the fire out . . . I wish I'd been able to get here sooner."

Lahela's heart twisted inside her chest. *This is my fault.* And no apology or glazed donuts were going to make it better, but she didn't know what else to do. "I wasn't sure how you'd be feeling this morning, so I brought you breakfast."

"You didn't have to do that."

"Should we go to your porch?" Her own porch looked so empty and sad now. Even though she'd had the rockers there for only a day, they had filled the space in a way that made it feel like home.

At his porch, they sat on two chairs, and she set the bag of donuts on a small table but paused when she held out his coffee. "Can you hold this?"

"My right hand isn't so bad." But he couldn't hide the slight wince when he took the coffee from her. "I'm sorry you were forced out of your home. Is the damage bad?"

"Captain Riser said it could've been worse." Lahela felt bad for saying so when she looked at the wounds on Mr. Dunn's hands. "He's got an arson investigator coming over sometime today to determine the cause of the fire."

Mr. Dunn's eyes widened. "An investigator?"

Lahela didn't want to go into all the details behind the suspicion. No reason to freak her neighbor out more than necessary. "Yes, and they might come by here to talk to you, is that okay?"

"Yes, of course." He set the coffee on the table. "Lahela, I will pay for all of the damage."

"Oh, no, that's not what this is about." She sat forward on the chair. "They're doing their job. If this was an accident"—she prayed it was—"my insurance will cover everything."

Mr. Dunn looked ready to argue, but the happy trilling noise coming from her cell phone stopped him. Last night, when she couldn't sleep, she gave all her contacts a special ringtone, so she'd know it was them calling. She silenced Daphne's call before sending a quick text that she was okay and would see her soon.

"You don't want to answer that?"

"No, it's my friend checking on me." She rose to her feet. "We're meeting up at church."

"Are you coming back?"

Mr. Dunn's question felt like he knew where her thoughts had gone. She glanced over at her sweet house. It appeared as lonely as she felt inside. "I hope to, but . . ."

"You don't have to be scared, Lahela." Mr. Dunn looked around the neighborhood. "We take care of our own. Rosemary was at my door first thing this morning, concerned about you. She's probably already forming a neighborhood watch team. We'll make sure nothing like this happens to you again."

"I appreciate that, Mr. Dunn, but the last thing I want is for anyone else to get hurt."

"We feel the same way about you." His lips pressed together for a second and his eyes turned glassy again. "In case you haven't noticed, we're not a bunch of spring chickens. It's

been nice having someone not collecting social security living here. You're like our daughter and we want to make sure
you feel safe."

Lahela blinked back tears. "Thank you, Mr. Dunn."

Homesickness set in as she drove away from her neighborhood. Many of her neighbors had first welcomed her
with baked goods, tips about Miracle Springs—including a
little gossip—and always waved whenever they saw her. She
didn't want to leave them, but if Mr. Dunn or anyone else was
harmed again because of her . . . she'd never recover from
the weight of it all.

ELEVEN

EYES—GUARDED. Smile—forced. Posture—uncomfortable.

Briggs didn't need years of working as a police officer to interpret Lahela's countenance while sitting in church. Two things kept him seated away from her at the back of the church: First, she was safe sitting with Daphne and her family, which included her father, Jack Crawford, a former Texas Ranger. And second, from his position he could watch for anyone paying extra attention to Lahela.

Or rather, unusual attention. Lahela had a magnetism that drew others to her—even if no one else but him could see how hard she was trying to appear like her normally bright self. The second the service ended, he made a beeline to her and invited her to lunch at a nearby café.

BRIGGS EYED Lahela's untouched ham sandwich. "Is your sandwich okay?"

"Yeah, I guess I'm not that hungry." She glanced at his own half-eaten turkey club. "You either?"

"Not really."

She tucked her hair behind her ear and her gaze slipped

away from his. "I'm sorry, I probably shouldn't have ordered anything."

"Lahela, please stop apologizing. I'd buy you a thousand uneaten sandwiches if it means sitting here with you."

Uneaten sandwiches? Had he really just said that? *Who buys eaten sandwiches, Briggs?* A burst of bubbly laughter from Lahela pulled him from his self-deprecation. Her smile reached to the corners of her eyes as she continued to laugh, no doubt realizing what he'd just said.

Since Trevor had shown up on Saturday, this was the first glimpse of the old Lahela he'd seen, and he wanted to do whatever it took to be the one who kept her smiling and laughing—even at his expense.

The attempt to keep her smiling was interrupted by a phone call from Nash. "Hey, man. I'm out with Lahela now."

"A date? It's about time," Nash practically yelled into his ear. From the smile playing on Lahela's face, she'd heard him. "Have you confessed all your feelings for—"

"I'll call you later." Cheeks flaming, Briggs silenced his phone. "Sorry about that."

"Nash needs to work on his indoor voice." She winked and then her playful tone shifted, brown eyes searching his face. "So, is this a date?"

"No."

Her face instantly flashed with hurt, and he stretched his hand across the table, taking hold of hers.

"*If* this was a date, it would be our first, and I have plans that don't include us staring at uneaten sandwiches in a noisy café."

Her eyes locked on his and filled with something that looked very much like hope. "Oh yeah? Where would it be?" She lifted a brow. "*If* it was our first date?"

He didn't have to think hard because he'd been planning this date in his head for months. *And all the dates after that.*

His cheeks burned again. "On our first date"—*not if,* he hoped she caught that—"I'd take you—"

Lahela's cell phone rang, startling her so much she jerked her hand from his. There was no mistaking the fear in her eyes. She cautiously flipped her phone over so she could read the screen and her shoulders relaxed a smidge, but her expression was full of anxiety when she looked up at him. "It's the police."

He nodded, expecting her to step away to answer the call, but instead she answered and put it on speaker.

"Hello?"

"May I speak to Lahela Young?"

"Speaking."

"Hello, Ms. Young, this is Officer Sandberg. I took your report yesterday."

"Yes, I remember." Lahela sounded as anxious as Briggs was feeling. He opened his hand to her and she slipped hers into his. "I'm here with my friend Briggs Turner. Do you have any news?"

"Yes, ma'am. Officer Blair spoke to a few of your neighbors to see if they saw anything suspicious." Lahela's grip tightened on his. "Mrs. Rosemary Truitt has a doorbell camera, and Officer Blair pulled video from around the time you arrived at your home to just before the fire started. There was a vehicle that drove by Mrs. Truitt's property twice before parking for a few minutes and then leaving. We couldn't get a license plate number, but the make, model, and description of the vehicle are a match for Trevor West."

Lahela's hand flew to her mouth, barely blocking her gasp. Her body stiffened even as she shook her head like she didn't believe it.

Anger pulsed through Briggs and he got up, moving to her side. Why hadn't he insisted Officer Sandberg find Trevor and pull him in for questioning? Lahela may not have seen the calls on his phone, but that didn't mean anything, considering this information. It wouldn't be the first time a stalker used a burner phone to antagonize their victim.

He reined in his emotions and focused on his next question. "So the fire *was* arson?"

"According to Investigator Sinclair, the origin of the fire started at the rocking chair, but she ruled out all spontaneous ignition and has sent the evidence to the labs. It'll take a few weeks, but she's classified the fire as arson, yes."

Lahela leaned into Briggs's side and he could feel her shaking.

"Ms. Young, we have officers bringing Trevor West in for questioning, and if we find out he's responsible, we'll have enough for you to file a protective order against him."

TWELVE

"TREVOR WEST did not set the fire, and no evidence was found on his phone that he's called or sent you messages or photos. We have no evidence."

Lahela pressed the stapler against the bulletin board and pinched the skin of her finger. *Ouch.* She'd come to school early this morning to distract herself from Officer Sandberg's explanation about why her ex-boyfriend wasn't being charged and why she wouldn't be able to file a protection order against him.

It wasn't him.

Trevor admitted he came by her house Saturday night only to apologize after what happened at the festival. According to him, he chickened out when he saw Briggs's truck and left, and he denied starting the fire.

But someone did start the fire.

She spent another sleepless night at Daphne's, pacing the floor until it woke up her friend. Daphne was an Army medic and working unusual hours while her unit was in the field for a training exercise. Lahela wasn't going to impose on her a second longer, and since the investigator was done, there was no reason why she couldn't move back home.

Home. Her gaze moved to the posters of Hawai'i on the

walls of her classroom. She'd taken so much effort decorating the space with bright, tropical colors, and decor like plumerias, palm tree fronds, a volcano where new spelling words flowed in the lava. She told her kids it was so they would learn to *lava* learning, and they embraced it with enthusiasm, using the term any time they enjoyed a subject she was teaching.

Ms. Young, I lava reading about butterflies. Ms. Young, I lava'd PE today, we played basketball. Ms. Young, I lava Hawai'i, can you tell me about the ocean?

Lahela lava'd her students, and walking into the classroom each morning reminded her that not everything about her decision to move to Texas was bad. But after all that had happened this weekend, she wasn't so sure anymore.

And that led her to look up the price of flights back to O'ahu and what an apartment would cost. Living on the islands wasn't cheap, and moving her whole life back there would cost her money she didn't have.

"So, I guess we're not meeting for Mocha Mondays anymore?"

Lahela turned at the clipped tone behind her and found Nancy standing there with two to-go cups of coffee, looking hurt. She'd completely forgotten about their standing coffee date. "Oh, Nancy, I'm so sorry."

Nancy set one of the cups down on Lahela's desk. "I brought this back since I was already there."

Guilt riddled her for letting her friend down. Again. "You didn't have to do that, but thank you."

"I know." Nancy's tone came out sharp, but then her shoulders relaxed. "But I figured there had to be a reason for you standing me up."

Lahela deserved Nancy's irritation, but she wasn't sure how much detail she wanted to go into. She at least deserved to know missing coffee this morning wasn't intentional.

"This weekend was rough."

The tight lines around Nancy's eyes softened a little. "What happened?"

The morning bell rang and Lahela was relieved. "It's a long story." Her eyes flicked to the posters. "And I'm a little homesick, I think."

Concern tugged at Nancy's features, erasing her earlier irritability. "You're not thinking about moving back again, are you?"

After Trevor broke up with Lahela, she was ready to eat humble pie and move home, but Nancy really showed up for her as a friend and encouraged her to stay in Texas.

"I just . . ." Lahela didn't want to lie, but she wasn't ready to admit the truth. "Miss home."

"If Hawai'i was my home, I'd be missing it too." Nancy smiled. "Forget about this morning. I'm ordering lunch for us today and you can tell me about your weekend."

Lahela wanted to refuse, but after letting Nancy down already this morning, she didn't feel like she could. "Sure."

NOTHING MADE YOU STOP thinking about your own troubles more than spending four hours with seven- and eight-year-olds—especially when it came to discussing the human senses. Somehow a strawberry-scented car freshener quickly began smelling like Damon's little brother's poopy diaper and Brady's dad's farts, causing her to cut short the lesson before it got worse. Because with second-grade boys, it always got worse.

Lahela never imagined she'd appreciate the distraction of boy humor more than she did today. She walked out the front door of the school and found Nancy sitting at the cement picnic table next to the fenced playground where their students were enjoying their lunch break.

Nancy started opening the takeout bag. "You hungry?"

"I'm starving." Lahela had just sat down when movement by the fence caught her attention. She squinted against the sun and saw a man talking to some students. Rising, she began walking in his direction. "Excuse me, can I help you?"

Either the man hadn't heard her or was ignoring her. Apprehension washed through her and she slowed her approach. The man's fingers were laced through the fence, and he leaned on it like it was holding him up.

Lahela looked back at Nancy, but she was already moving in the direction of the office, following protocol to alert the security officer.

She turned back to the man. "I'm sorry, sir, but you can't—"

"Don't tell me what I can't do." The man spun on her, rising to his full height, which towered over her by several inches. "That's my kid and you, this school, the law doesn't get to tell me I can't see him."

Lahela had no idea what the family situation was, but clearly law enforcement was involved.

"Sir, you really should leave."

"I said I'm not leaving!"

Lahela flinched, expecting him to come at her, but instead a hooded figure rushed around her and shoved the man backward. Before she could identify who had intervened, yelling drew her attention to Principal Maestros, Nancy, and the school security officer as they ran over. A police cruiser screeched to a stop, and two officers were already out of the car and charging toward the man. Thankfully, the students had already been shuffled off the playground, including the man's son.

"Are you okay, Lahela?"

She frowned at the scene unfolding slowly around her, realizing she knew that voice. Unease crawled over her skin when she met his eyes. "Trevor?"

THIRTEEN

"WHAT DID THE POLICE SAY?" Briggs steadied himself on the ladder. The sound of wood splitting caused him to pull back on the screwdriver he was twisting with more aggression than necessary to secure Lahela's new security system into place. He'd called her after school, hoping to revisit their date discussion, but the second he heard her voice he knew something was wrong. When she told him about the incident at school involving a volatile custody battle and then Trevor showing up, it took every ounce of self-control to not overreact. Going out to buy the best security system on the market and installing it the second she got home from school was *not overreacting* at all. "You filed a report, right?"

Lahela finished sweeping her porch and leaned the broom against the railing. She looked up at him beneath dark lashes. "Trevor didn't break any laws showing up at the school, and without a protection order there's nothing they could do but ask him to leave."

Briggs climbed down the ladder. He could see she was upset and that was the last thing he wanted. "I'm sorry, Lahela." He sighed. "I'm just ticked off and worried and, well . . ." He looked at the tool in his hand. "I really want to punch someone, but I'm trying to focus that urge onto something more productive and less illegal."

He watched the edges of her lips tip into a smile before she laughed and then covered her face with her hands.

"Sorry. None of this is funny," she said.

He set down his screwdriver, took her wrists, and gently tugged her hands down. "It's not, but hearing you laugh and seeing your smile . . ." She dropped her chin, but he was quick to tip it back up with the edge of his fingers so she was looking in his eyes. "I'm glad you still have reason to do both."

There was a battle warring inside him. He wanted to crush her in his arms and protect her until all the shadows disappeared, but he didn't want to take advantage of her vulnerable state.

Lahela stepped forward and cupped his cheek. "Thank you, Briggs, for everything."

All restraint snapped, and in the space of a breath, he pulled her into his arms and all the tension and worry and fear quieted.

"I don't know how you did it as a police officer." Her words vibrated against his chest. Lahela tilted her head back and met his eyes. "Is that why you moved back here?"

"It wasn't easy," he said. "Putting on the uniform felt like a calling on my life and I believed it was what God wanted me to do, but"—he took a deep breath—"I couldn't avoid the violence, pain, and suffering that comes with the job. It's dark, and I started to withdraw, become detached, and instead of appreciating the joy of life, all I could think of was the last hard call." He shrugged. "It took me coming home a few times to realize that I needed my people. The evil was blurring my faith, and I needed my family and friends to remind me that there's still good in the world." His voice became husky as he peered down at her. "Good people who are bright lights of promise for the kind of future I want."

There wasn't a single cloud in the sky, but there was a current crackling between them, and he couldn't help where his mind traveled when his eyes fell to her lips.

Lahela cleared her throat, and when she quickly stepped out of his hold, he worried he'd crossed a line. "We have an audience."

He frowned and she raised her brows to something behind him. When he casually turned, he spotted Lahela's neighbor peeking out of her window. When she saw Briggs, she dropped the curtain in place.

"See how safe I am?"

If he hadn't heard the smile in her voice, Briggs might've questioned Lahela's sanity. He remembered the tiny, elderly woman from the night of the fire, and she was about as intimidating as a newborn calf.

"What do I owe you for this?" Her focus moved to the box the security cameras came in.

"Nothing," he said. "Though I really wish you'd consider taking me up on my offer to come out to the ranch. We have a guest house and I'd love to introduce you to my family and show you the land."

"I appreciate the offer, Briggs, but I can't do that."

His need to understand measured equally with his need to do whatever it took to keep her safe. "If not at my place, then go back to Daphne's." He looked up at the camera he'd installed. "You're home alone, and as much as I trust the police to do their job, if you need them, they'll be here in minutes, but it's the seconds that count."

Lahela smiled. "I think you're forgetting about Rosemary. Did you know she's a member of the Pearls and Pistols group?"

"What is the Pearls and Pistols group?"

"I have no idea." Lahela giggled. "But it sounds pretty and scary."

Briggs didn't want to think about the eighty-year-old woman wielding a pistol. "Pretty scary is more like it."

Lahela and Briggs stood there staring at the now-empty window of Rosemary's house for a few seconds until they both burst into laughter. The sound and sight were a sweet balm to the weariness he'd seen Lahela carrying for the last few days.

The moment was cut short by a text message that drained the color from Lahela's face. Briggs took the cell phone from her hand and his blood ran cold at the message.

Unknown

There's nowhere I can't reach you. School.
Festival. Home.

His fist curled around the phone and he wanted to chuck it across the lawn. Without a word, Briggs guided Lahela into her house, closing the door and locking it.

"You should go to Daphne's—"

"I can't. She's in the field tonight."

"Then come home with me." The look on her face told him she wasn't going to do that either. "Fine. I'll sit in my truck and keep an eye out."

"Briggs, I can't ask you to do that."

"You're not asking and I'm not leaving. I will camp outside your house for as long as it takes to find this guy, but I am not leaving you."

"Briggs . . ."

She swallowed, her focus lingering on the darkness outside her home for several seconds, and Briggs prepared himself for her to argue. When she found his eyes again, all he saw was resignation.

"You can stay here."

FOURTEEN

BRIGGS TURNER was in her house. *On her couch.* Lahela paced her room, heart thumping erratically against her rib cage. Was he comfortable? Did he need an extra pillow? Did he know where the cups were in case he got thirsty in the middle of the night?

"I can hear you pacing."

Lahela froze and dropped her eyes to the old oak floors beneath her feet. "Sorry."

"Do you need anything?"

She pressed her hand on the wall separating her room from the living room. No, it wasn't a shared wall with her bed and her couch, *but* it was a thin wall. Her eyes widened. *What if I snore?!*

Kekoa had teased her on more than one occasion, saying she snored loud enough to wake up Pele, the Hawaiian goddess of volcanoes and fire, and even blamed her for why Kilauea was still flowing. *"Pele can't rest with your snoring, Sis."* And now, thanks to her annoying brother, she was going to stay awake all night.

"Lahela, you okay?"

She jumped, spinning to face her closed bedroom door.

Briggs was on the other side of her bedroom door. Without thinking, she swung it open and blurted, "I snore!"

She cringed and clamped a hand over her mouth. This was not the way to win Briggs's affection. *What if snoring is where he draws the line? And why isn't he saying anything?*

And why— Her attention was momentarily stalled on the realization that Briggs was standing there shirtless. The cut of his chest muscles moving with the slow steadiness of his breathing that certainly didn't match the erratic breaths coming from her.

"I was worried when you didn't answer." But the amused look he was giving her now didn't appear to be worried at all. "You okay?"

"I'm good." Her reply came out breathy. "Thank you for checking on me."

"I'm always going to be here."

His voice was low and husky, and Lahela didn't know who stepped forward first, but his fingers brushed against her neck, sending a trickle of chills dancing over her skin. His chin dipped and she could just barely pick up the scent of his aftershave as his eyes asked permission.

Lahela slid her hand up his arm until her fingers stretched into his hair, and she felt his warm hands at her back, gently pressing her into his body until his lips finally found hers. She closed her eyes, leaning into him and into the kiss. It was soft and tender and—too short.

Briggs pulled away and it delighted her to see the heady way his look confirmed it was too short for him too. "Good night, Lahela."

"Night, Briggs."

She closed the door and then tiptoed to the wall and pressed her ear against it. She touched her lips—they were still warm from the kiss.

"Lahela." His voice echoed through the wall, and she

pressed back as if he'd known she was standing there. "If you can snore louder than me, I'll buy you dinner tomorrow night."

The smile she was biting back unfurled widely across her face. "Briggs, are you using a bet to ask me out on a date?"

"Maybe, but you haven't heard me snore yet. The odds are definitely in my favor."

Lahela laughed and remembered what Briggs said about doing whatever it took to make her smile and laugh. He was a man of his word, and suddenly her desire to be on the other side of this wall, sitting on the couch, tucked into his arms, and feeling his lips back on hers was overwhelming.

"Good night, Briggs." She vaulted into her bed like a teenage girl. "May the odds be ever in my favor."

"Good night, Lahela."

Snuggling into her blanket, she reached over to make sure her alarm was set on her cell phone when it vibrated with a call from Nancy.

Lahela kept her voice low when she answered. "Hello?"

"Hey! What's wrong?"

"What? Nothing. Why?"

"Your voice sounds weird."

"I'm using my indoor voice," Lahela said. "Why are you calling so late?"

Nancy scoffed into the phone. "It's barely ten."

"On a school night." Her eyes flickered to the wall and she imagined Briggs's body sprawled out on her couch. Would her pillows smell like him after tonight? Was it weird to hope so?

"You still there?"

Lahela blinked, realizing Nancy had still been talking to her. "Yeah, sorry. It's been a long day." She flopped a hand over her eyes. No need to worry about snoring, she wasn't going to get any sleep tonight. "Um, did you need something?"

"There's something I need to tell you."

Lahela sat up at the change in Nancy's tone. "What?" All it took was a second or two of silence for the anxiety to return. "Nancy, what is it?"

Nancy released a sigh. "I spoke to Trevor."

She let that hang in the air for a second, unsure if she was surprised by it or that she was expecting something . . . worse? "What do you mean?"

"While you were giving your report to the police today at school, I went over and spoke to Trevor. He told me everything. About what happened at the fair, that he went to your house to apologize, but he saw Briggs there, and how the police questioned him about the fire—which by the way, why didn't you tell me about that?"

"I was going to." Did her answer sound as defensive as she felt? She didn't want to relive the terrible details of her weekend, but she wasn't trying to hide them either. "At lunch."

"Oh. And you thought Trevor would do that?" Again, there was an oddly accusatory tone in Nancy's voice. "I mean, he was an idiot letting you walk out of his life, but stalking you? You should've seen how upset he was today, Lahela. He's really worried about you, and I think maybe he's realized breaking up was a mistake."

Lahela dropped back against her pillows and relief eased through her, realizing what this was. Nancy had been Trevor's biggest fan and was nearly as upset as Lahela, maybe even more, when Lahela told her about their breakup. Even though it was Trevor who had called it off, it hadn't stopped Nancy from hoping for a second-chance romance that Lahela blamed on Nancy's obsession with romance novels.

However, if this was Nancy's thinly veiled attempt to get them back together, she was going to be very disappointed in how this story would end.

"I don't think Trevor is a bad guy." She kept her voice low. "And I wasn't convinced he was behind the calls or fire, but the police had reason to look into him. I appreciate he's sorry but, Nancy, that part of my life, with him, is over."

"Are you sure? Because there's nothing like a knight rising to the challenge of protecting his maiden."

Lahela rolled her eyes. "You need to read some nonfiction."

"Ugh. No thanks. There's enough nonfiction in the world for me." Nancy sighed. "Okay, well, I guess I just wanted you to know that if there were any lingering feelings for Trevor, I think he'd be open to rekindling th—"

"There aren't." Her voice was a little louder than she expected. "Feelings. For Trevor," she whispered.

"Fine. I just thought it was super romantic of him to show up today. And before you tell me that's the stuff of make-believe, there's a reason authors keep writing the hero rescuing the heroine tropes. It's the grand gesture that wins back her heart."

"I don't want him to win back my heart." Exhaustion weighed on her. Lahela wasn't going to explain how she'd been questioning whether she ever really loved Trevor in the first place. At least not tonight. "Look, let's meet up for coffee tomorrow since I missed Mocha Monday today."

"Ooh, Tea Tuesday. Sounds great."

With plans made to meet at the coffee shop, Lahela flipped off the light and listened to see if she could hear Briggs snoring. Nothing. Maybe if she buried herself beneath her covers, it would hide her snoring, but then that meant he'd win and there'd be no dinner. Smiling, Lahela folded her blankets down and prayed she snored loud enough to wake up Pele all the way from Texas.

LAHELA JOLTED UPRIGHT in her bed to the sound of the blaring alarm echoing in her ears. It took her a second to shake off the sleep and realize it was *her* alarm system going off. Fear pulsed heavy through her veins, and she scrambled out of her sheets, forcing her eyes to adjust to the darkness of her bedroom. She screamed when her bedroom door flew open. *Briggs.*

He was at her side, one arm wrapping her into his side as he helped her off the bed and walked her toward . . . her dark closet? She looked up at him and realized he was talking on his cell phone, his face the picture of calm against the panic thrashing against her rib cage.

"What's happening, Briggs?"

Pressing her deeper into his side, he met her eyes. "Someone tried to break in."

The coil of unease Lahela had been fighting all night to loosen tightened with a snap around her gut. Burying her face into Briggs's shoulder, she closed her eyes, hating that she wanted to be anywhere but here.

FIFTEEN

"WE FOUND A TASER, rope, and duct tape."

Briggs ran a hand through his hair and gripped the back of his neck. He met the eyes of Detective Michael Morgan. "They were going to abduct her."

The words soured in his stomach, and Briggs immediately wanted to take them back, make them not true, but from the grave expression on the detective's face and his own intuition, they were the terrifying reality.

Or the possibility. He didn't want to think about what could've happened if he'd not been there. The alarm system wasn't connected to the windows in the house, so when he heard the glass break, he immediately rushed to the panel and triggered the alarm.

His attention was fixed on Lahela sitting on her couch in sweatpants and a T-shirt, cocooned in the same blanket he'd been sleeping under a little over an hour ago. Officer Sandberg was there talking to her, but she looked . . . detached, like she was in shock.

Briggs balled his hands into fists. "Are you checking Trevor West?"

"We've got an officer with him now," Detective Morgan said. "But West says he was asleep and nowhere near here.

317

Look"—he tucked his pen into his pocket—"our crime scene techs have collected all of the evidence and will run it for fingerprints. We'll check them against Trevor's and see if we get a match. I'm sharing this with you because I know your background and I know you can explain to her"—his gaze traveled to Lahela—"why we're going to do everything we can, but that it might not be . . . enough."

Briggs gave a tight nod, understanding from the police perspective he was familiar with. But now as he stood on the other side of the badge—the victim's side—the only thing he understood was that someone out there came to Lahela's home tonight intending to harm her.

"Our K9 unit is going to keep working, but with the winds tonight, I don't know if they'll pick up a scent."

They're trying. Briggs blew out a breath. "And the cameras?" He knew the answer, but he had to hope. "Will your techs be able to enhance the images?"

"We'll do our best."

None of the cameras Briggs installed were able to catch a clear enough image of the shadowed figure as they approached or left the house. Maybe Lahela's neighbor's cameras caught something.

A knock sounded and he turned to see Daphne walking through the front door in her Army uniform. She beelined it to Lahela and wrapped her in a hug.

"If she plans on staying here, I'll have some officers patrol the neighborhood for the rest of the night." Detective Morgan handed Briggs a business card. "Let me know what she plans to do."

Once the detective stepped outside, Lahela lifted her vacant gaze up to Briggs. "What did they say?"

"They're going to test the evidence for fingerprints, look into the video, and they've got the K9 out there working. They're doing everything they can."

"But it won't be enough, will it?"

Had she overheard his conversation with the detective? He dropped onto the couch next to her and laced his fingers through hers. "The police are doing everything they can, and I will do everything in my power to keep you safe." Lahela had inched her way into his life and heart, and without warning, he realized he'd completely fallen for her. She had stirred dormant pieces of him to blazing life, and he meant it when he said he'd do anything to protect her.

"We're all going to help," Daphne said. She put a hand on Lahela's arm. "I know you didn't want to, but I called Kekoa."

Lahela's entire body stiffened as she swung her gaze to Daphne. "You did what?"

"Someone came here to hurt you, Lahela. He needed to know, your family needs to know."

"I told you not to call him." Lahela's face filled with color. "What did you tell him?"

"Nothing," Daphne said. "He didn't answer, but someone named Lyla answered and—"

"You had no right! You heard what the police said, there's nothing anyone can do—"

"There's nothing the police can do. But the same isn't true about what Kekoa and his team can do. They can help."

Briggs sat there confused. He knew Kekoa worked for a private contract agency, but he didn't know the details of what they did. If they could help, why was Lahela hesitant?

"I don't need their help." She pulled her hand free from Briggs and stood. "I knew this was a mistake. I never should've stayed here. I should've moved back home and then none of this would've happened."

Move back home? Lahela had wanted to leave? His chest heaved at the idea. He rose. "Lahela, it's going to be okay."

"No, it's not, Briggs." Her tone softened, and when she

looked at him, her eyes were filled with tears. "Look at all of this trouble I've caused."

"You didn't cause—"

"Excuse me." Detective Morgan entered the living room and held his cell phone up. "Ms. Young, do you have your cell phone?"

Lahela looked around and then went to her bedroom and returned with her phone. "I have two missed calls from the hospital."

"Here." Detective Morgan handed her his phone.

Briggs watched as Lahela took the call. He thought his stomach couldn't be twisted into a tighter knot, but the second that alarm washed over her pale face, he was wrong.

Lahela handed the detective his phone and turned to Briggs. "Nancy was in a car accident." Her voice cracked. "Someone tried to kill her."

SIXTEEN

"SHE COULDN'T TELL US much other than the color of the car and that it followed her for a few miles before slamming into her car."

Lahela tried to concentrate on Officer Hoffman's explanation, but the words felt like they were swimming around in her head. He was the officer she'd spoken to on the phone. The one who told her, *"It looks like someone ran your friend off the road."*

She'd replayed those words in her head as Briggs drove her to the hospital with Daphne following in her car. Now the two of them stood by her side, listening to Officer Hoffman tell them that Nancy suffered head injuries and a broken femur that required immediate surgery.

"Has her family been notified?" Briggs asked.

Officer Hoffman shook his head. "The only number we had for an emergency contact was Ms. Young."

"Lahela Young"—a short nurse with dark brown curls walked over—"Ms. Bart is out of surgery and in recovery. She can have two visitors at a time."

"I'll wait here," Daphne offered. "When you're done, we can go back to my place for the night."

"You should go home. I'll figure something out." Lahela set

her jaw. She wasn't intentionally trying to hurt Daphne, even though the look in her eyes said she'd done exactly that. Old fears of burdening her friends resurfaced and she needed to escape them. "I need to go check on Nancy."

Following the nurse to a dim room at the end of the hallway of the hospital's trauma floor, Lahela shoved the panic aside when she saw Nancy. She had bruises and scrapes on her face, her red hair tangled against the pillow, and her left leg was wrapped in bandages and elevated on pillows. Lahela reached down and clutched Briggs's hand. It was warm and strong, and he gave her a reassuring squeeze.

"She's still going to be groggy from the anesthesia, but you can talk to her and let her know you're here."

All Lahela could do was nod. When the nurse left, she went to Nancy's side and rubbed her hand, careful of the IV.

"Is he why you don't love Trevor anymore?"

Lahela startled when she heard Nancy's scratchy voice. "Hey, how do you feel?" Her tone came off a little too cheery for the setting and circumstances, but she hoped it would distract Briggs from what Nancy just asked. "Do you need anything?"

With half-closed lids, Nancy looked at Lahela. "Y-you're my best friend," she slurred. Her head flopped around, eyes widening more as she looked Briggs over. "He's got big muscles and looks like a cowboy. Do you have cows . . . boy?"

Briggs grinned. "Yes, ma'am."

Nancy's eyes opened fully and a lopsided grin filled her face before she cringed and reached up to touch the cut at the edge of her lip. "I like cowboys with matters . . . manters . . ." She frowned and tried again. "Manners."

"The nurse said you're going to feel a bit groggy from the anesthesia."

"I'm fine," she slurred again, before she grabbed Lahela's hand. "You're my bestest friend. Best friend forever. And I love you."

Guilt niggled at Lahela's conscience. They were certainly friends, but she had never considered Nancy her best friend. It had to be the anesthesia.

Nancy released Lahela's hand and then wiggled her finger at Briggs to come closer. He kindly obliged, leaning in.

"You have very nice hair. And muscles. And cows. But if you hurt my best friend, I will kill you."

Lahela's jaw dropped. "Nancy."

But Briggs just chuckled. "Understood."

"Good." Nancy's eyes started to drift closed but then shot back open. "My cat. I have to take care of Mr. Boots. He'll be scared." Her voice rose. "My cat. I need to get—"

"I'll do it."

Briggs looked at Lahela and she shrugged. She didn't even know Nancy had a cat.

"I can go to your house before school and check on—"

"No." Nancy tried to sit up, but her head just lolled to the side like a rag doll. "He's probably so scared. Please will you go . . . Mr. Boots." Nancy drew out the last word like she was well on her way to la-la land again.

"Okay, I'll go tonight." She saw the clear plastic bag on the counter with Nancy's items and dug through them to find her keys. "I've got your keys and—"

"She's out," Briggs said.

"You don't think she'll mind I just took her keys, do you?"

Briggs raised an eyebrow. "I'll be surprised if she remembers this conversation at all."

Lahela looked at Nancy's sleeping form. Her broken and battered body. It was hard to think someone would purposely run into Nancy's car.

Inside Briggs's truck, Lahela gave him Nancy's address and then leaned against the door trying to wrap her mind around the chaos of her life. Her family believed in God and relied on their faith—especially after losing Ikaia. But was her faith as strong? Right now it didn't feel like it.

"Do you want to talk about what happened?"

Lahela slid a look at Briggs. "Not really."

"Daph loves you, and not in the drugged-up confession way Nancy does."

Guilt pricked her conscience again when she didn't find Daphne waiting. She shouldn't have snapped at her like she did but— "She shouldn't have called my brother."

"Why?"

Lahela looked over at Briggs and he met her gaze. He wasn't pushing her for an answer but inviting her to share. What if she did? The last time she shared her feelings, it hadn't ended well.

It was weird how core memories were forever ingrained in the brain. Quick to pop to the surface with the same powerful emotions they held the first time.

"When my brother Ikaia died, my parents were distraught. We all were. Especially Kekoa. There's something indescribable about witnessing your parents cry and hearing their howling grief at night." Tears burned the back of her eyes. "Kekoa couldn't handle it and blamed himself. He left the island, making it feel like I didn't just lose one brother, I lost two. I think my parents felt the same way and I didn't want them to worry about me, so I hid my grief. I waited until I was at school and then I cried in the bathroom. My friends were there for me at first, but then as the days, weeks, and months passed, their lives moved on, but my life was stuck in a nightmare that I couldn't share with anyone. They stopped calling and hanging out with me. I don't blame them. It was my burden, not theirs."

The truck stopped, and Lahela realized they were at Nancy's house already. She started to reach for the door, but Briggs put a hand on her arm and remained silent until she faced him.

"Lahela, I'm so sorry you were abandoned by your friends when you needed them most." He reached his hand to her face and brushed his thumb against the tear running down her cheek. "Maybe they were too young to handle the grief, or didn't know what to do with it or how to make it better for you—but you didn't deserve to face it alone."

Emotion choked her, so all she could do was nod.

"We—Daphne, Nash, and I—are *never* going to abandon you. Ever."

"D-don't"—her voice broke—"make promises you can't keep."

"I never make a promise I don't intend to keep." He lifted her hand to his lips and kissed her knuckles, his gaze locked on hers. "Now let's go find Mr. Boots."

At the door, Lahela used the key to unlock it and then entered the house. "This feels so weird." Lahela searched the wall for a light switch, and when she flipped on the lights, she gaped at the mess. "Did someone break in?"

Briggs whistled. "I think your 'best friend forever' is a slob."

He wasn't wrong, but given the amount of furniture, papers, clothing, dishes, and trash filling Nancy's apartment, *slob* may have been too generous.

"How are we going to find the cat in this?"

"Divide and conquer." Briggs pointed to the hallway. "You take bedrooms and I'll take the front area."

Something about being in here made Lahela's skin crawl. The Nancy she saw every day at school was neat and tidy. Quirky, yes, but nothing to even suggest she was a pack rat at home. Squeezing her way through the hall, Lahela called out the cat's name. She really hoped he wasn't one of those cats that liked to jump out and scare their owners.

Behind her, Briggs was doing the same thing. The first room she came to was a bathroom packed with far too many bottles of hair product for a single person. But no cat.

Lahela twisted the knob on a closed door across the hall and flipped on the light switch. This room looked like an office and was quite organized compared to the rest of the house. There was a desk covered in papers and a wall that looked like some kind of vision board. Of course, Nancy would have a vision—

Wait.

She stepped farther into the room and eyed the photos and papers taped all over the wall. It was *her*. Dozens of photos and not just of her. Of Trevor and—

She gasped.

"Cat's not in the front of the—"

Lahela jumped and knocked into a box. It tipped, spilling a bunch of black cell phones across the floor.

"What in the world?" Briggs's forehead creased as he looked at the wall, and then his jaw clenched. "Lahela, call the police."

"Briggs." Her body started to shake.

He pulled her to his chest, his strong arms wrapped tightly around her as if he wanted to shield her from the truth of his words. "I think we found your stalker."

SEVENTEEN

BRIGGS NEVER IMAGINED he'd see so much of the inside of a police station once he left the Dallas PD.

Detective Morgan had set them up in his office and offered the use of his Keurig before stepping out to take a call from Officer Hoffman questioning Nancy at the hospital. Briggs set a cup of tea in front of Lahela. The shock of discovering Nancy's obsessive shrine had been as revealing as it was unsettling.

Lahela wrapped her hands around the tea. "I don't understand, Briggs. She was my friend. Friends don't stalk friends, right?"

Her voice wasn't hysterical, just matter-of-fact, like she was trying to make sense of the situation.

"Every stalking case I've worked was between domestic partners, but there have been cases where victims were stalked by ex-employees, friends, family members even. Each case varies based on the motivation behind the obsession."

"But why would Nancy be obsessed with me? I don't think I've ever done anything to upset her."

Briggs wanted to help Lahela understand, but the truth was, he didn't understand himself. The facts and evidence behind stalking rarely provided all the answers—there was a psychological component. And it was the latter that made the cases unpredictable and dangerous.

Detective Morgan entered his office and sat behind his desk. "I'm sorry that took longer than I expected, but I wanted to have as much information to give to you as possible."

Lahela reached for Briggs's hand, and he covered it with his own, hoping his touch would provide her with the courage to hear whatever was coming.

"Nancy confessed to almost everything."

Lahela sucked in a breath and Briggs tightened his grip on her hand.

"Including being the one who came to your home tonight."

Tears slipped down Lahela's cheeks, and she shook her head as if the truth was more than she could handle—or wanted to believe.

Briggs moved his chair close to hers, wishing more than anything he could protect her from the hurt. "You said she confessed to *almost* everything."

Detective Morgan nodded. "She denies starting the fire at your home on Saturday night, but she admits to being at the festival that day and driving by your home."

"She wanted to hurt me?"

"No," Detective Morgan said. "According to Nancy, she went to your house to scare you, hoping you would reach out to her or Trevor for help."

"It doesn't make any sense. Nancy knew Trevor and I were done." Lahela's voice held the same disbelief that was coursing through him. "Why would she think pretending to be a stalker would get us back together?"

Detective Morgan slipped on a pair of glasses and looked down at his cell phone. "In her statement, she said she saw how upset you were about Mr. West ending the relationship and she didn't want you to move. She began calling you from different burner phones to scare you so that you would call

Trevor and he could"—Detective Morgan cleared his throat—
"rescue you."

Briggs frowned. "I'm sorry?"

"She wanted Trevor to be my knight," Lahela answered for
Detective Morgan. "Rescue me like a damsel in distress, like
in her books."

Detective Morgan sat forward. "Do you have more information?"

"She called me tonight. We talked about what happened at
the school, and she mentioned Trevor might still have feelings
for me and that he was like a knight coming to my rescue
today." Lahela fell silent for a few seconds, before she glanced
up between them. "She's delusional."

"Most stalkers seem to have a break in reality." Detective
Morgan looked down at his phone again. "Ms. Bart claims
she was doing all of this because you were her best friend.
She was afraid of losing your friendship and was convinced
getting you back together with your ex would make you
happy."

Lahela hung her head. "It just doesn't make sense."

"Unfortunately, most cases like this never do," Detective
Morgan said. "But you're safe now, and we've got a judge who
signed a protective order for you." He shuffled some papers
and handed Lahela a sheet. "Ms. Bart isn't allowed to contact
you or come near you."

"So that's it?"

"For now." The detective's cell phone vibrated. He pushed
back from his desk. "That's the officer at the hospital. I'm
going to head over there and make sure we have everything
we need to charge Ms. Bart."

Briggs rose and held on to Lahela's hand as she stood.

They walked with the detective through the police station and parted ways at the front doors. Briggs didn't realize
how late—or early—it was until he saw the sun cresting the

horizon. He tugged his cell phone free from his back pocket to call Jett and let him know he'd be back at the ranch as soon as he could. He paused when Lahela yawned and noticed the dark circles beneath her eyes.

"Why don't I take you home, you can get showered and call in to the school and request a sub for your class, then I'll take you back to the ranch." He brushed away the hair lying across her forehead. "You're exhausted and need some sleep. You can rest in the guest house."

"I need to go to work, Briggs." She covered a second yawn. "It's too late to call a sub, and being at school with my students might be the only thing to keep me from losing my mind."

He opened his mouth to convince her that he was there to walk through this with her when his cell phone rang, startling them both. It was Barrett Brown's number. Frustration and exhaustion pulsed through him. Still, he answered. "Good morning, sir."

"Hopefully it will be," Barrett said, and that was enough to know Briggs wasn't heading to the ranch anytime soon. "Jett's already on his way to Esperanza Park. We have a missing hiker."

Briggs exhaled through his nose, his gaze locked on Lahela. He really wanted to get her back to his place to rest, but the temps in the mornings had dropped into the forties, and that spelled trouble for someone lost in the wilderness.

He told Barrett he would be at the park in thirty minutes and ended the call. The sky outside had barely begun turning pink. Someone out this early wasn't a novice hiker, which usually meant there was an injury keeping them from returning home. "I'll drive you home, but I think Daphne should drive you to school."

"That's okay." Lahela averted her gaze.

"Lahela . . ."

"It's okay, Briggs." She tried for a smile, but it fell far short. "I'll talk to Daphne. Just not right now."

"I'd feel better if she met us at your house. You've barely slept—"

"Go, Briggs." Lahela put her palm on his chest and rose on her toes to place a soft kiss on his cheek. "I'll be fine and call an Uber to get me home. Go find that hiker and then maybe we can discuss dinner plans."

His face split into a grin, and suddenly the exhaustion that had been weighing on him evaporated. He lifted her hand to his lips and kissed her knuckles. "I'll call you as soon as I'm done."

Briggs forced his feet to hurry to his truck. He didn't want to leave her side. He wanted to take her into the hill country on the back of his horse and spend the rest of his day whispering words to her while she was wrapped in his arms. He'd find this hiker as soon as possible so he could return to the woman wrangling his heart.

EIGHTEEN

THE DOORS ARE LOCKED. But that didn't stop Lahela from walking to her front and back door and checking again. She really thought knowing who was behind the stalking would give her back some sense of control or courage, but she was still fighting off the chill of reality that her coworker—*her friend*—was responsible.

It doesn't make sense. That's what was on repeat in her head on the Uber ride to her house. While she showered and changed. And when she got the kind call from Principal Maestros that a substitute had already been called in for her and that she was to take the rest of the week off.

Exhausted, she dropped onto her couch and stared out her front window. Her eyes inadvertently found the still-charred spot on the porch. *How did I get here?* The ache for home welled up inside her again.

The situation with the stalker—Nancy—was over. There was no need to leave, was there? Lahela chewed on her lip. *There's not, so why am I afraid to stay?*

Her attention shifted to the photo on her coffee table. It was of her, Daphne, Nash, and Briggs at their first taco night. It had been taken a week after Trevor broke up with her. She'd been a wreck, only functioning because she had a classroom of second graders depending on her to show up every day. And yet, in that week, Daphne had come over with movies and dinner. Nash had had cookies delivered to her. And Briggs . . . he had surprised her by showing up at her house with a list of chores she'd never given him. He changed her air filters in the house and the batteries in her smoke detectors, tightened the bolts on the front porch banister, and replaced the fluorescent lights in the laundry room. And when he was done with all of that . . . he mowed her yard.

With her world flipped upside down and her relationship upended, her friends had showed up. They allowed her to process the breakup and the fears that she'd made a huge mistake moving to Texas. Instead of running away, they walked her through it.

Daphne smiled up from the photo and Lahela swiped at a tear. She needed to fix things with her friend. Apologize. Daph had been trying to help and probably did the most responsible thing by reaching out to Kekoa.

Lahela frowned. It was weird her big brother hadn't called or stormed her front door yet though. That could mean only one thing—Kekoa was busy and probably hadn't received Daphne's message yet. Good. That gave Lahela a chance to call and let him know everything was okay *before* he overreacted.

She went to her kitchen where she'd left her cell phone on the counter. The pages of takeout menus flapped from a sudden cool breeze. The door to her laundry room was open, and the cold air was coming from the window Nancy broke last night.

A chill skirted down her spine, but Lahela shook it off. She found a piece of cardboard on the ground outside the door that led to her backyard. It looked like it had been used to temporarily seal the window. Shards of glass still littered the area, so she grabbed a broom and dustpan to sweep it up. *What had Nancy been thinking?*

Sunlight glanced off a large piece of glass lying in the grass, and Lahela bent over to pick it up. She dropped it when the sharp edges sliced into her hand and fingers.

"Lahela."

She screamed, backing into her door as she lifted her gaze to see Trevor standing there. "W-what are you doing here?"

Trevor's eyes moved to her hand. "You're bleeding."

"It's fine." It wasn't. Bright red blood dripped from her hand, and she clutched it to her chest and backed toward her house.

"It's not." Trevor started to take a step toward her.

"Stop!"

He did, looking startled by her shout. He stepped back and lifted up his palms. "I just came by here to check on you. The police came to my house and told me about Nancy. I had no idea."

Lahela wanted to believe him, but after everything that had happened, could she trust him? The hammering in her ribs said no. At least not until she heard the whole story from Detective Morgan. "It's fine."

"It's not. You're really bleeding."

Blood had already soaked into her shirt. "I just need to get a towel and put pressure on it." She took a step back, but her heel caught the edge of the doorstep, and she lost her balance, falling to her bottom.

"Lahela!"

"Don't touch her!"

Trevor froze at the gravelly voice behind him. He looked back, and his shoulders relaxed a bit when he saw it was just her neighbor. "I was just trying to help her."

"You've already done—" Mr. Dunn's gaze landed on her bloody shirt and hand. He whipped his head around, his eyes glaring, and stabbed a finger at Trevor. "What did you do?"

"Nothing, man. She cut her hand on the glass."

"I'm calling the police."

"No, Mr. Dunn." Lahela pushed herself to her feet with her good hand. "He's telling the truth."

Mr. Dunn narrowed his eyes on Trevor. "You need to leave."

She didn't know what it was about Mr. Dunn's tone, but it pushed Trevor back a few more steps.

Trevor looked upset and scared. And like he wanted to say something else but changed his mind. He gave her a nod and then disappeared around the corner of her house.

"Let me get a look at that." Mr. Dunn was at her side. He carefully pulled her cut hand from the shirt, and she looked away. "Looks like you might need stitches."

"Really?"

"Come on." He closed her back door and then started leading her around the house. "I'll drive you to the hospital."

"No, that's okay. I can drive." Probably. *And bleed out in my car.* That thought made her feel a little lightheaded.

"Nonsense. You're hurt and I'm going to take care of you."

Briggs's words about accepting help returned, and she relaxed. "Thanks."

They walked across the street and up his driveway, and Lahela paused. "Why is Janine's car covered?"

"Oh"—he opened his front door and ushered her inside— "it's supposed to rain today."

Lahela had never been inside Mr. Dunn's house, and it was as she expected. The front was divided into a living room and formal dining room. The furnishings looked like they were probably the same ones his wife had chosen when they were married, and the house had a musty smell that tickled her nose.

A painting hung over the mantel of a man, a woman, and a young girl. Assuming it was a family portrait, Lahela had no idea Mr. Dunn had a daughter.

"She's pretty, isn't she?"

Lahela smiled but wasn't sure if he was referring to his wife or the girl. "Is that your daughter?"

He handed her a thin towel for her hand and nodded. "Crystal. She was the light of our lives."

Was? Lahela looked around the living room, pausing on each of the framed photos, and noticed there weren't any with Crystal older than she looked in the painting. Eight or nine maybe.

"I miss her every single day. Both of them." Mr. Dunn's voice turned strange, and an uncomfortable feeling settled over her. "You remind me of Crystal."

In the painting, Crystal had short blond hair, blue eyes, and the same fair skin as her parents. Nothing about them looked the same.

"Obviously, you don't look like her, but she had a bubbly personality. Like you. Always friendly." He swallowed and looked at Lahela, but those blue eyes that always seemed fatherly were empty now.

Lahela's hand began to throb. A pounding that kept cadence with the eerie pounding of her pulse. She moved toward his door, suddenly anxious to get out of there. "Uh, I think I can drive myself to the hospital."

But Mr. Dunn's hand was around her arm, squeezing tightly, and she found it weird that the thing she noticed as he dragged her backward was that the blue sky outside didn't look at all like it was going to rain.

NINETEEN

"SOMETHING'S NOT RIGHT." Briggs secured the latch on the horse trailer. He and Jett had spent almost three hours searching for a man named Joe Smith with no luck. "The man's name doesn't even sound real."

Jett grunted. "Might be. Look."

Briggs turned to see Barrett Brown marching their way. The man normally had the soft expression of a teddy bear and rarely showed emotion, but from the tight expression creasing his features, Briggs expected steam to come out of his ears.

"What's wrong?"

"We've tried calling the number of Jim Smith, the man who called in the missing hiker, and the number's not working."

Barrett wiped his brow even though the temperature was barely registering in the sixties. "We've accounted for the only vehicle in the parking lot and it doesn't belong to our hiker."

"A false call," Briggs offered. It wasn't common, but there were times when someone reported a missing hiker only to learn they weren't missing at all.

"Maybe. It's almost Halloween, maybe some kids thought this would be a funny joke," Barrett answered. "I hate this holiday."

"Not a fan of kids, myself," Jett added—even though it was clear that wasn't what Barrett meant.

"You're young." Barrett closed the tack box on the trailer and locked it. "You're supposed to say that."

Briggs caught Jett making a face like Barrett's excuse was completely wrong. He would've teased him if not for the tension thrumming through his chest. If this was a false call, whether by kids or not, it bugged him because it had taken him from Lahela.

"You awake?" Jett waved a hand in front of Briggs's face. "Your phone."

He pulled out his phone and saw Daphne's name on the screen. "Hey, Daph."

"Hey, have you talked to Lahela?"

Something in his gut twisted, but remembering the way Lahela and Daphne ended the night, he shook it off. He looked at his watch. "A few hours ago. I got called out for a search."

"Oh, sorry. I didn't mean to interrupt—"

"No, the search has been called off."

"Okay, um, well, I wanted to talk to Lahela after last night, and I picked up a coffee to take to her at school, but they said she took the day off."

Briggs sighed with relief. "I'm glad. She was exhausted this morning."

"Yeah, so I came by her house . . ." Daphne's tone set off alarms in his brain. "Her car's here but she's not."

"What do you mean?"

"I knocked and she didn't answer. I called her phone and she didn't answer. Maybe she's still mad at me?"

Yes, Lahela had been upset with Daphne, but he couldn't see her not answering Daphne's calls. Something wasn't right and he didn't like the eerie similarity to the nonexistent missing hiker.

"Are you there now?"

338

"Yes," Daphne answered. "I'm at her front door. It's locked."

That was good. "Go around the back and knock on the door. See if you can see into her bedroom window. I know she was exhausted, so she might be asleep."

"Okay." He waited, listening to Daphne's breathing and the sounds of her walking to Lahela's backyard. "Briggs, there's blood."

"There's blood?" His voice pitched and instantly drew the concerned attention of Jett and Barrett. "Where?"

"At the back door by her laundry room. The door's unlocked. Lahela!"

He ran a hand through his hair, feeling helpless just standing there listening to Daphne call for Lahela. His face must've revealed his distress because Barrett mouthed the word *Go*.

That was all he needed. He ran to his truck, jumped in, and started the engine, all while keeping the phone to his ear. "Daph, is she there?"

"No. The house is empty." Daphne sounded breathless. "And I found her cell phone in the kitchen."

"How fresh is the blood?" Briggs forced himself not to imagine the worst. "And how much?"

"It's dark and I don't know. There's some big drops on the— Oh, there's a little blood on the glass. Maybe she cut herself."

"I'm on my way back to town." He accelerated down the highway. "I should be there in twenty minutes."

"There's an urgent care two blocks from here. I'm going to head there and call the closest hospitals to see if she's there. I'll call you as soon as I find her."

"As soon as I find her." He shivered. Nancy was at the hospital, so there was no reason to believe she could do anything to Lahela. But— *Trevor.* Detective Morgan hadn't mentioned if Trevor was involved with Nancy's plan, and so far, he'd been able to provide an alibi for all the incidents. What if there was more to the story than Nancy confessed?

TWENTY

WHERE WAS SHE? Lahela could tell she was sitting, but her head felt heavy, like she'd been asleep for hours. She would've thought this was a nightmare except for the immense pain radiating down the side of her face. Dim sunlight filtered around her and there was a strong smell of gasoline. A garage. That's where she was.

"Y-you shouldn't have made me do that." Lahela flinched as Mr. Dunn walked into view. He pressed a cold pack to her head. "I don't want to hurt you."

"Mr. Dunn, what are you doing?" Lahela trembled, causing the old rolling desk chair to rattle. Both of her hands were cuffed to the arms of the chair. "Please."

He set the cold pack down and looked into her eyes. "I told you, call me Jesse." He started to unwrap the towel from her bloodied hand. "The bleeding is slowing down. I think if we keep this clean, it'll be all right. I'll use glue to help with the scarring."

"Mr.—" His eyes snapped up to hers. "Jesse, I can't feel my fingers."

His brow pinched. "That's concerning." He slowly pried her clenched fingers open and studied her cut. "I'll keep an eye on it."

Panic surged up Lahela's throat and she felt like she was going to be sick. "M—Jesse, I don't feel well."

He sat on a stool. "That's probably from the hit to your head. I knew you were going to fight back. I was hoping you wouldn't, but that's just like my Crystal. A fighter."

The way he kept comparing her to his daughter freaked her out. Maybe if she could get him to talk about her—or at least what happened to her—it would give Lahela time to think of a way out of this.

"You've never told me about Crystal. What was she like?"

He stood and went to the sink next to the washing machine and filled a cup with water from the faucet. "She was so bright. Always asking questions and smiling. She never met a stranger."

Lahela searched the space around her, looking for something she could use as a weapon. There was a tall metal shelf a few feet away from her that separated the laundry area. She spotted a pair of garden shears. Using her toes, she started to roll her chair toward the shelf, but the wheels screeched against the cement.

Mr. Dunn looked back and Lahela held her breath. Maybe if he saw enough of his daughter in her, he wouldn't do whatever it was he planned to do. And then a horrifying thought filled her mind. What if he'd done something to Crystal?

"Where's Crystal?" She forced the words out. "What happened to her?"

He met her questions with silence for several seconds before he finally turned to face her. "I should've been watching. I told Janine I was, that Crystal was safe with me, and we'd only be at the park for an hour. There was this tree and Crystal wanted to show me she could climb it." He frowned. "It wasn't very tall and had a thick trunk. Kids climb trees all the time and I didn't see any harm. Crystal started and she was doing so well. But then she got to a branch and it snapped right out from under her. She fell and hit her head. They told me it was instantaneous."

Lahela understood grief, and despite current circumstances, Crystal's story hurt her heart.

A cold sweat broke out across her skin. Who was going to find her? No one knew where she was. No one was coming.

"Janine never forgave me. Never trusted me again." His cold tone flicked her attention back to the sad smile he gave her. "That's why I need you."

"I don't understand . . . Jesse." She hated calling him by his first name. "We're neighbors . . . friends. What did I do?"

"Do?" Mr. Dunn looked genuinely confused. "You didn't do anything. Don't you see? I'm going to take care of you. Keep you safe."

Was he referring to the fire? The stalking? Trevor?

"I'm safe, Jesse. The police caught Nancy. She can't hurt me now."

"Oh, I know." He poured some pills into a bowl and began smashing them. "I saw her outside your house. I went to confront her, but that alarm went off and scared her away. I couldn't let her get away. I had to protect you."

Bile climbed up her throat. "You? You were the one who hit her?"

"To protect you." He dumped the pills, now a white powder, into the glass of water and stirred it with a spoon. "But soon you won't have to worry about her again because I will keep you safe."

"Jesse, what're you going to do?"

He started for her. "I'm going to take you away so I can keep you safe."

"Take me away"—her voice broke—"where?"

"To Janine."

Lahela's panic swelled. He was taking her to his dead wife?

She had no idea what that meant, but she wasn't going down without a fight.

"Drink this and when you wake up, you'll be in your new home."

She waited until he was close and then kicked his kneecap as hard as she could. Mr. Dunn dropped to the ground immediately, and the glass of whatever he was about to make her drink crashed next to him.

Lahela tried using her feet to roll the chair away, but it was stuck on a hose. Mr. Dunn placed his palm against the wall to help himself up. There was a fury in his eyes that terrified her. He limped toward Lahela and raised his hand like he was going to strike her again, but a doorbell echoed from inside his home.

They looked at each other, and she opened her mouth to scream, but he was faster than she expected, even with an injured knee. He wrapped a hand around her mouth while the other reached for something. She squirmed in the chair, but he was much stronger than his seventy-something years, and using his teeth, he ripped some tape and pressed it against her mouth. Silencing any attempt for her to scream for help.

Mr. Dunn leaned in next to her ear. "Stay quiet for Daddy."

TWENTY-ONE

BRIGGS PRESSED the doorbell at Mr. Dunn's again. He rubbed the back of his neck, unable to rid himself of the unease snaking through him. He called Detective Morgan, and he confirmed Nancy was still in the hospital. Then the detective asked about Lahela.

That was when Briggs's world had tilted.

"What do you mean?"

"I heard on the police scanner that her neighbor Rosemary called in after hearing an argument," Detective Morgan said. *"But she said it was fine because Lahela went with Mr. Dunn."*

"Who was she arguing with?"

"Rosemary said a young man, she thought it was you at first but said the guy left in a car and she knows you drive a truck."

"Trevor."

"I've already sent officers to find him."

Briggs would feel no relief until he knew where Lahela was and that she was all right. Especially after seeing the blood on her back stoop. Daphne hadn't called him back, and his hope that Mr. Dunn was home was evaporating with each passing second. But he didn't know where else to go.

He was about to leave when the door swung open. "Mr. Dunn?"

344

"Hello, Briggs. How can I help you?"

For a second, Briggs was at a loss for words. He wasn't expecting Mr. Dunn to be there. "I'm looking for Lahela." Behind Mr. Dunn, his living room was empty. "Ms. Rosemary said Lahela walked here with you."

Mr. Dunn wiped at his brow. "That ex-boyfriend of hers was nosing around the front of her house and then he walked into the backyard. I wanted to make sure Lahela was okay. She was bleeding but said it was from the glass and it didn't look serious."

Briggs frowned. "Where is she?"

"She left."

"Left?"

Mr. Dunn shrugged. "I offered to take her to the emergency room, but she said she was okay." He scratched his chin, and Briggs noticed dark residue in his nails. Was that Lahela's blood? Mr. Dunn dropped his hand and looked at his nails. "I guess I got some of her blood on my hand when I was wrapping her hand. I would've done a better job, but she seemed like she had somewhere to go."

"What do you mean?"

"I dunno, but I'm afraid she's really considering moving back to Hawai'i." He shook his head. "I tried to tell her she should stay, that we'd miss her, but I think she just wants to get away from here."

Briggs needed to find Lahela *now*. "You don't know where she went? Did she walk? Leave with someone?"

"I'm sorry, I don't know." He stepped back, his hand on the door as he smiled at Briggs. "You let me know if you hear from Lahela."

"Yeah, okay."

Mr. Dunn closed the door on him. Briggs always thought the man had a bit of an odd overprotective fatherly connection to Lahela, but if that were true . . . why wasn't he more concerned that Lahela seemed to have disappeared?

Briggs looked across the street to Rosemary's house. She had the doorbell camera that caught Trevor's car the night of the fire. Maybe she'd have footage of Lahela. He started down Mr. Dunn's driveway and then paused. A weird feeling overcame him.

Briggs started walking again but stopped after a few feet and looked to his left. The green Volvo that belonged to Mr. Dunn's wife was covered. That was it. The thing that was different.

Shaking his head, Briggs walked down the rest of the driveway. He was about to cross the street when that niggling feeling he used to get as a police officer warned him that something wasn't right. He turned around.

TWENTY-TWO

SWEAT HAD MIXED with Lahela's tears, and both were running down her face by the time Mr. Dunn limped back into the garage. She worked to steady her breathing, which was almost impossible to do with the duct tape covering her mouth, but she didn't want Mr. Dunn to notice she wasn't in the same spot he'd left her in.

While he was gone, she'd tried to get to the shears on the metal shelf, but they were out of reach. She tried to use her feet to knock them down, but after her third attempt, the only thing she'd managed to do was knock over a plastic watering can that thankfully fell into a laundry basket.

Panicking, she ran out of time to roll her chair back to its original spot before he came back into the garage, and she prayed he wouldn't notice.

"Let's try this again." His face twisted in pain as he limped to the faucet with another glass. Pulling out a bottle of pills, he opened the top, then shook a few into the bowl and began smashing them. "Your friend, I think he really cares about you."

Her friend? Briggs? She whimpered against the tape. Briggs had come looking for her. Desperation overrode fear and she squirmed in the chair and kicked at anything her feet could reach to make noise.

Mr. Dunn looked over his shoulder at her. "He's gone."

Her shoulders fell and she cried, the tape muffling her sobs. This was not how it was going to end.

"I thought he might be the one." Mr. Dunn refilled the glass of water and then poured the crushed pill powder into it like he had before. "But not even Briggs could keep you safe."

Lahela kicked angrily and her foot connected with the shelf, causing it to shift a little. Eyes widening, she snapped them to Mr. Dunn to see if he noticed, but his back was to her. Moving over a few more inches, she used her toe and pressed against the shelf a little harder. She felt it give beneath the pressure. With enough force she might be able to kick it over on top of Mr. Dunn. She had no idea how much it weighed, but there were boxes and tools that might just be heavy enough to pin him down. What she'd do after that, she didn't know.

The only problem was that she'd have to wait until he was closer, and that put her at risk of being caught beneath it too. It was a risk she was willing to take.

"No, that boy isn't good enough for my girl." Mr. Dunn took a slow step toward her, his face tight with the pain she had inflicted on his knee. "Briggs can't keep you safe, but I will. I will prove to you and to Janine that I am a good father and I can keep you safe."

Mr. Dunn took another step toward her, and she refocused her thoughts on the mission. *One more step . . .*

But he stopped and she looked up to meet his smirk. "I'm old but I'm not dumb."

He stretched his arm out, and she flinched thinking he was going to hit her, but instead he grabbed the edge of her chair and spun her around so that he was at her back. And her feet were nowhere near the shelf.

"Another kick like that first one and you'll force me to discipline you." He pulled on the chair so it felt like she was going to fall backward. Her heart pounded in her ears, and she gripped the chair with her hands, ignoring the searing pain from the cut on her palm. "I'm going to tell you what's going to happen next so you're not scared, okay?"

Lahela shook her head and her eyes filled with tears.

"This can be easy if you want it to be."

It was like her body was acting on its own accord for survival and she nodded.

"Good. I'm going to grab your hair to pull your head back, but I'll be as gentle as I can. This will open up your throat and then I'll pour the water down. It's best if you don't fight it, otherwise you might choke and we don't want that, do we?"

Again, her head moved without her telling it to. She whimpered against the tape again and searched his eyes for any sign of compassion, but there was nothing but an empty void.

"I'm going to remove the tape and I don't want to hurt you, but if you scream, I will."

Lahela clenched her jaw and this time she forced herself to nod in agreement, but the second that tape was removed she was going to scream for her very life.

TWENTY-THREE

"HELP! SOMEBODY HELP!"

Like the starter's gun to begin a race, Briggs was sprinting toward Mr. Dunn's front door at the sound of a woman's voice. He pounded his fists on the front door. "Lahela!"

"Briggs!"

He spun on his heel and ran to the garage. Is that where the noise came from? "Lahela!"

No answer. Instead, he heard scraping and scuffling coming from inside the garage. He reached for the handle and tried to pull it up, but it didn't move. He yanked out his cell phone and dialed 911 while running back to the front door.

He tried the handle, but the door was locked. It was solid wood, but that didn't stop him from punching and kicking at it. "Lahela!"

As quickly as he could, he gave the 911 operator his information and location. Then he went to the garage door and pounded on it. "Mr. Dunn, there's nowhere for you to go. Let her go."

A loud grunt was the only response he got. He needed to get inside this garage now. Spinning around, he looked at the covered Volvo. Would there be a garage door opener inside?

Briggs ripped off the cover and was relieved when he saw

the garage remote attached to the visor. He checked the door, but it was locked. Behind him, he grabbed a smooth river rock from the flower bed and smashed the window. The car's alarm went off, giving away Briggs's advantage.

All his police training told him he should never go into a situation blind, but experience working the job said seconds counted when the police were minutes away. This was Lahela's life, and he wouldn't waste a single second.

He smashed the garage door button and heard the motor kick on as it began lifting upward. Moving to the edge, he crouched, and when there was enough room, he rolled under and popped to his feet.

"Briggs, watch out!"

Lahela's warning came just as Mr. Dunn lunged at him with an open box cutter in his hand. Briggs grabbed Mr. Dunn's hand and redirected his momentum so that he twisted the man backward and shoved him to the ground, causing the box cutter to slip from his grip.

Mr. Dunn groaned but rolled over and reached for the box cutter. But his attempt was foiled when a large shelf crashed over him.

Briggs's natural inclination was to go to Lahela, who sat handcuffed to a chair, but he needed to check on Mr. Dunn.

"Is he alive?"

The man's body lay motionless, and there was blood trickling from a gash on his head, but there was movement in his chest that suggested he was still breathing.

"Yes." Briggs got to Lahela just as the first sounds of sirens met his ears. He checked her face, running his hand along the angry red mark on her cheek. *He'd hit her.* Rage raced through him, and he forced himself not to go over there and kick the old man. He crouched in front of Lahela, his eyes tracing the rest of her face before moving down to her hands. He gently cradled her injured hand and looked up at her. "The police will take the cuffs off and there's an ambu—" His voice broke and the sting of tears burned his eyes.

"Briggs, I'm gonna be okay."

He rolled her as close to him as possible and threaded his arms around her waist and dropped his head to her knees. "I've never been so scared in my life."

"Me either." Lahela rested her forehead on his shoulder and whispered, "Thanks for sticking around."

Lifting his head, he gazed into her dark brown eyes. "I'm not going anywhere, Lahela."

CLOSE TO AN HOUR LATER, Briggs had kept his word. At least until Detective Morgan pulled him away so he could take his statement while Lahela was getting her hand checked by the EMT. And even then, Briggs was only three steps away. He'd counted.

He was grateful her injuries were superficial and would heal, but he wasn't sure about her heart. He wouldn't blame her if this *was* the final straw to send her back across the Pacific. But he wasn't ready for her to leave. He wouldn't stop her, but if she did decide to leave, Briggs wanted to be sure she was making the decision for the right reasons.

"The damage on Mr. Dunn's car matches the impact on Nancy Bart's car," Detective Morgan said. "Rosemary's camera caught him leaving his house in the Volvo a few minutes after Lahela's alarm went off. Crime scene will confirm, but it looks like he's the guy who ran Nancy off the road. He's also confessed to setting the fire to the chairs and calling in the false missing hiker report."

Briggs seethed. "Another charge to add to the rest and keep him in jail."

Stalking charges on their own were hard to prosecute because the crime was so nuanced the laws often fell short of protecting the victims. The more criminal charges they could add, the higher chance of keeping the stalker behind bars for a very long time.

"I've seen some pretty weird stuff in my career, but this one might take the cake."

Briggs thanked Detective Morgan for his work and then crossed the three steps back to Lahela's side. She lifted her gaze to meet his and smiled.

"Hey," he said.

"Hey." She waved her freshly wrapped hand. "They're forcing me to go to the hospital."

"That's good." He brushed his fingers across the cheek that wasn't hurt. He physically ached to see the spot where Mr. Dunn had hit her, and it was probably going to take a whole lot of praying to stop wanting to hurt the man. "You've been through a lot, and we all just want to make sure you're okay."

"We?"

Briggs tipped his head, and Lahela looked around him to find Daphne hanging back near the police cruisers parked along the curb. She gave a shy wave, looking more self-conscious than he'd ever seen her. "She didn't want to impose, but she wanted you to know she's here for you. Whenever you're ready."

A tear slipped down her cheek, and he brushed it away. "I'm ready." She sniffled and then her expression turned bashful. "But I'm also ready for that dinner you promised me."

Briggs grinned. "Oh yeah?"

"Mm-hmm."

Tension crackled between them, and Briggs searched her eyes, hoping to find the answer to his question. Was she going to leave? Was the hope flickering in his chest for a future with Lahela going to be snuffed out? Was—

Commotion behind them turned their attention to the

sudden movement of the police jogging toward the street. Detective Morgan was at their side, his hand on his service pistol at his waist.

"What's going on?" Briggs moved in front of Lahela, reaching one hand behind him for her to hold on to as he searched for the threat. "What is it?"

"There's a man trying to get to Lahela. He's threatened two of my officers and—"

"Wait," Lahela cut in, putting a hand on Briggs's shoulder to peek around him. "Does he look like a Hawaiian Fabio?"

Detective Morgan frowned and then spoke into his radio. A second later, his frown deepened. "Yes," he said with some hesitation.

Lahela groaned. "That would be my brother."

TWENTY-FOUR

NOVEMBERS IN TEXAS might be her new favorite thing. Lahela tipped her head back against the Adirondack chair and soaked in the sun shining from the bright blue sky. She closed her eyes and breathed in the blended country scent of the animals grazing in the nearby field and the smoky scent drifting from the BBQ pit.

Briggs was right. There was something cathartic about being in the natural beauty of the country. And in the two weeks since the incident, Lahela had quietly enjoyed the solitude at Briggs's family ranch.

"You okay, Sis?"

Solitude that included her big brother checking on her every five minutes.

Lahela opened her eyes, shielding them from the sun, and pinned a stare on Kekoa. "You're worse than Mom and Dad."

"Psh, you're lucky I'm the only one here." Kekoa dropped into the empty chair next to her. "Garcia had to keep Lyla from coming with me." He squinted like he was searching the distant terrain. "Can't be certain she's not got eyes out there somewhere."

"Are you serious?"

"The whole team was worried about you." He eyed her. "All

of them were ready to come down here, but you know Lyla always takes it to the next level."

Lahela laughed because he was right. Lyla was the feistiest of Kekoa's team, but it meant a lot that all of them had accepted her as part of their 'ohana. Her eyes moved to where Daphne, Briggs, and Nash were huddled around the smoker.

Each of them had accepted her in the same way. Become her 'ohana here in Texas and didn't leave her side when things got hard.

"They're good people, Sis," Kekoa said like he'd read her mind. "'Ohana."

"I know." And she did, but that didn't just fix her fear that one day they'd leave her. "You know, when you left Hawai'i after Ikaia died, you didn't just leave Mom and Dad. You left Makalena and me too. I know it was hard for you. Extra hard, but when you left . . . it made me afraid I was going to lose everyone I loved."

Kekoa swallowed and he twisted his gaze away from her, wiping his eyes. "I'm sorry, Sis. I never meant to hurt you or make you afraid."

She reached over and squeezed his giant hand, grateful he was here.

AFTER DINNER, Briggs walked her to the fence by the horse pasture. "I know you're thinking about leaving and I don't want to pressure your decision, but I do want to make sure you have all of the facts before you decide."

Lahela was about to interrupt him, but he twisted to face her, tipped up his Stetson, and had such a purposeful look in his eyes that she wanted to hear what he had to say.

"We need you. You've told me that you're afraid of being

a needy friend, but the truth is *we're* the needy ones. Daph, Nash, and me."

"What are you talking about?" She hadn't meant for her question to come out on a half laugh of disbelief, but she couldn't help it.

Briggs took her hand in his and spun her so she could see where Daphne, Nash, and Kekoa were talking and laughing at the picnic table.

"Have you noticed that Daphne doesn't have any girlfriends besides you? She's got her older brothers, Fish and Finn. Me. And Nash. She doesn't have girlfriends because once upon a time—"

"She was teased about being a tomboy," Lahela finished for him, remembering the story Daphne confessed to her a few months into their friendship. Those childhood friends had scared Daphne into believing something was wrong with her because she would rather ride horses, watch football, and not gossip about boys. "I think she's perfect."

"That's just it. You've shown her that she doesn't need to change who she is to have a girlfriend. And she definitely needed one to discuss all of the things us boys are not equipped to handle." He gave a little shudder and Lahela hid her smile. "And Nash. He's a workaholic, but for some reason he's made hanging out with us for taco night a priority. You've brought joy and fun back to his life. And Finn and Fish, well, I go back to the whole girl-talk thing."

Lahela faced him. "And you?"

Briggs inhaled deeply, his eyes falling to their intertwined fingers before meeting her gaze. "I thought leaving the police department in Dallas and moving home would help me find my place. I've always had this idea of what my life was going to look like. It was like a puzzle and all I had to do was keep adding pieces to complete the picture, but it began feeling like I was forcing the pieces. No matter what I accomplished or how I grew in faith or where I moved, the big picture still felt incomplete . . . until I met you. You are the light and the joy and the fun I didn't know I was missing. You are a piece of my puzzle, Lahela."

He gently pulled her closer, closing the space between them as he stared down at her.

"I need you because you are the piece that begins the picture of the life I want."

Lahela's heart danced beneath her ribs. She was falling in love with this man. "So I'm like an edge piece because those are the most important pieces of the puzzle, right?"

Briggs smiled and she couldn't help letting her gaze fall to his lips. "Yeah. You're the piece I want to finish the puzzle with. Only you. Please don't leave."

"One thing you should know about me, Briggs. I love puzzles and I've never left one unfinished."

His eyes lifted to hers, a fire in them that matched the one warming her entire body. She leaned into him and closed her eyes, anticipating the gentle touch of his lips on hers and then—

Clapping. Slow clapping that was painfully recognizable. *Brothers.*

"Bruh, that was epic."

Briggs groaned and pulled back, his eyes still on her. "When does he fly back to DC?"

"This should get him on a plane quickly." She tugged Briggs by the collar, removed his Stetson, and pressed her lips against his.

Briggs deepened the kiss, clearly understanding the assignment. And maybe Kekoa made a gagging noise and maybe she heard him scrambling to get away, but she didn't care because all she cared about was the way her lips moved with Briggs's in a kiss that was both tender, heated, and everything she hoped for.

If breathing wasn't a necessity, Lahela wouldn't have pulled back, and from the hooded expression Briggs was giving her—neither would he.

"That was worth waiting for." His breathless voice feathered over her skin.

"One more thing you should know about me, Briggs." She flattened her palms over his chest and enjoyed the feel of his heart beating beneath her fingers. "I think waiting is overrated."

With that, their lips met again, and Lahela knew she was finally with her people. And finally with her person.

ACKNOWLEDGMENTS

Dear readers, thank you for spending time in Miracle Springs, Texas! I hope you enjoyed Briggs and Lahela's story. When I began brainstorming ideas for a new novella, I wasn't sure who my heroine was going to be, but there was something about Kekoa Young's little sister that I saw in *Fatal Code* that made me want to explore her a little bit more. I ended up loving her quiet, unassuming personality (especially compared to Kekoa's), and I'll admit, it was more painful than I imagined torturing her with a stalker. These are the woes of a suspense author, I suppose. ;)

This story wouldn't be in your hands without the great team at Revell and my agent, Tamela Hancock Murray. It's a privilege to be a part of this great collection with Lynn and Lynette. Thank you for your support. I'm incredibly grateful to Joy Tiffany, Ashley Johnson, and Rachel Scott McDaniel for reading early drafts and helping me make this story so much better. Early morning writing and editing sessions are much more tolerable with good friends. Thank you, Emilie Haney, Christen Krumm, and Steffani Webb, for your unwavering encouragement.

To my husband and family, y'all are the best and I'm blessed. I'm so grateful God has given me the opportunity to do what I love, and I hope every word I write honors him above all.

Lastly, if you want to learn more about the Hawaiian Fabio or Daphne Crawford's cousin Colton, be sure to check out the SNAP Agency and Harbored Secrets series.

Want another thrilling romantic suspense novella collection?
Pick up *Targeted* next!

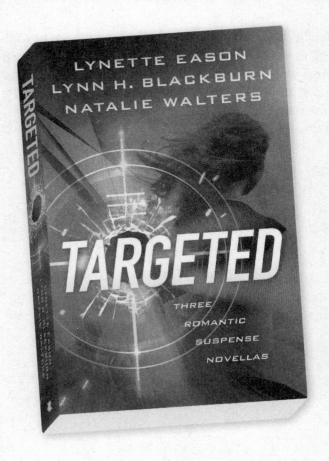

If you loved *In the Dark* by Lynette Eason, don't miss the rest of the Lake City Heroes series

If you loved *Downfall* by Lynn H. Blackburn, keep reading the Gossamer Falls series

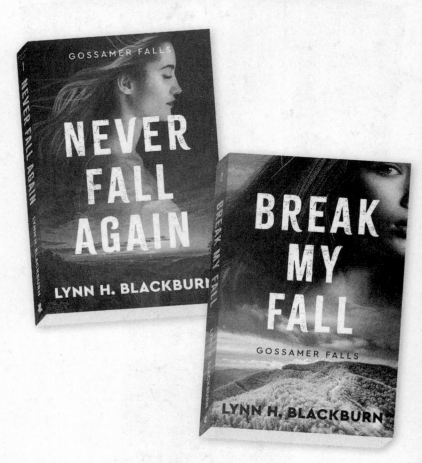

If you enjoyed *Perilous Obsession* by Natalie Walters, you'll love the rest of the SNAP Agency series